THE
TREASURE KEEPERS

THE TREASURE KEEPERS
A NOVEL

Henry D. Schreiber

YELLOW HYDRANGEA BOOKS

THE TREASURE KEEPERS: A NOVEL
by Henry D. Schreiber

First Edition: July 2020
Printed in the United States of America
ISBN: 978-1-7347785-0-2

PART 1
NETTLE CREEK

Happiness resides not in possessions, and not in gold.
Happiness dwells in the soul.

– Democritus

Chapter One
BICENTENNIEL

Pastor Elwood Martin followed the flashes of reflected sunlight to their source, a few steps past Eula Belle Elliot's granite gravestone. His six foot frame stooped, groaning from the ten pounds of excess weight around his waistline. He combed his long, thin fingers around and under clumps of grass. Nothing. He took a step backwards, keeping eyes down, continuously scanning the ground. Once again, he probed his fingers back and forth through the grass. Nothing. As he slowly rose from his crouch, the flashes reappeared within an arm's length of his right shoe. He grabbed at the bright spot and plucked the treasure, a coin, off the ground. After rubbing it on the cuff of his white dress shirt, he nodded his approval at the bicentennial quarter. He cheerfully flipped his discovery in the air. His dark brown eyes followed its high arc until becoming sidetracked to the steeple of Twin Falls Presbyterian Church. At the top of its spire glistened a large golden cross.

Pastor Martin sighed at the sight of the steeple. Silas' riddle – *Why did the hawk sit on the church steeple?* – had tormented him all day. No hawk perched there tonight. *Had he really expected to see a hawk there?* He shrugged and flipped the coin again.

Pastor Martin pocketed the quarter and restarted his short stroll from the parsonage through the cemetery to his church. The backdrop of Nettle Mountain jutting from the Blue Ridge always imparted in him a sense of awe in God's creation. This summer evening, the double rainbow that settled over neighboring South Mountain after a quickly moving thunderstorm amplified his reverence. He paused a moment to enjoy these breath-taking sights. Then again, he was quickly distracted by the sounds of bluebirds chirping and flitting in the wild rose bushes as well as the smell of a freshly mowed church lawn. Once he neared the church, he spontaneously broke into whistling "The Wonder of It All," one of his favorite hymns.

Hydrangea shrubs with abundant assortments of large pink, blue, and purple blooms greeted him at the church's back entrance to its Fellowship Hall. When Pastor Martin opened the door, the aroma of freshly baked cookies further welcomed him. He had arrived early to help arrange tables and chairs for the scheduled event. But the church's sexton, Reese Coleman, and his wife, Mabel, had already been tending to the hall's preparation, evidently for quite a while.

"Pastor Martin, I've set up about seventy chairs – think that's enough?" queried a shuffling, bald-headed Reese.

"Let's go for about a hundred." Pastor Martin smiled as he surveyed the hall, instinctively plopping the newly-found quarter in the offering plate just inside the door. "I have a feeling this event might be quite popular tonight."

"No problem."

Pastor Martin turned to see Mabel, her gray hair in a bun, proudly carrying a tray from the kitchen. "My goodness, Mabel, I smelled your chocolate chip cookies as soon as I arrived. Now the sight of them is making my mouth water." He scrutinized the table in front of him. "Wow – quite a selection! There's your persimmon pudding squares. . . . Oh, and do I see your always delicious lemon bars? And a fresh-cut arrangement of your prize-winning gladiolas; you know I just love those bright red ones."

Mabel, wearing a floral print dress, beamed. Pastor Martin had never seen Mabel in anything other than a dress or a skirt and blouse; she had been raised in an era in which proper Southern women did not wear slacks or jeans. She shoved the tray of still-warm cookies in front of him. "Why don't you sample one or two to see if they're fittin'?"

"I think my waistline expanded by an inch when I first saw them."

Pastor Martin grabbed a couple. He popped one in his mouth, savored the taste, and applauded, "Mmm . . . My, my Mabel! No one, absolutely no one, bakes a better cookie than you. Just heavenly! You've outdone yourself in preparing the spread on the table."

Mabel grinned from ear to ear. "I knew you wanted tonight to be special."

This gathering would be the last in the summer-long celebration of Twin Falls Presbyterian Church's 200th anniversary of its founding. Pastor Martin expected a large turnout, with not only many members of his congregation but also a large contingent of curiosity seekers attending. Seating would be needed, or so he thought, for those from the local Irish Creek community, as well as historians and news reporters.

Tonight, instead of its regular Wednesday night Bible study, the church was doing something that hadn't been done to anyone's knowledge – open the large safe in the secluded basement of its sanctuary. It had remained locked and undisturbed for over a century. No one still living knew what treasures it might contain.

† † †

Twin Falls Presbyterian Church sat in the small hamlet of Cornwall, next to the confluence of Irish Creek flowing into South River – a rural area of Virginia's Rockbridge County, at the southern extremity of the Shenandoah Valley. Cornwall was once a bustling city in the latter part of the 19th century. As a result, the Twin Falls congregation had hundreds on its membership roll. The church once boasted it was the largest in the county. But now Cornwall consisted only of Twin Falls Presbyterian Church surrounded by a few scattered houses and trailers. On any given Sunday most church pews were empty. Membership had declined to a few dozen; and, like many rural churches, a steadily aging congregation accounted for most of those churchgoers.

Elwood Martin had been the respected minister of Twin Falls Presbyterian Church for more than two decades. Although in his early-fifties, he looked much younger. His cherub-like face eschewed wrinkles, and his pompadour of hair defied any graying of its naturally dark brown color. Few hairs ever strayed out of place. Even so, his habit of running his hands through his head of thick hair always reset his natural coiffure. Only his bushy moustache, totally gray and mismatched to his brown mane, indicated his true age. He once shaved this moustache, but strangers then mistook him for the famed entertainer Liberace. They'd ask for his autograph and for pictures with him; he quickly grew it back.

The pastor's personal and spiritual life, though, suffered a significant setback three years ago, when he joined the ranks of divorced ministers. One week after his step-daughter Arany departed for a West Coast college, his wife Dot announced she no longer wanted to live in the glass house of a pastor's wife. She packed her bags to find a new life in North Dakota.

During his next couple years of melancholy, Pastor Martin struggled to comprehend, much less effectively preach, God's Word. He suffered through bouts of depression. Phone calls from his ex-wife belittled him, harping on his shortcomings throughout their marriage and demanding more money for alimony. She cackled at his attempts to reason with her. Dot did everything in her power to prevent Arany from having any contact with her step-father. She succeeded. He then felt abandoned by his step-daughter. His self-confidence was shattered.

But, through compassionate counseling from Silas Clark, his longtime friend and confidante in the Twin Falls congregation, he recovered to once again become a pious and faithful servant of God. Still every day he prayed and yearned for Arany, albeit not her mother, to reenter his life.

† † †

About a half hour before the scheduled start of the Wednesday night event, a handful of church members and Pastor Martin congregated around the refreshment table. They talked. They munched. They sipped freshly-brewed iced tea from plastic cups.

The characteristic creak of the back door opening interrupted their banter about the afternoon thunderstorm. A petite young woman, with a camera hung around her neck and a backpack slung over her shoulder, entered the Fellowship Hall. She and the church clique mutually surveyed each other. Her blue eyes eventually locked with those of Pastor Martin. He returned her gaze, as she confidently traipsed over to him in front of the table.

She thrust out her hand and in a high-pitched voice declared, "Hi. I'm Kit King, a reporter for *The Lexington News-Gazette*. I assume you're the minister?"

Pastor Martin cordially shook her hand: "I'm Pastor Elwood Martin. Welcome to Twin Falls Presbyterian Church." Chuckling, he added, "I suspect sporting the cross pendant may have given me away."

"Well, that and you just looked like a preacher," she shrugged with a twist of her head to shake her long brown hair away from her face. She pulled a notepad from her backpack and unenthusiastically stated, "My editor assigned me to cover your church opening an old safe. May I ask you a few questions to provide some background?"

"Sure," Pastor Martin answered. He shivered in discomfort at her shrill voice piercing his ear drums. Snickering to himself that her speech disqualified her as an on-air reporter, he continued, "So, have you visited Twin Falls Presbyterian previously?"

"Nope, I'm just finishing my summer internship with *The News-Gazette*. Up until six weeks ago, I'd never even been in this county. I grew up around Richmond. I'll head back there for my senior year at VCU in another couple weeks."

Pastor Martin frowned – *Shucks, the local newspaper didn't even see fit to send a regular reporter to cover our big event.* He quickly found his smile, though, and spread his arms. "I'll be glad to answer your questions. We have a few minutes before the formalities start."

Pastor Martin and Kit drifted a few steps away from the group, but not before Kit grabbed one of Mabel's cookies.

"It felt like forever to get here from Lexington," Kit screeched. "Once I turned onto South River Road, I just saw the railroad tracks on one side and the river on the other for miles. Only a few isolated houses and farms, as well as lots of woods. I wouldn't have known I'd arrived in Cornwall except for the sign. Why's there such a large church – I peeked into the sanctuary and saw seating for several hundred – way out here in the boondocks?"

"Well, let me give you a little historical context." Pastor Martin looked past her out the window at the cemetery, repeating a narrative he'd told many times previously. "The church's sanctuary was built in 1886. At that time, Cornwall – or rather Crowder as it was called back then – was a rail hub. The Irish Creek Railroad connected to the Shenandoah Valley Railroad. Crowder was one of the largest communities in this county. The forests on the slopes of the Blue Ridge supplied an abundance of chestnut, poplar, and oak. The fertile flatland around South River yielded rich harvests of grains such as wheat, corn, barley, buckwheat, and flax." He hesitated, then added, "South River farms were also famous for their potatoes, apples, watermelons and, in particular, paw paws –"

"Huh? Paw paws?" Kit glanced up from her note-taking. She pranced in place, moving her weight from left to right leg and back again, not standing still for any length of time – yet another of her annoying mannerisms to Pastor Martin.

"They taste like a blend of bananas and citrus," he explained matter-of-factly. "Many consider this fruit a delicacy. Paw paw trees were native and abundant in this area, although only a few are now left."

"Well, I think I'll stick to eating fruit I know, such as apples and peaches," she giggled.

"Cornwall was quite different back in the late 1800s," he continued. "This area had several general merchandise stores, brick kiln, iron foundry and machine works, distillery, tanbark factory, boarding house, livery –" Pastor Martin paused, realizing Kit was furiously scribbling notes. He ran his hand through his hair, then said more slowly: "And several sawmills, grain mill, stave factory, blacksmith shop, molasses mill, cannery, and . . . other businesses that I probably left out."

"Wow – what happened to make them leave?" exclaimed Kit, as she cleared her face of wayward strands of hair with a brush of her hand.

"Buena Vista, that's what," he smiled.

"I don't understand?"

"Around 1900, most industries moved to Buena Vista, the new city taking shape along the Maury River. Nowadays, there's no trace left of Cornwall's businesses except for a few crumbling stone foundations."

"Are there any jobs left out here in the backcountry? How many members are left in your church?" Kit asked rapid-fire.

"Well, it's not really the back woods," he shook his head. "We're not that far out in the country. Most locals commute to jobs in Lexington or Buena Vista. Some lumber hardwoods or cut pulpwood. Others do cattle farming. And we have about fifty to sixty, including children, who regularly attend church."

Kit nonchalantly turned her notepad back to its first page and perused her reminders for questions. "Oh, I assume the opening of the safe tonight isn't the only activity scheduled to commemorate your church's bicentennial. Are there other happenings?"

Pastor Martin grimaced – *She hadn't done her homework; other events had previously been reported in her newspaper this summer.* Rubbing his chin, he transformed his expression back to a smile. "The church had a homecoming service about two months ago – it featured the return of Rev. Cecil Potter, the church's only living retired minister. It also included messages from our governing Presbyter and the leader of the regional Synod. This ceremony was followed by a covered-dish banquet. Then, a couple weeks ago, we had a combination revival and church picnic under a big tent at Twin Falls –"

"Yeah, I stopped at Twin Falls on the way here," interrupted Kit, "about two or three miles downriver from Cornwall. By the way, why's the church named after Twin Falls instead of

Cornwall, or its previous name . . . whatever that was?" She quickly flipped back a few pages in her notes.

"Crowder."

"Yep, that's right – here it's in my notes," she pointed to the entry in her notepad.

"Let's delve into a few more details of our church history," declared Pastor Martin, as he calmly folded his hands in front of him. "The original church structure 200 years ago was indeed built on the east bank of the South River across from Twin Falls. It lasted about twenty years before being washed away in a flood. The next sanctuary and additions were built a little farther back from the river, but burned to the ground in 1885. The church leaders then decided it'd be more convenient for the congregation to move closer to the population center, to the outskirts of the town. They finished building the current sanctuary here in 1886 and this Fellowship Hall in the 1950s – obviously without changing the name of the church."

"I can understand why the location across from Twin Falls was chosen for the original church. The falls are absolutely beautiful," Kit squealed, continuing to prance in place. "But why're there so many 'No Trespassing' signs?"

Shaking his head in dismay, he frowned, "Through the years several people slipped to their deaths while climbing the rocks around the falls. And at the base of Twin Falls was a popular swimming hole for locals and students, until new owners closed it because of liability concerns. Our church, though, still performs baptisms from the bank of South River across from Twin Falls. In fact, one of the highlights of this summer's revival was the baptism of the first grandson of Reese Coleman." Pastor Martin pointed toward Reese who was half-asleep on one of the chairs.

Several curious members of the church milled about Pastor Martin and Kit. A few greeted their minister with a handshake, a pat on the back, or a passing "Hello."

Kit glanced at the clock on the wall. "I guess it's about time to start. Thanks for taking time to respond to my questions." Kit turned to walk to the refreshment table, but spun around as if doing a pirouette. "On my way here, I have to admit I was worried about getting lost and driving right past the church. But one of my coworkers told me I couldn't miss it along South River Road. That it had a big dead tree and an ugly – um, um I mean unique – sculpture in front. Indeed, he was right. By the way, is there any reason why y'all don't cut down the dead tree in front of the church? It looks like it's been dead for a while."

Pastor Martin smiled, "Yet more history for you. When the church building at Twin Falls burned down, legend has it that a large white oak tree next to the church survived. An acorn from this tree was planted at the new construction in Cornwall to symbolize its connection to the founding Twin Falls location. So, the tree is now over 125 years old and showing its age, but isn't totally dead – it has some patches of leafy branches amongst its rotting limbs. The church membership is split on cutting it down. Half wants to get rid of the eyesore. The other half wants to keep it as a sign of the continuing legacy of our church. They're superstitious; they worry that removing the tree may coincide with the demise of the congregation."

"Interesting," Kit mulled, as she jotted furiously on her notepad. "One final question – Is there any significance to the large sculpture of the hunter and bear on the other side of this almost dead tree in front? Strange – but I hear this is bear hunting territory."

Pastor Martin put his hands over his mouth, but couldn't keep the deep belly laugh inside. "Oh my . . . It's actually of Jonah being swallowed by the whale, or great fish." He glanced again at the clock on the wall and continued, "You might want to ask Peggy Lauderdale, our church historian, for the full story of this brass sculpture."

"Oh!" Kit exclaimed, much too loudly in her high-pitched voice. She headed for the refreshment table.

Pastor Martin was always astounded that the church's ruling session, about thirty years before his arrival, allowed the Jonah-and-the-whale monstrosity to grace its grounds. But there it was – the size of a small shed next to the Twin Falls Presbyterian sign in front of the church – to welcome everyone.

Chapter Two
BEETS, TURNIP, and TATER

Pastor Martin scanned the room – lots of empty chairs. The audience consisted of about twenty people, mostly the same congregational members he could rely upon to attend the usual happenings at the church. No outsider from the community was present. The regional newspapers from Roanoke and Staunton, despite invitations and promises to attend, did not; nor did any of the television stations from Roanoke and Lynchburg. Only Kit King, the student intern from the local weekly newspaper, *The Lexington News-Gazette*, and a reporter from the monthly paper, *The Rockbridge Advocate*, deemed the event suitably newsworthy. Not even a representative of the local historical society showed up. Pastor Martin's initial optimism had evaporated.

He opened the festivities with a subdued welcome and an invitation to grab a few more homemade cookies and snacks. He followed with a prayer. But as soon as he said, "Let us pray," it hit him. *The hawk is a bird of prey. That's why it roosts on the church steeple.* A sense of self-satisfaction in solving Silas' riddle rejuvenated him. *It was as if Silas uncannily knew he'd need a shot of encouragement.* By the time he reached "Amen," he was grinning from ear to ear.

"Tonight we'll be opening the large safe in the basement of the church's sanctuary," Pastor Martin now thundered, while he rearranged several sheets of handwritten notes on the podium.

"The safe hasn't been opened in generations. In fact, no one in the church has any recollection of it ever being opened. No one knows the combination to the safe. When we relocate to the basement, you'll see that the safe is the size of a large refrigerator with its legs and part of its base cemented into the floor. The current sanctuary, erected in 1886, was essentially built around the safe. Initially, the safe sat on a dirt floor; then, at a later date, a concrete slab was poured around it so that its legs are now partially buried. Its size and weight are such that it'd now be impossible to get it through the door out of the cellar. Antique dealers have identified the production of the safe as circa 1880's by its serial number, 0014, and its manufacturer, Sargent & Greenleaf." He surveyed the audience. Upon noting many bored stares and more than one yawn, he skipped to the bottom of his notes. "This safe has survived several floods, most notably you'll see the high water mark on its front and sides from the catastrophic aftereffects of heavy rain due to the remnants of Hurricane Camille in 1969. This line from the South River floodwaters is about a quarter the way up the safe. Camille wreaked the most devastation ever seen in the Cornwall community as well as the South River area."

Pastor Martin then turned to a man sitting on the front row. "Sam, could you please stand for a minute?"

Sam, revealing an ever-present scowl and slicked-back hair, rose only momentarily. He seemed oddly out of place in a three-piece suit whereas all other attendees dressed informally. Pastor Martin pegged him as looking like one of Al Capone's henchmen plucked out of an old episode of *The Untouchables*.

"We've hired a professional safe cracker by the name of Sam to open the safe as we watch," Pastor Martin continued. "He's traveled about 150 miles to get here, all the way from Richmond, in order to break into the safe and –"

"A professional safe cracker by the name of Sam?" interrupted Doug Sullivan, a grizzled old-time reporter from *The Rockbridge Advocate*. He sarcastically snarled, "Gimme a break! Tell us more about him?"

"Can't do," Pastor Martin chuckled. "One of the conditions for him agreeing to break into the safe was not to ask any questions about his background. I can only assume for obvious reasons. I don't have his credentials. His fees were underwritten by one of our church members, Silas Clark. Silas' only comment was that he had impeccable references from the Richmond police department."

Sam sat motionless. He maintained a blank stare on his face.

"And tombs, not safes, are buried under churches," scoffed the same reporter. "Why was the safe put in the basement when it was being built in the first place?"

Pastor Martin shrugged his shoulders. His eyes lit up mischievously. "Let's hope the safe isn't operating as a tomb."

Giggles spread throughout the audience.

Pastor Martin looked around the room and smiled, "Any other questions before we reconvene in the basement?"

"Why now?" asked Doug Sullivan. He impatiently tapped his pen on his notepad.

"It's our 200th anniversary – something fun and interesting . . . as well as unusual when compared to the normal activities associated with an anniversary," Pastor Martin replied. "Silas Clark has actually been after us for many years to open the safe – that there might be something of consequence or value therein. By the way, please keep Silas in your prayers. He wanted to be here tonight, but his continuing heart condition and other more recent problems preclude him from venturing out of the assisted care facility in which he now resides."

The hand of Kit King, the intern from *The News-Gazette*, shot up. "Anyone have any idea what might be in the safe?"

Reese Coleman not too discretely put his hands over his ears. He whispered too loudly to his wife: "Her voice screeches like fingernails scraping across a blackboard." Mabel shushed him, then gently wagged her finger in his face to behave.

"No one knows," Pastor Martin responded to Kit. "Some guesses are the church's original land grant for its Twin Falls property dating back to the early 1800s. Or maybe the deed to the property on which the church and cemetery sits here in Cornwall. Evidently, a cemetery existed at this location for several decades before the church was built here. Maybe, old church records and other documents and items of historical consequence." After a dramatic pause, he snickered, "We can always hope for some cash." He then pointed to a grand-motherly figure on the left side of the front row. "Perhaps Peggy Lauderdale, our church's historian, can offer other possibilities."

Peggy Lauderdale rose from her seat, adjusted her glasses, and cleared her voice. "Those are the usual things that might be expected. Some people think there could be artifacts from the Civil War – it's well known that Professor Thomas 'Stonewall' Jackson of VMI was a frequent visitor to this church at Twin Falls before the war, as was Robert E. Lee after the war. I personally think the safe is where we'll find the missing records that describe the prosecution and excommunication of a prominent church elder, Herbert Grant, for moonshining during prohibition. The old session minutes describe these records as being sealed, but never mention where they were stored." She giggled and added, "One thing for sure, it doesn't contain anything after World War II or someone would've remembered the safe being opened."

"My daddy always said the church's basement was haunted," bellowed Faye Tolley, at about 30 years old one of the younger individuals in the crowd. "He told me the ghost of Hubie hides in the safe and oozes out to patrol the basement on nights of the full moon."

Kit stared wide-eyed at Faye.

"Fortunately it's another week until full moon," Pastor Martin wise-cracked.

A chorus of laughter rose from the crowd.

Peggy Lauderdale, sitting back down in her chair, shook her head and sighed. She glanced at Kit. "Don't let them scare you. Pastor Hubert Sumpter was murdered by a deranged parishioner in the basement of the church in the 1890s. This ghost story keeps the children from wandering down there."

Kit raised her hand and looked toward Peggy. "Ms. Lauderdale, just out of curiosity . . . Pastor Martin suggested I ask you about the story behind the quite distinctive sculpture in the front of the church. He says –"

"What does that have to do with the price of eggs in China?" Faye pooh-poohed loudly. "I thought we were talking about the safe."

Audible snickers circulated throughout the audience.

Now a grandmother with frizzy gray hair, Peggy despised irrelevant questions, a trait well-known by all church members. She retired several years previous as a middle-school history teacher with a reputation for maintaining strict discipline in the classroom.

Reese Coleman mumbled, "It's a whale of a story!" His wife, Mabel, elbowed him in the ribs to keep quiet, while others around him snorted.

Peggy once again rose from her chair. "Some in this area cynically refer to us as 'The Whale Church,' much to my displeasure. My father – George Lauderdale – headed the session that accepted the beautiful brass sculpture that graces our grounds. Over fifty years ago, Silas Clark arrived in the county from New York City as a young engineer hired by the Lee's, now Mohawk, carpet factory in Glasgow –"

"Excuse me," intruded Kit. "But is this the same Silas Clark that Pastor Martin just mentioned?"

Peggy shot daggers at Kit. "Yes!"

Peggy took a deep breath and continued her story. "Afterwards Silas got a job with Kennametal – a maker of industrial coal mining and drilling equipment. His education had been in metallurgical engineering. In his younger days before moving to Rockbridge County, he had also been an artist who created this wonderful brass sculpture. So, when he relocated here, he also transported this sculpture from New York City. By the way, since joining the church more than fifty years ago, Silas has been the pillar of the church's community, serving as a ruling elder for many terms as well as the church's sexton and manager of its cemetery up until several years ago. In effect, he managed all the property concerns of the church for many decades. He did everything required to keep the church running smoothly not only in terms of its facilities but also in its worship services –"

"Excuse me," interrupted Kit again. "The question was about the sculpture, not Silas Clark."

Peggy growled, "It's impossible to separate the art from the artist. This sculpture is a work of great art that tells the story of Jonah. Perhaps if you would've taken the time to study it, you would've seen that!" She abruptly took her seat.

Kit scrunched her face wondering how many times previously Peggy had defended the questionable beauty of this downright ugly sculpture.

† † †

The attendees filtered out of the Fellowship Hall, walked around the side of the building, then down the outside steps to the only entrance to the sanctuary's basement. The undersized wooden door eerily and loudly screeched, when opened.

At the first creak of the door, Faye Tolley gently touched Kit King on her shoulder from the rear. "Yah-Hoo! Did-ya just hear the ghost of Hubie?"

Kit jumped. Faye cackled.

All were greeted by the stereotypical stuffiness, low-hanging pipes, cobwebs, and bad lighting of an old cellar. An antiquated furnace, along with its long-abandoned coal bin, occupied a sizeable portion of the space. The musty smell of furnace smoke still lingered. Past workmen deemed it easier just to leave the now-defunct furnace in the basement, even though it had long since been replaced by an adjoining propane-fired one.

Once the group crammed into the basement, Sam sat in a chair positioned in front of the safe. He methodically cracked his knuckles one at a time, then put a headset over his ears. He plugged a wire into the headset. This connected to an electronic device already taped to the safe next to the spinner of the combination lock. He nodded to Pastor Martin.

Pastor Martin explained to the onlookers that Sam previously informed him the electronics amplified the sound of the lock's tumblers. He also pointed out that the bottom quarter of the safe was totally rusted – a sign of the high water mark from Camille. Finally, he glanced at Sam, announced, "Let's open it up," and took a few steps back into the audience.

Before Sam could even turn the lock one rotation, Kit blurted, "Hey Sam, how long will this take?"

Sam turned, wrinkled his eyebrows, scowled at Kit, and snarled, "I need quiet." He spun back to the safe and carefully twirled the lock, concentrating on the sounds of the tumblers rotating and slipping into place. After about three minutes of watching Sam slowly spin the tumblers back and forth, the audience became conflicted – waiting in eager anticipation, but already tiring of no immediate action. They whispered loudly amongst themselves.

"Safecracking ain't a spectator sport," Reese Coleman sighed.

"Quiet!" shouted Sam, with face to the safe.

Everyone hushed.

Minutes later, Sam addressed the audience: "Two spins to the right to 23; turn left passing 11 once and stopping at 11 on the next rotation; then turn right to 3. Combination is 23-11-3."

Everyone froze.

Sam repeated louder: "23-11-3. Someone might wanna write it down."

The crowd looked at Pastor Martin. He pulled out a pen from his shirt pocket and fumbled around for a piece of paper on a cellar shelf.

"Got it!" he said, while he scribbled the numbers on the paper.

Sam turned the handle. The lock disengaged with a loud clack. He slowly rose from his chair, smoothed out his suit, removed his electronic gizmos, and stepped back from the safe. Motioning for Pastor Martin to come forward, he grinned, "Please have the honor of opening its door."

Pastor Martin weaved his way to the front of the safe. Others maneuvered to get the best view of the safe's door, craning their necks in that direction. Kit squeezed through the crowd to get a photograph. The disinterested Sam started to pack up his gear.

Pastor Martin pulled on the handle. It failed to open. He yanked again. Nothing.

He turned to Sam, who was still stuffing his equipment in a bag. "Hey, Sam, it won't open."

"Not my problem," shrugged Sam. "It's unlocked – that was my job."

Pastor Martin gave several more hard tugs. Still nothing. "Sam, it won't open," he repeated in exasperation.

"I guess the safe's rusted at the bottom part of its door's seal. Pull harder," Sam grumbled.

Troy Montgomery, a tall, muscular, and young lumberjack, as well as a congregant, dressed in his best flannel shirt, bib overalls, and NASCAR baseball cap, stepped forward. He looked like he could pick up a small car with little effort. "Hey pastor, lemme give it a try."

Faye Tolley whispered to Kit: "Strong as an ox, rough as a cob. By the way, the only time he ever takes off his cap is when he's in the church sanctuary or during the National Anthem. I think he sleeps in his NASCAR cap."

"But quite the handsome specimen," Kit whispered back. "Is he married?"

"I don't think he's looking for a city girl," Faye scoffed, rolling her eyes.

Troy pulled on the handle. Nothing.

He spat on his hands, rubbed them together, and wiped them on the legs of his overalls. He grabbed the handle and yanked with more vigor. Nothing. He angrily gave another mighty tug. Nothing.

"Aaaargh!" he loudly grunted during the fourth pull. "I feel a little movement."

Ed Painter, a beanpole of a guy with large framed glasses, suggested, "Maybe we need a hammer or some WD-40."

"I think I have both in my pickup," announced Preston Hughes. "Just a minute, Troy, I'll run out and git 'em before you bust a gut."

"That doesn't surprise me," laughed Ed. "You've got a regular workshop in your truck's cab. And, I suspect you have ole' Rebel in the bed of the truck."

"Of course," Preston returned the laugh. "I don't go nowhere without Rebel." Rebel was Preston's prize Plott hound, one of his bear-hunting dogs. Preston lived to hunt – turkey, deer, bear, or whatever was in season. He wore camouflage everywhere.

Preston returned with a hammer and a WD-40 can. He sprayed so much WD-40 on the door's seal that liquid dripped onto the concrete floor, then handed the hammer to Troy.

Bang-*bang*! Bang-*bang*! Bang-*bang*! Bang-*bang*! Bang-*bang*! Bang-*bang*! Hammering echoed throughout the cellar, as Troy attempted to crack the rust sealing the safe's door shut.

Troy gave the hammer back to Preston, and yanked on the safe's handle. Nothing.

He huffed. "I felt it give a little more. Preston, give it a few more whacks with the hammer."

Bang-*bang*! Bang-*bang*! Bang-*bang*! Bang-*bang*!

Troy rubbed his hands on his bibs, took a strong grip of the handle, and pulled. The door groaned open. The flash of Kit King's camera exploded into the safe's now-exposed cavity.

A stuffy smell emanated. The safe's contents peered back.

"Oh my," exclaimed Pastor Martin, standing next to Troy. He stepped back.

Kit followed her camera flash to grab a quick look into the safe. "Another safe. That's all? A smaller safe within a larger safe."

Estelle Harris, who doubled as the church organist, snuffled, "Maybe it'll be like a set of Russian dolls – and have yet another smaller safe nested within this one as well."

"That's weird," commented Preston, holding his spray can and hammer. "Why would anyone lock a safe within another one?"

Pastor Martin looked around anxiously and found Sam who had already retreated to the cellar steps with his packed equipment. "Hey Sam," he shouted. "Can you open this other combination safe?" He noted that this smaller safe was in near pristine condition.

Sam shook his head. "Not part of the deal," he griped. "Contract was to open one safe – and just one safe. No money, no open."

"Give me a moment." Pastor Martin galloped by Sam up the cellar stairs.

Sam dropped his bag. He waited impatiently on the bottom step. People milled about the cellar. They coalesced into small groups. They kept asking the same question over and over: "Why did someone put a safe into a larger safe?"

The clock ticked. Pastor Martin returned in a few minutes. He announced to the waiting crowd as well as Sam: "Silas Clark says he'll pay any additional fees."

The people cheered.

Sam methodically pulled out his electronic gear from the packed bag. The groups continued their discussions.

Pastor Martin had Troy and a robust young farmer, Harry Whitmer, pull the second safe, the size of a large microwave, out of the larger one and place it on a nearby table in full view of the gathering.

"Whew. Was that heavy?" exhaled Harry, wearing the attire of modern tractor-driving farmers – denim shorts and a T-shirt. Emblazoned on the front of his shirt was "My master walked on water. John 6:19."

"Not that bad," grinned Troy.

Once he got a view of the smaller safe, Sam's eyes lit up. "Wow – amazing. A Terwillegar – top-of-the-line safe in 19th century America." He stroked the safe. "In this condition, the safe itself is worth a couple thousand dollars. It'll be an honor to open it." Sam quietly set up his equipment on and around the safe – about a hundred pounds of glossy steel metal with a red and yellow Terwillegar insignia painted on front.

Chitter-chatter continued to fill the basement. "What might be in the safe? Why is one safe inside another?"

Finally, Sam yelled, "Quiet!"

He concentrated on the task at hand. Five minutes passed. He smiled and pulled off his headset. "It's unlocked. Combination: 40-19-21."

The audience politely applauded the feat.

Sam looked at Pastor Martin. "40-19-21." Pastor Martin stared at the safe, lost in his thoughts.

Sam repeated louder: "40-19-21." Preston Hughes, standing next to the pastor, gave him a nudge with his elbow, returning him to reality.

"Well," Sam glibly remarked, "Are you gonna write it down?"

Pastor Martin finally obeyed. He wrote the combination on the same piece of paper as before.

Sam turned the safe's handle. "It's all yours, pastor." He smirked, "You should be able to open this one by yourself – no rust."

People jockeyed to get a better view of the safe. Pastor Martin jerked it open. Kit's camera blindly took a picture of the safe's content. Simultaneously, a loud crash reverberated through the cellar.

Faye Tolley gleefully hollered, "The ghost of Hubie Sumpter is out. And he's mad!"

Kit, face white and heart thumping, breathlessly spun around. Her eyes locked on the exit door.

"Oops," sheepishly mumbled Preston Hughes. "Just an empty jar I knocked off the shelf. Careful of the broken glass."

Kit's adrenaline quickly plummeted. Relief replaced panic. She turned to Faye and spluttered, "That wasn't funny."

Peggy Lauderdale sighed and pointed at the safe, "So what's in it?"

Pastor Martin pulled out a stack of yellowed pages and a small burlap sack, about the size of a small jewelry carrier.

"What's in the bag?" queried Kit, as she shook her hair out of her eyes. Her camera flashed, taking more pictures.

Peggy Lauderdale excitedly cried, "Read the pages. What do they say?"

The crowd was abuzz.

"Wait a moment. Let's open the bag first." Pastor Martin took charge. He gently slipped the string from around the bag's top, then poured the contents into his hand. His eyes grew as wide as saucers. The flash on Kit's camera popped several times; yet more pictures.

Two crude coins, about an inch-and-a-quarter in diameter with a gold luster, tumbled into his palm. He held one up to show the crowd. More flashes resulted in more pictures.

"On one side is stamped 'C.S.A.,'" he announced. He flipped it to the other side, "And on the other '1 oz.'"

A collective gasp seemed to momentarily suck all the air from the basement.

"Gee, Pastor Martin," Charlie Whitesides scratched his brow. "Are they gold?"

"They sure appear that way – gold coins as if crudely made from metal poured into a homemade mold. I guess they must be one ounce coins. That's what they feel like," replied Pastor Martin.

"C.S.A. – Confederate States of America – Is that what it represents? I've never seen confederate coins before."

"I didn't think the Confederacy minted coins, much less gold coins."

"Could C.S.A. stand for anything else?"

"Two ounces of gold – How much are they worth?"

"I guess that depends on whether they're gold."

Sam quietly slipped through the crowd and out the cellar door, knowing his services would no longer be needed. No one noticed his broad grin.

"What do the pages say?" fussed Peggy, hands on her hips. "Maybe they'll explain the coins."

Pastor Martin returned the coins to their bag and to the small safe. He held up the eight pages, handwritten with splotchy ink. Yet more flashes and more pictures by Kit. He read slowly, stumbling on words often misspelled, scribbled, or smeared to a hushed and astounded audience.

Testimony of Beets Campbell
August 28, 1886

This be the story of me and my brothers - Turnip and Tater. Pa be farmer up Irish Creek. Pa say he name us for the crop he be harvesting at time of our birth. Says so he could remember when we be birthed. Me be eldest. Pa says Turnip be two years younger. Tater be two years younger than Turnip.

Pa cut wood. His mules haul logs to sawmill at Crowder. After Rockbridge Foundry open upstream from Crowder, Pa build kiln. Pa make charcoal from wood for furnaces. Pa farm, grow lots of corn. Pa make squeezings into shine - always share, never sell. Pa work hard. We never have money.

Pa and Ma take me and Turnip and Tater to Presbeetarian Church by Twin Falls every Sunday - ride the wagon down and back. Pa say Pastor Elijah Hughes --- he always speak the Word. Pa say Pastor Elijah be a broom maker when not Sunday. Everyone buy Pastor Elijah brooms - sweep sin from house. Pa say his daddy helped build 1st church at Twin Falls.

Eight winters before the war Ma go to store in Crowder for salt and flour. Ma never return. Pa tell sheriff she be kidnap. Sheriff say she left. Pa mad. After Pa die, widow Layton tell me that Ma run off with shoe salesman from Connecticut. Pa has bad bad hate for Yankees and anything Yankee.

Me apprentice at Rockbridge Foundry when me be 12. It be hot dirty work. Old man Taylor at Foundry pay Pa for me working. It be six winters before the war. Me live with cousin Mamie and her man in Crowder. Me learn to read and write, unlike my dumb brothers, from Mamie.

Me work under Mr. Tankersley - he be forgemaster for old man Taylor. Me learn to work iron - make molds and tools. Make chains, plows, carriage parts, stuff. Every fortnight Tankersley have me make delivery

> *to Lexington and VMI. Me deliver horse-shoes, nails, swords, medals - bring back stuff to repair. VMI stuff me deliver to Professor Jackson - to be called the Stonewall. He always want horseshoes me forge - say they be best. Stonewall tell Tankersley he want Beets to forge VMI military medals.*

Pastor Martin flipped to the next page, then paused. The mesmerized audience milled impatiently. He held up the page. "It's impossible to read the next couple of paragraphs. There's one big black ink blot covering the top half of the page."

Heads nodded in agreement.

"Interesting story. But what's it got to do with the gold?" blurted Kit. "Who's Beets Campbell? Why's his story in the church safe?"

"I haven't a clue," Pastor Martin shrugged. "Anyone ever hear of Beets Campbell?"

Head shakes indicated negative responses.

Peggy tapped her right foot irritably. She sneered at Kit. "Perhaps the rest of the pages will shed light on the gold."

Pastor Martin continued reading.

> *Pa die the winter three years before the war. Doctor from Crowder say Pa die of consumption of shine. On his deadbed, Pa make me promise to care for Turnip and Tater, to bad hate all Yankees, to love Jesus, and to protect Campbell land. Pa have land round Big Bend Creek and Nettle Creek off Irish Creek. I quit work at Foundry. Me and Turnip and Tater farm and timber.*
>
> *Me and Turnip and Tater be chopping trees next to Irish Creek where Big Bend Creek enter - just upstream from Duck Pond. We use logs to build shed. It be two winters before Yankees attack us. It be hot day in*

summer - Turnip dunk his head in Irish Creek to cool down and gulp water. Turnip saw glitter in a wash. He follow it under water and pick up rock chip - look like gold flake. Me and Turnip and Tater tell no one.

That summer we follow the trail of gold flakes up Irish Creek. We have not much time - cut logs for Decker's sawmill, wood for the Tribbett tanbark factory, and make charcoal for old man Taylor's Rockbridge Foundry. We never have money. Turnip and Tater have taste for shine like Pa. We pan for gold flakes in Irish Creek. We find small nuggets up to where Nettle Creek enter Irish Creek - find no gold in Irish Creek upstream from Nettle Creek. Dumb Tater find out why it call Nettle Creek - step in patch of nettle-weed and spend two fortnight scratching itch away.

The next summer through winter me and Turnip and Tater follow the trail of gold flakes up Nettle Creek. Gold flakes about half way up to its spring. Me and Turnip and Tater explore uphill from the last gold flake in the creek. Me find a few small nuggets - a trail of gold. Then, me find the vein - me having the sharpest eye - underneath a bramble bush on rock slope.

Me keep promise to Pa. Me make Turnip and Tater ride with me to Presbeetarian Church at Twin Falls every Sunday. Yankees start war in spring. Pastor Elijah preach sermons telling about responsibilities to Confederacy. He say Jesus want all to join army - shooting a Yankee is like shooting the Devil. And he say Jesus want all to give to support Virginia and Confederacy. Me keep other promise to Pa - hate all Yankees.

Me and Turnip and Tater decide after a Pastor Elijah sermon to give our gold to the Confederacy. Jesus and Pa be proud.

Me ride to Lexington and tell Professor Jackson - he say to tell no one about gold. He have me ride with him to Richmond to see governor John Letcher. Professor Jackson know Honest John, also from Lexington. Honest John send Professor Jackson - he make him Colonel Jackson - to take command at Harper's Ferry. Honest John excited about Nettle Creek gold - he say to tell no one about the gold. He say me and Turnip and Tater need to serve Virginia and South by mining gold. Me tell Honest John me can make gold into coin for the treasury - he happy. Honest John tell me to contact him after several hundred pounds ready to ship.

Honest John send me back with letter to Rockbridge officials ordering me and Turnip and Tater exempt from conscript. Me tell him letter be not needed - we shoot first. Rockbridge Local Militia have sense to stay away from Irish Creek. Leader of militia - LT Amos Lackey - be little pipsqueak. Honest John say he tell Rockbridge powers that the Campbell farm is secret prison for Union soldiers. Campbells will get Yankees to talk - Honest John not so honest. LT Lackey and his gutless troops stay clear of Irish Creek and Campbell brothers.

Me and Turnip and Tater work mine. Turnip and Tater dig, me make coin - make mold, melt gold in kiln, and pour into mold. Pure gold into 1 ounce coin, $25 pieces. We keep farm and cut logs. Only time we leave Irish Creek be to cart logs to

Decker's Sawmill, for Turnip and Tater to get their shine, and every Sunday to hear Pastor Elijah. Summer of 1863, Pastor Elijah work church into a frenzy - Yankees kill our Stonewall. Tater want to join the army to kill Yankees. Turnip get him drunk instead.

Summer of 1864, me and Turnip and Tater ride to church. Pastor Elijah not there. News that Yankee soldiers raid Lexington and burn VMI make Pastor Elijah follow Jesus into battle there. Church elders say Pastor Elijah be martyr to South.

The next page stuck to the preceding one. Pastor Martin tried to gently pry them apart, first from the top, then from the bottom.

"I've read a lot about Pastor Elijah Hughes," offered Peggy Lauderdale, as Pastor Martin kept trying to separate carefully the two pages. "He indeed was a character – the pastor of Twin Falls during the Civil War, a nut case, and a real-life Bible thumper. He quoted Scripture to justify his hatred of Northerners. I read that he was so incensed at the Yankees during Hunter's Raid on Lexington and VMI that he singlehandedly charged a regiment with his gun blazing and bayonet drawn. He claimed he was leading an army of angels –"

"And I suspect his imaginary angels were no protection to him," interrupted Preston Hughes with a chuckle.

"Hey, Preston," Ed Painter laughed, "you any relation to the Bible-thumping preacher?"

Feeling confident, Pastor Martin gave the sheets a final pull. A large hole appeared in the middle of the page. The color of its paper differed from that of all other pages. It also appeared to have gotten wet, then dried – and crumpled, then smoothed out. He shook his head. Red-faced, he gasped, "I don't think we've lost much of the story. I'll skip over what remains on this page, just a profanity-laced diatribe about Yankees." He continued with his reading on the next page.

Several fool Yankee soldiers in a scavenging party ride up Irish Creek - Turnip shot em all. We let the buzzards, skunks, and possums pick em clean. Honest John replaced as governor - got message to me that our secret be known by President Jefferson Davis. Me need send him gold coin when ready.

Spring 1865, Turnip and Tater come to the end of the gold in the quartz vein. Me finish about 500 pounds of gold as 1 ounce coins. Turnip ride to Richmond - tell President Davis that gold ready for shipment. President Davis tell Turnip we be true patriots. President Davis make arrangement to have train pick up gold at Crowder station. We deliver gold coin in wooden boxes to station - train never show up. I hear news that Yankees chase President Davis from Richmond to Danville. All trains head South from Richmond.

Troops of marauding Yankees begin to move around the county. Several fools come up Irish Creek seeking revenge for Campbell prison camp. Buzzards ate a'plenty of 'em. Turnip and Tater stumble upon a lone dying Yankee up on the ridge near our mine. Tater shoot the Yankee horse to get the saddle and colors. Turnip and Tater went to scavenge the soldier's weapons - Yankee had blisters full of puss all over him. The next day, Turnip and Tater catch fever and die. I bad hate Yankees.

Me bury Turnip and Tater next to the mine. Me let buzzards eat the Yankee and the Yankee horse on the ridge. Me be all alone. Me need to protect our gold from the Yankees. Me pick up three caskets from

Charlie Hardin in Crowder - load gold coins into the caskets. Me haul em to cemetery in Crowder. Everyone stay away - Me spread word that a Yankee soldier give Turnip and Tater poison disease. Me bury em in cemetery. Graves of gold mark by flat rocks with chiseled TC, TC and Y.

Yankee carpetbaggers descend on Crowder. Me stay up on Nettle Creek. Me blow up the mine - no more gold anyway.

South has not yet risen again against the Yankees. Me be on my deadbed; no heirs. Me keep promise to Pa - hate Yankees and love Jesus. Buried coins now belong to Twin Falls Presbeetarian Church. Me put two coins in new safe at church. As me write testimony today, building of Twin Falls Presbeetarian Church next to cemetery almost finish.

"That's the end!" Pastor Martin looked up to stunned silence from the crowd.

Kit broke the quiet. "500 pounds of gold bullion. How much is that worth in today dollars?"

Pastor Martin grabbed his smartphone from his shirt pocket. "Right now it's a little over $1,200 per ounce."

"And 500 pounds is 8,000 ounces," Ed Painter chimed in. "So that's almost ten million dollars."

"Ten million dollars – we'll be dancin' in tall cotton," Faye Tolley mimicked a quick jig in celebration.

"Oh, my!" exclaimed Mabel Coleman, taking a seat in the only chair.

"Wow – the real Confederate gold," hollered Charlie Whitesides.

"It could be worth even more. The 8,000 coins are so rare that no one even knows that they exist."

"First step," Pastor Martin said, papers shaking in his hand. "We need to analyze the metal in these two coins. Is it really gold?"

"My grandson just did an experiment in his science class identifying a metal by its density – mass per unit volume," added Peggy Lauderdale. "Perhaps he could measure the density of one of the coins at school."

Doug Sullivan, ever the skeptical reporter, shook his head. "Y'all are just plain crazy . . . and gullible. Beets, Turnip, and Tater – Get real? And a hidden gold treasure from the Confederacy – come on?"

"I've heard others with those names – or rather nicknames – but not all three in the same family."

"But, yeah – I've heard there were plenty of Campbells up on Irish Creek in the past."

"The story seems unbelievable, yet believable."

Kit gulped, "Now, that's what I call a real story – in fact, a real treasure. I should be able to get my editor to put out a special edition of the paper, instead of just posting on the internet, without waiting until next Wednesday. I can write up the story as an exclusive for *The Roanoke Times* or call the TV station. And I have pictures. This could be the big break in my career." She threw her camera and notepad in her bag, and headed up the cellar stairs in a full sprint.

"Pastor Martin, what're you going to do with the testimony and gold coins?" queried Peggy.

Pastor Martin stuttered, "Ah . . . Ah . . ." He took a few steps away from the crowd and immediately ran into a cobweb. He swatted it off his face.

"Cat got your tongue, pastor," laughed Ed Painter. "First time I've seen you speechless in a long, long time."

"Funny," commented Pastor Martin as he cleaned the remnants of the cobweb from his forehead. "Well, first let's make sure the letter and coins are authentic."

"Mining gold up Irish Creek makes sense," pondered Ed. He pointed in the direction of the back wall, to the northeast. "After all, there's that Irish Creek tin mine up there – a working mine long ago. Why not gold as well?"

"I always thought Crowder was changed to Cornwall, after its namesake in England, in the 1890s because of the tin mine – with both being mining communities and all. Maybe they knew about the gold mine back then too," added Alice Jane Grant. Speaking in her characteristic raspy voice, she excitedly added, "I've always heard there was gold in that mountain up Irish Creek. In fact, my granddaddy Joe Hubbard supposedly had a prospect up there, but he got chased off."

"And my grandpappy always told me about a gold mine on the other side of the Blue Ridge – at Buck Mountain. About ten miles as the crow flies from Nettle Creek," related Troy Montgomery, with thumbs in his bib straps.

"Then there's the legend of Yankee Horse Ridge," roared Preston Hughes. "Indeed it was named after a Yankee soldier's horse that died there during the Civil War. Maybe Tater Campbell will now go down in history as the shooter to help the horse along on –"

"Just one problem that I can see," scoffed Reese Coleman, the oldest man in the crowd. "I've been all over our cemetery and thereabouts in my 86 years here on this earth. I don't reckon I ever saw one, much less three, graves as described in the letter."

Chapter Three
TREASURE HUNT

The ringing jolted Pastor Martin awake. He rolled on his side and automatically pushed the off button on his alarm clock. The ringing continued. He squinted at the alarm clock next to the ringing phone – 6:01 AM. He rolled onto his back and stretched, shaking at least some of the sleep from his brain. When the phone rang this early, his mind immediately jumped into emergency mode – *What happened? Who died? Where am I needed?*

By the fifth ring, he sat up on the edge of his bed. He coughed to clear his voice. "Hello, this is Elwood Martin."

"Good morning, Reverend Martin. I'm Sparky Peters, a field reporter for the morning show of Roanoke WDBJ Channel 7. I was hoping to interview you about –"

"What?" Pastor Martin staggered out of bed, then flipped on the light switch. "When?"

"This morning. I'd be interviewing you live, on the air."

"Do you realize it's not even daylight yet?" Pastor Martin shuffled across the room and parted the curtains in the bedroom window.

"But it will be soon. In fact, you must live at the house on the other side of the cemetery. I just saw someone peeking out a window over there. The breaking news overnight has been the discovery of a cache of Confederate gold at your church. Just a quick interview, please."

Pastor Martin saw the WDBJ satellite truck, along with several cars, parked on the shoulder of South River Road in front of the church cemetery. Light beams from flashlights darted across the cemetery. Trying to gather his thoughts, he stammered, "But . . . but breaking news – we only had the opening of our safe last night. And your reporter wasn't even here."

"Would half an hour give you enough time? We'd do the broadcast in the 6:30 time block – perhaps do half the interview in the cemetery, then finish the other half in front of the opened safe. There you could show the letter of Beets Campbell and his gold coins."

Pastor Martin, now fully awake, headed for the bathroom. "OK, I'll walk over to your truck," he decided. "Meet you there by daybreak."

Pastor Martin hastily showered, then toweled off. Walking back into the bedroom, he noticed the phone blinking. The digital display on its base flashed three – three messages in less than five minutes. He ignored them. He dressed and snuck another look out the bedroom window. Two more satellite trucks, near the WDBJ truck, were parked on the other side of the cemetery. The phone rang. After six rings, the answering machine clicked on.

Downstairs he microwaved a mug of coffee left over in the pot brewed yesterday. He sipped the coffee as he scurried out the back door under the cover of dusky light, with no time to admire the blooming red rose bushes and a kaleidoscope of colors from flowering zinnias. The daily regional newspaper, *The Roanoke Times,* had already been delivered to the box at the end of his sidewalk. He returned through the back door, unseen, and retreated to the kitchen table. He paid no heed to the constantly ringing telephone; instead he quickly flipped to the Virginia section of the paper. The headline – "Confederate Gold Located" – with a subheading of "$10,000,000 of Gold Buried in Twin Falls Presbyterian Church Cemetery" jumped out at him. Its byline featured Kit King reporting an exclusive in cooperation with *The Lexington News-Gazette.* A spread of pictures included the front view of the church highlighting its

Jonah-and-the-whale sculpture, the safe within the opened safe, and a gold coin inscribed with C.S.A being held by him. The article took up most of the section's front page.

Pastor Martin grabbed his cell phone and headed out the front door with a refilled coffee mug in hand. He sighed, for the irony of the situation didn't escape him. Last night, he yearned for press coverage of the big event at his church and got very little; now today, he wanted some quiet time to investigate the discovery, and what he got was media frenzy.

The sun started to peek over the Blue Ridge as Pastor Martin strode briskly across the church parking lot. He caught a glimpse of first light reflecting from the golden cross at the top of the church steeple – still no hawk. Then, instead of admiring Nettle Mountain in the distance, he was dumbfounded by the numerous cars and trucks parked helter-skelter around the church. A scan of the cemetery picked up clusters of people, some with shovels and others with metal detectors, flitting about the gravestones. He stopped in his tracks – *Oh my goodness, we've created a giant treasure hunt.*

Arriving at the middle of the cemetery, he bellowed, "No digging in the cemetery. Please respect the gravesites. All are welcome; but do not disturb this hallowed ground."

Treasure hunters, heads down, ignored the announcement and continued milling about the cemetery. Pastor Martin groused at the sight of two men jousting with metal detectors for a prime location in the older part of the cemetery; and he gently scolded a teenage girl for digging with a trowel next to a headstone. He even saw Kit King on her hands and knees intently surveying the ground close to the cemetery wall, remembering that Kit had left the safe opening ceremony before Reese Coleman's revelation that there weren't any graves in the cemetery matching those described by Beets Campbell.

Pastor Martin dialed Reese. He answered on the first ring.

Before Pastor Martin said a word, Reese spoke, "I hear it's a zoo over at the church. I should be there in about five minutes."

"Thanks Reese. You might want to give our big fellows, Troy and Harry, calls as well. See whether they can help keep order here at the church. People are all over the cemetery."

"Golly gee," Reese chuckled, "we got ourselves a real gold rush."

"Yep, everyone's looking for the TC and Y grave markers."

"Hrmmph," Reese hissed, "the ones that ain't there."

Pastor Martin groaned as he looked around the cemetery once again. "Maybe call the sheriff's department to give them a heads up as to what's happening here."

"Will do. From the chatter I'm picking up on my police scanner, though, a deputy is on his way for traffic control," Reese replied.

Pastor Martin then called Peggy Lauderdale.

Seeing his name pop up on her caller ID, she answered before the phone finished its first ring. "Pastor Martin, I hear you're a popular fellow this morning. I'm watching the Channel 7 morning show. They just announced that Sparky will be interviewing you shortly."

"Yeah," Pastor Martin half-laughed. "I'm heading across the cemetery as we speak. Peggy, can we meet later this afternoon? We need a strategy. Perhaps first put a transcript of the testimony and pictures of the gold coins on our website," he rambled. "We also need to determine whether the testimony of Beets Campbell is real, or at least consistent with the history of the region."

"I'm one step ahead of you," crowed Peggy. "Last night, I was in the county library until almost midnight. My librarian friend snuck me in after hours. As someone said at the safe opening last night, the writings of Beets Campbell are unbelievable, but yet believable."

"Hmmm," Pastor Martin mulled.

"I'm planning to do some more research and make phone calls," added Peggy. "I'll see you around three o'clock at your church office. Actually I see you already. The camera is on you as you're walking toward it – and a beautiful sunrise behind you."

"Yep," Pastor Martin sighed, "It's Show Time!"

It all made sense – she thought. Carlene "Sunshine" Clutterbuck had just gotten off the phone with her sister, who told her about Kit King's news flash from this morning's *Roanoke Times*. Sunshine always felt something unsettling about the Twin Falls cemetery, ever since her granny's burial there when she was five years old. Afterwards, every time she visited granny and other family members at this cemetery, creepy-crawlies oozed from every pore of her body. *Something just wasn't right there.* Now she understood – *It wasn't the presence of those six feet under, but the confused spirits of those not buried properly. The gold in the caskets must've displaced the spirits of the Campbell brothers and the Yankee. Their spirits were still trapped outside their graves and drifted about the cemetery like lost souls.*

Sunshine realized she needed to seize this once-in-a-lifetime opportunity. She grabbed her Bible, opened it to Chapter 8 of Matthew, glanced without hesitation at the paragraphs following verse 28, and yelled, "Hallelujah. Jesus ordered the spirits in the possessed man to 'Go.' And these spirits went into a herd of pigs." Her green eyes sparkled with joy; her husband Clarence always said her eyes released rays of sunshine. She waved the Bible in the air. She praised her Lord God Almighty for showing her the way. Finally, she beamed, "In the name of Jesus, I'll send the wandering spirits in the cemetery into pigs. The pigs will lead me to the graves of gold, to the final resting places where the spirits wanna go. Indeed, where Jesus commands their spirits to go!"

Sunshine always had a smile on her face, along with a few freckles on her cheeks. She was short, barely five feet in height, and skinny. Clarence told her she was so thin she could take a shower in the barrel of a shotgun. But she had plenty of spunk, as well as notions.

Sunshine hurried to a cluttered bedroom where she ran a comb through her bleached blonde hair. Gazing into the mirror, she made a mental note to trim her pageboy that night. Clarence might notice it looked a little straggly around the right ear. She whisked bright red lipstick on her narrow lips and complemented it with dangly earrings, her favorite ones with concentric circles. A self-made purple concoction of paw paw, pomegranate, and vanilla bean extracts sat in an unlabeled bottle on her nightstand; she splashed a few drops behind each ear. Clarence found its citrusy smell intoxicating. On her way out of the room, she grabbed two cheap necklaces with cross pendants from the dresser top.

Sunshine ran from the small house trailer, badly in need of painting and roof repairs, through a yard littered with miscellaneous engine parts, beer cans, and cigarette butts. The cast concrete statue of Jesus riding a donkey seemed oddly out of place. Her first stop was at the rickety shed that doubled as Clarence's kennel for his hunting dogs. A chorus of baying hounds announced her arrival. She snatched two tracking collars, ones used to electronically follow hunting dogs, from a shelf. *Clarence definitely wouldn't be happy with her borrowing the collars, but he'd understand.* At the far end of the ramshackle property, peppered with sumac trees and overgrown weeds, was the pig sty, home to Grunt and Hamm. She grabbed two apples from the feed bin to attract the 400 pound gray-and-white behemoths and scaled the fence in one jump. Grunt and Hamm slogged through the mud to greet her. Clarence hadn't been happy that she'd named the pigs, even less happy that she'd tamed them.

The pigs resisted when Sunshine fastened the antenna-topped electronic collars around each of their withers, using bungee cords as extenders, and attached the cross necklaces around each neck with baling twine. Grunt was especially upset, pushing her into the mud. She tried to wipe the mud from her tank top and jeans but ended up just smearing most of it about the jeans. But she had no time to waste on cleaning – she was a woman on a mission.

Fortunately, Clarence had already hooked up the stock trailer to "Ole Brownie," his battered 1984 Dodge Ram pickup truck, and had backed it up to the loading ramp attached to the pigs' pen. He had planned to take them to market that afternoon. *Clarence wouldn't like her borrowing his truck, but when she returned with a truck full of gold, he'd understand.* She loaded Grunt and Hamm, becoming even muddier in the process, then threw a pick ax and shovel in the truck bed.

Ole Brownie clattered from her and Clarence's small farm in Arnold's Valley, just south of Natural Bridge, to Twin Falls Presbyterian Church at the other end of the county. It was late morning by the time Sunshine arrived at the traffic jam surrounding the Twin Falls cemetery. But it was her lucky day; a car pulled out from its parking space on the shoulder of the road in front of the church. She squeezed the rusted trailer into the spot, backing it at an incongruous angle into the ditch just next to the Jonah-and-the-whale sculpture. Ole Brownie stuck out onto the road, blocking traffic.

Sunshine jumped out of the truck, impervious to the honking car horns. She quickly dropped the ramp to the trailer and screamed, "Go, in the name of Jesus," to the lost spirits in the cemetery. The antennae on Grunt and Hamm would retrieve the spirits and return them to their rightful gold-containing burial spots. *Clarence would be proud of her for bringing home the gold treasure.*

After a few tentative steps off the trailer, Grunt and Hamm wildly snorted, squealed, and sprinted. The commotion surrounding them in the cemetery and on the highway drove them absolutely crazy. Two very large and scared pigs galloped haphazardly throughout the tombstones. Sunshine followed, yelling "Go, in the name of Jesus" and thinking their frightful grunting was due to them corralling the lost spirits, not their fear of people and noise. Treasure hunters scattered, using shovels and metal detectors to ward off the stampeding pigs. The pigs, with antennae on their backs and crosses dangling from their necks, headed in the general direction of the stone wall on the opposite side of the cemetery.

Hamm barreled over, instead of around, the headstone of Eula Belle Elliot, Sunshine's granny, and toppled it. Sunshine dropped to her knees at the stone, now flat on the ground. She cried, begging forgiveness from her granny. Then, at top speed Grunt and Hamm had Kit King, still searching on her hands and knees, in their sights. She froze. Troy Montgomery came running and picked her up like a sack of potatoes. He deposited her at a safe distance from the pigs. The pigs finally took refuge next to the stone wall on the far side of the cemetery, near the large sycamore tree looming on the wall's other side. They were squealing in panic, trying to simultaneously blast through the wall and jump over it. They weren't successful with either.

Kit gawked wantonly at her knight in shining armor, who showed no interest in her.

Troy and Harry then herded Grunt and Hamm along the stone wall away from the road toward the parsonage, where they penned them in its back yard. Troy retrieved Ole Brownie and stock trailer, then backed the trailer to the gate at the parsonage's yard. Grunt and Hamm calmly loaded after rooting and denuding the plants and shrubs in the pastor's back yard.

Reese Coleman, aided by Pastor Martin who'd been giving an interview at the edge of the cemetery, consoled Sunshine at her granny's grave. Reese uprighted the granite stone and promised the mud-encrusted Sunshine that all was okay. He'd cement her granny's headstone back in place tomorrow. Meanwhile, Sunshine kept blabbering that the gold was hers, that the spirits of the Campbell brothers and the Yankee led the pigs to their graves over by the cemetery wall.

Pastor Martin and Reese rolled their eyes.

Pastor Martin tried to reason with Sunshine that the pigs were just running to the spot farthest from the people, while Reese called her husband Clarence at his job at Ruley's Auto-Body Shop. Reese knew both Clarence and Sunshine. In fact, Sunshine used some of her special ginseng tea to help Reese's wife, Mabel, with digestive issues several months ago. It had worked.

Sunshine's face glowed upon realizing her Clarence was on his way. *He'd understand; he'd claim the gold as theirs.* She raised her arms to the heavens and shouted, "Praise the Lord." The crowd of onlookers, who'd gathered about her, collectively took a few steps away.

Pastor Martin gently touched Sunshine's shoulder and cautiously asked, "How are you?"

Smiling, she responded, "Fine . . . as fine as a frog's hair."

† † †

"Sorry I'm a little late, Pastor Martin," Peggy apologized as she entered his church office at 3:14 without knocking. "But, geesh, I think this is the first traffic jam I've ever encountered getting to the church. Cars were backed up quite a ways down South River Road."

"Not only cars," Pastor Martin got up from his desk chair to greet Peggy, "but telephone calls as well. I convinced Alice Jane to come in to answer the church telephone. Reese, Troy, and Harry have been out in the cemetery all day."

"Plus a sheriff's deputy is directing traffic at the crossroads of South River and Irish Creek Roads," Peggy laughed, "and the church's parking lot is full. Have you ever seen such a sight?"

"In fact, Twin Falls made the national news with all my interviews." Pastor Martin hoarsely added, "The Confederate gold story is going viral on the cable news channels."

"Everyone likes a treasure hunt, much like a big payout in the lottery." Peggy paused, then grinned, "As well as a greased pig scramble. Everyone's talking about the pigs running amok through the cemetery. "

Pastor Martin shook his head. "Some stuff you just can't make up."

They shared a laugh, while drifting to his desk.

"I guess you won't be entering any of your roses and zinnias in the county fair this year," Peggy kidded.

"But maybe a few blossoms of hogsweed," Pastor Martin sighed, as he instinctively straightened his necktie. Having a second thought, he loosened the tie and unfastened the top button of his white dress shirt. He smiled, "It's been a long day."

Pastor Martin directed Peggy to take a seat in front of his desk. The only adornments on the faded green walls in his small office were an old painting of the church and diplomas for his graduation from college and seminary. One wall was covered with bookshelves overflowing with papers and volumes. On its center shelf sat open an autographed copy of *The Holy Spirit: Activating God's Power in Your Life* by Billy Graham, surrounded by more of Billy Graham's books. On the other shelves, a layer of dust covered books ranging from C. S. Lewis' *The Screwtape Letters* to *The Da Vinci Code* by Dan Brown, the latter a present from Silas Clark.

Pastor Martin sat in his office chair, which emitted a characteristic creak. "Well, tell me what you've found about the Beets Campbell testimony."

"Where should I start?" snickered Peggy, as she plopped a stack of books and papers onto the edge of his desk.

"How about with the Campbells – any Beets, Turnip, or Tater . . . especially Beets?" probed Pastor Martin.

"Well, it's not an easy question to answer," responded Peggy. "There's nary a Beets, Turnip, nor Tater Campbell on land or census records. But then these might have been their nicknames and not given names for legal purposes. It would've made things a lot easier if Beets would've given his father's name, instead of just Pa, in his testimony. Indeed there are several Campbells identified as being land owners up Irish Creek. Most lived at the nexus with Big Bend and Nettle Creeks. They had names like Charles, James, John, Joseph, and Cyrus. There was a Cane as well."

"Didn't think they grew sugar cane around here," teased Pastor Martin.

"There aren't any Campbells in the Irish Creek area anymore. But I talked to some of the old-timers around here. They told me tales about the Irish Creek Campbells – in particular, you didn't want to be found trespassing on their land. They were a rough crew. My uncle told me this morning that his grandpa used to tell him stories about them – no one messed with them. On a good day, they might give you a warning shot . . . but, he said, they'd never give a Yankee a warning shot. It was almost as though they were stuck fighting the Civil War into the 20th century."

Pastor Martin rocked back in his chair with his hands interlaced behind his head and exhaled audibly.

She continued, "My uncle didn't remember any of their names, except for one. He said that this Campbell achieved folk hero status as a bear hunter up around Nettle Creek. He went by the name of . . . get this . . . Spud Campbell. Evidently, the Campbell clan must've loved their root vegetables."

Pastor Martin murmured as he rubbed his chin. "So, Beets might be credible, but not proven." He ran his hands through his hair. "How 'bout gold mining in the area?"

Peggy rustled through her papers and thrust a topographic map in front of him. She stood and pointed to an X she had marked on the map. "A tin mine was way up Irish Creek, on a tributary called Panther Run. In fact, Panther Run is just upstream from where Nettle Creek enters Irish Creek. The entrance to the tin mine was on this side of the Blue Ridge near the community of Montebello. A trace of the mine's entrance is still there." Peggy flipped through more pages, then pulled out a page of notes. "This mine operated off and on from 1884 to 1919. It produced 17 tons of tin from the 3200 tons of mined ore."

Pastor Martin strummed his fingers on his desk. His gaze wandered out the office door to where Alice Jane was talking to a visitor.

Peggy directed him back to the map. "And the mine is within a few miles of Yankee Horse Ridge, where legend has it being named for the location of an exhausted Yankee horse that died there in the last days of the Civil War."

"Seems consistent thus far with the story of Beets Campbell," mused Pastor Martin. "The landmarks of Nettle Creek and Yankee Horse Ridge are indeed close to the abandoned tin mine."

Peggy pulled a pamphlet from her stack of papers. Pastor Martin grabbed it from Peggy's outstretched arm and flipped through its pages.

"I got in touch with a scientist from the Virginia Division of Mineral Resources," Peggy said. "He provided me with technical articles produced by the Division that dated to the 1990s. Their analyses showed anomalously high concentrations of silver and gold in certain areas of Yankee Horse Ridge – or, in other words, around Nettle Creek. They claim such is consistent with gold in underlying or nearby bedrock. Although the author of one study didn't find any visible gold nuggets, he didn't preclude a gold vein being in the area. He did find some telltale signs of gold's possible presence, such as pyrite – that is, fool's gold – as well as a mineral called arsenopyrite." Peggy pointed to a second X on the map. "Finally, he found what might have been a vestige of an opening to a mine half-way up Nettle Creek, about where described in the testimony of Beets Campbell."

Pastor Martin stared at the X on the map, as he fiddled with the pencil in his hand.

"And then the scientist said – off the record – that he'd heard folk tales of gold being mined in the Irish Creek – Nettle Creek area," Peggy added. "In fact, some people still pan for gold in Irish Creek – but find nothing of any consequence."

"Well, I guess there might be some basis for all this gold folk lore," he contemplated.

Peggy smiled, "And there's more. It seems that the stories are true of Joe Hubbard – I think Alice Jane indicated he was her grandpa – making a gold claim on Nettle Creek at the turn of the 20th century. Oddly, soon after the claim, Joe went missing. No one in her family ever wanted to talk about him, other than he was a prospector."

"It gets more and more interesting," Pastor Martin pondered, as he used his pencil to drum on the desk.

Peggy checked her notes. "Oh – one last thing about the gold. Some small gold mines or prospects were worked in the late 1800s and early 1900s east of the Blue Ridge. Buck Mountain, as was mentioned last night, as well as Jack's Hill mine, Colleen prospect, and Ivy Creek prospect – all within twenty miles or so of Nettle Creek. But most of Virginia's gold was mined further east in a band from northern Virginia to Orange County. The last mine in Virginia closed right after World War II." She hesitated, then continued. "And one reference I found stated that, because of labor shortages, essentially no gold was mined in Virginia during the Civil War."

"To paraphrase the old saying," Pastor Martin chuckled, "there's gold in them thar hills!" Peggy nodded, as he queried, "Did you find out anything about the story of Beets and ties to the Civil War?"

"I had a long discussion with Clayton Bodie, a local historian, and checked many reference books in the local library," Peggy smiled. "Indeed Stonewall Jackson traveled to Richmond to see Governor John Letcher, nicknamed Honest John, in the early days of the Civil War. So, I guess it's possible that Beets could've accompanied him – just as possible, but nowhere recorded, is that Beets met Professor Jackson during deliveries from the Rockbridge Foundry to VMI. It is recorded, though, that the Rockbridge Foundry supplied horseshoes and other metal goods to VMI."

"Possible – but the question is whether it actually happened?" contemplated Pastor Martin, as he returned his pencil to his desk and with his fingers twisted the chain from which his cross pendant hung around his neck.

"The bottom line is that it's hard to say for sure," confided Peggy. "Then at the other end of the war, during the frantic days of April 1865 when Confederacy President Jefferson Davis relocated the capital from Richmond to Danville, Virginia – legend has it that ten million dollars, in today's money, worth of gold and silver went missing –"

"Interesting that you quote ten million dollars," he took a deep breath. "The same as we estimated for the gold mined by Beets Campbell and his brothers."

"Just speculation suggested by Mr. Bodie, but it could be that Jefferson Davis and the Confederacy anticipated the arrival of this gold from the Campbell brothers in the closing days of the war. Maybe the long lost Confederate gold, although many historians discount its existence, isn't buried in Danville – or, for that matter, anywhere. The 'real' Confederate gold might never have left its original location in Rockbridge County."

"So, once again, possible," he shrugged, "but did it really happen?"

"But, if Beets' story is true," Peggy mused, "we've got several million dollars of gold buried in our cemetery."

Pastor Martin thought for a moment. "What is it that Reese always says?" He laughed, "And if frogs had wings, they wouldn't bump their rumps when they jumped."

Peggy shared the laugh. "That's right . . . if, if, if."

He then pointed at a heap of notes on his desk. "Look here, Peggy, I've already got messages and calls from numerous academic historians and self-proclaimed Civil War experts wanting to inspect and study the testimony of Beets Campbell. Some claim it has the potential to change many views about Civil War history."

"That's what Mr. Bodie said as well," Peggy nodded. "Also, the events described by Beets in his testimony are consistent with the history of Twin Falls Presbyterian."

"But the conclusive proof," Pastor Martin reared back in his chair, causing another loud creak. "Just where's the treasure hidden? Where're Turnip's, Tater's, and the Yankee's grave markers?"

"Well, not here in the cemetery next to our church. Neither Reese nor any other old-timer in the church, or even in the Irish Creek area, remember seeing gravestones identified by TC or Y." Peggy shrugged, "There aren't any other nearby cemeteries where the burial of this treasure could've been done. Although there're several family cemeteries way up Irish Creek and one at Bethesda Baptist over on Old Buena Vista Road, there's nothing with such gravestones, or anything that would be comparable over this time period."

"Let's hope we find 'em, before the treasure hunters hone in on 'em." He rose from his desk and stared out the window at the activity in the cemetery. He shook his head in disbelief.

"What next? My 'to do' list might have room to include some of your ideas," she joked.

"Two things for tomorrow," Pastor Martin deliberated. "First, take one of the gold coins and see whether it's actually gold. Maybe a chemist at one of the colleges could help you out."

"I'll make inquiries. I suspect a chemist, or even a jeweler, might provide more authority than my grandson determining its density to prove its identity," Peggy teased.

He turned back from the window. "Second, take one of the pages of the original testimony and copies of the rest and see whether they're authentic for this post-Civil War period."

"I'm one step ahead of you there. I've already contacted a Civil War document appraiser in Charlottesville. He's expecting me tomorrow morning."

"Great – we have a plan," Pastor Martin escorted Peggy to the office door. "Say, let's meet again tomorrow afternoon, same time. In a sense, we're racing against the treasure hunters descending upon our cemetery in search for the graves. I hope we don't have any modern day grave robbers."

"Word is already out that the location of the graves is a mystery," Peggy said as she started to exit the office.

"Well, I'll also announce that I'll have a press conference late tomorrow to, at least, address some questions concerning the authenticity of the coins and document."

Before Pastor Martin returned any phone calls, he marched out to the Twin Falls Presbyterian sign, next to the Jonah-and-the-whale sculpture, in front of the church. There he posted the title of his sermon for the Sunday worship service – *Our Treasure Map*.

† † †

Friday morning's *Roanoke Times* headline – "New Confederate Gold: Old Hoax" – greeted Pastor Martin over his breakfast of reheated coffee and microwaved frozen sausage biscuit. The news report included a full transcript of the testimony of Beets Campbell. But questions were raised whether Beets' account and the accompanying gold coins were real, neither having yet been authenticated. Several pundits proclaimed Beets' entire testimony to be a fairytale, as believable as pigs being spirit transporters. And a plethora of shovel toting people had been unable to locate any stones with TC and/or Y on them in the church cemetery. Although the Twin Falls Presbyterian Church cemetery had Campbell tombstones, the article reported none dated to the 1860s era.

Pastor Martin looked at his watch. He groaned – 8:50, ten minutes until his first appointment of the day at the church. Every twenty minutes Alice Jane had scheduled him for a different phone or live interview with journalists from all over the state. He didn't look forward to repeating answers to the same questions – Where's the gold? Why hadn't the safe been opened years earlier? If someone finds the graves, does the church share the treasure with them? Are the Campbell brothers real?

He exited the parsonage through the backyard. It looked as though it'd been hit by a tornado with uprooted shrubs, broken branches, and dead flowers strewn all about. The marauding Grunt and Hamm even managed to mangle most of the manicured grass lawn.

Pastor Martin had telephoned the Clutterbucks last night to check on the wellbeing of Sunshine. Clarence answered; and he wasn't happy. Sunshine had planted herself next to their pig pen to protect Grunt and Hamm. She wouldn't let him take his pigs to market. She claimed they still possessed the spirits of Turnip, Tater, and the Yankee because the pigs weren't able to release the spirits into their gold-laden caskets. She demanded to return with Grunt and Hamm to the cemetery, but he had all keys to Ole Brownie. On the other hand, Clarence kept asking, "And you say, 'xactly how much gold's buried there?"

As Pastor Martin passed through his now-bent backyard gate, he looked directly at his church and stopped. A deep peaceful breath accompanied his sight of the church steeple rising majestically into the backdrop of Nettle Mountain. Still, no hawk on the steeple.

His calm was short lived. Another riddle attributed to Silas immediately jumped into his mind. Reese Coleman confessed to him yesterday, after most treasure hunters departed for the day, that Silas refused to tell him the answer to a riddle. Reese and Mabel had visited Silas at the nursing home the previous week. Silas presented them with a riddle, then whispered in Reese's ear: "The answer is a secret." Reese fussed at Silas for not telling him the riddle's solution. But Silas just hooted and hollered in laughter, so much so he couldn't get his breath and they had to call for a nurse. Pastor Martin placated Reese somewhat by telling him that Silas plays the same game with him by not telling him the answer. But now this new riddle confounded him, just like the riddle about the hawk on the church steeple. His mind kept spinning – *If I have it, I don't share it. If I share it, I don't have it. What is it?* He initially thought money, or food, as possible answers; but they didn't quite fit. Pastor Martin focused, once again, on the church steeple. His calm returned with a chuckle to himself – *I'm trying to find ten million dollars of gold treasure and instead I'm preoccupied with solving a stupid riddle.*

On his walk to the church, Pastor Martin shook his head in amazement at the treasure hunters. Similar to yesterday morning, they descended like a swarm of locusts on the two-acre cemetery. Even the skepticism of today's news articles didn't diminish their enthusiasm. Still, no one found anything. Reese enjoyed the attention; he set up a chair and tent at the edge of the cemetery. A steady stream of reporters, self-proclaimed historians, and treasure hunters debated possible locations of the Campbell treasure with him in the shade. The women of the church, led by Mabel Coleman, supplied coffee, lemonade, and iced tea, as well as cookies, for the cemetery visitors under an adjacent tent. Along South River Road, an enterprising young man hawked gold-colored tee shirts emblazoned with an artist's rendition of Beets Campbell with C.S.A. coins in one hand and a shovel in the other. The activities took on a carnival atmosphere under brilliant blue and sunny skies, but customarily humid air.

† † †

Pastor Martin suggested to Reese that seventy chairs should be more than sufficient for the five o'clock press conference in the church's Fellowship Hall. Several minutes before the hour, Reese added another thirty chairs. Still, reporters and bystanders stood against the walls of the packed room. Cameramen from several television stations jockeyed for the best positions. Microphones were taped to the podium; wires were everywhere. Reese fretted that circuit breakers would pop.

Pastor Martin and Peggy Lauderdale arrived at a noisy Fellowship Hall a few minutes late. All could readily identify him as the preacher, attired in black slacks, white shirt, pastor's collar, and a four-inch wooden cross pendant. He scanned the crowd as he walked to the podium, recognizing many journalists who had interviewed him over the past two days. Doug Sullivan, the reporter for *The Rockbridge Advocate*, sat scowling in the back row. Once at the podium, with Peggy standing next to him, Pastor Martin spotted Kit King with her notepad and camera on the front row. She must have come straight from the cemetery; she had grass stains on the knees of her jeans. But he did a double take at the presence of the couple – Sunshine and Clarence Clutterbuck – sitting next to her.

Pastor Martin took a deep breath. Flash bulbs popped; video cameras rolled. His hands sweated. He welcomed all, offered a prayer, and introduced Peggy as doing most of the leg work for the information being supplied today.

He took another deep breath. "Let me first give you an update on the coins found in our church safe. Are they gold? Robbie Jones, owner of Hamric & Sheridan Jewelers in Lexington, examined one of the coins today. He attests that the coin is indeed pure 24K gold. A chemistry professor at VMI measured the density of the coin to be 19.3 g/mL, an exact match for gold. Dr. Dan Harrison at this college indicates it's hard to fake this density by mixing a little gold with other common metals, all of which have lower densities. The coin was exactly 1.0012 ounce in weight – so it had been accurately albeit crudely made. Finally, Dr. Harrison agrees with Mr. Jones that indeed the coin is pure gold bullion. Dr. Harrison also used an instrument to prove –"

"Was the coin dated to the 1860s?" interrupted Doug Sullivan.

"It's my understanding that it's impossible to determine when the coin was made," Pastor Martin sighed, "only inferences from its inscription of C.S.A."

"But the Confederacy never minted gold coins," yelled a curly-headed reporter from the left side of the room.

"Well," Pastor Martin swept a bead of sweat from his forehead with his sleeve. "The testimony of Beets Campbell explains why these were unique."

"But how do you know they weren't fraudulently produced in someone's basement last year?" shouted another reporter. "Can't you chemically age date the coins, like scientists put ages on historical artifacts all the time?"

Pastor Martin had no chance to answer; more reporters yelled other questions simultaneously. The crowd buzzed. Pastor Martin flapped his arms, motioning for quiet.

"All I can tell you at this time is that the coins are pure gold," he stated, "just as Beets described in his testimony."

Peggy and Pastor Martin switched positions with Peggy now at the podium. "I met today with a document examiner, Dr. C. Hamilton Hollandsworth, an expert who's testified in many court cases on the legitimacy of historical manuscripts. He specializes in Civil War materials and is certified in the field. Dr. Hollandsworth authenticated the writings of Beets Campbell. He verified the document was written on paper consistent with that manufactured in the decade after the Civil War. Also, ink and penmanship are consistent with that of that time period. No chemical analyses have yet been performed on the paper or ink. In conclusion, nothing in the recently discovered testimony of Beets Campbell has been discredited or proven false."

Kit King, as she shook her hair from her face, voiced the question of many. In her shrill voice, she squealed, "But it hasn't been proven true either. Where're the gravestones with TC and Y chiseled thereon?"

"Yeah, where's the gold buried?" bellowed one of the treasure hunters, rising from his seat on the back row and shaking his fist in the air. Reporters shouted questions lost in the background noise of a rowdy audience.

Pastor Martin jumped back to the podium, pleading with the crowd to be quiet, so he could respond.

"The gold's location is problematic," yelled Pastor Martin over the residual clamor. "We still haven't discovered the grave markers of Turnip Campbell, Tater Campbell, as well as the Yankee in our cemetery, or in any neighboring cemetery. We, as well as lots of other people, are searching for these stones. We do ask everyone to respect the property of Twin Falls Presbyterian Church in their search. We agree that 'the proof of the pudding,' so to speak, is the existence of these three graves. We will continue our search for –"

"Are you gonna release the pigs again in this search?" laughed one of the reporters standing on the side of the room.

"Let us know so we can get it on film this time," chimed in a cameraman for a Lynchburg television station.

Pastor Martin stole a glance at Sunshine and Clarence. Sunshine smiled. Her green eyes radiated joy, impervious to snarky remarks.

He sighed, "Any serious questions?"

Another reporter's hand shot up. "I see your sermon this Sunday is entitled *Our Treasure Map*. Will you be providing further information in your search for the gold at that time?"

"I invite everyone to attend my sermon," Pastor Martin coyly grinned.

† † †

The next morning was unusually brisk, requiring a sweater; but the sun rising over the Blue Ridge guaranteed a pleasant day, much like the past few days. Pastor Martin moseyed out to the tent that Reese Coleman had erected at cemetery's edge. He sat on a lawn chair next to Reese, both sipping their coffees along with a breakfast of church cookies.

Reese pointed to a scrawny little man under the old oak tree in front of the church. "That fellow has been here dawn to dusk for the last two days. He just seems to sneak around, like he's trying to hide what he's doing – gives me the creeps. His metal detector is top of the line, a real Cadillac. Supposedly, yesterday he found a cuff-link from the Civil War uniform of a Union soldier under the oak."

"He seems upset that another person is also metal detecting around the tree," observed Pastor Martin, as he took another sip of coffee.

"He's quite territorial," laughed Reese. "I've heard him called 'Slick' by others, who claim he hails from Bratton's Run, near Goshen."

When not entertaining visitors at the tent, Pastor Martin and Reese discussed the Saturday morning newspaper articles about their church treasure. One article reported on the "New Gold Rush" and the near impossibility of finding a shovel or a metal detector on any store shelf in Rockbridge County. Another,

"Cemetery Tourism," described the influx of people searching for the grave sites of Turnip and Tater Campbell as well as the Yankee. Attendance at previous meccas in Rockbridge County – the grave of Stonewall Jackson and the tomb for Robert E. Lee – paled in comparison to recent visits to the Twin Falls Presbyterian Church cemetery. It had become a *bona fide* local tourist attraction much like Natural Bridge. And a final article, "Whale of a Treasure," playfully compared the size of the church's unique welcoming sculpture to the dimensions of three coffins containing the potential cache of Confederate gold coins.

A treasure hunter, holding a metal detector, stopped by the tent for a cup of coffee, while her young son, clutching his miniaturized detector, grabbed an iced tea. They told Reese and Pastor Martin of their fun family outing searching for the buried Campbell treasure. The tow-headed boy, no more than nine years old, pulled out two coins – a wheat penny and a modern dime – from his pocket and proudly displayed his current findings.

Reese smiled, "Keep looking, sonny, you might discover gold coins to add to that collection!"

"My mommy says this wheat penny is worth a quarter." The boy happily pointed to his penny with his other hand. Mother and child quickly returned to their adventure.

Reese then turned to Pastor Martin. "You know," he said, "there've already been lots of coins found in the cemetery and around the church. Most of them are relatively recent coins, except for a few buffalo nickels and Liberty dimes."

Pastor Martin responded, "I've also heard lots of pop tops and bottle caps have been found."

"Many of the caps are from beer bottles," Reese laughed. "Betcha didn't know of all the parties on Saturday nights in the cemetery years ago. But you know – a sheriff's deputy told me that he couldn't understand why all the people were searching for the gold treasure here with metal detectors – that they wouldn't penetrate deep enough to find treasure six feet below ground."

"Yeah, that's what I've been told as well," Pastor Martin added, "I've just been hoping that someone stumbles upon the gravestones with TC or Y on them."

"Unfortunately, no one has found 'em yet." Reese then opened a small plastic box next to his chair and showed Pastor Martin. "Here're several earrings, all in need of a mate, that our amateur treasure hunters have found and donated to the church's lost-and-found. Mabel tells me no silver or gold, just stainless steel."

"Wow – a real treasure trove," Pastor Martin, snickering, rooted through the box. "I like the one with the dangly bars on it."

"But also included in the stash is a silver dollar – 1842 vintage – and its finder donated it to the church, said it's worth a little bit of money for the church coffers."

"Interesting," Pastor Martin inspected the coin closely.

"But even more interesting is that the silver dollar wasn't found in the cemetery – rather in front of the church near Jonah and the whale."

Chapter Four
TREASURE MAP

Pastor Martin walked to the pulpit and looked out over the filled sanctuary Sunday morning. Joy filled his heart and soul. He had experienced similar joy earlier on his walk from the parsonage to the church – the beauty of Nettle Mountain, the wisp of the soft breeze, the blooming flowers, and the infinite presence of the Holy Spirit. He praised the Lord with all his energy.

That morning, when he had arrived at the church, Pastor Martin decided against his normal attire of an open-collared white shirt adorned with his silver cross pendant. Today, he dressed in his Presbyterian finery, a flowing black robe accompanied by a golden stole with large embroidered purple crosses at each end. Every pew in Twin Falls Presbyterian Church was jammed with people, even in the balcony which hadn't been opened for seating in his entire tenure. Pastor Martin recognized his fifty or so church members and several of the reporters. Most of the over four hundred people, though, were visitors – or, as he called them, potential members. But, he fully accepted the reality. The church guests were only nosy or seeking the map for finding the gold treasure buried years ago by Beets Campbell.

Pastor Martin motioned for the ushers to open the front doors. A gust of wind whooshed throughout the sanctuary. "Let our singing be heard all over Cornwall, up Irish Creek, and down South River to Twin Falls," he thundered.

The sanctuary's stained glass windows shook with a rousing rendition of the hymn "God in Heaven Hath a Treasure." Afterwards, Pastor Martin raised both of his arms heavenward and boomed, "Our treasure is Jesus Christ! Praise our Lord!"

The service continued with the call to worship, liturgy, confession, and offering.

Pastor Martin read the Scripture for the day from the Gospel of Matthew 6:19-21 & 24 from his pulpit Bible.

> [Jesus said –] "Do not store up for yourselves treasures on the earth, where moth and rust destroy, and where thieves break in and steal. But store up for yourselves treasures in heaven, where moth and rust do not destroy, and where thieves do not break in and steal. For where your treasure is, there your heart will be also. . . . No one can serve two masters. Either he will hate the one and love the other, or he will be devoted to one and despise the other. You cannot serve both God and money."

Pastor Martin transitioned smoothly into his sermon. He hesitated from the pulpit as he scanned the pews, then picked up his Bible, thumped it, and raised it over his head with his right hand.

He roared, "Here it is – the map to your treasure! It's not the letter of Beets Campbell locked in the church safe, such is a treasure on the earth which Jesus warns us not to store up. Instead we need to look for the treasures in heaven."

He paused, then asked, "How do we get to the treasure there? Here is your map!" He offered his Bible to the audience, holding it out from his body and toward the sanctuary. "The Bible is the map – the Bible is the way to find Jesus and, through Him, find the treasure of God in heaven. As Jesus said, money or gold is not your treasure. What will you seek?"

Pastor Martin zipped down from the pulpit, jumped off the stage in front of the choir, and skipped on the manicured red carpet down the center aisle of the church. He abruptly stopped halfway to the back. He opened his Bible, challenged everyone to look in the Gospel of John 14:5-6, as he thundered from memory:

> Thomas said to Him, "Lord, we don't know where you are going, so how do we know the way?"
> Jesus answered. "I am the way and the truth and the life. No one comes to the Father except through Me. . . ."

He continued skipping down the center aisle, stopping just before the last row. Every set of eyes in the sanctuary were riveted on Pastor Martin. Peggy Lauderdale appeared from the narthex carrying a cardboard box. She handed him a pocket New Testament from it. He showed the New Testament to a visitor sitting next to the center aisle, thumped it, and announced, "This is your personal map to the treasure, to Jesus and your great reward in Heaven." He handed him the book.

Pastor Martin bestowed more New Testaments on random worshippers in his procession back to the front of the sanctuary. After he arrived at the pulpit, Peggy distributed all the remaining books. She quietly said, "Here's your treasure map," along with each individual presentation.

Pastor Martin kept the audience spellbound with the rest of his sermon. As he neared the end, he reiterated, "The goal isn't to discover point X on a map; but the goal is to be with the Father in heaven. How do you get there? It's not by finding stones marked TC or Y. It's by finding God in heaven. And the way, the only way, is through Jesus Christ."

Someone from the sanctuary yelled, "Praise the Lord." A chorus of people roared, "Praise the Lord."

Pastor Martin stood stunned – no one had ever spontaneously yelled out words of praise during his lifetime of sermons. He didn't miss a beat, though. He thumped his Bible, and bellowed, "This is the real map. Spiritual treasures are more valuable than material treasures of gold. Would you rather walk on gold-paved streets in heaven or keep searching for millions of dollars of gold in our cemetery? Let's not lose sight of what's really important. Amen."

A crescendo of "Amen" echoed through the crowd.

Pastor Martin again motioned for the ushers to open the front doors when the congregation sang "Jesus, Priceless Treasure" as the closing hymn.

† † †

Pastor Martin tried to visit Silas Clark at Faithful Care, Silas' nursing home in Buena Vista, weekly. Unlike the past few sunny days, Monday started drab. Fog sat on the mountain ridges; and overcast skies peered through the low-hanging, dark clouds. Pastor Martin gently knocked on the open door, then entered room 79.

Silas always described his room as cramped Spartan – a hospital bed and small nightstand occupied half the room, while the other half sported a wooden chest of drawers, a worn recliner, and a card table which doubled as his desk. A small television, usually turned off, sat on the top of the chest of drawers, and a folding chair at the card table. A picture window gave a view of an equally Spartan central courtyard. This room was destined to be Silas Clark's home for the remainder of his life.

This same description could have been used for most of the rooms at Faithful Care. But Silas' personal imprint included a faded water color painting of Twin Falls Presbyterian Church on the only open wall, and a tattered Bible and a smattering of puzzle books on his table. A small omnipresent bouquet of fresh flowers on the window sill brightened the room somewhat from its dull gray paint and commercial carpeting.

Silas, dressed in sweatpants, a pullover shirt, and bedroom slippers, sat slumped over in his wheelchair at the table. Each time Pastor Martin visited, Silas' slouch seemed to worsen. And over the course of the last half year, his weight had withered to 120 pounds, down fifty pounds from his prime. His prominent nose matched his equally prominent shock of white unruly hair. Wire-rimmed spectacles added to his aging appearance. Several weeks previously, he had fallen, not only breaking a hip but also several leg bones, putting him in the wheelchair. But despite his failing health, he always seemed to be in good spirits.

Recognizing Pastor Martin by his distinctive footsteps in the hallway, Silas greeted him without looking up from his newspaper. Before Pastor Martin could say a word, Silas kidded, "Hey, Elwood. What's a six letter word meaning 'goober?' It starts with a 'p.' Also has an 'a' and a 't' in it. I initially thought 'pastor,' but it doesn't fit."

Pastor Martin smiled. "Very funny, Silas – so you're getting back at me for not visiting last week."

"Would I do that?" Silas turned toward his minister. "I'm just cranking out the daily crossword . . . and testing your brain power."

"By the way, I like your bright purple shirt," Pastor Martin snickered. "Does it glow in the dark so the nurses can see you at all times?"

"You should try more color in your wardrobe instead of your white shirts," Silas laughed. "If I had to do it over again, I'd have honed my eccentricities at a much younger age."

"Peanut! See whether 'peanut' fits," Pastor Martin proudly stated. "I thought you'd be finished with the puzzle by now; it's almost eleven o'clock."

"Nope, just started – Sudoko was harder than usual."

"I think every time I come in here, you're doing a puzzle," ribbed Pastor Martin, as he walked over and sat on the chair facing Silas at the table. "I see you still have the daily word jumble and crytoquote yet to do in today's *Roanoke Times*."

"Yep," replied Silas, as he wrote O-U-E-H-R-A on the margin of the newspaper and rotated it to show Pastor Martin. "What letter comes next in this sequence . . . in fact, the next letter also completes the sequence?"

Pastor Martin stared at the six letters: "Can I have a clue?"

"Oh, Elwood. Think about it. The next letter would be the seventh one."

Pastor Martin forced himself to look at the letters for a few more moments, then turned the paper back to Silas. "I've got nothing," he admitted, shaking his head.

"OK – I'll be more direct with my clue. What comes in a group of seven?"

"Maybe seven days in a week . . . or continents of the world . . . or the seven dwarfs in *Snow White* . . . but I still don't see any connection to your letters."

"It's 'U,'" smiled Silas.

Pastor Martin combed his fingers through his hair.

"Think second letters of the days of the week . . . you're hopeless," added Silas.

Once again, he stared at the sequence of letters. "Oh, I see," replied Pastor Martin as a smile slowly formed. "Geesh . . . Not only doing but also creating puzzles – morning, noon, and night."

"Yep, my current recipe to ward off senility," Silas chuckled. "I don't need mental ailments to complicate my physical ailments. I've been thinking about a quote in today's paper attributed to Satchel Paige."

"He was one of the truly great baseball pitchers of all time," Pastor Martin nodded.

"He said 'How old would you be if you didn't know how old you are?'" Silas turned his head slightly. "By the way, the German chocolate cake over there on the dresser is for you."

"Huh? I don't understand," exclaimed Pastor Martin.

"Nurse Laura – that is, Laura Armstrong – dropped it off for you this morning . . . just like she left cookies for you the week before last, and a pie the week before that. I think she's sweet on you," laughed Silas. "I'm sure she'll stop by my room if she knows you're here."

Pastor Martin's face turned bright red.

"Laura's cooking is as good as Mabel Coleman's . . . so enjoy the cake. In fact, Mabel during one of her visits here told Laura that the way to your heart was through your stomach. You needed someone to cook for you, because your cooking was so bad you couldn't fry a snowball." Silas erupted into a belly laugh.

Pastor Martin shrugged his shoulders. "Well, Silas, no snowballs today, too warm. Just low-lying clouds, damp, and dreary."

"Yeah, if you poke a stick at the sky, it'd probably rain."

"Well, I see you haven't lost your sense of humor."

"Nope, just lost my ability to walk," chuckled Silas. "And lost the ability of my heart to function normally . . . but heaven forbid, not my humor. And, Elwood, I hear you're becoming a real Bible-thumper." Silas picked up his Bible from the table and thumped it several times with his hand. "Reese stopped by yesterday afternoon and said you're thumping Bibles in your sermon, just like ole' Elijah Hughes from the Civil war era."

Pastor Martin took the Bible from Silas and gave it a few thumps of his own. "Just trying to focus people to what's really important."

"Yeah, I hear that opening the basement safe ended up opening, in a sense, the proverbial can of worms," cackled Silas. He paused, then added, "As well as unleashing a couple of pigs." Silas could barely mouth the words without breaking into another full-fledged laugh.

"I don't even want to talk about pigs," groused Pastor Martin.

"Yep, I guess you're looking forward to your next ham dinner," teased Silas. "So there's lots of excitement over at the church – on a treasure hunt for gold instead of seeking Jesus, despite your sermon."

"Yep – news reports, as you've probably read in the paper, are listing it as the discovery of the long lost Confederate gold," sighed Pastor Martin. "But we still haven't found where the gold is buried. Only that it's supposedly somewhere in our cemetery."

"Why haven't you found it yet?" A broad smile developed slowly on Silas' face.

"Well, for obvious reasons," Pastor Martin shrugged. "The gold is buried in three graves marked by simple stones with the initials TC, TC, and Y. We haven't found them, after an exhaustive search by lots of people over the last few days."

Silas giggled.

"What's so funny?" queried Pastor Martin.

"Well, why didn't you ask me? I took care of the cemetery for many decades."

Pastor Martin gulped.

"I've been waiting for several days for you to show up so I could tell you."

"I see a cell phone sitting next to you on your table," Pastor Martin grumbled. "Did you think about using it?"

"Funny. More entertaining this way; your expression is priceless."

"Well," Pastor Martin tapped his foot. "Well, are you going to tell me?"

"Of course, but only by a fluke of luck do I know." Silas' eyes flickered. "One day many years ago, I was weed-eating on the outside of the stone wall on the east side, the oldest part, of the cemetery. As you know, the church owns about a hundred yards past the wall. Anyway, I went too deep, got into the dirt, and broke the cord. I saw a rock long concealed below the disturbed ground. Curiosity got the better of me. I cleared a little more of the dirt and found what I thought was a flat rock marker for a grave. A well-worn TC appeared to be chiseled on the face of the rock. Nearby, I then found two more adjacent rocks, one with another TC and another with a Y."

"So they exist!" Pastor Martin exhaled deeply, rearing back in his chair.

"I didn't think too much about it at the time," confessed Silas. "I knew they might be quite old – but first I thought more than likely just marked the graves of criminals, or perhaps graves of slaves, or maybe unbaptized infants that the church didn't think sufficiently worthy to belong in the cemetery." While Pastor Martin sat wide-eyed, Silas rambled, "Then I rationalized that because two had 'C' as the last initial, both belonged to the same family, with 'Y' meaning unnamed youth. Another possibility is that the stones were separated from the rest of the cemetery when the church built the wall, I think back in the 1920s during the depression. Perhaps they accidently left them outside."

"Where are they?" Pastor Martin yelled in excitement.

"Know where the big sycamore tree is?" Silas paused and coughed.

Pastor Martin breathlessly nodded.

Silas continued, "As I remember, about ten or so paces from this tree toward South River Road. I think the stone markers were covered by a few inches of dirt about six feet outside the wall. Years ago, I tried to keep the scrub brush from growing on them when I had time, but it kept getting ahead of me. So I suspect there's a couple decades worth of brambles, weeds, and small trees growing on them by now."

Pastor Martin jumped out of his chair. With a broad grin, he turned to the door. "Gotta go! You know what I'll be doing this afternoon."

He scooted half-way across the room before Silas called, "Just a minute. Don't forget your German chocolate cake from Laura on the dresser."

Pastor Martin screeched to a stop.

Silas looked down at the crossword puzzle in the paper. "By the way, Elwood – what does one call a pastor in Deutschland? I'll give you a hint . . . it's not a goober."

"You think I don't know," snickered Pastor Martin. "I've visited Germany . . . and know some German. The German word for pastor is 'Pfarrar.'"

"Nope – It's a 'German shepherd.'"

Pastor Martin groaned, grabbed the cake, and scurried to the door. Once again, he skidded to a halt and turned to Silas. "One more thing, I have a riddle for you."

Silas' eyes lit up, ready for the challenge.

"If I have it, I don't share it. If I share it, I don't have it. What is it?"

Silas chuckled, "I see Reese has been complaining to you."

"You're tormenting him by telling him the answer to the riddle is a secret."

"But the answer," Silas hooted, "is . . . 'a secret.'"

Chapter Five
GOLDFINGER

The steady afternoon rain didn't deter Pastor Martin from investigating the bombshell revelation of Silas Clark. He flagged down Charlie Whitesides and Ed Painter as they passed the church; both were volunteer fire fighters who had just gotten off a call with the South River Fire Department. They sloshed through the wet underbrush outside the cemetery wall with chainsaw, weed-eater, several loppers, cutters, and shovels.

Meanwhile, around the church, only a handful of treasure hunters braved the rain. Ed remarked that all the rest must be city folk. Or fair weather hunters, Charlie added. Pastor Martin recognized Slick with his metal detector still slithering around the old oak tree in front of the church.

Pastor Martin walked ten paces from the sycamore tree and six feet from the wall. He marked the spot with a small red flag. Over the course of the next hour, he and his crew cleared Russian olive bushes, multiflora rose, wild raspberry, brambles, Devil's shoestrings, small trees, and trash undergrowth from the swath of land around the flag. The rain continued unrelenting, but the three treasure seekers were equally unrelenting. Then, trying to pull the roots of a wild grape vine from the ground, Pastor Martin tripped and fell into a pokeberry stalk ripe with dark purple berries. He got up half-way before slipping and tumbling back down into a stick'um bush. Charlie gave him a hand up. Both Charlie and Ed laughed at the sight of their preacher – mud splattered, purple stained shirt, and little green fuzz-balls stuck all over jeans and socks. Charlie kidded the pastor that he'd be picking "beggar lice" off his clothes all night, while Ed teased him that he looked and smelled as though "he'd been rode hard and put up wet."

After clearing the patch, they skimmed the top two to three inches of weeds, grass, and soil – rapidly becoming mud – from the surface. Rain soaked them thoroughly.

Then, all of a sudden, Charlie's shovel slid over a large flat rock; and he brushed the wet dirt off its top. "Whoopee!" he screamed ecstatically. He dropped his shovel and pushed his arms upward.

Pastor Martin and Ed skidded over to Charlie. Three drenched souls stared at the rock. Chiseled on its top was TC. They celebrated with high fives which quickly transformed into hugs and random up and down jumping. Thirty minutes later, they uncovered the other two stones and outlined all three with red flags. With each discovery, they yelled joyfully.

"Wow," Charlie exclaimed, as he leaned on his wet shovel. "The testimony of Beets is actually true."

"I have to admit – I didn't believe it to be real." Ed rubbed the four-day stubble on his face, adding yet more mud.

Pastor Martin laughed almost smugly: "And Silas only missed his description of their location by four paces and two feet."

Intrigued by the revelries of Pastor Martin and his team, three of the treasure hunters from the cemetery joined them on their side of the fence. They helped party. Muddy handshakes and congratulations were the order of the day.

After the merriment, Ed scraped some residual mud off the Y marker. He exhaled deeply and asked, "How do we prove that the graves actually contain gold instead of bodies, before we start digging?"

"You sure know how to throw water on a party," growled Pastor Martin.

As they started to pack up their mud-encrusted equipment, Pastor Martin observed a none-too-happy Slick throwing his metal detector in the back of his beat-up Ford pickup and kicking up stones as the truck pealed out of the church's parking lot.

News of the discovery spread like wildfire throughout the church, the Irish Creek community, and Rockbridge County.

Pastor Martin retreated to the parsonage, depositing his clothes in a trash can rather than making any attempt at picking the multitude of "beggar lice" balls and at bleaching intense purple stains from them. He found time to relax a few minutes in a warm shower, squeezed in amidst the many congratulatory telephone calls. Reese and Mabel Coleman brought a jug of home-made apple cider by the parsonage to help celebrate the good news. Pastor Martin shared slices of Laura's German chocolate cake.

Mabel looked sternly at Pastor Martin: "It would've been nice for you to invite Laura to join us."

He quickly changed the subject, though, by sharing the answer to Silas' "secret" riddle with Reese.

"Just like Silas. Always pulling people's strings," Reese griped.

After a half hour visit, Pastor Martin escorted them onto the front porch. All heard the same distinctive sound ingrained in their ears from four days earlier – a combination of squealing, snorting, grunting, and rooting. They peered around the side of the house to see a rush of activity at the exposed graves of Turnip, Tater, and the Yankee. Ole Brownie was parked alongside South River Road with the ramp down on the stock trailer.

The constant rain had subsided to sporadic drizzles. Pastor Martin jogged through the cemetery, skidded his bottom over the top of the rock wall, and stood face to face with Sunshine and Clarence Clutterbuck. Grunt and Hamm, meanwhile, grubbed and slogged through the quagmire forming on top of the grave sites. The pigs appeared calm, not crazed like the other day in the cemetery.

Panting, Pastor Martin wiped the rain from his face. His khaki pants were uncomfortably wet. His white button-down shirt was getting there. And his dress shoes were caked in wet mud.

Sunshine smiled, "All is well. The spirits have returned to their rightful place. They were just lost in the cemetery. They needed to go over the fence just like they told Grunt and Hamm. They led me in the direction of the gold the other day in the cemetery."

Pastor Martin remained speechless, slack jawed. He cut his eyes to Clarence.

Clarence pounded a large yellow stake into the ground. On top, a sign displayed his name. He shouted, "I claim the gold buried here to be the property of Clarence Clutterbuck."

Pastor Martin shook his head in incredulity.

† † †

Pastor Martin knocked the phone off its base as he woke from a deep sleep. While he retrieved the fallen receiver, the digital display on the alarm clock showed three minutes after four o'clock.

"Hello, Elwood Martin speaking," murmured Pastor Martin.

"Reverend Martin, this is Deputy Steve Hickman from the Rockbridge County Sheriff's Department. I met you this afternoon. At that time, my partner and I convinced the Clutterbucks to take their pigs and leave your cemetery. You might –"

"What's wrong?" Pastor Martin interrupted, his mind quickly ticking off possible catastrophes about to be disclosed.

"Well, we stumbled upon some activity next to your church cemetery."

Pastor Martin jumped out of bed and fumbled his way to the bedroom window. He peeked around the shades. "I see lights over at the far side of the cemetery. What's happening?"

"We were driving by your church when we picked up some lights just outside your cemetery wall . . . the same place as Clarence Clutterbuck staked his gold claim. A couple of locals with flashlights and shovels tried to dig up the grave sites marked by red flags. Our head lights spooked them. They ran – but not very far. One tripped over a branch. The other ran into the sycamore tree." Deputy Hickman half-laughed, "I suspect their running ability was affected by the two empty six-packs of beer we also found at the site."

"Yet more treasure hunters," groaned Pastor Martin.

"Yep, just like the Clutterbucks," agreed Deputy Hickman. "But these two guys claim they had the church's permission. One of 'em is well known to us – Alvin Thompson. He goes by the name of Slick." Deputy Hickman chuckled, "But them running and doing the digging at four in the morning make their story quite suspicious."

"No . . . no permission." Pastor Martin recalled a disgusted Slick from the afternoon. He added, "I guess we should've secured the site. But it was getting close to dark when you left earlier."

"These yahoos dug down about two feet at one spot – we'll be taking them in for trespassing."

"Okay," Pastor Martin said, as he turned on the bedroom lights. "Many thanks for your diligence. I'll be out there in a little bit to check; I won't be able to get back to sleep anyway."

"Just a suggestion," added Deputy Hickman, "the church might need to hire a private security firm to guard the graves. Scavengers and vultures are always looking for a quick buck."

After putting the phone down into its cradle, Pastor Martin sat back on his bed for a moment. He shook his head, mad at himself – *Geesh, I need to be more careful with protecting a financial bonanza for the church. What an oversight on my part?*

He reached for the phone, despite the ungodly hour.

† † †

Even before daybreak, Troy Montgomery, the broad-shouldered lumberjack in his bib overalls and NASCAR baseball cap, arrived at the church with his old tractor trailer loaded with freshly harvested oak logs. He used his mobile crane to stack the large logs, about three feet in diameter and 24 feet long, in a pile on top of the TC, TC, and Y graves under the watchful but sleepy eyes of Pastor Martin.

Troy jumped out of the cab of his crane and chuckled, "Well, pastor – that should discourage any digging. That's what I call security without hiring a guard."

"Yep, that should do the job," agreed Pastor Martin. "How much do you estimate the logs weigh?"

"Oh, you have at least several many tons of logs stacked there. Unless someone brings in heavy equipment like this crane, they ain't gonna be able to move 'em."

"Thanks for temporarily donating the logs, Troy."

"No problem, I already had 'em on the trailer ready to take to the Shumate lumberyard," smiled Troy. "Just let me know when you want 'em moved; and I'll load 'em back up. It'll only take a little bit."

"Not sure when that'll be. The church needs to be certain there're no bodies and just gold six feet down before we start digging."

† † †

A few days later, Pastor Martin called a special meeting of the church's ruling elders after Sunday church service to discuss the status of the alleged gold buried by Beets Campbell. All, as well as everyone else who read a newspaper or watched television, knew the key component of Beets' testimony had now been confirmed. And the site of the three graves was safely protected under tons of logs.

While the session, the group of ruling elders, waited for Etta Shields to arrive, Hansford Cash peppered Pastor Martin with questions: "Why didn't you, Charlie, and Ed just start digging when you found the marker stones? Why did you stop, creating the need for security?"

"I think most will agree that we need to confirm that something other than bodies is buried there. We didn't want to dig up bones," replied Pastor Martin, who glanced around the table.

He saw everyone except Hansford nodding in agreement. The session then heard a distinctive clomp-climp-clomp-climp-clomp-climp-clomp coming down the hallway.

Hansford sneered, "That's Etta and her high heels. Five . . . four . . . three . . . two . . . one . . . and arrival," as Etta walked through the doorway. Etta stomped past Hansford to take her chair at the table. Hansford gasped. The smell of too much cheap perfume also branded Etta.

"So – what do we do next?" asked Alice Jane Grant, relieved Etta's entrance had broken Hansford's accusatory questioning.

"I did some research and made some phone calls," Pastor Martin said. "Found out that the method of choice used to detect a buried body is GPR, ground penetrating radar. It's sort of like using radar to identify aircraft in the sky. But you look down instead of up. Evidently companies specialize in doing this. They push something that looks like a lawnmower over the site; its radar pulses provide a map of what's below the surface."

"So, it'll give a definitive answer whether gold or bodies are buried there?" Alice Jane beamed, as she opened a piece of hard candy and popped it in her mouth. She had several handfuls of assorted candies in her oversized pocketbook, and was known as the "candy lady" to the children of the church, distributing candy every Sunday morning. "Problem solved!" she added.

"Well," Pastor Martin sighed. "The representative I talked to wouldn't provide a guarantee, especially when he found out our soil composition. Wet clay is the worst type of soil for GPR to penetrate. But he thought the GPR could definitely distinguish between metal and human remains."

"What will GPR cost?" Hansford griped. "Anything described by an acronym is never cheap." Hansford always thought of himself not only smarter than anyone in any room – having been elected a county supervisor in his younger days – but also more handsome. The comb-over of his few straggles of hair which appeared to be glued in place, though, seemed to discount, at least, the latter attribute.

"Most estimates are in the range of several thousand dollars," confessed Pastor Martin.

"Wow," exclaimed Hansford. "The church doesn't have that kind of money."

"But a few thousand dollars to get a ten million dollar payout seems like a good investment to me," Preston Hughes countered.

"Can't spend what we don't have," groused Hansford. "You all should have just dug up the graves Monday without asking questions."

The group sat in silence. Pastor Martin looked around the table. "While you ponder that problem, we may have another. Our Presbyter, Rev. Royster Van Guider, called yesterday. To make a long story short, he claims the buried gold treasure belongs to the UAPC (United American Presbyterian Church), not to Twin Falls. He argues –"

"What?" squawked Hansford.

"Didn't Beets' testimony say he left the gold to Twin Falls Presbyterian Church?" fumed Peggy Lauderdale.

"That's right," agreed Pastor Martin, "but Rev. Van Guider thinks that –"

"Isn't he a Yankee from Connecticut?" interrupted Alice Jane.

"Wonder whether he's related to that salesman who wooed Ma Campbell over a century ago?" wise-cracked Hansford.

"Indeed, he's from Connecticut originally, and he'd been an Associate Presbyter somewhere up North before being recruited as our Presbyter last year," Pastor Martin offered. "I just wanted to give you a heads up that UAPC believes any gold belongs to them. Rev. Van Guider has talked to his bosses at the Synod and national levels. I told him that I didn't think our session would see it that way."

"That's right," Hansford, Peggy, Alice Jane, Etta, and Preston responded in unison.

"But first we need to see whether there's indeed gold buried in the graves," Etta said. "As y'all know I work as a secretary in a VMI engineering department. One of the professors, Jim Squire, in the electrical engineering department has invented numerous devices, one a robot that rids a wooded area of ticks, and –"

"So what?" interjected Hansford rudely and much too loud. "We're talking about gold, not ticks."

"Let me finish," barked Etta. "Another device that Professor Squire developed is a machine that locates coal miners when trapped in a mine – say, by an explosion or a cave-in. Someone described it to me as a 'thumper' device, using the echoes of sound waves to locate bodies underground. Maybe he could use it to see whether we have bodies or gold in our graves."

"Might be worth a try," Alice Jane replied.

Everyone nodded in agreement, except Hansford.

Hansford growled, "Just dig. There aren't warm bodies there; if not gold, there're only bones."

"I'll give Professor Squire a call in the morning," volunteered Pastor Martin. "Hopefully, he'll be able to help us."

"And charge us an arm and a leg," fussed Hansford.

† † †

The next day, Pastor Martin sent an e-mail to the church's ruling elders –

> I talked with Professor Jim Squire at VMI this morning. I have some bad news and some good news, but mostly good news.
>
> First, the bad news: he indicated that his device to locate trapped miners is not applicable for our purposes.
>
> But, the good news: he indicated that he could easily modify a commercial metal detector to identify metal buried six feet below the surface. A store-bought metal detector is usually good to find metallic things no more than two feet deep.
>
> Professor Squire says all he needs to do is match the induction of the ring in the normal metal detector with a larger loop made with wire or copper tubing. He also provided more explanations beyond my comprehension. The bottom line is that he said he can manufacture this modified detector in a few days in his laboratory – at NO EXPENSE to the church. All we have to do is contribute an operational store-bought metal detector. Charlie Cathcart had a spare one and already donated it. I delivered it to Professor Squire today.

"Sounds good," replied all the ruling elders except Hansford Cash. Later that same day, Pastor Martin sent another e-mail to the elders –

I devised a test for Professor Squire's proposed detector. Harry Whitmer has agreed to use his tractor to dig several post holes about six feet deep. We'll bury some old animal bones in one, a piece of steel in another, and a small bronze statue in yet another, before we use Professor Squire's device for the TC and Y graves. Perhaps we'll be able to have this issue resolved by the end of the week.

This time Hansford Cash sent back a snarky comment –

Perhaps you could bury the Jonah-and-the-whale sculpture as one of the test objects. Kill two birds with one stone.

† † †

Fog enveloped the Twin Falls cemetery at daybreak. Pastor Martin woke to the racket of heavy equipment and the smell of diesel fumes. Troy Montgomery was hard at work loading his logs back onto the tractor trailer. The illicit and unfinished digging of Slick and friend was still evident after clearing the logs.

The fog had burned off by the time a crowd of about fifty curiosity seekers gathered. Word had gotten out. When Professor Squire, also a Colonel in the Virginia Militia and now dressed in his military fatigues, arrived with his modified commercial metal detector, the throng cheered and dubbed it "Goldfinger." It was made of wooden 2X4s outlining the shape of a low four-sided pyramid, with four wheels close to the ground, wire strung around the square base, and metal detector attached to the apex. Harry Whitmer waited with his tractor and backhoe on standby next to the graves in anticipation of the desired result.

The crowd stood entranced as Professor Squire swept his freaky-looking metal detector over the first test hole. It made the machine click wildly. He swept the metal detector over the second hole. Silence. The third test hole repeated the initial click-click-click-click-click-click.

Professor Squire smiled broadly. "Metal is buried in holes one and three," he announced. "No metal in hole two. The detector cannot distinguish between steel and brass."

Pastor Martin grinned and yelled, "That's right. It worked."

The crowd gave a collective shout of approval.

Pastor Martin escorted Professor Squire to the graves. Each time he swept "Goldfinger" over one of the graves, the detector clicked wildly. Professor Squire set the detector on the ground, then turned to the crowd: "Definitely metal and not bones. The metal deposit is about two feet wide by six feet long for each of the three locations."

"About the size of a casket – but filled with metal and not a body," exclaimed Pastor Martin, as he raised his arms as if to signal a touchdown.

The crowd drooled at the thought of the contents.

Harry cranked up his tractor and positioned it at the base of the first grave, the one identified by the Y stone marker.

A sheriff's deputy sprung from the crowd and approached Pastor Martin. He gave him a handful of sealed envelopes and said, "Sorry to do this to you, but consider yourself served. In the envelopes are several court orders for you not to open the graves. There seem to be numerous claims to the gold that might be buried here."

Pastor Martin kicked the ground and motioned to Harry to shut the tractor down.

Chapter Six
REAL CUTE

The next day under clear blue skies, Pastor Martin visited Silas Clark. As usual, Silas sat slouched in his wheelchair at the card table he used as his desk. He had the daily newspaper, which was opened to the puzzle page, in front of him. But Pastor Martin immediately realized something was different in his room. A sock monkey dressed in a bright red vest and matching knit hat sat on the window sill. Its arms were wrapped around the flower vase containing a spray of fresh red carnations and Baby's breath.

Once Silas caught a glimpse of Pastor Martin, he started whistling – quite badly, as the tune was interspersed with fits of wheezing. After a loud cough, Silas caught his second breath. He whistled for a few more moments, before getting winded.

"Whatcha whistling, Silas. It sounds somewhat familiar?" Pastor Martin kidded as he walked over to the table.

"I'm just in the mood for whistling," Silas replied. "Look at this 'whatzit?' puzzle – it's a puzzle in which you determine the familiar phrase or saying."

Silas showed Pastor Martin the words in the paper –

WHICH WEIGH
WITCH WAY
WYCH WHEY

Pastor Martin stared, furrows forming on his brow.

Silas continued his poor attempt at whistling. "Elwood, I'll give you a hint," he finally said, "think of a movie starring Clint Eastwood and Clyde."

"Clyde who?"

Silas laughed. He shook his head and continued whistling and wheezing.

Pastor Martin shrugged, "Halloween brew."

"Ah, Elwood – what kind of saying is that. What am I whistling?"

"Sorry, I'm sort of distracted today."

"Geesh, and I kept giving you a hint . . . Every Which Way! . . . remember the movie with Clint and the orangutan." Silas laughed.

Pastor Martin, without thinking, looked at the sock monkey.

"That's a monkey, not an orangutan," teased Silas. "And he's named Joe, not Clyde."

Pastor Martin finally groaned, "I get it; your whistling was really a hint. The theme song of *Every Which Way But Loose!*"

"It took long enough," Silas hooted. "To change the subject, I hear the church's customized metal detector attracted quite a crowd at the cemetery yesterday. Did you know that Edison, Einstein, Pavlov, and the Curies attended your festivities; but Ohm didn't."

"Huh?"

"Yeah . . . Edison found it to be illuminating, Einstein thought it was relatively interesting, Pavlov drooled at the opportunity to be there, and Pierre and Marie Curie radiated enthusiasm. But Ohm resisted being there," Silas chuckled.

"Very funny," Pastor Martin deadpanned. "You're just full of yourself this morning."

"Now, Elwood, what's this about you being distracted this morning?" queried Silas. "I heard that the VMI professor proved there might very well be gold in the graves. The church may be on its way to riches."

"Ha," Pastor Martin growled. "That's just the point. Everyone wants the riches."

"Yeah," Silas scowled, "I also heard the Sheriff stopped the proceedings just as y'all were getting ready to dig."

"His deputy delivered a stack of legal papers initiated by people who want the buried gold. Since then, I've received notices from other lawyers who intend to file claims for the gold. Two people assert they're direct descendants of Beets Campbell; one claims to be a relative of an uncle of the Campbell brothers; several more are relatives of Jim 'Spud' Campbell who they argue is the same as 'Tater' Campbell; and yet a few more individuals hail from Connecticut and maintain they're descendants of the half-siblings of Beets and his brothers from his run-away mother. Even Clarence and Sunshine Clutterbuck retained a lawyer who contends some obscure centuries old finders-keepers law gives them the rights to the treasure. Then the Commonwealth of Virginia also claims the money since the Campbell brothers entered into a oral contract with Governor Letcher to supply the gold for their purposes; the U.S. Attorney is alleging the money is theirs, essentially as spoils of the Union winning the Civil War; and even the Valley Presbytery has put forward a legal claim for the treasure. Who knows who else will file a claim?"

"Wow – what a lineup?" exclaimed Silas. "Even the Presbytery?"

"Evidently, when Twin Falls became part of the UAPC back in the 1980s, we agreed to all our property being held in trust by the Presbytery. They argue that the gold is part of the property that they're holding in trust for us; and as a small rural church we couldn't possibly put the ten million dollars to proper use. They argue they're legally responsible for it. Can you believe that?" Pastor Martin sputtered in frustration.

"Unbelievable, they're all comin' out of the woodwork . . . they must smell the gold."

"Not only that, now it's gonna cost us money," Pastor Martin groused. "Our ruling elders aren't happy about having to hire a lawyer, or actually a legal team, to represent our interests. We're likely to be legally outgunned."

Silas squirmed in the wheelchair to regain a more comfortable position. "Elwood, know what I just found out today?"

"What?"

"I always thought that the apple was what caused the downfall of man in the Garden of Eden, but I found out it was actually the pear."

"Huh," replied Pastor Martin, confused.

"Nope – it wasn't the fruit on the tree that caused all the trouble in the Garden of Eden. It was the pair on the ground."

"Ha, Ha!" Pastor Martin half-laughed and rolled his eyes.

"I suspect the only people who'll end up with a financial bonanza from Beets Campbell are the lawyers who'll keep the case alive long enough to suck up most of the ten million dollars, if indeed it does exist. They, and the people they represent, are a bunch of money grubbers. I can only guess how Beets Campbell and his brothers would've handled those who make claims on their gold. They would've left a string of bodies in their wake."

"That's the truth!"

"Tell you what, Elwood, I have the money to underwrite retaining my lawyer Dick Dawes on the church's behalf. He's the best lawyer in the Shenandoah Valley. Maybe he and his law firm, Dawes Steck & Dawes, can at least get the court to approve opening the graves, even though they really aren't graves or even in the official cemetery. All sides should want the potential treasure to be confirmed – to see what there is to claim or to divvy up. I'll give him a call to get things moving, if that's okay with you."

"I'm sure the ruling elders and congregation will be most grateful."

"No problem," smiled Silas. "I don't have much time left in this world before my heart goes CLUNK. I might as well use my money to do some good. I still can't believe the Presbytery is laying claim to the gold – after all, Twin Falls could use new facilities, as well as fund a mission program, just as much as the greater Presbyterian Church."

"Once again, Silas, many thanks," sighed Pastor Martin, as he placed his hand on Silas' hand. "By the way, you might remember that Peggy Lauderdale is writing an update on the history of the church, also in connection with our 200th anniversary. The last history about Twin Falls Presbyterian was written fifty years ago, so she's just focusing on these last fifty years, covering most of the time you've been a member of the church. One chapter is going to focus on 'funny' happenings – so she thought immediately about your purported shenanigans. You accepted responsibility for some, and some for which you never denied. So, could you jot down some of your recollections for posterity? Peggy will edit them."

"My shenanigans – now, now, Elwood," Silas grinned sheepishly. "Would I have done such things?"

Pastor Martin chuckled, "You're sneaky mischievous. Remember about ten years ago when I announced that the topic for my sermon would be the story of a donkey speaking to Balaam? When everyone arrived for church that Sunday, a whole herd of donkeys grazed in front of the church. You want me to believe that you had nothing to do with that!"

"You give me too much credit," smiled Silas. "HeeHaw, HeeHaw!"

"And then there was the time when an outhouse showed up in the front yard of a previous pastor, I think John Richardson, after he complained of the toilet not working in the parsonage. I hear he didn't have a keen sense of humor."

"And despite the fact that it was a luxury model, a two-seater," Silas deadpanned.

"Do I need to jog your memory of other happenings? Like the peanut butter on the communion wafers, the quarters glued to the church sidewalk . . . and then there's that infamous Easter egg hunt years ago. I'm surprised you didn't have the kids following clues that led them to the top of the Blue Ridge just to get the surprise gifts," Pastor Martin shook his head and smiled.

"I think I get the gist." Silas looked out the window, and a devious smile slowly formed.

"I wouldn't expect anything other from you." As Pastor Martin rose from his chair, his eyes once again caught a glimpse of the sock monkey on his sill. He pointed, "So, I assume that Joe has moved in with you."

"Yep, 'twas a present from nurse Laura. She makes them for the residents here at Faithful Care. She's quite talented and creative."

Pastor Martin nodded in agreement.

"I almost forgot. Nurse Laura said she left some pieces of homemade apple pie for you. It's in the refrigerator at the nurse's station."

"Yum," Pastor Martin licked his lips. "A few more pounds of weight gain."

Silas deadpanned, "Did you know that the fattest knight at King Arthur's round table was Sir Cumference?"

"Huh? Sir Cumference?"

"Yep," Silas giggled, "He acquired his size from too much pi."

† † †

The next week, Pastor Martin arrived at room 79 in Faithful Care to see Silas sitting once again in his wheelchair at the room's table. Halfway into the room, Pastor Martin hesitated. Silas' eyes were closed. The puzzle page of the newspaper rested on the floor. Joe the sock monkey hugged the side panel of Silas's wheelchair. Pastor Martin considered turning around and letting Silas nap.

"Good morning, Elwood," Silas suddenly spoke, without opening his eyes. He fidgeted to raise his drooped shoulders.

"I didn't realize you're awake," replied Pastor Martin, as he picked up the puzzle page from the floor and walked to the chair across the table from Silas' wheelchair. "I see you're not working any puzzles this morning."

"The crossword and Sudoku were super easy, so they're already finished. Instead of doing the rest of the puzzles from the newspaper, I've just been thinking – remembering some of my science and engineering from years ago." Silas smiled from ear-to-ear: "Did you know that you can never trust an atom?"

"Huh?"

Silas laughed, "Yeah, never trust an atom because they make up everything."

"Real cute," laughed Pastor Martin.

"Seriously, though, Elwood, I was thinking about the novel metal alloy I developed when I worked at Kennametal. You know brass is an alloy of copper and zinc; and bronze is an alloy of copper and tin. My alloy was made of copper and tellurium. You know what it was called?"

"Not a clue," shrugged Pastor Martin, "I've never even heard of tellurium. But I guess its alloy would be something like brass or bronze . . . maybe brellium or brellurium."

"Nope," Silas deadpanned, "it was called 'cute.'"

"Huh?"

"Yep, cute," Silas smiled. "Isn't that just cute?"

"What're you talking about?"

"I guess I'll have to explain it to you," Silas laughed to himself. "The atomic symbol for copper is Cu, while that for tellurium is Te. Put them together; and what does it spell? C-U-T-E."

"You're full of yourself today – what a surprise," snickered Pastor Martin, "and I thought you looked tired."

"I hear you got another surprise when you opened the graves."

"Yep – your lawyer Dick Dawes got the judge to allow us to open up the graves. I can't believe he got the legal system to move that fast." Pastor Martin reared back in his chair. "Then the rest of the good news is that the other lawyers – or rather their clients – are losing interest in the case. But the bad news is that there's likely not 500 pounds of gold."

"Well," smiled Silas, "there might be some gold . . . or maybe an I.O.U."

"Yeah, or maybe not," Pastor Martin shook his head as he repositioned himself in his chair. "As you've probably heard, when Harry extricated each wooden coffin box from the graves with his tractor, they fell apart. Each one had only scrap iron in it plus a safe. The safe was the same make and model – a Terwillegar – as the one in the large safe in the cellar; in fact, all are exact duplicates, the same vintage, except for their serial numbers. The mystery deepens."

"So I guess you'd like me to contact Sam to get the safes open."

"Yep."

"Consider it done. I'll have him call you to set up a time," Silas said matter-of-factly.

"The sooner he does it, the better," Pastor Martin replied. "Church members are a little anxious to discover what's in 'em. Hansford is getting especially cranky."

"Arnie Rubin, down in room 42, is quite cranky as well," Silas offered. "Police were called into his room here at Faithful Care today."

"My goodness! Isn't he over ninety years old."

"Yep, the police got him for resisting a rest," Silas howled.

"With that one I'm gonna leave," Pastor Martin rose and stretched. "I can't take any more of your fun at my expense."

"Oh, don't be such a party pooper." Silas' expression turned suddenly somber: "Before you leave, though, you should visit Ricie Horn. The doctor saw her yesterday."

"She's in room 92, I think."

"The strangest thing – her brain scan the week before showed spots of radioactivity inside her skull."

"I've never heard of such a thing."

"Supposedly it's a quite rare condition. It's called cranium uranium," Silas hooted.

Pastor Martin shook his head and started to walk away.

"Seriously, though, before you leave today, nurse Laura said for you to stop by the nurses' station." Silas gave Pastor Martin a wink. "Says she has some homemade frozen meals for you – ones you can heat up in the microwave."

"Laura sure is nice to me," blushed Pastor Martin. He gazed upward. "She's also quite beautiful – both in her looks and her spirit."

"Well, why don't you ask her out?" asked Silas. "I can attest that she's very caring, and not just caring for my physical needs. We've also had more than a few prayers together. She may not be Presbyterian, but at least she's Methodist. You know, she lost her husband to cancer in his forties."

"Oh, I don't think I have a chance with her," Pastor Martin shook his head. "I'm sure she has lots of men knocking at her door. Dot always called me quite boring."

"Geesh, Elwood, you're just clueless."

"I just don't know," Pastor Martin once again shook his head. "Maybe?"

"Have you ever heard what happened when two hydrogen atoms met?" smiled Silas.

"What?"

"One of the hydrogen atoms said, 'I've lost my electron.' The other said, 'Are you sure?' The first hydrogen atom replied, 'Yes, I'm positive.'"

✝ ✝ ✝

Sam, dressed immaculately in his tailored suit, arrived at Twin Falls Presbyterian Church with his equipment immediately before Wednesday night Bible study. Pastor Martin escorted him to the sanctuary basement. The three safes recovered from the fake graves were lined up next to their twin recovered from the large safe. A dozen church members welcomed Sam, then stood around in small groups in whispered conversation. Sam prepared his gear. The media storm about possible Confederate gold had evaporated – not a single member of the press, not even Kit, attended this safe cracking.

Sam wise-cracked, "I don't feel the excitement, or even love, compared to when I was here the last time."

"Somehow I don't think 500 pounds of gold is stuffed in the safes," Pastor Martin replied. "The safes feel about the same weight as just our empty safe. Most of the people here think they're also empty."

"Well, we'll see what's in 'em in a few moments. At least the person who buried 'em had class in his choice of safes – three more Terwillegars," smirked Sam.

"But who buried them? We're questioning whether Beets Campbell and his brothers ever existed – that it's all been a ruse," shrugged Pastor Martin.

Sam methodically worked the tumblers on the first safe. After about five minutes, he yelled, "51-1-26."

"Got it," Pastor Martin replied. This time he came prepared with the sheet of paper recording the combinations of the previous safes.

Sam turned the handle slightly. Pastor Martin stepped in to open the safe. A single burlap sack, same size and appearance as the one in the first Terwillegar weeks ago, sat alone. He poured its contents into his hand. Out tumbled two crudely-made gold coins with the C.S.A. logo on one side and 1 oz on the other.

An air of fulfilled disappointment filled the basement.

Pastor Martin walked among the Wednesday night group showing them the coins. "Well, if nothing else, the bullion value of the gold in the sack is, at least, more than two thousand dollars, just like the last one."

"Not sure what to believe anymore," commented Peggy Lauderdale. "Were these coins really made by Beets Campbell for the Confederacy? If so, why just a handful, instead of lots of them as claimed in his testimony?"

"I wonder what's in the next safe?" asked Troy Montgomery.

Sam worked on its combination. Several minutes later, he yelled, "18-23-10."

Once again, Pastor Martin dutifully recorded the combination and opened the safe. And, once again, an identical small burlap sack contained two gold coins with identical inscriptions as the previous ones.

"Why would Beets claim he buried over a hundred pounds of gold in each grave, then only have two ounces in each? It just doesn't make sense," pondered Peggy.

"Yeah – why even put anything in the safes?" questioned Alice Jane Grant.

"And why have just two coins in each?" added Peggy, throwing up her hands in disappointment.

"Anyone wanna guess what's gonna be in the third safe?" laughed Troy.

Sam hooked up his amplifiers to the final Terwillegar. He methodically and slowly spun the dial on the combination lock.

After several minutes, he removed his headphones. "32-1-17," he called out.

Pastor Martin repeated the routine, writing down the safe's combination on the piece of paper and opening the safe. He peered in the safe, as he blocked a view of its contents from the others with the safe's door.

"Wow!" he exclaimed. He turned to the crowd with an expression of wide-eyed astonishment on his face.

"What's in there?" several people jointly shouted.

Pastor Martin turned with a small burlap sack in his hand and a smile on his face.

"What a surprise?" Peggy said sarcastically.

Pastor Martin, yet again, recovered two more one ounce C.S.A. gold coins from the bag. "So we're down from ten million dollars to about ten thousand total."

"Instead of 500 pounds of gold, we have eight ounces," added Alice Jane.

"Oh, Beets, why have you forsaken us?" Preston Hughes shook his arms in mock exasperation.

Chapter Seven
SOLVING PUZZLES

The meeting of the ruling elders of Twin Falls Presbyterian Church began with a frustrating discussion of the current status of the testimony of Beets Campbell.

"What a fiasco?" Hansford Cash cynically declared. "We should never have opened the safe in the basement. It created one problem after the other. What an ending to our 200th anniversary celebration! We're the laughing stock of the county."

"We have eight ounces of gold coin," replied Etta Shields, not at all feeling consoled by her own response.

"Is any part of the story of Beets Campbell true?" asked Peggy, discouraged. "After all, he's shortchanged us by over 499 pounds of gold."

Preston Hughes shook his head. "Where do we go from here? All I see are dead ends in our treasure hunt."

"Well," Pastor Martin chimed in, "I talked to a gold buyer up at Rocky's Antique Mall. He suggested that we put the coins up for auction. Perhaps they're worth more to coin collectors than as pure bullion. Appraisers have nothing to compare them to – they're not even supposed to exist."

"Perhaps only put up one coin to auction to find out the value," suggested Alice Jane, "before we commit to selling all eight of them."

"An antique collector from Virginia Beach has offered to buy the first Terwillegar safe, the one in pristine condition, for four thousand dollars." Pastor Martin added, "And the other three for two hundred each, since they've suffered from being buried and exposed to the elements underground."

"At least we'll see some money for our efforts," chuckled Preston.

"What're we going to do with the testimony of Beets Campbell?" queried Peggy.

"Historians and the media seem to have lost interest after the discovery of safes instead of a fortune of gold in the three fake graves," shrugged Preston. "The safes led nowhere! One can only conclude Beets Campbell is a fraud."

"But who would've perpetrated the hoax?" wondered Alice Jane out loud.

"I have an idea," Hansford cackled. "Why don't we use some of the money we profit from the sale of the safes to remove the ugly sculpture of Jonah and the whale from the front of the church? Jonah looks like some moonshining redneck. You can't even tell whether he's being swallowed or spit up. And, the whale looks like it was created in the abstract by a drunken Picasso." Hansford scanned the elders to see who agreed.

"Geesh, Hansford, get off your high horse," Peggy replied. "The sculpture has been part of this church for more than fifty years. Every year you've served on the session you want to get rid of it."

"Perhaps you should get off your high horse, Peggy," muttered Hansford, "Just because your daddy was the one –"

"Okay, let's hold on, you two," interrupted Pastor Martin. "Let's keep our discussion civil. Everyone is aware of the sensitivity in debating the fate of this sculpture – with Silas, the donor and artist, in failing health."

"Last year, my motion was defeated with a four-to-two vote, and that was before the hullabaloo about the Confederate gold. It may be time to revisit the issue. I think I may have the votes, now that we have a possible source to fund its disposal," Hansford smiled confidently.

"I've researched the issue. We just can't get rid of the sculpture. It's still owned by Silas," asserted Peggy. "The sculpture is officially just on loan to the church, although it passes to the church on Silas' death."

"Well, let's just move the sculpture then. Perhaps to the rear of the church?" suggested Hansford. "Or maybe to the area of the fake graves outside the cemetery wall? Hide it so people can't see it. It's just plain dreadful."

Preston spoke, "I don't like the sculpture either, but we have to realize that Silas doesn't have any heirs – or none that anyone knows about. To be quite blunt – we don't want to do something to upset him until he dies – he already has, and for many years, covered over half the annual budget of the church. I think he also had some quite valuable patents when he worked for Kennametal."

"Let's wait," all the ruling elders echoed, except Hansford.

Alice Jane changed the subject: "Does everyone realize that the church has gained almost thirty regular churchgoers, hopefully to become members, since the treasure hunt began?"

"I did a survey of these new worshippers," said Etta. "Surprisingly, a quarter said they were impressed by the church and Pastor Martin after their curiosity led them here, another quarter wanted to affiliate themselves with a potentially rich church – not sure whether they'll stay here –, and the other half were fascinated by the whale sculpture. Can you believe that?"

"What?" Hansford and Peggy exclaimed in unison.

"Well, it looks like we finally got Hansford and Peggy to agree on something," Preston joked.

Etta continued, "One family indicated that any church willing to put an ugly sculpture in the front would also be willing to accept sinners like them. The church would be just like Jesus. Also, once they told the story of Jonah and the whale to their children, the kids wanted to play around the sculpture every Sunday. Another family pointed to Scripture in 1 Peter 3:3-4 that beauty should not come from outward adornment in God's sight, but instead should be that of one's inner self. And, similarly, yet another quoted 1 Samuel 16:7 which says that the Lord does not consider another's appearance, which man does, but the Lord looks at the heart. So – yet more reasons to keep the sculpture."

Hansford frowned and stared out a window.

Peggy smiled broadly.

"Anything else to discuss?" Pastor Martin looked around the room.

"How about the oak tree out front?" Hansford bellyached. "Can we, at least, get rid of that eyesore?"

"As you're aware, some in church oppose that, since legend has it that the tree originated from the oak tree at the Twin Falls site," replied Pastor Martin. "A local arborist has placed the age of this tree at about 125 years, consistent with being planted at the time of the building of the church sanctuary here."

"Let me surprise everyone, again," Peggy contributed. "I actually agree with Hansford. My grandson has nurtured several oak seedlings planted from acorns collected off this tree two years ago. All are quite healthy. Let me propose, then, to remove the old tree and replace it with one or more of these seedlings. What would be a better time than now to do so? This will provide a symbol of our church's renewal at our 200th anniversary."

"Great idea – have a rebirth from a seedling of the tree that itself was a rebirth of the original oak at Twin Falls," put forth Preston.

"I think we can get Troy to cut the tree down and remove the wood," added Pastor Martin. "We'll only have to pay to remove the stump and perhaps backfill some dirt."

"We can designate some of the proceeds from the sale of the safes to do so," suggested Alice Jane.

Everyone agreed.

† † †

The next visit of Pastor Martin with Silas in room 79 at Faithful Care interrupted Silas in the midst of working his daily crossword puzzle. Joe the sock monkey sat with his arms crossed next to the newspaper on the table. The angle of the sunlight entering the window seemed to accentuate the pallor of Silas' skin, even whiter than Pastor Martin's last visit.

Before greetings and pleasantries, Silas asked, "What's a ten letter word that has as its fifth and sixth letters 'h' and 'q' respectively – it's one of the big words in the puzzle? The clue is 'dancing soil?'" He showed Pastor Martin the puzzle.

"I haven't the foggiest idea," Pastor Martin responded. After a few moments of feigned thought, he giggled, "Why don't you ask Joe?"

"It might start with an 'e,'" added Silas, ignoring his pastor's suggestion.

"Still nothing."

"Let's go with 'earthquake,'" Silas concluded. "Let's also try another big word – in the theme of the puzzle, it should also start with an 'e,' and it looks like it ends with 'er.' The funny clue is 'noble-stuck-in-the-mud flask?'"

"I don't even understand the clue."

"You might want to think of some chemistry and lab glassware," Silas smiled.

"Still nothing"

"Let's write in erlenmeyer," Silas stated. "Haven't you ever heard of an Erlenmeyer flask? It looks like I'm not gonna get any help from you today. I'll finish the crossword later."

Pastor Martin nodded his head in agreement. "Your crossword clues confuse me instead of help me," he laughed.

"Talking about other clues that confuse you," added Silas. "When are you going to ask out Laura Armstrong, my nurse here, on a date?"

"Oh, Silas, she's way out of my league – I don't think she'd even give me a second glance," groused Pastor Martin. "Dot once said that she didn't have to worry about me having an affair, that no other woman would ever want me."

"Forget what Dot said, Elwood. Here's your next clue. Laura gave me a message to give you – stop by the nurses' station before you leave. She wants to talk to you."

"Why would she want to see me?"

"I think she made some homemade yeast rolls for you."

"That sounds absolutely delicious," responded Pastor Martin. "I think she just has sympathy for an old guy who can't cook."

"You're just hopelessly clueless!" Silas threw up his arms. "To change the subject, I hear that Hansford went one for two at the session meeting this past Sunday. The oak tree is coming down, but my sculpture is staying."

"You have good sources, as usual. I'm glad we don't discuss national security secrets among the ruling elders," Pastor Martin replied. "The information would be out in the public before the meeting ends."

"Any more activity on the Beets Campbell front?" questioned Silas.

"Just going to sell the Terwillegar safes. Maybe put out one of the C.S.A. gold coins to auction to see whether they're worth more than just the bullion. Other than that, we're sort of at an impasse on what to do," answered Pastor Martin. He hesitated, "Do you have any suggestions?"

"Actually I do," snorted Silas. "Let's do a riddle."

Pastor Martin rolled his eyes. "What does a riddle have to do with anything?"

"Humor me. Five hundred begins it; five hundred ends it; and five is in the middle. The first of all the letters and the first of all the numbers are in between. Put it all together and you spell the name of an ancient biblical king."

"You really expect me to figure that out?" confessed Pastor Martin.

"Ah, give it a try," laughed Silas.

Pastor Martin thought for a moment. "Well, I guess the name must have an 'a,' the first letter . . . and a '1,' the first number, in it . . . unless zero is the first number. Do I get clues?"

"Let me read a passage in Isaiah to you."

"Does it have the name of the biblical king there?"

Silas smiled. "The verse I'm going to read is Isaiah 11:3 – but because I'm into numbers with this riddle and Isaiah is the 23rd book in the Bible, I could say I'm reading from 23-11-3." Silas took a piece of paper and wrote "23-11-3" in large block numbers.

Pastor Martin stared at the numbers. He leaned his elbow on the table and propped his chin up with his hand. He glared at Silas: "And?"

Silas grinned broadly. He picked up his Bible, opening it to his bookmark. "Well, the passage in part reads, 'He shall not judge by what his eyes see or decide by what his ears hear.' Or, another way to look at the passage is that things aren't as they seem at first glance."

"So? What does that have to do with the riddle?"

"The answer to the riddle is DAVID," smiled Silas as he wrote 'D-A-V-I-D' in block letters on his piece of paper. "You had to translate the numbers as letters."

"I don't understand."

"The numbers had to be put into their Roman numerals. That's the code, the key to solving the riddle," Silas pointed at the letters "D" and "V" on his paper.

"How was I to know that?" Pastor Martin responded. "I guess it would've helped for me to know the Roman numeral for five hundred is 'D.' But you said this riddle would provide guidance on the church's next step with our Beets Campbell debacle – How?"

Silas handed him the piece of paper with "23-11-3" and "DAVID" on it. "Here. Just take this paper back with you to your office and re-read the verse in the Bible."

Pastor Martin obediently folded the paper and stuffed it in his shirt pocket. He looked to the heavens, praying for God to provide guidance.

"By the way, I think Laura wrote her address and phone number on the bag of rolls."

"That's right, I need to pick up the rolls on my way out." Pastor Martin slid back his chair, stretched his legs, and stood.

Silas laughed, "Why was the mole of oxygen molecules excited when he walked out of the single's bar?"

"Is this another joke?" Pastor Martin put his hand on his forehead. "My head hurts."

"He got Avogadro's number," smiled Silas.

"Ha-Ha," replied Pastor Martin without laughing.

"Remember 23-11-3," Silas wrote the numbers once again on another piece of paper.

"God, give me patience in a hurry," Pastor Martin threw up his arms, exasperated.

"Persistence is the key," Silas chuckled. "Quite often, the reason you can't solve a puzzle isn't that it's too difficult, it's that you didn't try long enough. Keep thinking about it. Everything can change in the blink of an eye. The solution to most puzzles is usually 99% persistence and 1% enlightenment."

"God, give me the 1% enlightenment in a flash," Pastor Martin grinned.

Chapter Eight
STRANGLE OR HUG

Just after noon the same day, Pastor Martin returned from his visit to Silas. At his desk, he munched on his lunch of a cheeseburger, fries, and Coke, picked up at Hardee's in Buena Vista. Reese Coleman shuffled into Pastor Martin's office mad as a hornet. Reese whined that Silas had done it to him again. Silas presented him with a riddle and wouldn't tell him the answer. Reese scuffled back and forth in front of the desk fussing how he was supposed to be compassionate to Silas because of Silas' failing health, and yet Silas was so infuriating at times. So much so that he wanted to figuratively strangle him. Pastor Martin sighed, knowing Reese would baffle him with the riddle too.

Reese finally spouted, "I can travel from there to here by disappearing, and here to there by reappearing. What am I?"

The only clue Silas would give Reese was a verse from Isaiah – that things weren't as they seemed to be. Pastor Martin smiled and ate another fry. Reese griped how was he to solve the riddle if he didn't know what here and there were. And Silas wouldn't tell him. And Silas only responded with his galling laugh.

As Pastor Martin finished his burger, he asked Reese to repeat the riddle, although he held little hope he'd be able to solve it. Reese recited the riddle. Pastor Martin doodled THERE and HERE next to each other on the burger wrapper, then HERE and THERE.

Pastor Martin threw his pencil in the air and jumped up from his desk. He shouted, "The letter 'T.' That's the answer. I got the riddle."

Reese shook his head, still not understanding why "T" was the answer. Pastor Martin did a little victory dance in front of his desk and gave Reese a bear hug in celebration.

Later that afternoon, Peggy Lauderdale stopped by Pastor Martin's office. She needed to pick up a gold coin to show yet another appraiser. Pastor Martin retrieved his piece of paper with all the safe combinations from the file drawer in his desk; then Peggy accompanied him to the basement. He looked at the paper for the combination, 23-11-3, for the large safe that now housed all the gold coins. He verbalized the numbers as he opened the safe: to the right several times to 23, then left to 11, and right to 3. The safe clacked open. Pastor Martin grabbed one of the small burlap bags. He slid a gold coin out and handed it to Peggy. Once she left with the coin, Pastor Martin strolled back to his office.

Pastor Martin heard his telephone ringing as he walked down the hallway to his office. He increased his pace to a jog. About to grasp the door knob, he tried to shift the paper with the safe combinations from his right hand to his left. In his haste, the paper fluttered to the floor.

The Presbyter, Rev. Van Guiden, droned on and on to him for the next half hour about Pastor Martin's responsibilities as the chair of the newly-created *ad hoc* lay ministry committee for the Presbytery. Although Rev. Van Guiden emphasized its importance, Pastor Martin knew the reality – lots of time, formulate a report, report filed for posterity.

Dismayed by the extra work, Pastor Martin plodded to the doorway and bent over to retrieve the errant piece of paper. Silas' piece of paper slid from his shirt pocket. After picking them both up, he placed them side by side on his desk mat. He sat in his creaking chair. He mindlessly unfolded the paper from his pocket. His eyes immediately focused on the "23-11-3" from the unfolded paper setting right next to the "23-11-3" on the paper with the safe combinations.

He recalled Silas's words – *23-11-3 . . . Isaiah, the 23rd book of the Bible, chapter 11, verse 3 . . . things are not as they seem.*

He grabbed his well-worn Bible from the edge of the desk and placed it next to the paper with the safe combinations. "40-19-21" was next. He flipped to the table of contents. The Old Testament had 39 books, so book 40 was the first book, Matthew, of the New Testament. Pastor Martin quickly turned to Matthew 19:21 and read, "Jesus answered [to the wealthy, young man]. 'If you want to be perfect, go, sell your possessions and give to the poor, and you will have treasure in heaven. Then come follow me.'"

Pastor Martin closed his eyes – *To whom, if anyone, is this passage directed. To me, to the church, . . . to Beets Campbell and his brothers? It doesn't make sense. It's like Silas giving clues for a riddle.*

Next combination was "51-1-26." Pastor Martin counted from book 40, or Matthew, up to book 51. Colossians, one of the letters of the apostle Paul. He paged along to chapter 1, verse 26 – "the mystery that has been kept hidden for ages and generation, but is now disclosed to the saints."

Next combination was "18-23-10." Pastor Martin counted to book 18, which was Job. He quickly found chapter 23 of Job, verse 10 – and read, "but he knows the way that I take; when he has tested me, I will come forth as gold."

Pastor Martin trembled. Things were hitting close to home. *Are the passages telling me that we have a mystery of hidden gold and maybe that Beets Campbell gave it to the church? They haven't told me anything I didn't know beforehand. But all this was preceded by a warning that things are not as they seem. What am I missing?*

One more safe combination: "32-1-17." Pastor Martin counted to book 32; he was surprised it was Jonah. He quickly turned to chapter 1, verse 17 – "But the Lord provided a great fish [whale] to swallow Jonah, and Jonah was inside the fish for three days and three nights."

Inside the whale – could it be? But that means it's not Beets Campbell, it's . . .

He laughed, as he closed and thumped the Bible's cover.

Indeed the Bible was our treasure map after all – not only for finding our heavenly treasure but also for the earthly treasure!

Pastor Martin burst out the office door. He ran down the hallway and hit the outside door at full speed. He almost took a tumble as he bounded down the two steps to the sidewalk. He dashed to the front of the church, every few steps skipping with joy. As he was gasping for breath, he looked into the open mouth of the whale of Silas' sculpture.

Unlike the oxidized patina of the brass comprising the sculpture, the inside belly bottom of the whale was still bright and shiny. *Could it be – hidden in plain sight all these years? But that would mean . . .*

At that moment, Pastor Martin didn't know whether to strangle or to hug Silas. Shaking his head, he took a step back and stared at Jonah. He laughed so hard that he fell to the ground – Jonah was neither being swallowed nor spit up. Jonah was pointing into the whale!

Chapter Nine
SECRETS

That night, Pastor Martin returned to Faithful Care for his second visit on the same day. As he entered room 79, someone sat at the table talking to Silas. He looked vaguely familiar to Pastor Martin. The two men were working on a crossword puzzle. Joe the sock monkey sat on the table, and the Bible was still opened to chapter 11 in Isaiah.

Silas looked up to see a beaming Pastor Martin, looking as though he had the Energizer Bunny trapped in his body. Pastor Martin kept combing his hands through his coif. For once, it was mussed. Silas grinned. Pastor Martin stared at Silas' visitor; minus the slicked back hair and expensive suit, he looked just like Sam, the church's safecracker. Tonight, he was neatly dressed in khakis and a pull-over knit shirt, with wavy brown hair.

"Gee," Silas exclaimed to Pastor Martin: "it looks like you've just had a eureka moment. But first, I need a word for my crossword puzzle. It's a biblical clue – it says 'type of man Boaz was before he married?' Eight letters and ends in '-ess.'"

Pastor Martin was taken aback, his enthusiasm temporarily abated. "Well, Boaz was quite wealthy and was kind to Ruth before he married her. She just showed up to help in the harvest of his fields. So maybe 'kindness' might be the right description. And it's even eight letters."

"Nope, it looks like it starts with an 'r' as well."

Pastor Martin thought for a moment and laughed, "how 'bout 'ruthless.'"

"Bingo!"

Pastor Martin shook his head and chuckled. "Sort of like the ruthless treasure hunt that you put me as well as the church through."

Both Silas and Sam snorted in laughter.

Sam offered Pastor Martin his chair, but he declined and continued standing. Pastor Martin added, "Indeed, my mind is still clicking." He pointed at Silas. "Could it be that you orchestrated this elaborate Beets Campbell puzzle? I just looked into the very shiny belly of our church whale."

Both Silas and Sam replied in unison: "It's about time."

Pastor Martin turned to a smiling Sam: "Well, Sam, I assume you really aren't Sam, nor are you a professional safecracker."

Sam smiled, "Actually I am Sam, Sam Kegley. I'm a part-time actor, and a full-time banking executive. Silas and my father grew up together; my father and he were best friends throughout grade school, then college in New York. In fact, Silas is my godfather. After numerous years of only trading Christmas cards, I moved to Richmond and we once again got together, especially after he entered this assisted care facility. He contacted me when he needed help with his scheme."

Pastor Martin turned to Silas, whose eyes were closed, and asked, "How much gold is in the whale's belly?"

Silas opened his eyes weakly and replied, "I'm tired; Sam knows the story."

"Actually, about the same weight as the fictional Nettle Creek gold – 500 pounds give or take some. So, in current dollars, it's worth about ten million dollars."

Pastor Martin added, "And it's been just setting there in front of the church for the past fifty years."

"Yep," confirmed Sam.

Pastor Martin then queried, "How did Silas get the gold?"

Sam gathered his thoughts, then confided, "Silas married the love of his life, Patty, in his last year of college. Silas' dad was an insurance agent; so as a wedding present, he paid the first five years premium on a two-million dollar life insurance policy on the groom as well as one on the bride. He said it was to protect his future grandchildren. Unfortunately, Patty was in a tragic car accident before they even graduated from college."

"Yeah, Silas told me about the accident but not the insurance policy," interjected Pastor Martin. "And that he never married or even had a relationship again."

Tears trickled down from Silas' eyes. Pastor Martin searched his pockets. He gave Silas a handkerchief.

"Silas didn't want the money," continued Sam. "He wanted Patty. The week after Patty's burial, he and my father went to my father's church, not Silas' church; and the sermon was based on the parable in Matthew about the rich young man being asked by Jesus to give all his money away and follow him – "

"So 40-19-21 referred to him, not to Beets," interrupted Pastor Martin with a laugh.

Sam gave a subtle nod. He added, "Anyway, Silas took that sermon as a message directed to him. My dad said Silas didn't want to be defined by his money but by his deeds to support his faith."

"Like a sign from above?" Pastor Martin walked over to the window and smelled the fresh yellow and red roses in a vase on the window sill.

Sam continued, "My dad suggested that before Silas donated all the money and followed Christ, they should have a 'whale' of a time for at least one night. At that time, Silas was an aspiring engineer. But, my dad said Silas also had the delusion that he was an artist."

"I am an artist," Silas expressed mock outrage.

"Well, we'll let history decide – I assume Hansford Cash would debate the point," snickered Sam. "As my dad told me the story, Silas must have misinterpreted him about the 'whale' of a time – instead Silas bought gold bullion with the insurance check and put the gold in his sculpture of Jonah's whale that he was working on at that time. He traded the two million dollars for about 500 pounds of gold which he put in the belly of his whale sculpture. Through inflation, it's now worth ten million. He kept about a half pound of gold in reserve."

"I actually made the sculpture of a giant fish as the Scripture says," Silas muttered. "It's not a whale. People misinterpret my art!"

"Why not just give the money, or rather gold, to the church decades ago?" Pastor Martin had a puzzled look on his face.

"I asked him that as well when he first recruited me for this performance," answered Sam. "Silas was embarrassed; he considered the gold as his backup if he couldn't make it on his own – that the sculpture was only on loan. He was worried that his faith wasn't that great – just like the rich young man. But, after a few years at Twin Falls Presbyterian Church, he was ready to give this fortune to the church. By that time, though, he wanted to do something unique in this gift – and he was into puzzles and having a good time with pranks. Evidently, his plan was long-term, as the graves were dug inconspicuously decades ago when he was the custodian of the cemetery and the church grounds. Such gave the fake graves many years to blend with their surroundings. He had also purchased the four small safes from an out-of-state antique dealer, and surreptitiously hired a real safecracker to open the large empty safe in the cellar years ago. He simply fed me their combinations for me to announce."

Pastor Martin shook his head: "I must admit you're a mighty good actor."

"I've been trying to get you and the ruling elders of the church to open that safe to put everything in motion for the past decade," grumbled Silas. "But, y'all just sat there – and I thought I would be just as stubborn and out-sit y'all."

Sam then added, "By the way, Silas at one time wanted to be a novelist before he became an engineer; he took several creative writing classes in college. He also researched the local history for quite a while. He even built a homemade kiln, mold, and stamp to manufacture the phony confederate coins – it helped that he's a metallurgical engineer."

"Why did Silas choose Twin Falls Presbyterian Church for this gift?" asked Pastor Martin. "It's my understanding that the sculpture was given to the church on loan, even before Silas became a member of the church."

Silas laughed, but it brought upon him a brief wheezing fit.

Sam shrugged his shoulders: "I don't know, I always thought the events were reversed." He looked at Silas, who turned away in thought.

Silas turned back to address Sam: "I guess I or your father never mentioned that part of the story to you. It's quite interesting."

Silas became quiet, closed his eyes, and feigned sleep.

"Silas, I know you're not sleeping. Tell me the rest of the story," insisted Pastor Martin.

"Well, okay – as Paul Harvey would say, 'here's the rest of the story.' My sculpture and I both came to Rockbridge County, once I accepted the position as an engineer at the carpet factory. I rented a house for about a year, but kept the sculpture in storage. In that time I visited numerous churches in the county – and decided whichever church would accept the sculpture as a gift to place in front of the church, I would join that church and relocate to that area of the county. Surprisingly, the Twin Falls Presbyterian Church seemed enamored with the sculpture – which even I now admit is not the prettiest sculpture."

"Out of curiosity, how many churches rejected your offer before you moved into your house in Midvale, just north of Cornwall?" Pastor Martin asked.

Silas laughed, "Y'all were number twelve. One church even called the sculpture an abstract representation of Noah and the Ark. How could someone mistake a fish or whale for an ark? I considered at one time that I might have to develop a plan B. So it was simply an act of Providence on the part of Twin Falls' congregation fifty years ago. As I understand, it was Peggy Lauderdale's father who encouraged the session to accept the offer of the ugly duckling of a sculpture – he said he could see into the heart of the monstrosity. I also remember him looking into the whale's mouth and smiling. I believe he may've had a sneaking suspicion."

"An amazing and fascinating story," smiled Pastor Martin.

"Silas said he wrote up the scheme for Peggy Lauderdale's 200th anniversary history book," added Sam. "He thought it would be a good way to end the book with the discovery of a ten-million dollar gift – and yet start a new era, sort of a rebirth for the church. He called it a whale of a story."

Pastor Martin smiled broadly

Sam paused, then handed Pastor Martin a document that had been setting on the table. "All signed and legalized, this transfers the sculpture from Silas to the church. It's no longer just on loan. In the document, he indicates that the gold is a gift from him for the exclusive use of Twin Falls Presbyterian Church. He said the sculpture can stay where it is – he designed it so that you just have someone take a blowtorch and drop the belly from the whale."

"Troy can probably do it. Just use the money from the gold as the church wishes." Silas yawned and wiggled in his wheelchair.

"Ten million dollars for the church – just think of all the needs the church can supply to the struggling folks . . . like Jesus would have done with the money from the rich young, or maybe old, man: 40-19-21 . . . we can help the widow Hostetter, and also the struggling Higgins and Duncan families. So much good can be done here – we can use this earthly treasure to lead to heavenly treasures. And, not just in the Cornwall area, but everywhere. I guess I'm rambling, but things just couldn't get any better."

Silas returned to working on the crossword puzzle on his table.

At that time, Laura passed by Silas' room and realized Pastor Martin was visiting. She entered and exchanged pleasantries with Sam and Silas. Hands on her hips, she turned to Pastor Martin. "Elwood, I'm tired of waiting for you to ask me out. I have two tickets to the Christian music festival at Glen Maury Park in Buena Vista on Friday night. Why don't you come over to my place for dinner, then you can take me to the concert?"

"I stand corrected – it just got better."

Topics for Discussion
NETTLE CREEK

1. What would be your response if a church member donates an ugly painting or family heirloom to display in your church?

2. Often times, lottery winners of multi-million dollar prizes become less happy. They simply cannot cope with the windfall as the new rich. What would you propose as a course of action if your church was suddenly entrusted with a ten million dollar gift?

3. The oak tree in front of the Twin Falls Presbyterian Church symbolized both a change as well as a continuous thread to its history. It's often said that the only constant in life (whether an individual or the church) is change. Does one have to change to survive?

4. Discuss the appropriateness of the underlying theology (parable of Jesus) used by Sunshine Clutterbuck to support her treasure hunt using Grunt and Hamm.

5. Solve the following word puzzles that Silas might have used to confound Pastor Martin or Reese Coleman:

    a. Who's the person one level under the convent sister in the religious hierarchy?

    b. How did Silas give out the batteries?

    c. A dentist and a manicurist married. How did they fight?

    d. With what do you measure grass?

    e. Name three consecutive days without using the words Monday, Tuesday, Wednesday, Thursday, Friday, Saturday, or Sunday.

6. Each of the following represents a saying, as might have been used by Silas as a puzzle. Solve each:
    a. <u>BBBBBBB</u>
    b. WOWOLFOL
    c. RE   RE
    d. **THREW** and

7. Why do you think Silas created a treasure hunt for his gift to the church, rather than simply providing the church with a check? If Silas had passed away before the treasure was discovered, do you think Pastor Martin would have persisted and solved the puzzle?

8. Florence Scovel Shinn, an American artist, said: "Giving opens the way for receiving." Provide illustrations of the truth of this saying from this story.

9. Jonah is sometimes called the "reluctant prophet." Compare the biblical story of Jonah and the whale (great fish) to the tale of Silas, who might be called the "reluctant philanthropist."

10. The opening quote for this story is, "Happiness resides not in possessions, and not in gold. Happiness resides in the soul." Compare this quotation to the message of Pastor Martin's sermon on *Our Treasure Map*.

ANSWERS to Questions 4 and 5:

4. a. second to nun.   b. free of charge.   c. tooth and nail. d. a yardstick.   e. yesterday, today, and tomorrow.

5. a. a beeline.   b. wolf in sheep's clothing.   c. repaired. d. through thick and thin.

PART 2

BIRD FOREST

Henry D. Schreiber

Now when He [Jesus] saw the crowds, He went up on the mountainside and sat down. His disciples came to Him, and He began to teach them, saying:

>Blessed are the poor in spirit,
>for theirs is the kingdom of heaven.

>Blessed are those who mourn,
>for they will be comforted.

>Blessed are the meek,
>for they will inherit the earth.

>Blessed are those who hunger and thirst for righteousness,
>for they will be filled.

>Blessed are the merciful,
>for they will be shown mercy.

>Blessed are the pure in heart,
>for they will see God.

>Blessed are the peacemakers,
>for they will be called sons of God.

>Blessed are those who are persecuted because of righteousness,
>for theirs is the kingdom of heaven.

Blessed are you when people insult you, persecute you, and falsely say all kinds of evil against you because of Me. Rejoice and be glad, because great is your reward in heaven, for in the same way they persecuted the prophets who were before you.

— Matthew 5:1-12

Chapter Ten
JOYFUL PATH

Pastor Elwood Martin stood nervous as a tick outside Laura Armstrong's front door. Decades had passed since he'd last been on a date. His quivering hand held a spectacular bouquet of hydrangea, delphinium, and iris, all in varying shades of blue. Carolyn at University Florists had guaranteed the flowers would impress anyone. Elwood breathed deeply, wiping a bead of sweat from his forehead. He took stock of himself – straightened his belt and re-tucked his new burgundy button-down shirt into his equally new khaki slacks.

As Elwood's hand came down to knock on the door, a dog started to bark wildly. The yapping, though, seemed to emanate from a back room in the house. Meanwhile, Elwood's knock aborted midair. He heard an earsplitting shriek, then Laura screaming "No!" and "No, Barney, No!" rapid fire. Frantic barking continued nonstop.

Elwood turned the doorknob. Unlocked. He burst through the door. Pulse racing, he dashed down the hallway. The noise led him to the kitchen. Laura was bent over shouting, "No, Barney, No. Come!" again and again at a black Scottish terrier. Barney danced back and forth. His barking was broken only by periodic snapping. He was in a standoff with a visibly irritated snake, not a run-of-the-mill garter or black snake but a four-foot long copperhead. Barney had it cornered. The snake kept unsuccessfully striking out at him. Barney paid no mind to the panicked and worried Laura.

Elwood quickly surveyed the kitchen and found the door of a likely closet. He grabbed a broom. Waving his hand at Laura to catch her attention, he shouted, "When I shove the broom between Barney and the snake, grab Barney."

Laura nodded.

Elwood returned the nod. "On 3 – . . . 1 . . . 2 . . . 3."

Elwood slammed the broom down. The copperhead struck at the broom, sinking its fangs into the straw bristles, then retreated back to a corner. Simultaneously, Laura snatched Barney's tail. She slid him toward her and whisked him into her waiting arms. Barney squirmed furiously, trying to jump back into the fray with the snake. Laura wrestled him into a bedroom. Barney continued to bark loudly, scratching on the bedroom door.

Elwood fruitlessly tried to pin the snake with the broom. Instead, the copperhead slithered into the gap next to a nearby refrigerator, then hid behind it.

Laura returned to the kitchen trembling and wiping tears. Elwood gave her a comforting look and gently touched her on the shoulder.

He pointed to the space between the refrigerator and counter. "It's back there."

"You came at just the right time," she exhaled. "I was so, so worried about Barney getting bit by the copperhead. And I hate snakes, all snakes."

"I understand. I'm far from being a snake-handling preacher-man," he ribbed kindly.

"At least we know where it is," she sighed.

Barney continued to bark in the bedroom.

Elwood peered into the gap next to the refrigerator. "Do you have a hoe?"

Laura hurried out to a woodshed. She quickly returned carrying both a hoe and a shovel. Together she and Elwood wiggled the refrigerator from its cubby hole between the kitchen counter on one side and the pantry on the other. They kept their eyes glued to the floor behind the refrigerator. The water line to the ice-maker, though, limited the distance they could wrest the refrigerator from the wall. And the hissing copperhead had coiled behind this plastic water line at the far corner. Elwood leaned over the kitchen counter to position himself. He tried to slip the hoe up to the snake; he couldn't just whack it because of the plastic tubing. The snake struck at the hoe and bounced back. Elwood unsuccessfully tried to pin it, though succeeded in corralling it to the opposite corner of the cubicle. The copperhead struck out time and again. Elwood now had a better angle. He gave a quick chop with the hoe. Not fatal, though the snake writhed at the hit. Two more quick thwacks, followed by a mortal chop to the copperhead's neck. Elwood took a deep breath – *mission complete and without the hoe even slicing the linoleum or water line.*

Elwood smiled at Laura, vigilant on the other side of the refrigerator and firmly gripping her protective shovel in hand. He gave a thumb up. "Got it. Crisis over!"

Laura returned the smile and relaxed.

Barney maintained his barking.

Suddenly, the smoke detector howled and flashed. Both Elwood and Laura jumped at the deafening screech. On the other side of the kitchen, smoke billowed out of the oven as well as from the top of the stove.

Laura quickly turned the burner knobs off and slid the smoking frying pan and pot to empty burners. She flipped on the fan of the stove vent. She pulled a baking dish from the oven. Smoke rolled out, while she furiously fanned the fumes from herself. Elwood opened windows. Smoke detectors from other rooms shrieked, drowning out Barney's barking.

Elwood propped open the back door to the kitchen.

Laura pointed to the door. "Might not want to do that," she excitedly hollered, "I'd rather have the smoke than another snake wander in."

He nodded and closed the door. "Any box fans in the house?"

"Hall closet!" Meanwhile, Laura also raced to the thermostat in the hallway to turn the HVAC fan to high.

Elwood positioned the fan to blow the kitchen smoke out a window. He also collected the now-dead snake and threw it over the backyard fence into the woods. Laura released Barney from captivity. He sniffed around the kitchen, more concerned with lingering snake scents than smoke. She joined Elwood outside to let the smoke clear and escape the noise. Barney followed, sniffing the air and ground, trying to recapture the smell of the snake.

Laura and Elwood smiled warmly at each other. Their smiles evolved into laughing.

"What a way to start a first date?" Laura threw up her arms.

"I have to admit you had my pulse racing," Elwood chuckled. "I initially came running in the house thinking you were being attacked by some guy named Barney."

Barney turned his attention to Elwood. He snuffled around Elwood's leather shoes while Elwood ruffled the top of his head.

"I worried about Barney getting bitten." Laura held back a tear.

The last smoke detector finally went silent.

"Emergency over. Both snake and smoke eliminated," Elwood announced.

Laura shook her head. "As well as dinner eliminated . . . I suspect everything's been burned to a crisp."

They plodded back to the kitchen. They peered at the charcoal briquettes which once had been homemade biscuits, the blackened pancake shapes that would have been chicken picatta, and the scorched rice. The steamed broccoli seemed to have survived. The cherry pie on the counter too, although Laura indicated both would probably have a smoky flavor. As she walked to the trash can with the burnt food, Elwood watched intently – quite beautiful in her jeans and red blouse, with a simple gold necklace. Her earrings, sparkly gold figure eights, entranced him – a perfect complement to her twinkling eyes.

Laura was understandably upset at the ruined dinner. But Elwood suggested an alternative plan. They could eat at the Kerrs Creek Ruritan Club Chuckwagon at the music festival, though their famous hamburgers would be a poor substitute for chicken picatta. Laura promised picatta with its citrusy sauce and capers would be in his future.

On their way out the front door, Laura paused. She saw the bouquet of flowers strewn on the hallway floor, whether fallen off or blown off a small table. Elwood had thrown them there in his race to the kitchen. He picked up the smoked flowers drooping from a lack of water, as Laura gathered scattered petals and leaves.

He pointed the flowers toward her. "Here's a once wonderful bouquet."

"A perfect match to a once marvelous dinner," Laura giggled.

Elwood and Laura, along with Barney, enjoyed the rest of the evening eating burgers on paper plates, drinking Dr. Peppers from the can, listening to music, talking, and greeting friends. They sat on lawn chairs and relished each other's company. Each discovered that Silas, ever the matchmaker, had fully educated them about each other.

Elwood didn't want the night to end.

"Tonight has gone by much too fast," he stammered, as he escorted Laura to her front door. "I wish tonight would last forever, for infinity." His face turned crimson.

Laura smiled and gave him a gentle hug. "Coincidentally, just today, Silas mentioned that there're only two infinities – yesterday and tomorrow. One is past and gone forever, and the other stays forever out of reach." She chuckled, "There's always tomorrow. Tonight was certainly memorable, in more ways than one."

Laura kissed Elwood softly on the cheek. His pulse raced the fastest that night, but this time with joy and hope.

Pastor Elwood Martin stopped in mid-stride as he entered room 79 of Faithful Care. His eyes locked on the ornate box in the middle of Silas Clark's table. Joe the sock monkey sat quietly next to the box. Everything else in Silas' room remained the same – from the neatly made hospital bed to the vase of fresh flowers, today multicolored dahlia and zinnia, on the window sill.

Pastor Martin made nary a sound as he stared at the box. Silas, as usual, was slouched in his wheelchair doing the puzzles from the daily newspaper. Without looking up, Silas happily proclaimed, "Good morning, Elwood. Have a seat. I'm halfway through the crossword." Silas seemed to have an uncanny awareness of happenings about him.

"A great morning, indeed. It's already a warm and sunny day." Elwood walked over to the table and took a seat.

Elwood scrutinized the wooden box, about the size of a lunch pail. It was elegant in its primitive simplicity, a profound work of art constructed from oak with inlays of walnut. An angel decorated the side closest to him, while two tulips, painted red, bracketed the initials "J.P." on the front. The box literally glowed in the sunlight streaming through the window.

"OK, Elwood – let's see how you're doing on puzzles today." Silas peered at the crossword in front of him.

"Why do you do this to me, Silas, quizzing me every time I visit? I can never get the words for the –"

"It looks like the theme for the puzzle is type of temperature scales," Silas interrupted. "Already, Fahrenheit and Kelvin have been two of the words. Let's go to 32-across; its clue is 'Mailed a report card?'"

Elwood scrunched his face. He remained mute.

"The word looks like it starts with a 'c' and ends with an 'e,' and has ten letters. The clue ends with a question mark indicating that it's clever or fun."

"Well, I don't have a clue," Elwood shrugged, "and I'm not having fun."

Silas smiled. "Let's go with 'Centigrade.'" He printed the letters into the crossword squares.

Elwood shook his head, then rolled his eyes.

"Let's see whether you're any better on 53-across. This word also starts with a 'c' and has seven letters. The clue has you fill in a blank. It says, 'Looking into a microscope, we can see a cell; but can a 'blank?'" Silas tapped his pencil on the table.

"Why do you punish me like this?"

"Oh, Elwood – just let this old man have some fun." Silas cupped his hand over his mouth and gave a token sympathy cough.

Silas looked tired in his wheelchair. His heart was slowly wearing out. Hospice was already aiding in his care. But today, as usual, Silas was nattily dressed, clean-shaven, and his tuffs of hair neatly combed. Silas was ready, fully committed to Jesus Christ, and at peace with his destiny with his head held high.

"I have no idea," Elwood said after a few moments of feigned contemplation. "Are you gonna tell me the answer?"

Silas picked up his pencil. "C . . . E . . . L . . . S . . . I . . . U . . . S." Then, he pronounced, "Celsius."

Elwood fidgeted in his chair, with a confused look in his eyes.

"Looking into a microscope, we can see a cell; but can a 'cell see us.' Cel-si-us," Silas pronounced syllable-by-syllable. "Yep, the cell sees us as well."

Elwood groaned, and stole another glance at the box on the table.

"Okay, most importantly." Silas put his pencil down and glared at Elwood: "Your first date with Laura? How did it go?"

"Enchanting," Elwood responded with star-struck eyes. "It was wonderful."

"Is that all you're gonna tell me?" Silas fussed. "Here I am – I set you up with my nurse. She has you over for an unforgettable 'almost' dinner at her house, then y'all go to a music festival. And you invite her to your church service on Sunday morning – and have dinner together again that night. And you summarize all that for me in just a few words."

"I don't kiss and tell," Elwood snickered.

"So you've already kissed?" Silas shot back rapid-fire.

"Ah. . . ah . . . ah," Elwood blushed a deep red.

Silas smiled, satisfied. "No need to tell me anything more. Laura's already been in to check on me and dispense my meds this morning. I found out everything – and I mean everything." Silas laughed, "I especially liked the part about the smokin' hot dinner."

Elwood returned the laugh. "I'm just so, so captivated by her charm and beauty."

"Oh, beauty, that's right," Silas grabbed a magazine from the stack on his table, then thumbed through one called *Mental Floss*. After a few moments, he said, "Here it is. This article says an artist and writer by the name of David Lance Goines developed the Helen system to measure beauty."

"I don't understand – a beauty scale? The Helen system?"

Silas cleaned his glasses with a tissue, then continued, "Just like Centigrade and Celsius are scales to measure temperature, the Helen scale gauges beauty. It's based upon the beauty of Helen of Troy. Legend says her beauty launched a thousand ships; so one Helen is that standard amount of beauty. Thus, to launch one ship, you need one-thousandth of a Helen or a millihelen. So, where would you place Laura on this beauty scale?"

"A kilohelen!" Elwood bellowed, while raising his arms in jubilation.

"Wow - a thousand Helens of beauty, enough to launch a million ships," Silas turned his face to a wide-eyed Laura standing in the doorway to the room.

Elwood slowly followed Silas's gaze to the doorway, still unaware of Laura's presence. "But that's only because I didn't know the prefix for anything bigger."

Laura blushed. "How sweet, Elwood. I'll see you tonight. I can't tarry now; Mrs. Esche needs me in room 22." Laura put her hands on her hips: "And Silas, you're just impossible!"

"I'll be there a little before 6 o'clock," Elwood beamed.

Laura walked away with a broad smile.

Elwood turned back to Silas. "We're having dinner together tonight."

"I know," Silas confessed. "My inquisition of Laura earlier got that information."

"By the way, how long was Laura in the doorway listening?"

"She heard all about the Helen measurement system," Silas chuckled. "I think she was quite impressed with your response."

Elwood blushed again. "I hope she was also impressed by my sermon yesterday," He stole another glance at the box, then pointed at it. "What's the –"

Silas talked over Elwood's attempted query. "Indeed Laura was. I think she'll become a regular at Twin Falls Presbyterian Church. Whatcha gonna talk about this coming Sunday?"

Elwood sighed and droned, "In anticipation of the meeting of the ruling elders after church, I'll be delivering a sermon based upon Luke's biblical verse on 'from everyone who has been given much, much will be demanded –"

"and from one who has been entrusted with much, much more will be asked,'" Silas interjected by finishing the verse; then added, "Sounds good, I look forward to hearing about the details of your message next week."

"The ruling elders are soliciting ideas from the congregation on what to do with the millions you donated to the church; I'll try to give them a nudge in the right direction," Elwood emphasized. "We'll be meeting this Sunday to plan our course of action – but you can imagine that the requests are already pouring in from charities and people with their hands out."

"I guess it's the church's equivalent of winning the lottery."

"And just like lottery winners, our church's life will never be the same." Elwood stole another glance at the box.

"Hopefully, the change will be for the better. One reads stories of lottery winners not gaining happiness from the money won," Silas weakly raised his arms for emphasis.

"Only one thing for sure so far," Elwood smiled. "The fund has been named the 'Patty Clark Memorial Fund' in honor of your late wife. Her life insurance policy provided the gold that you hid in your Jonah-and-the-whale sculpture in front of the church."

"How sweet," Silas uncharacteristically had a few tears well up. Quickly regaining his composure, he added, "I hear Troy Montgomery's oxy-acetylene torch had no problem dropping the gold out of the whale's belly."

"No problem. You designed it perfectly. 498.23 pounds of gold to be exact – it's already been traded in for dollars – ten million and change." Elwood chuckled, "One person who's getting quite a ribbing is Hansford Cash – he wanted to trash that sculpture all these years."

"Yep, that's quite a hoot about Hansford," Silas smiled. "He stopped by to visit last week; and, while here, he ate a big piece of humble pie. We had a good time."

Elwood finally blurted, "I can't take it anymore. What's the story behind the wooden box on your table?"

Silas laughed, "Oh, you noticed."

"Of course I did," Elwood fussed, "Your room has been the same every day for the past few months – nothing ever changes but the puzzle books and magazines in the stack on the table, the flowers in your vase, and now where Joe is sitting."

"I knew I could outwait you. I knew you'd eventually ask me about the box. It's unusual and quite beautiful. How many Helens of beauty would you give it?"

"Quite a few," Elwood replied. "It has very intricate woodwork. Quite remarkable – what's the 'J.P.' stand for?"

"Don't know." Silas handed the box to Elwood.

"Even more remarkable, I see nary a nail or screw – the box is fitted together with interlocking joints." Elwood turned the box around and saw the matching angel inlay on the opposite side panel and the painted floral inlays on the rear. Elwood opened the lid to the box – Nothing inside. "But why do you have it?"

"Had it brought from my house to give to you," Silas chuckled.

"But why?" Elwood set the box back down on the table.

Silas expressed mock horror. "Do I need a reason?"

"You don't need a reason; but I'm sure you have one. You're always plotting and orchestrating this and that," Elwood laughed.

"Just thought you might like it. Got it in a carton of stuff I bought at an estate auction years ago at a local firehouse – not sure which one. As I remember, no one else bid on it, so I gave a dollar for the whole carton of supposed trash. This small box in it caught my attention, so I spent some time cleaning it up."

"Well, it's quite nice – I can see why it fascinated you." Elwood picked up and admired the box once again.

"An antique dealer told me that it dates back to the 1800s, probably pre Civil War. She said it was most likely a box – sort of like a jewelry box – given to a daughter, probably teenager, to start her dowry collection. She offered me a pretty penny for it."

"But why're you giving me this box?" Elwood queried. "My initials aren't 'J.P.'"

"Well, I'm downsizing some of my things I have in my house – for obvious reasons." Silas paused. "My doctors have already started the countdown. I thought you might be able to tell others that the 'J.P.' stands for Just Praying or Jesus Preacher, or something like that."

"Or maybe Joyful Path," Elwood added. "After all, that's the path to everlasting life."

Elwood and Silas shared a hearty laugh.

"Okay," Elwood granted, but then added suspiciously: "You're not starting me on another treasure hunt – or a wild goose chase – or something, just like opening old safes for the last few weeks trying to find your hidden Confederate gold."

"Me – Oh, come now. Would I do that?" Silas chuckled, "Just consider it a gift from a dying parishioner – your consolation prize for finding the ten million dollars for the Twin Falls Presbyterian Church coffers."

Elwood suspiciously shook the box. Nothing.

† † †

Laura's house was only a few miles from the parsonage – a quick jaunt down South River Road, then onto Old Buena Vista Road toward Lexington, and a right on Borden Grant Trail for less than a mile. Accordingly, Elwood left the parsonage for their dinner date promptly at 5:30 that afternoon. Ten minutes later he arrived at her well-maintained brick rancher with a white picket fence surrounding the front yard. Her nearest neighbor lived about a quarter mile away in this rural area of the county. As he scanned the rocky woods surrounding two sides of the property, he smirked, hoping they wouldn't be visited by a copperhead tonight.

Barney, full of energy, greeted and accompanied him down the sidewalk. Elwood knocked, and without breaking stride went into the house along with a scampering Barney. Laura gently kissed him on the cheek as he entered the kitchen. Elwood reciprocated with a gentle hug. A jealous Barney nosed Laura on her ankle demanding and receiving several pats on his head. Wonderful garlic-laden aromas filled the air.

Laura Armstrong bustled about finishing dinner preparation while maintaining a conversation with Elwood. She was a couple inches shorter than Elwood, and a few years younger, with warm and enticing brown eyes that perfectly matched her wavy brown shoulder-length hair. Her complexion literally glowed. She was quick to smile, always pleasant. Walking the hallways of Faithful Care as a registered nurse had cultivated her athletic physique. Thoughts swirled in Elwood's mind – *Talented cook, beautiful woman . . . How lucky am I? . . . Caring nurse, virtuous Christian . . . How blessed am I?*

The dinner consisted of a tossed salad, delicious baked spaghetti, garlic bread, and steamed broccoli – as well as dessert of scratch-made carrot cake with cream cheese icing. Afterwards, he helped wash and dry the dishes. Laura and Elwood had quickly become comfortable in each other's presence. She even allowed him to feed Barney supper that night.

Elwood excused himself to go to his car. Barney joined him. Elwood retrieved Silas' wooden box from the back seat of the car and plopped it on Laura's kitchen table.

Laura picked up the box and shook her head. "I saw it on Silas' table this morning. I asked him about it, but he just grinned and changed the subject."

"Yep, he's a lot better in getting information than in giving it," Elwood sighed. "He gave the box to me . . . and for no obvious reason, other than giving his pastor a gift. Silas said it's somewhat valuable and dates back to the 1800s as a dowry box."

"It's definitely beautiful," Laura nodded, as she inspected it from all angles. "But I don't accept he did it for no reason – especially after he toyed with you on the gold treasure hunt at your church." She paused, then laughed, "He played you like a banjo."

"Indeed, I called him out on that, but he denied that the box was anything but a gift."

"The woodwork is intricate," she mused, "quite remarkable, in fact. A skilled carpenter must've made it."

Laura opened the lid to the box, then turned it upside down. She thought for a moment, opened the box again, and turned it upside down again. Elwood watched as she got up from the table and retrieved a ruler from a kitchen drawer.

"You know, Elwood, the depth of the box is about five inches on the inside, but eight inches on the outside. The wood on the sides is less than a half- inch thick. Could there be a space for hiding something in the bottom of the box?"

"Please – don't add any mystery," Elwood groaned. "Silas said it's just a gift."

Laura flipped the box over again, placing it in front of Elwood. "Look here, the tongue and groove boards go lengthwise on the inside, but crosswise on the outside. Why?" She taunted in delight: "A secret compartment?"

Elwood shook the box several times.

"I hear nothing." He exhaled, "Probably much ado about nothing."

"This is a box from Silas we're talking about," Laura laughed.

He thumped the box's bottom. "And what might be in there?" he grumbled.

Laura placed her hand on Elwood's shoulder. He felt her warmth sweep through his body. She retrieved the box from him, and shook it.

"Hmmm," Laura pondered. She pushed and pulled on the box's bottom, then handed it back to Elwood. "Here, you try it for a while. I'll be back shortly."

Elwood tugged and fiddled again with the bottom and sides of the box. Nothing.

From her computer desk in the next room, Laura yelled, "Hey, Elwood. Try to slide up the front panel or the right side panel. It looks like that's how most secret compartments are designed. The boards in the panel are sliced in half with the outer part being able to slide up or down."

Elwood tried to move the right side panel up and down. Nothing. He wiggled the front panel. Still nothing.

Laura came back to the kitchen table and reached for the box. "Let me try."

"Don't trust me to do it right?" kidded Elwood.

She duplicated his attempts at sliding the right side and front panels. Nothing.

"I told you so," he grinned.

She hesitated, staring at the box cupped in her hands. She tried the left side panel. Up it slid, smooth as silk. "Hah – Hah. 'J.P.' or the maker of the box must've been left-handed instead of right-handed."

"Or maybe just overly clever."

They peered into the concealed compartment. Laura squirmed a book out of its tight quarters. She gently set it on the table in front of them. It was obviously old with its leather cover hanging by threads to the pages.

"Well, it has 'J.P.' written on the front in a fancy script," Laura noted. "Matches the initials on the box."

Elwood opened the book. He quickly reacted to the yellowed and brittle first page: "At least it's written in handwriting very different from that of Beets Campbell. Thus, if this is another of Silas' ruses, he's being ingenious again."

"It's very neat and flowery writing, but larger than usual – like the writing of a young girl. Sort of looks like a journal."

Gently turning the page, Elwood started to scan it as Laura peered over his shoulder. He caught a whiff of her intoxicating perfume. His head unconsciously turned to allow his nose a more pronounced smell, momentarily losing his focus on the journal.

Laura reacted to his response. She likewise turned her head, then kissed him gently on the forehead. "The perfume's called 'Purple Magic.' A friend gave it to me." She grinned, "Said it's a secret concoction made here in the county by a woman who goes by the name of Sunshine. You might know her."

Elwood rolled his eyes. He breathed another fresh waft before returning to the book.

"Only the first few pages are used," he sighed. "Let's see what it has to say."

"Nothing dated, or even numbered," she added.

Elwood returned to the first page. He read slowly and hesitatingly through the outdated penmanship and ink splotches.

> Mother gave me this journal. She traded eggs for several weeks to Elsie, our neighbor down the path a bit, for the book. It is for me to record my thoughts. Mother said she had one when she was growing up.
>
> I miss going to school. It has been a long time since my sisters and I went to school when we lived in Campbell country.

Elwood looked up from the page and gasped, "Campbell country – Don't tell me that 'J.P.' is somehow connected to Beets Campbell and his brothers. Is this yet more ramblings of Silas' imagination?"

"My goodness," Laura groaned as she gently rubbed Elwood's back: "Would Silas do this to you yet again?"

"It sure makes me leery." He shook his head, but continued reading.

> My wish is to be back in the classroom of my old schoolmarm Mrs. Tarpley. She never smiled. She hit my knuckles more than once when she didn't like my penmanship. But it was school. Mother teaches us at home when she has time. Not very often, only a little each day between chores. We no longer have books. Mother teaches us from the family Bible. Father is gone most of the week. He works at the distillery next to the big creek. He comes home Saturday night and leaves before

daybreak on Monday. Even then we rarely see him. He chops wood, repairs sheds and house, plows the field, and digs out the root cellar.

Today was a normal day – I collect water in the buckets for the house from the stream, bring wood inside for the cooking stove, look after Johnny and Lizzy while mother and Rachel dig taters, chop some carrots for dinner, and wash pots and dishes. We live in a cabin at the end of a long path from the big creek. Our nearest neighbors, the Andersons, are about a fifteen minute walk down the path. Father says to stay clear of them. Father says they aren't good people. We walk over an hour to get to the general store along the big creek. Upstream is the church and the distillery. We have no horses and donkeys like we had back in Campbell. We have to walk everywhere. We don't go many places – too many chores to do.

I yearn for the days when we were back in Campbell. Father owned land and house, had horses and oxen and men to work the fields for him. Mother made new dresses for me instead of me having to wear Rachel hand-me-downs. This is the second summer we've lived at the cabin. Father's parents live on the other side of the mountain from the cabin. Mother says we had to move because men took over our land. Why did God let them do that?

Elwood put the journal down on the table. "You know, Laura – it sounds like a typical pioneer story."

"I agree; I wonder when it was written?" Then, as she gently placed her hand on top of his, she half-laughed, "Instead of a rags-to-riches story, it's a riches-to-rags story. Not really conducive to another treasure hunt choreographed by Silas."

Elwood nodded and returned the laugh.

Laura thumbed through the pages of the journal. "Not yet half-way. And some of the pages have been torn out in the book's middle."

Elwood resumed reading where he left off.

Yesterday was special. Father played his fiddle on the front porch. Mother sang and taught us words to songs. My favorite song is Barbara Allen. Rachel and I danced. Father played fiddle every weekend back in Campbell.

The leaves are beautiful. I collect leaves of many different colors and shapes to put over top our winter turnips. Father says God paints each leaf.

It is a sad day. Rachel left with father. They left this morning to walk over to Kerrs Creek to grandma's house. They hoped to get a ride with a wagon on the road. Grandma is sick and Rachel will care for her. I will miss Rachel. Mother says I will have to do more chores for I am now the oldest child in the house.

Before turning the page, Elwood fidgeted in his seat to regain a comfortable position.

I sat by the stream on the rocks today. Wonderful creation of God. Moss on the rock and minnows in the stream. I found a crayfish under a rock and saw red birds

129

singing in the bushes. One of the bushes had pretty white flowers. I prayed to God to take care of Rachel.

Father came home early. He gave me a pretty box. He told me I could start collecting things that I might need after I get married. He showed me its secret space to store my valuables. This journal fits perfectly there – to hide my thoughts and words. I have no valuables yet. Father says he made the box from scrap pieces of wood at work.

The forest around the cabin is always filled with birds – all colors: blue, red, yellow, white, all shades of brown. All sizes. Father showed me the jays, thrushes, and waxwings. He shot two quail last week. Mother cooked them with gravy. At night, we hear owls and whip-o-wills. I wonder whether Rachel hears the same sounds at Kerrs Creek.

The entire family walked to church today. The preacher read from the Bible and spoke for a long time. He yelled about people not having enough faith in Jesus Christ, that if they had faith they would not sin. Those people with faith will go to heaven and the sinner to hell forever. Charlie Ward spoke to me afterward. He says he is smitten by my beauty. On the walk back home, father told me to stay away from him – he had bad morals. But he sure is handsome.

Jesus

Elwood hesitated, "Wonder whether this one word entry was intentional?" Laura shrugged, as Elwood turned the page.

My Uncle Samuel came yesterday. He surprised my mother. He spent the night, then left. I thought of jumping in his carriage and heading back to Campbell with him. But mother is sad. Her brother David died.

Weather is changing. Getting quite cold. I need a better coat. All the leaves have fallen from the trees.

Father finished the root cellar. He worked on it for over a year. The cellar is not underneath the house but hidden on the side of the hill. He told mother he had to hide its entrance so that others do not steal from them. He doesn't trust the Andersons next door. Anderson is a thief. He also told mother about lots of gold in the root cellar. Father seems out-of-sorts. He reads the Bible to us the rest of the day. He reads over and over from Matthew 5 about the Blessed Eight – we take them to memory. I wonder whether father hid gold in the root cellar. I hear them talking about mother inheriting money from her brother back in Campbell.

Blessed are the Blessed Eight.

"Oh, Oh," Laura interrupted. She sarcastically smiled, "Correction from my previous analyses . . . it might actually be a riches-to-rags-back-to-riches story. And hidden gold, no less?"

"Starting to sound suspicious," Elwood nodded.

"Let's finish the last page," she sighed. "Just four more entries."

Father takes me around the mountain to see Rachel. Long walk. Rachel and I have picnic next to the creek. Father gives Rachel a note and a stone. He tells her it's from the root cellar. She puts it in her box.

Father says that I am now a woman. He wants to show me what is in the root cellar. I told him I already saw the cellar. Mother and I took some apples and preserves there. He says he wants to show me what else is there. He takes me there with the setting sun. He says he designed it so that the setting sun coming up the cove shows the entrance. He says it's a little off now but will match up at the winter solstice which is still a couple weeks later. He shows me how to get through the back wall of the root cellar. Unbelievable, so much gold, I could never imagine anything close to what I experience there. I remove several pages from the center of this journal to record what I see.

I try to ask father about the root cellar and the gold. Instead he reads to me over and over from chapter 12 in Luke – to whom much is given, much is expected; and from the one who has been given with much, much more is asked. He says he is on a joyful path. He reads from other verses. I am not sure what it all means – so much gold, shining in my eyes.

Elwood paused, opened his mouth to talk, shook his head, then continued with the final entry in the journal.

Snow fell all night and continues to fall – over a foot deep and still snowing. Winds howl outside and through the cracks in the house. I see drifts outside that are higher than I am tall. Father is at work. I am with mother, Maggie, Letty, Johnny, and Lizzy huddled next to the fireplace. We cover with all our blankets. Mother says the temperature must be below zero. No one wants to move away from the fireplace. Mother says I need to bundle up and go outside to get wood – and to the root cellar and get some preserves to eat. Maybe I'll find my father's Joyful Path?

Elwood and Laura stared at each other, astonished.

Laura finally spoke, "And it just ends. I wonder whether 'J.P.' and family survived the blizzard? I wonder whether the story is real, or another one of Silas' made-up tales? Do you believe it?"

"Well, just like the 'Testimony of Beets Campbell,' this one has enough facts to make it intriguing, but not enough facts to let you know exactly who, what, and where," mulled Elwood. "Indeed it has all the markings of another one of Silas' fictional adventures."

"So I guess you're gonna talk to Silas tomorrow," she offered. "It's my day off at Faithful Care; and I have some chores to do."

But Elwood was lost in his thoughts. "To whom much is given, much is expected . . . everyone who has been given much, much will be demanded . . . to whom much is given, much is expected . . . everyone who has been given much, much will be demanded . . .," mumbled Elwood, mussing his hair with both of his hands.

"What're you talking about?" queried Laura.

"If this is one of Silas' treasure hunts, how would he have known?"

"Known what?"

"Silas asked me today about the topic of my sermon for this Sunday. I responded it'll focus on the phrase from Luke, chapter 12 – 'from everyone who has been given much, much will be demanded,' or depending on the biblical translation, 'to whom much is given, much is expected.'" Elwood paused, then looked upward: "How would Silas have known to include that specific verse in 'J.P.'s journal, if indeed it's his writing?"

"Maybe coincidence," Laura offered, "or maybe it is what it is – an old journal found in an old box."

Elwood took a deep breath. "But that's not all. I also kidded with Silas today that J.P. could be the initials for Joyful Path."

Chapter Eleven
A PORTAL TO HEAVEN

The smell of fried bacon hit Pastor Elwood Martin as he turned the corner to Silas' room at Faithful Care. Clattering of breakfast dishes sprung from the large dining room at the end of the hall. Pastor Martin caught sight of Betty, a nurse's aide, rolling Silas in his wheelchair up the hallway toward him. He greeted both and took over for Betty in returning Silas to room 79.

"Gee, Elwood," Silas chuckled. "I'm surprised to see you here today . . . and so early. You, of course, know that Laura is off."

"Oh, so you're really surprised?" Sarcasm oozed from each word spoken by Elwood.

"Of course, two straight days and two visits," Silas snickered. "Plus if Laura isn't here."

"I'm here to see you," Elwood tersely replied. He quickly added, "About the box – "

"I had a conversation with the Lord last night," Silas interrupted.

"Huh?" stammered Elwood. "You're not that close to the time yet."

Looking up solemnly, Silas slowly whispered, "I asked God what a million years meant to Him? The Lord replied 'a minute.' Then I asked Him what a million dollars meant to Him? The Lord said 'a penny.' I then asked Him whether he could spare me a penny." Silas leaned closer to Elwood: "And you know what God said to me?"

"What?"

"The Lord told me: 'Yes, in a minute.'"

Elwood grumbled, "Got me again," then laughed.

He pushed Silas' wheelchair to the table in front of a half-finished Sudoku puzzle. He noticed that the fresh flowers in the vase on Silas' window sill today were white carnations, yellow roses, and Baby's breath. Joe the sock monkey also sat on the window sill, but next to a sheet of paper taped to the window. Elwood ignored both.

"Once again, what I came to see you about –"

Silas cut Elwood short: "I was also pondering over dinner yesterday our theological discussion from several months ago – back before you even read about Beets Campbell and his exploits. It was about the origin of faith. We both agreed that my, as well as your, personal faith was primarily a gift of God's love to each of us."

"That's right, but –"

"And I argued with you that if such were the case," Silas slid the Sudoku puzzle aside: "we should more often profess statements of God's love in worship services instead of statements of our faith."

"Indeed I remember, sort of like the chicken and the egg. Which came first – God's love or your faith?" Elwood folded his hands together on the table. "I challenged you to write your own personal statement of faith, your own Apostle's Creed in a sense. But being the obstinate person you are, you wrote a statement of God's love – and called it Silas' Creed."

"You used my Creed in the worship service the following week," Silas proudly grinned.

"And I also recall the congregation was underwhelmed. We went back to the Apostle's Creed the week after that," Elwood smirked, "and Silas' Creed faded into obscurity. But what I really wanted to talk to you about –"

"I've been working for a few weeks on my statement of faith in the Holy Trinity – one that would be appropriate for a scientist or engineer, like me." Silas stroked his chin. "I thought

I might need one for judgment day. Joe has the statement. Why don't you grab it from him?"

Elwood reluctantly shuffled the couple steps over to the window, resigning himself to first listen to Silas. After setting Joe aside, he carefully peeled the tape from the window pane. He glanced at the sheet of paper, then scrunched his face. "This isn't a statement, it's some sort of a graph."

"My statement of faith takes the form of a phase diagram," Silas announced.

"A what diagram?" Elwood muttered, as he plopped in his chair at the table.

"A phase diagram – didn't you learn anything in your science classes?" Silas teased.

Elwood set his elbow on the table and propped up his forehead with his hand. "It's been a long time," he mumbled, then stared at the graph on the paper for a minute or so.

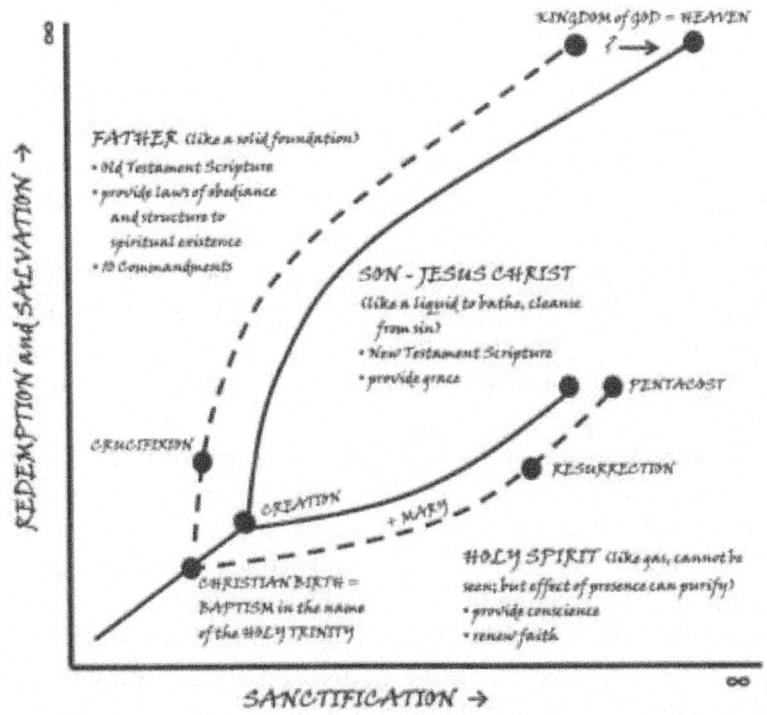

Elwood looked up from the graph and at Silas. Elwood's eyes were wide open, like those of a deer caught in the headlights of an approaching car.

Silas smiled. "A phase diagram for water, for example, displays the stability regions of the three forms of water – solid ice, liquid water, and gaseous steam – at various pressure and temperature conditions. I have faith in the truthfulness of water's phase diagram as published in chemistry texts even though I didn't personally determine or obtain the measurements. Similarly, I summarize my statement of spiritual faith in this phase diagram for God – in a sense, stability regions for the three forms of God. Although I haven't personally experienced every event in my diagram, my God has blessed me with the love and faith to accept its truth."

"I understand the words in the diagram," Elwood confessed, "but its organization is pure mumbo-jumbo."

"My God embraces a Holy Trinity – that is God as the Father, the Son (Jesus Christ), and the Holy Spirit simultaneously," Silas spoke as if delivering a lecture. "But, at any given time as shown in this diagram, I may experience a manifestation of God in just one of these forms of the Trinity. Under certain special conditions, I may experience two manifestations of God at the same time as shown by the lines, or all three as shown by the point where the lines intersect. These manifestations of God are the same, but yet not the same – sort of like the three forms of water are the same, but not the same. God the Father, God the Son, and God as the Holy Spirit are all one, but interact with me in different ways at different times."

"I hesitate to ask. Why solid lines and dashed lines?"

"The addition of a solid, such as sugar or salt, to water expands the stability region of liquid water at the expense of ice and steam. In my diagram, the solid lines represent the Old Testament God. Then, to take the phase diagram analogy one step further, the addition of Mary as the mother of God's Son expands my interaction with Jesus Christ, as shown by the dashed lines. My personal commitment to Jesus Christ is a way to understand and worship God. For, like water is the most common phase of water, Jesus is the most common experience or entry point to God. My love by God is through the grace that Jesus Christ provided to all, including me, through Himself."

Elwood stared blankly at Silas' phase diagram of the Holy Trinity. "Just fascinating, only you could've come up with something like this," he murmured.

"I thought I'd skip telling you about triple points and critical points on my God diagram," Silas continued, impervious to Elwood's sarcastic critique. "But note that I've the Father, Jesus, and the Holy Spirit all present at both the creation as well as the new creation, one's baptism. Then I've developed another triple point or critical point at infinite sanctification and infinite redemption, in a sense heaven – once again the Trinity will manifest all three forms simultaneously to us."

"You . . . You've lost me," Elwood stumbled on his words. "I don't think I'll be using your statement of faith anytime soon in our worship service; it'll drive people away."

Silas laughed. "Indeed, they'll probably question your sanity if you present a God phase diagram as a statement of faith. On the other hand, there's one thing I couldn't figure out – that is, whether to keep the dashed line parallel (after Christian birth) to the solid line (creation) on the approach to heaven, or have them connect as shown in my graph? If I keep them apart – I end up with a second heaven."

Elwood nodded reluctantly. "Here's a thought – If you keep the lines parallel, maybe you don't actually get a second heaven but another pathway to heaven. Sort of like the front door and the back door."

Silas leaned both arms on the table and cupped his chin in his hands. "But would both doors go through Jesus? They must. The only way to heaven is through Jesus Christ."

Elwood paused. "That's true, that sort of contradicts my idea of two different doors. Maybe it's not really a second door, but a portal – a way or window in which you could, in a sense, sneak a peek at heaven while still on earth."

"Hmm, that's an interesting concept," Silas agreed, "especially in light of some of the descriptions of near-death experiences of people. So – in my phase diagram, if I keep the two lines parallel, the portal to heaven might explain this phenomenon as well." Silas stared out his room's picture window.

"While you think about that," Elwood interjected, "Let me ask you something as well?"

Silas returned his gaze to Elwood.

"Laura and I opened a secret compartment in the 'J.P.' dowry box you gave me. Is this another one of your treasure hunts?" Elwood momentarily locked eyes with Silas'.

"Don't know what you're talking about?" Silas shrugged.

"A girl's journal was hidden in the bottom of the box," Elwood reiterated louder.

"Don't know anything about that feature of the box."

"J.P. writes in her journal about gold hidden in a root cellar. Sounds similar to your story of gold buried by Beets Campbell in the cemetery of the church?" Elwood appealed, "You can, of course, see why I might be suspicious."

Silas shrugged again. "I swear I know nothing about a journal. I just bought the dowry box, along with the remaining contents of a cardboard box, at an auction. No more, no less." His shrug transformed to a laugh, "It would be kinda funny, though, to toy with you again . . . but it's not something I'd do to Laura."

"Okay," Elwood nodded, albeit somewhat dubiously. "The dowry box was part of some 'trashy stuff' you purchased as one lot at an auction?"

"Yeah," Silas said, "I have all the stuff still in the original carton."

"Do you think there might be anything else in it related to the 'J.P.' dowry box and journal?"

"Nary a clue," Silas shook his head. "I haven't looked in it since I bought it several decades ago." He pointed to his nightstand next to the bed. "Grab my house key there. The cardboard box is in the basement. If I remember correctly, it's on the top shelf, near the middle, of the shelving just to the right of the water softener. I think it's an old Mogen David wine box."

Elwood remained quiet.

"Take the entire carton home with you – to be quite blunt, it'll be one less thing for my estate to worry about after I kick the bucket."

"That's really being blunt," Elwood said, "and if I can be equally blunt – you're sure you're not pulling my strings for another treasure hunt or the like, one involving 'J.P.'?"

"I swear." Silas smiled, and added, "If I'm lying, may lightning strike me dead as I sit here in my wheelchair!"

† † †

Elwood played fetch with Barney in the yard, while waiting for Laura to return home from her scheduled chores. Barney loved to chase after a rubber chicken, his favorite toy. But, Barney hadn't yet mastered the second part of fetch; that is, he failed to return the rubber chicken to the thrower. Instead, with chicken in mouth he scampered just out of arm's reach of Elwood. Intermittently, Barney growled and vigorously shook the chicken. Then, Elwood chased Barney around the yard until grabbing the rubber chicken, after which the game turned into a tug-a-war. The toss, retrieval, and romp on the grass repeated itself numerous times.

As Laura's car turned into her driveway, she caught a glimpse of Elwood, Barney, and the rubber chicken lying side by side in the front yard. Barney snatched the chicken. But he ran slower than normal to the gate to welcome her. She debated which of her two men – Barney or Elwood – were more tired from their playtime.

A short time later, Elwood, along with Laura in the passenger seat and Barney on the center console, backtracked to the Twin Falls Presbyterian Church parsonage – then continued the short distance north to a small hamlet. About a hundred yards past the Midvale sign, they turned into a long driveway to Silas' house, a quaint clapboard Cape Cod, painted white and trimmed in green. The surroundings felt peaceful, albeit a bit overgrown. The part-time groundskeeper, who Silas had hired after becoming a resident at Faithful Care, accomplished only minimal maintenance on the lawn and gardens.

"Beautiful," Laura exclaimed. "You've been here before to visit Silas?"

"Yes, many times," Elwood responded. He pointed to a large fenced-in area behind the house, "Back there, you can see the remnants of Silas' vegetable garden. He grew lots of anything you can imagine."

"What did he do with it all?"

"One of Silas' ministries," Elwood smiled, "he supplied peas, beans, tomatoes, lettuce, carrots, corn, potatoes, red beets . . . and many other veggies to church members and the needy in the area."

Barney, nose to the ground, explored the hedges around the house. The scents drew him to the vegetation around a holly bush at the edge of the front flower bed. For the next five minutes, he pounced on imaginary, hiding critters. Laura and Elwood sat on the wooden swing on the wrap-around front porch.

"What happens to the house after Silas is gone?" Laura asked.

"Don't know. But Silas has indicated that his will is in order – that his lawyer, Mr. Dawes, has a copy and is the executor."

"The only people who regularly visit Silas at Faithful Care are church friends," offered Laura. "And Sam Kegley stopped by a handful of times."

"I suspect that Sam, his godson, may be in line as well for a sizable inheritance." Elwood continued. "Silas has no living relatives to my knowledge."

"He's quite popular among the workers at Faithful Care – they love to banter with him about a whole range of subjects."

"Well, let's hope Silas hangs in there as long as possible," Elwood remarked.

"But now, we've things to do," Laura smiled. "Time to go in!"

With Barney back on his leash, they went inside where sheets covered most of the furniture. A large oil painting above the fireplace mantel showed a young Silas with his bride, Patty, at their wedding. The portrait entranced Laura. On an adjacent wall hung an original and captivating water color of Jesus blessing a resurrected Lazarus. Elwood focused on the artist's signature in the lower left hand corner, one whose name he couldn't read. They walked hand in hand from the living room to the kitchen.

The wooden steps screeched and groaned on their descent to the cellar. The stale smell and damp feeling of a dirt floor greeted them. And a sole light bulb supplied weak illumination to the entire space. Flickering shadows gave it an eerie aura – Laura suggested they not tarry. Elwood quickly found the set of shelves next to the water softener. Only one box, the one displaying the Mogan David logo, set on the top shelf. Stuffed next to it was a pressure canner on one side, and canning supplies on the other.

Laura rummaged through the box. After shuffling its contents a bit, she withdrew her now grungy hand.

"Silas said we can take the box along with us to sort it out," Elwood offered

Laura wiped her hand of its muck and grease on the side of the box. "From my perspective, it looks like a pile of junk."

† † †

Elwood plopped the cardboard box on his kitchen table. It emanated a musty cellar smell. The cardboard had softened from decades of high humidity. Basement dust and cobwebs covered its contents.

"Silas said he paid a dollar for this box," he said, as he rifled through the contents.

"I think the price was too high," Laura laughed. "There're several pieces of rope – all of them old and frayed. And some moth-eaten pieces of cloth. Looks like your treasure hunt could end here."

"Well, wow – here's a small clay jug with some cracks in it – looks like someone made it in an elementary school art class. And a rusted horseshoe," Elwood dryly added.

Laura plucked a large piece of metal from the box. "Now here's something interesting. A piece of rusted steel – sort of a cube, but it has a bunch of rods molded into the top. On the bottom it's stamped 55.85 ounces." She thought for a moment, doing some mental calculations. "That's a little over three pounds. If solid steel, it should weigh a lot more. It must be hollow." Laura shook it. Nothing. "Weird, I've never seen anything like it before."

Elwood gave the steel cube a fleeting glimpse, then grubbed his hand inside the box. "Here's a glass jar of crooked nails, a cracked canning jar, and an empty as well as broken cigar box."

Laura set the cube on the table. "And a bicycle pedal, leather strap, broken wax candle, cracked ruler, magnifying glass, and a butterfly broach."

"Something usable, maybe you can wear the broach," Elwood kidded.

Laura shook her head and smiled.

"There're a few pieces of oily burlap," Elwood wiped his hands one at a time on his pants. "There's something inside this one piece." He unwrapped the burlap and handed the contents to Laura.

"Just an old piece of copper pipe; but wait, it's something else interesting," Laura rolled the pipe in her hand. "Bingo – look, it has the initials 'J.P.' on its side. It's a piece of copper pipe with caps on both ends and soldered shut."

Elwood mulled, "And 'J.P.'s father worked in a distillery where copper pipe would've been available. We might have something here."

Laura looked in the now-exposed bottom of the cardboard box. "Just some old horseshoe nails, a couple pieces of broken wood, four marbles, some small circular pieces of scrap metal, pieces of broken plaster, and dirt – that's all that's left in the box. The steel cube and the copper pipe seem to be the only things of interest. Do you have a tubing cutter or a hacksaw to cut the pipe – to see what might be inside?"

Elwood headed to his toolbox in the garage. Meanwhile, Laura fiddled with the copper pipe, about an inch in diameter and a foot in length.

Holding the tube on the edge of the table, he carefully sawed next to a capped end. Once the end fell off, he tapped the cut end on the table. He immediately viewed rolled up paper inside and carefully slid two pages out.

"They look like the missing pages from J.P.'s journal," Laura observed.

"You read 'em this time," he said and handed them to her.

Laura smoothed the yellowed pages with several torn edges, and cleared her throat.

> *Revelation of Judith*
>
> *Father showed me how to open the stone door to get behind the wall of the root cellar. He told me that by going in I would enter a portal to heaven. He said it was a window through which I could sneak a peek of heaven.*

"Whoa there," Elwood interrupted, flabbergasted. He gulped and held his head in his hands. "In my discussion with Silas this morning, he showed me a diagram to support his statement of faith. I suggested that if he made a slight change, he would actually create a portal to heaven in which one could look through a window to sneak a peek. Wow – just wow! Unbelievable!"

"So this is a fake document, another one of Silas' exercises in creative writing."

"No . . . no . . . no," Elwood stuttered, "You don't understand. I made the statement – portal, I can't remember the last time I used that word or even heard the word; and sneak a peek – it wasn't Silas, it was me. Just like the passage from Luke 12 in 'J.P.'s, or I guess Judith's, journal yesterday. Creepy; it makes me shudder." He took a deep breath: "Please continue."

> *Father told me to close my eyes when I entered into the space behind the root cellar. Afterwards I could slowly open them in order to allow my eyes to adjust. The door closed, but even with my eyes closed I was aware of a bright light. I smelled a sweet odor, much like a hyacinth blooming in the springtime. I felt warmth about me, as*

though I was a baby held by a mother. I felt movement even though I wasn't walking. I heard a low rumbling which transformed into a deep chant shouting Holy, Holy, Holy – with time it transformed slowly into a high pitch singing. I opened my eyes. Everything about me glistened gold. Did my Father make this room behind the root cellar out of gold bricks? Where did the light come from?

Out of the light walked Jesus. He called me His precious child and took my hand. I said "Here I am, Lord." I felt love. He told me that my mother and father were of great faith and love, as was I. He said that my father tried to help others to his own harm, but never lost his faith. He told me to keep my faith, even though bad things happen on earth. I would see heaven. I will soon be in heaven with Him.

Jesus walked me through a gate on a road of gold. Angels sat around on silver chairs. They played music on harps and sang songs of praise. In a distance, I saw God sitting on an immense gold throne. Jewels were everywhere in the stones that lined the road. But the road, chairs, harps, thrones were not really the objects that I know on earth – they are indescribable. Jesus told me that heaven is not made of the same material as is the earth. The smells and tastes were also indescribable. I entered a field with souls happy and praising God. I drifted into a sleep.

I awoke and my father was staring at me in the root cellar.

They sat in silence. They stared into each other's eyes. Elwood took a deep breath. He got up from the table and paced the kitchen floor. Barney woke from his nap and nosed Laura on her ankle. She picked him up and mindlessly stroked his back.

"This is getting stranger by the moment. Revelation, the last book of the Bible, gives John's vision of the end times and heaven. Now we also have the Revelation of Judith – Judith 'P.'s description of heaven with Jesus as a tour guide." A wide-eyed Elwood re-took a seat at the kitchen table.

"It's almost too amazing. Silas may be up to his old tricks again," bemused Laura. "I still don't totally trust him – especially coming on the heels of him leading you on the wild goose chase, or wild whale chase, for Confederate gold."

"But if the treasure is real gold hidden in a root cellar, or the metaphorical gold in a window to heaven, it may be well worth it. Maybe it'll be even more valuable than finding ten million dollars of gold in a whale's belly." He sat silent for a moment, then snickered, "But, I have to admit I'll proceed cautiously."

"Where do we go from here?"

"Hmmm," he reflected, "we know a girl named Judith P. had an older sister Rachel and younger siblings Maggie, Letty, Johnny, and Lizzy. They all lived with their mother and father somewhere within a good walk's distance from Kerrs Creek and in a time frame of the 19th century. They were prosperous in Campbell country, and lost it all before they came to another part of Rockbridge County to be near kinfolk. What else?"

"They lived in a cabin with the Andersons as neighbors; and the father worked in a distillery by a creek. And, of course, the father built a very unique root cellar. The journal ends with a blizzard," Laura added.

"Well," Elwood laughed, "we've narrowed it down to a location somewhere in the western half of Rockbridge County and a time frame in the 1800s. It sure would help to have a last name."

"Maybe something is inside the steel cube, just like Judith's Revelation was in the copper tube?" Laura suggested.

Elwood picked up the cube, rolled it in his hands, and investigated it closely. "No 'J.P.' anywhere on it like the dowry box, journal, and copper pipe."

"But maybe it has something hidden inside it? How about using your hacksaw to cut it open?" asked Laura.

"I have to admit that it's piqued my curiosity," he replied.

"I counted the rods on top. Why are there 26 small steel rods molded into one side of a steel cube . . . and exactly 55.85 ounces as its weight?"

"I worry that cutting it open might destroy what's inside it, or its exterior?" Elwood mused, "Maybe I'll show it to Silas tomorrow – see whether he has any ideas?"

"Or admit his shenanigans," Laura added. "I'll go with you to Faithful Care to get his input, even though I'm off work again tomorrow."

"But I have to admit," Elwood confessed, "the opportunity for a pastor to open a portal to heaven is as enticing as catnip to a cat."

Chapter Twelve
A GENTLE WHISPER

Laura and Elwood announced their arrival at room 79 of Faithful Care with a rap on the open door. Laura gently squeezed Elwood on the shoulder and whispered, "I win – gerberas, a type of daisy, today." Elwood lost; he had predicted sunflowers would be in Silas' vase of daily fresh flowers. Elwood clutched Laura's hand as they walked into the room. His other hand carried the strange steel cube. She also brought a fresh apple turnover in a small Styrofoam container for Silas.

"Gee, a together visit. Are y'all gonna make an announcement already?" Silas gushed.

Laura blushed.

Elwood groaned, "It's just been days, not months, since we first went out –"

"Any nary a day you haven't been together," Silas interrupted. "And this is the third day in a row that Elwood is visiting me."

"It must mean that you're his favorite person to visit," Laura teased.

"Or I'm closer to dying than I think," Silas chuckled. "With all these visits, Elwood, when are you going to work on your sermon for Sunday – or are you just gonna wing it?"

"Or maybe I'll just get Joe to substitute for me," Elwood kidded, as he caught a glimpse of the sock monkey perched on one end of the curtain rod over the window.

"What's that in Laura's hands? – I think I can already taste the smell," Silas drooled at the sight of Laura's container.

"I baked you a fresh apple turnover this morning."

"And I can attest they're absolutely delicious," Elwood interjected, "but, Laura dear, I thought you made me the apple turnovers – and Silas just got the one that's leftover."

"Do I detect a little jealousy amongst my menfolk?" Laura laughed as she playfully poked Elwood in the ribs. Then, bowing as she presented the box to Silas, she added, "And, Elwood dear, I even came on my day off from Faithful Care to visit my sweet Silas."

"All I have to say, Elwood," Silas added, "it's a good thing I'm not thirty years younger – I'd give you a run for your money in courting Laura."

Silas opened the box and grabbed a nearby fork. He pushed a small bite into his mouth. "Scrumptious!" He closed his eyes and relished the moment.

"These turnovers were made with the last of my apples. I'm going to have to head up to Effinger to pick up another bushel of Granny Smiths," Laura remarked. She turned to Elwood, "Maybe we can drive up there next week."

"Sounds like a good idea," Elwood nodded his head in agreement. "It's a picturesque jaunt along Buffalo Creek up to Colliers Creek. I need to stop at nearby Oxford Presbyterian anyway. We can do both at the same time. The pastor there, Bart Guthrie, has some papers for me to pick up – committee work for the Presbytery."

"Whatcha got in your hands, Elwood?" Silas inquired, as he took another bite of apple turnover. "You have my curiosity buds cranked up, just like Laura stirred up my taste buds."

"We discovered it in your Mogan David wine box," Elwood offered. "It's a steel cube that has no obvious use."

Silas inspected it, shook it, and tapped on it.

"Interesting! But first it's not steel, it's cast iron. Remember I'm a metallurgical engineer," Silas laughed. "It's hollow. The tubes of iron molded into its top are weird. And it doesn't look like it was ever a part of something else."

"Any ideas on what's inside it?" Laura asked.

150

"Why?" Silas set the cube on his table.

"Your auction box had a sealed piece of copper pipe, inside of which was a document titled the 'Revelation of Judith,'" Elwood interjected. "This Judith, a girl from the 1800s, is most likely the 'J.P.' of the journal and dowry box. She described a visit to heaven accompanied by Jesus. Interestingly, to quote her, she described it as looking through a portal to sneak a peek of heaven."

"Fascinating," Silas smiled and pointed a finger upward. "You also mentioned a portal to heaven in our discussion about my phase diagram yesterday."

"Odd, to say the least," Elwood sighed. "Anyway, we thought that this quite strange hollow steel, or rather iron, piece might contain some clues to the identity of Judith P. I didn't want to destroy it without showing you."

"I'd like to read the 'Revelation of Judith' sometime – hopefully I'll be going to heaven, maybe sooner rather than later," Silas laughed. He hesitated, then continued, "That would make Judith one of a select number of people who've returned to earth from heaven – Elisha and his young servant, Ezekial, Jesus, and of course John. Anyone else?"

"Yep, both Stephen and Paul make the claim," Elwood added, "And Judith's father saw through this portal as well, according to her revelation she recorded."

"I've often wondered about Lazarus," Laura pondered, "Was he, or his soul, in heaven for the four days before Jesus raised him from the dead?"

"It's puzzling that no one in the Bible wrote about Lazarus' experiences for those four dead days," Silas added, with a smirk.

Silas inspected the iron box once again. He counted the iron tubes on top. He set it down and looked out his window as he scratched his brow.

"You look like you're thinking about something," Elwood offered.

"Yeah, I thought it's interesting that there're 26 tubes on top." Silas then flipped the box over, "and has a weight of 55.85 ounces stamped on the bottom. It's amazing."

"I agree – but to what purpose, if any?" Elwood queried.

"Laura," Silas smiled, "Betty, one of the CNAs here at Faithful Care, is taking courses to get her nursing degree. Every now and then I help her with her chemistry assignment. I think she usually brings her chemistry book along to work most every day. Could you track her down and borrow her book for a moment?"

Silas' comments elicited puzzled shrugs from both Elwood and Laura. But Laura took off, and within a few minutes returned with the textbook. She handed it to Silas.

He pointed to the inside front cover. "The periodic table of the elements – in a sense, the vocabulary of chemists. There's iron with chemical symbol 'Fe' in the middle of the table. See what two numbers are in the block with iron?" He looked at Laura and Elwood: "I know those numbers from memory – I used them almost every day at work at Kennametal."

"26 and 55.85," Laura and Elwood answered in unison.

"The atomic number of iron is 26; and its atomic mass is 55.85 – an iron box decorated with 26 iron tubes and a marked weight of 55.85 ounces. Somehow, I don't think it's a coincidence," Silas said.

"Does the cube being made from iron have any significance?" Laura pulled the open chemistry text in front of her. She pointed to the periodic table. "Why not a copper cube with 29 tubes and 63.55 ounces stamped on it – or an aluminum cube with 13 tubes and a weight of 26.98 ounces – or some other metal?"

"Perhaps because the iron cube would be the easiest and cheapest to make," Silas answered. With a mischievous glint in his eye, he added, "Heck, even the fictional Beets Campbell could've made it in the pre-Civil War era at the Rockbridge Foundry."

"With comments like that, I'm getting suspicious again," Elwood fretted.

"No need to worry," Silas laughed and raised his arms in defense. "Lightning hasn't struck me!"

"Okay – but what, then, does the cipher on the iron cube mean?" asked Elwood.

"Maybe we'll know once we see what's, if there's anything, inside," offered Laura.

"One disconnect though," Silas proffered. "You mentioned that the happenings with Judith occurred in the 1800s. If the numbers on this box signify the atomic number and atomic weight of iron, this iron box couldn't have been made in the 1800s. The atomic number represents the unique number of protons in an element's atom – I think Rutherford coined the word 'protons' only in about 1920. The modern periodic table followed soon after."

"I guess what you're saying is that the numerical references of 26 and 55.85 would only be relevant if the iron box was made post 1920," Laura interjected.

"Or constructed by some 19th century chemistry genius who knew things that weren't to be known until many decades thereafter," Silas chuckled.

"Or we could delve into science fiction with time travelers," Elwood added sarcastically.

"Take a hacksaw or sledge hammer and see whether anything is in the cube – you have me interested too," Silas proposed.

Elwood laughed. "Laura suggested that approach last night."

"By the way," Silas took on a serious tone, "I just read about this man who was going through some difficult times. He lost his job and injured himself. So he went to see his pastor where he ranted about his problems. He told the pastor that he had prayed and prayed, but God didn't do anything about his situation. He finally shouted, 'I've been a good person all these years, I've begged God to say something to me to help me. But nothing! Why doesn't God answer me?' The pastor, sitting across the room, said something, but it was so softly said that the man couldn't hear it. The man stepped closer and asked 'What did you say?' Once again the pastor spoke words too faintly for the man to hear; so the man got so close he was next to the pastor's chair. 'Sorry,' the man said, 'I still didn't hear you.' The pastor spoke once more. 'God sometimes whispers,' he said, 'so you might need to move closer to hear Him.'

Sometimes the gentle whisper is louder than the booming thunder."

Elwood smiled.

"Maybe God is whispering clues to us," Laura contemplated.

"That also reminds me," continued Silas, impervious to the comment of Laura, as he pointed to the top of the window. "See Joe looking down at us. He's been listening to us. He's a good listener. What do you have to be in order to listen?"

"Huh?" Laura and Elwood responded in unison.

"I'll give you a hint. The answer is spelled with the same letters as 'listen.'"

"So you have to be 'something' in order to listen; and the something is spelled with the same letters as listen, L-I-S-T-E-N," pondered Laura out loud.

A few moments of silence followed as Laura and Elwood considered the riddle.

Finally, Laura spoke up excitedly: "You have to be S-I-L-E-N-T, silent, in order to listen."

With a rascally smile, Silas pushed the iron cube off his table, making a loud racket as it dribbled on the floor. Both Laura and Elwood jumped.

Silas laughed. "Sometimes, though, you have to hear the whisper through the thunder."

† † †

Laura and Elwood returned to the parsonage. With the hacksaw, Elwood started to cut open one end of the iron cube. He quickly learned one basic tenet of materials chemistry – iron is much harder than copper. After ten minutes with Elwood sweating profusely and his arm tired, he hadn't advanced very far, but far enough. The cut allowed Laura to peek inside with the help of a flashlight.

Elwood wiped his brow with his sleeve. "I think I'm gonna give it a whack with the hammer. Maybe it'll make it easier to cut."

"Go for it," answered Laura. "I see a piece of paper in there. It's not breakable."

Elwood swatted the cut edge of the cube, as Laura held it tight over the rim of the kitchen table. The end of the iron cube cracked off.

"That's right," deadpanned Elwood, "cast iron is more brittle than steel – that's why people use steel instead of iron."

Laura peered into the cube and withdrew a notecard.

76·9·8·37:59·99·5·39·52·75·95:58·25·52·75
ARPD/HPON/HTHHE
27·3·68·16:24·53·6·19
53·16·13·53·13·1·GD:NA
HE·27·75·49·90·53·95·16·BE:N

They stared at each other.

"Let me state the obvious," Elwood shrugged. "It's written in some sort of letter and number code. Why didn't whoever just write out what they wanted to say?"

"One thing confirmed is this message wasn't written by Judith 'P.' I don't think she had a typewriter in her cabin," said Laura.

"How does the message tie into the periodic table of the elements, in particular that of iron? Why codes and clues?" Elwood turned to Laura: "Despite his denial, it sure smells like one of Silas' puzzles."

"It's still a clear day – no lightning yet," Laura smiled as she kissed him on the cheek.

He hugged her in return. "Perhaps God is whispering instead of yelling to us."

Chapter Thirteen
BIBLICAL QUOTES

Laura anxiously telephoned Elwood several times from work at Faithful Care in the morning. She called from her cell phone as she dashed from one room to another needy resident's room. She fretted about Barney, having dropped him off at Elwood's house on her way to work. For the first time, she entrusted Elwood with Barney's total day care. Elwood kept assuring her that Barney and he were in the process of some serious male bonding.

Yet another buzzing call button, this one interrupted Laura's lunch. The oxygen tubing in room 8, Mrs. Eastridge, had pulled loose from the concentrator – a quick fix for Laura. Then a flash of inspiration struck as she reconnected the oxygen – *Oxygen in room 8. Oxygen has chemical symbol O and atomic number 8 in chemical lingo. Like iron is Fe and 26 respectively on the periodic table. It's a code to go from numbers to letters as well as from letters to numbers. Perhaps, that's what the strange iron cube directed to be done with its notecard.*

Laura searched for her co-worker Betty. She tracked her to Silas' room. Betty was helping Silas cut his food into bite-size pieces, while Silas was giving her a tutorial on the importance of the octet rule in generating Lewis dot structures. Laura was quickly in and out of Silas' room after borrowing Betty's General Chemistry textbook, then went back to the lunch room.

She opened to its periodic table, her decoder for the iron box's message, and picked up a pencil.

Room 22 buzzed. Mrs. Esche needed her. *Why the periodic table as a decoder? – Laura considered in route to room 22 – Perhaps, because chemical elements make up everything on earth, the periodic table ties these elements to the earth's creation. But Judith P. in her revelation emphasized that things in heaven were unlike those on earth. What would a decoder periodic table for heaven look like? And who wrote the coded message in the iron box? As Silas explained, it couldn't have been Judith P.* Laura convinced Mrs. Esche that it wasn't time for her medicine, that such was dispensed every day after dinner, not lunch.

Upon her return to the lunch room, she made the conversion on a piece of paper. It actually worked. She wrote –

OsFORb PrEsBYTeReAm CeMnTeRe =
    Oxford Presbyterian Cemetery
Ar·Pd/H·Po·N/H·Th·He = 1846/1847/1902
CoLiErS CrICK = Colliers Creek
I·S·Al·I·Al·H··Gd:Na = Isaiah 64:11
He··Co·Re·In·Th·I·Am·S··Be:N =
    2··Co·Re·In·Th·I·Am·S·4:7 =
    2 Corinthians 4:7

She picked up her translation, then ran down to and burst into Silas' room.

"Good afternoon Silas, I need to borrow your Bible," squawked Laura.

"Well, good afternoon to you as well," responded a bleary-eyed Silas. He had almost drifted into his post-lunch nap, and fought off a yawn. "First a chemistry text from Betty and now a Bible from me . . . What's up?"

Without answering, Laura quickly moved Joe, who had been sitting on top of Silas' Bible, and went straight to two biblical passages.

I·S·Al·I·Al·H··Gd:Na = Isaiah 64:11

Our holy and glorious temple, where our fathers praised you, has been burned with fire, and all that we treasured lies in ruins.

He··Co·Re·In·Th·I·Am·S··Be:N =
2··Co·Re·In·Th·I·Am·S·4:7 =
2 Corinthians 4:7

But we have this treasure in jars of clay to show that this all-surpassing power is from God and not from us.

She proudly slid her decoded message along with transcribed biblical verses to him. "I solved the iron cube puzzle," she announced.

Silas studied her results. He smiled, "Seems interesting – could there be some treasure in Oxford Presbyterian's Cemetery on the way to Collierstown?"

"I need to call Elwood," exclaimed Laura. She reached for her cellphone with one hand as she grabbed her translation from Silas' table with her other.

"What do the biblical verses mean?" Silas asked.

But Laura already had her back to him on the way out the door.

† † †

"Barney's next to me on the couch getting his belly rubbed," Elwood began as he answered Laura's phone call. "He's training me to do my work – preparing Sunday's sermon – while sitting on the couch instead of at my desk. I must admit this couch sermon is starting to sound better than my typical desk sermon."

"Amazing," Laura sarcastically responded, "Barney's not only best buddies with you now but also your consultant on sermons."

Laura excitedly related her findings to Elwood.

"Oxford Presbyterian and Colliers Creek," Elwood sighed.

"Well, it looks like we need to find something in Oxford Presbyterian Church's cemetery with the dates 1846, 1847, and

1902 on it. And it's clearly this church in our county, up by Colliers Creek," Laura said.

"I agree. But what about the two biblical quotes – one about the fire destroying our treasure and the other about treasures in jars of clay?" he wondered.

"I've been thinking," she replied. "For the first verse, I have nothing. But the second refers to a jar of clay. Wasn't there a cracked clay jug in the carton of Silas' trash?"

Elwood quickly headed for the Mogen David box stashed on the parsonage's side porch. Without even rustling through the box's junk, he snatched the clay jug sticking out its top. He hurried to the kitchen.

"Yep, it's here. I also grabbed a hammer to see whether a treasure's inside," he laughed.

"Do it," she said.

She heard a loud crack and smash.

He sighed, "Nothing."

Before Elwood had a chance to pick up the pieces of the clay jug, his phone rang again. He smiled optimistically; Laura must have had another idea. His hopes, though, were quickly dashed. He recognized the number on caller ID. That number of his ex-wife Dot rang at least once a week since the discovery of the gold treasure at Twin Falls Presbyterian Church. He considered not answering, not listening to her alcohol-fueled ramblings. But such would delay the inevitable. She'd continue to dial his number every few minutes until he answered.

As always, she demanded increased alimony payments, now that he was a millionaire. His attempts to explain the money belonged to the church, not him, were futile. Venom poured from her mouth to describe his lack of positive attributes – cheap, lazy, worthless, stupid, lying. That he remained calm fed her anger even more.

He asked about Arany, about how his step-daughter's college studies were going. Dot exploded, "It's none of your business." She then harangued him about not providing more financial assistance to her daughter. Before hanging up, she proudly cackled, "Arany cares nothing about you, only me."

Elwood closed his eyes, trying to replace thoughts of Dot with those of Laura.

Barney barked; he took off yapping to the front door.

Ding-dinga-ding . . . Ding-dinga-ding . . . Ding-dinga-ding.

As Elwood shuffled down the hall to answer the doorbell, he heard a distinctive rumble outside, loud enough to hear over Barney's barking. Ole Brownie was idling in his driveway. He sighed – *Another demand for the church's gold.* Repressed visions of the lost spirits of Turnip, Tater, and the Yankee supposedly jumping into Grunt and Hamm resurfaced in his mind.

He cautiously opened the door to a smiling Sunshine Clutterbuck. He caught a whiff of her enchanting perfume. He couldn't help but return the smile; her eyes complimented her scent, both radiated streams of joy.

Without even saying any pleasantries, Sunshine pointed to a fence post in the front yard. Elwood was taken aback. A box turtle perched on top of the post, at least three feet off the ground.

"You know what they say when you see a turtle sitting on a post?" Sunshine continued to point to the turtle.

Elwood murmured, "Huh?"

Barney, growling suspiciously, sat next to the right foot of Elwood. Sunshine kneeled onto the porch and stroked Barney's head with a gentle pat. He immediately rolled onto his back. Sunshine rubbed his belly while Barney stretched.

Sunshine rose and pointed once again to the turtle on the fence post. "You know it must have had help in getting there." She grinned from ear to ear.

Elwood glanced from turtle to Sunshine to Barney, then back to Sunshine. He took a deep breath. "Indeed, the turtle must've had help to get there. Just like you think you helped the church find the gold treasure, but –"

"Yesterday, that's what I thought," Sunshine interrupted. "I'd been reading my Bible and praying to Jesus – searching for a sign from above so I could claim the gold. But this morning Jesus spoke to me. He explained to me that I didn't help you find the gold. Jesus helped you find it."

Elwood stood mute.

"Jesus directed me to the 8th chapter of the Gospel of Matthew, specifically to verse 39," Sunshine continued. "Like the Pharisees had asked Jesus for a miraculous sign, I too asked Him for a sign. Jesus gave them, and you, the sign of Jonah."

"That's right," Elwood nodded. "Jesus wouldn't give the Pharisees a miraculous sign, except for telling them about the sign of Jonah. But I received no –"

"You found gold in the belly of Jonah's whale – the sign of Jonah," Sunshine raised her arms to the sky. "So you are a person greater than Jonah. You will find spiritual gold – you will be with Jesus."

"Ah . . . ah . . . ah," Elwood stammered. "That . . . that's not really the sign of Jonah." But Sunshine's words had blindsided Elwood. Thoughts of him being with Jesus, just like Judith P. and her father being with Him swirled in his mind. *Sunshine couldn't have known about "The Revelation of Judith."*

Sunshine bowed her head. "The men of Nineveh repented at the preaching of Jonah. I likewise repent at your preaching and for trying to trespass on your earthly treasures. The words of Jesus, spoken in the Gospel of Matthew, say you will be with the Son of God. For the sign has been given to you. Remember me when you obtain your spiritual treasures."

Elwood tried to respond, but Sunshine placed her fingers on his lips and shushed him.

She quickly retrieved a small corked bottle from her pocket and handed it to Elwood. She whispered, "A present – some 'Purple Magic' – for your lady friend."

Chapter Fourteen
FROM ZERO TO HUNDRED

Today was the second Sunday of December. On every month's second Sunday at Twin Falls Presbyterian Church, the adult Sunday school class looked forward to its long-established tradition of "Stump Your Pastor." Members of the class anonymously submitted questions ranging from the trivial to the deeply theological into a box. After devotions and a prayer, the teacher of the class, Hansford Cash, drew one question from the box. Pastor Elwood Martin then had no more than ten minutes to answer, before the class continued with their regular lesson.

"Gee, Pastor Martin, the box is getting mighty full." Hansford began the festivities by sticking his hand into a box full of folded yellow notecards. "We may have to get a bigger box. After all, our class has almost doubled in size these past few months."

"We could expand 'Stump Your Pastor' to twice a month," interjected Peggy Lauderdale.

"Or have Pastor Martin answer a couple questions, instead of one, in ten minutes," added Ed Painter.

"I guess everyone wants to stump their pastor," Elwood laughed. "Whatcha got for me today, Hansford?"

Hansford unfolded a notecard. "What's the temperature of hell?" He looked over at Pastor Martin. "I just pick 'em; I didn't write this one."

"I hope the questioner is asking out of curiosity, not because he's wondering what to pack on his way there?" Elwood kidded.

The fifteen members of the class enjoyed the tease.

"Maybe it would've been more appropriate for the questioner to ask about the temperature of heaven," laughed Hansford. He set the timer to ten minutes. It started ticking.

Elwood thought for a moment. "The Bible has many verses referencing hell – depending on the version, it's described as unquenchable fire, eternal fire, perpetual fire, furnace of fire, or punishing fire. What's the temperature of a fire that lasts forever?"

He surveyed the class for a response.

Members of the class looked sheepishly at each other. Many mouthed "Don't know."

Alice Jane Grant finally stated, "Probably a couple thousand degrees."

Pastor Martin nodded politely, but left the answer hanging. "Then, there's Revelation in which John writes about being thrown into molten brimstone. That's liquid sulfur. Scientists calculate this temperature to be around 750°F – quite hot. Can you imagine the stench of burning sulfur as you are being basted in this brew? Having to smell rotten eggs or a skunk for eternity is bad enough, but being scalded in the sulfur at the same time would be even worse."

"Just the thought of the smell makes me gag," added Peggy Lauderdale.

To a chorus of giggles, Elwood continued, "But then, others have described the burning in hell as a dark fire. That description seems paradoxical – fire should be giving off light, not darkness. Perhaps the adjective 'dark' is meant metaphorically. In the same vein, *Dante's Inferno* depicts hell in nine levels, with the ninth or worst being extreme cold. What would be the rationale for hell being cold? One might argue that it's the farthest from God's warmth, God being the source of light and warmth."

"So, Pastor Martin – Is it cold or hot?" asked Ed Painter. "Are you just covering all your bases?"

"You're starting to sound like a politician," kidded Hansford.

"Well, let's just say that hell would be very unwelcoming. No one wants to experience hell on a first hand basis," Elwood chuckled. He hesitated, then became serious: "What would you find more uncomfortable for eternity – a burning, sweltering heat or a freezing, blustery cold? What would be more hellish – dying in a burning house or in a blizzard? Or even worse, in a burning house during a nighttime blizzard – now that would be a very dark fire!"

"I'm confused, Pastor Martin. So is hell very hot or very cold?" asked Troy Montgomery. "As you say, two extremes of temperature, which is it? It can't be both."

"Well," Elwood rubbed his brow, "very hot and very cold may not be quite as far apart as you might think. Our good friend Silas, who'd been your teacher for many years, had this same discussion with me in private a year or so ago."

"By the way, how's Silas doing?" Alice Jane Grant asked.

"He gets tired easily," Elwood responded, "but he still maintains his wit and mental sharpness. And does his daily puzzles."

Hansford picked up the timer and waved it to catch Elwood's attention. He pointed to the digital display, 4:32 left in the ten minute countdown.

Elwood nodded. "In this case, Silas had a very interesting perspective on describing hell based on the science underlying extreme cold and extreme heat. All of you are quite familiar with Silas challenging your preconceived notions with his unique blend of mischievousness and seriousness."

"Don't we," interjected several members of the class.

"Supposedly, the coldest theoretical temperature is absolute zero, where things and atoms no longer move. This temperature is $0°$ on the Kelvin scale, or below $-400°$ on our more common Fahrenheit scale. That's cold! If you're thrown into that situation, you'd freeze solid immediately – much like God turned Lot's wife into a statue of salt in a blink of the eye. But the coldest attainable temperature is a fraction of a degree above absolute zero – one can never achieve absolute zero. On the other hand, what's the hottest temperature? You might think a high temperature, maybe infinite temperature. But Silas showed me a graph that indicated that heating something past a positive infinite temperature flips it to a negative infinite temperature – then it becomes assigned a less negative temperature as it gets yet hotter. So the hottest temperature theoretically becomes a fraction of a degree below absolute zero. The bottom line is that the coldest temperature is approaching absolute zero from the positive side, while the hottest temperature is approaching absolute zero from the negative side."

"You're really starting to blow my mind," interjected Troy.

"Yep, that's what I told Silas as well," shrugged Elwood, "but this perspective may also have theological implications with respect to hell. This scientific analysis espoused by Silas may be beyond comprehension to many, but it does show that there may not be that much difference between the coldest cold and the hottest hot – only absolute zero, less than a single click on the temperature scale separates them. Mortals may have to go through infinite temperatures to get from one to the other, but maybe not so for hell – perhaps you are punished with all-encompassing hot and cold simultaneously at absolute zero."

"Are we having 'Stump the Pastor' or "Confuse the Flock?'" Alice Jane queried.

"So would this be analogous to getting hot and spicy chicken wings, then dipping them in a cool ranch sauce – hot and cold at the same time?" mulled Peggy.

"I guess that would be a good analogy – except instead of being something hot and cold and pleasant to your taste buds, imagine something hot and cold and torturing your sensory system." After a hesitation, Elwood added, "Perhaps something described as a dark fire!"

"Geesh, Pastor Martin," Troy interjected, "I wanted just one number, a temperature, and instead we got a lecture."

"Not sure whether it was a scientific or theological lecture," deadpanned Ed.

"Yep – What we thought was a simple question yielded a mind-blowing answer," Hansford shook his head. "I'll be wondering for the rest of our class, and probably the rest of the day, whether I'd be burned or frozen by a dark fire. Hope I'll never find out, though."

A nervous laugh echoed throughout the class. The timer buzzed.

† † †

Less than an hour later in worship service, Pastor Martin spoke from the pulpit. In his introduction to the Scripture reading, he stressed the preceding verses which told the Parable of the Faithful Servant (or the Parable of the Doorkeeper). In essence Jesus warned His disciples that they must be ready – not asleep, or distracted – because He will return at an hour when they might not expect Him. Then, Elwood read that day's Scripture, Luke 12:41-48 –

> Peter asked, "Lord, are you telling this parable to us, or to everyone?"
>
> The Lord answered, "Who then is the faithful and wise manager, whom the master puts in charge of his servants to give them their food allowance at the proper time? It will be good for that servant whom the master finds doing so when he returns. I tell you the truth, he will be put in charge of all his possessions. But suppose the servant says to himself, 'My master is taking a long time in coming,' and he then begins to beat the menservants and maidservants and to eat and drink and get drunk. The master of that servant will come on a day when he does not expect him and at an hour he is not aware of. He will cut him to pieces and assign him a place with the unbelievers.
>
> That servant who knows his master's will and does not get ready or does not do what his master wants will be beaten with many blows. But the one who does not know and does things deserving punishment will be beaten with few blows. From everyone who has been given much, much will be demanded; and from the one who has been entrusted with much, much more will be asked."

Elwood scanned the congregation before starting his sermon. "A very powerful message from Jesus. The Scripture starts with Peter asking Jesus a very straightforward question – that is, to whom is the parable directed? Peter desires a one word answer, them or us, but instead gets a lecture."

Elwood grinned and gave a nod to Troy sitting in the second row of pews. Troy responded with a thumbs-up sign.

"It's sort of like a child asking a parent a yes or no question and getting an earful instead," Elwood continued. "In His answer, Jesus tells His disciples they bear an enormous responsibility, to teach and ready the people for His return. The disciples have already been taught by their master. But the people do not yet know the right way. In a sense, the people can use as an excuse, 'ignorance is bliss,' but not the disciples. For the disciples, responsibility entails accountability."

Elwood pointed his index fingers from both hands at his chest. "Similarly, preachers might be judged more harshly than their congregation. I'm supposed to guide my flock. What do I use for guidance?"

He picked up his Bible and held it in his hand: "It's in here – the words from Jesus Christ. Everyone needs to read the Word; I need to encourage you to read the Bible and to explain it to you. There's not only individual responsibility but also collective responsibility for me, and for all of you once you also become disciples of the Lord."

He hesitated a moment. "Let me merge this message from Jesus with a quote that's been attributed to one of our great, arguably our greatest, president – Abraham Lincoln. He supposedly said, 'Nearly all men can stand adversity, but if you want to test a man's character give him power.' It's easy for the weak to be gentle. But can the powerful use their authority to be gentle and show mercy? During the Civil War, Lincoln had almost absolute power, yet he never abused that power. He never turned anyone away; he believed in second chances and pardoned many. For many, power corrupts – but Lincoln couldn't be bribed, the power didn't go to his head, he remained a loving man. Robert Ingersoll, a biographer, described him as 'knowing no fear except the fear of doing wrong.' Abraham Lincoln held political power over his people – he used that power wisely to unify a country. Jesus provided His disciples with spiritual power over the people. Jesus then told His disciples to use that power wisely, for they will be held accountable to unify the people in His Word. In summary – God will judge the disciples, leaders, and believers more harshly if their followers are not ready. In addition, they should do so humbly – without a smidgen of pride in doing so."

Elwood pulled a pouch from his pocket, shook it, then poured eight gold coins into his hand. He juggled them back and forth from one hand to the other, as he walked from the pulpit down to the front of the sanctuary.

"Twin Falls Presbyterian Church now finds itself in a position of economic power," he began. "For some reason, God has entrusted us with ten million dollars – He has given us much, much more than almost any other church. What are we to do with this cache of cash? I hope we'll do well with it – for we will be judged more harshly than those without such funds. Those are the words of Jesus, not me. Let us not be corrupted by this earthly possession. We should not be concerned with gathering physical things, but in gaining treasures for the kingdom of God. These dollars should be used as our jewels of the spirit. If we go back a little bit in Luke chapter 12 . . . back to verses 33-34 – Jesus said 'Sell your possessions and give to the poor. Provide purses for yourselves that will not wear out, a treasure in heaven that will not be exhausted, where no thief comes near and no moth destroys. For where your treasure is, there your heart will be also.' Let our heart be with God and not with possessions. We have been given and entrusted with much, so we will be expected to do much – yea, even demanded to do much. The question is – Will we?"

Elwood walked back to the pulpit, while Hansford Cash carried a box and strolled down the center aisle from the narthex. Elwood smiled, "Let's have some fun . . . maybe even a modern-day parable to illustrate my point. Because you've been told the Word, much more is expected of you. Hansford Cash, one of our elders, will be passing out envelopes to each person – man and woman, young and old, member and visitor – randomly here today. The envelopes all look the same. All, but one, have blank sheets of paper therein. That unique one has a hundred dollar bill in addition to the paper. Don't open your envelope until you get home. One person will get a hundred dollar bill – it's yours to do with as you wish. No one but God knows who has the hundred dollars. Will you use it to add to your possessions, or will you use it to gain treasures in God's kingdom. You've been entrusted with it. What does God expect, or demand, you to do with it! Amen."

† † †

The church session met immediately following the Sunday worship service. Hansford Cash, Peggy Lauderdale, Alice Jane Grant, Ed Painter, Preston Hughes, and Etta Shields joined Pastor Martin as moderator.

Hansford confessed, "As chair of the property committee, I came prepared. I have a list of fourteen major needs of the church – from replacing the roof on the sanctuary building, to replacing the carpet throughout the entire church, to resurfacing the parking lot. Then, there's also a long list of deferred maintenance. I thought all items on our wish list could be funded by part of our ten million dollar windfall –"

"And now I see you're feeling guilty after hearing the sermon today," interjected Peggy.

"That's right. Maybe we should fund these items as we always have – through our annual operating funds on a hope and a prayer," Hansford said sheepishly.

"I guess the right thing to do, according to Scripture, would be to give the money to the poor or for mission work – to spread the Word," added Alice Jane, "just like I spread candy to the children of the church every Sunday."

"The main question then is the logistics – who, how much, how to spread out the giving," contributed Etta.

"That's right. The difficulty is in the details. How to identify the needy; How much of the money goes local versus regional, national, and international; How much of the ten million is used each year; Do we maintain the principal and just use the interest?" Peggy pondered out loud.

"I think we all agree in principle not to use the money for our own purposes here at the church, except for our disadvantaged members," summarized Preston.

Everyone nodded in approval.

"I also think we should organize, say, a ten year plan where we distribute about a million dollars plus interest each year to make a major impact in our giving instead of distributing just the interest." Hansford snickered, "Keeping the principal, all ten million dollars in reserve, would feel like we're hoarding our possessions. Or to say it differently: to whom much is given, much is expected."

"I agree," said Peggy.

"Hansford and Peggy are agreeing on everything," laughed Etta. "Wow!"

"Let's just appoint an *ad hoc* committee to put together a plan for the distribution – using the general guidance of a ten-year program. I suggest Pastor Martin, Peggy, and Alice Jane," Hansford proposed.

"Sounds good," everyone shouted in unison.

As the meeting started to break up, Hansford shouted, "I have one more question to add to the session agenda today – if our pastor can give out a hundred dollar bill during his sermon, is his salary too high?"

"Might be a way to increase attendance at church even more – give out money," laughed Peggy.

† † †

"Elwood, your messages today – both in Sunday school and your sermon – were truly inspirational," confided Laura as they snuggled on the sofa in the parsonage that night. Barney rooted his nose in between them, collecting pets and scratches.

"Thanks, and the church is doing the right thing, doing what is expected of them."

"I was somewhat disappointed though," giggled Laura.

"Why?" Elwood immediately got defensive.

"I just got a blank piece of paper. No hundred dollar bill for me!" kidded Laura.

"Silas must be wearing off on you," he responded with a laugh.

"I've been wondering, though," she added, "What are you, actually we, chasing with respect to Judith P.'s journal, revelation, and root cellar – earthly or spiritual treasures?"

"Gold and earthly possessions, once found, can always be given to the poor – extreme wealth isn't in my life's game plan. My heart doesn't seek such treasure," confided Elwood. He thought for a moment, then turned and gently kissed Laura on the cheek. "But my heart treasures you."

Laura snuggled into Elwood's shoulder, forcing Barney to grudgingly reposition himself onto Elwood's lap.

"I keep dreaming about a tour of heaven with Jesus as guide, like Judith P. described," he spoke softly. He hesitated, closing his eyes as his thoughts drifted to the sign of Jonah, or his being with Jesus according to Sunshine. He breathed deeply and opened his eyes. "But then I worry, especially in light of today's Scripture, that 'from the one who has been entrusted with much, much more will be asked.'"

"I see your point – what would be expected, or demanded, of you if you find this treasure of spiritual gold," whispered Laura.

Chapter Fifteen
GIFTS

Elwood picked up Laura mid-afternoon in his gray Subaru, still reliable even after its odometer showed well over 200 thousand miles. Her shift at Faithful Care had ended at 3 o'clock. Their first destination was Oxford Presbyterian Church, their second nearby Effinger Fire Department to buy apples. Elwood drove toward Lexington before skirting the city, passing the old Kennametal plant, and heading into the southwestern region of the County. A few miles past Lexington, the two-lane Collierstown Road began to follow Buffalo Creek upstream. Scattered houses and woods interspersed with the fertile farmlands.

During the drive, Laura discussed the logistics of her newly proposed outreach program for Twin Falls Presbyterian Church. She wanted to establish weekly meals for the shut-ins of Elwood's church community. Spurred by his sermon to effectively use the gift each was given by God, Laura planned to prepare meals and accompany Elwood to homes of the elderly and disabled – a visit and a healthy meal. She already had the enthusiastic support of Mabel Coleman and a bevy of other homegrown cooks in the congregation. Elwood reminisced about the previous night's scrumptious kale salad Laura had prepared, and how before last night he thought he didn't like kale. He agreed totally that others would likewise cherish her gift of cooking.

Reaching across the car's console, he put his hand over Laura's, and gave it a gentle squeeze. "If you cook for them like you do for me, this meal will be the highlight of their day – or even their week."

At Murat crossroads, they traversed a bridge over the creek and turned sharply to the west. Laura admired the native beauty of Buffalo Creek – wide, wild, and rocky. Elwood remarked that he'd heard the creek described as an ideal fly-fishing spot for trout.

Once the fire house and old schoolhouse came into view, Elwood made a sharp turn to the south onto Blue Grass Trail, which continued to track Buffalo Creek upstream. After only a couple minutes, Oxford Presbyterian Church appeared on a wooded knoll about 400 yards off the main road. Its small sanctuary overlooked a three acre cemetery. The Virginia Historical Marker along the road disclosed that Presbyterian settlers built a log fort, which doubled as a place of worship, at that site in 1758. A stone church replaced that structure after the Revolutionary War; and in 1866 local citizens, many of whom were Confederate veterans, constructed the present brick church on part of the original foundation.

No one was at the church or cemetery. Oxford's pastor left a manila envelope of documents in the church mailbox for pick-up by Elwood. After parking in front of the church, Laura and Elwood bundled up in coats, stocking hats, and gloves. They hopped out of the car into the wintry cold and a blustery wind under cloudy skies.

Elwood surveyed the cemetery. "It looks like the oldest tombstones are closest to the church. They stretch down to the ridgeline, although some newer markers are scattered throughout."

Laura opened her pocketbook. She showed Elwood a torn piece of paper on which she'd scribbled 1846, 1847, and 1902.

"Still can't figure out why three dates would be on Judith P.'s tombstone," mulled Elwood. "I wonder whether she was born in 1846 or 1847."

A squirrel scampering up a nearby oak tree distracted Laura. She grabbed Elwood by the arm. "Hey, Elwood, there's a squirrel collecting an acorn. Better watch out, he might mistake us for his next nuts."

Elwood burst into laughter. "Yep, we're crazy . . . We're plodding through a cemetery looking for something we don't know even exists. Not too long ago, I searched the Twin Falls' cemetery doing the same thing."

They wandered into the cemetery hand in hand. Within a few steps, Elwood found a tombstone for George Bare, 1848-1911. Their optimism quickly grew. After a few more steps, Laura located the grave of Elizabeth McHenry, 1847-1922. But then, they continued to search for about ten minutes without any match, or anything closer to the dates or name.

Farther down toward the ridgeline, Elwood spotted a weathered tombstone. "Here's the marker for 'Ann Armstrong, wife of William.'" Although some of the numbers were quite fuzzy from corrosion, he identified her birth date as May 7, 1800, and death on August 13, 1834. "I wonder whether she's any relation to your late husband."

"Good question," Laura mused, "I haven't done any genealogy on his family, but I think he did have some relatives from this area. Ann Armstrong died at thirty-four – quite young."

Elwood added, "I don't see any William buried nearby. Did he remarry?"

"Perhaps Ann wasn't on good terms with William."

They continued for a while longer, getting less and less hopeful as they neared the ridgeline with graves having more recent dates. And they were getting cold; Elwood put his arm around Laura to draw her closer.

In unison, they yelled, "That's it!"

The square white marble monument with a pagoda-like top, about eighteen inches on each side and about four feet high, stood majestically with inscriptions on each of its four sides:

IN MEMORY OF A MOTHER AND FIVE CHILDREN WHO PERISHED IN THE SNOW STORM OF THE 17TH OF DECEMBER 1846 BETWEEN THE HOUSE MOUNTAINS.

MARY ANN MOORE,
 WIFE OF JOHN PETTICREW, AGED 41 YRS
 AND 10 MOS.
JUDITH ANNIE, AGED 14 YRS AND 7 MOS.
MARGARET JANE, AGED 12 YRS AND 10
 MOS.
LETITIA, AGED 10 YRS AND 11 MOS.
JOHN THOMAS, AGED 8 YRS AND 4 MOS.
MARY ELIZABETH, AGED 6 YRS AND 8
 MOS.

THE HUSBAND AND FATHER ON HIS
RETURN HOME THREE DAYS AFTER THE
SAD EVENT WAS THE FIRST TO DISCOVER
THAT HIS HOUSE WAS IN ASHES AND HIS
WIFE AND FIVE CHILDREN COLD IN DEATH.
--- JOHN PETTICREW – FEB 1805, AUG 1848.

THIS MONUMENT WAS ERECTED BY A
SYMPATHISING COMMUNITY IN 1847.
REPLACED BY THE CITIZENS OF BUFFALO
AND COLLIERSTOWN 1902.

"Hmmm," Elwood contemplated. "Judith Annie Petticrew, our Judith P.; as a fourteen year old, she perished in a snowstorm in 1846, monument erected in 1847, and replaced in 1902. A perfect match."

"And a house in ashes, probably burned in fire, and lying in ruins – I guess that explains the one decoded biblical verse as well," added Laura.

"But it's freaking me out," Elwood shook his head. "A house on fire in a blizzard! Dark fire! My words from Sunday now almost seem prophetic."

"Your coincidences continue," Laura echoed.

"What a tragedy, though," Elwood whispered with a tear in his eye. He removed his stocking cap. Laura and Elwood knelt solemnly at the monument's base, while he offered prayer.

"All the pieces of the coded puzzle are starting to fit together," Laura wondered out loud. "One piece, though, is still missing – where's the clay jar?"

"On the other hand, we now know that the Petticrew cabin must've been between the House Mountains, in the area that most locals call the saddle."

"Why isn't the oldest daughter, Rachel, buried with the rest of the family?"

"And why did the monument have to be replaced?" Elwood sighed.

Elwood and Laura hastily walked back to the car. They were cold.

† † †

The drive from Oxford Presbyterian to the Effinger Volunteer Fire House and Rescue Squad Building took only a couple minutes – not even enough time for the car's heater to blow warm air. Laura had Elwood drop her off at the side entrance, while he circled around back to a refrigerated shed. Within a few minutes, Laura appeared with Jay, a jovial, portly man. He was Effinger's retired fire chief turned apple huckster and event organizer *extraordinaire*. Selling apples from local orchards was one of the many fundraisers of the fire department.

"Is this the million dollar preacher?" Jay kidded, "The one who found ten million dollars of gold hidden in plain sight in the front of his church."

"The one and only," Elwood laughed.

"And you're only buying one bushel of Granny Smiths?" Jay spoke to Laura.

"That's right," she responded.

Jay hesitated, then playfully smacked Elwood in the shoulder. "You're only buying one measly bushel of apples for Laura. Whatcha gonna do with all your money? You should be buying a bushel of apples for every single person in the county from this poor old fire department. We could use a new fire truck."

"Next time, I'll remember to bring the church's check book."

"Be sure you do," Jay laughed and turned to give Laura a hug.

"By the way," Elwood interjected, as he loaded the box of apples into the back of his car. "Do you know anything about the Petticrew family? They supposedly died when their cabin burned in the 1840s in this neck of the woods – up in the saddle of the House Mountains?"

"I've heard and told the story many times – sort of folklore on this side of the county," Jay replied. "But one correction, they didn't die in a burning cabin – they supposedly were murdered during a snowstorm and tossed outside, then the killer set the cabin ablaze."

"Murdered?" gasped Laura.

Jay paused. Suspiciously, he inquired, "What's your interest in the Petticrew massacre?"

"We think we may've stumbled upon the journal of Judith Petticrew," Elwood naively confided, "one of the daughters who perished in the fire, or snow."

"Yeah, sure," Jay scoffed. "Was the journal carved in stone instead of written on paper to survive the fire?"

"Elwood and I are still trying to authenticate it," Laura smiled at Jay. "In fact, we only discovered her last name and date of death less than a half hour ago at the Petticrew monument in the Oxford cemetery."

"The original monument was constructed the year after their death, but then replaced in 1902." Elwood added. "Do you know why?"

"A bolt of lightning shattered the original," Jay warily answered. "My grandpa said he never saw anything like it, just blasted to pieces and marble chunks seem to have melted."

Laura poked Elwood in the ribs and whispered, "Not really God whispering."

Elwood smiled at Laura, then turned back to Jay. "Do you know any more about the Petticrew family?"

"The best person to tell the whole story is the widow Reynolds; she knows all the details by heart." He removed his "Effinger F.D." baseball cap and smoothed his hair. "She comes to suppers at the fire department all the time. I think she traces some kin back to the Petticrews."

"Do you think she'd mind if we stopped by?" asked Laura.

"She loves to tell the story – but it's a fair ways to drive, yonder over on the other side of House Mountain, and it's gettin' late," Jay offered, replacing his ball cap.

"No problem," Laura and Elwood responded in unison.

"There's several ways to get there, but the easiest is . . . go about a hundred yards down the road, take a right onto Toad Run . . . it'll merge into Beatty Hollow Road . . . and take you to route 60, West Midland Trail."

"Okay, I'm with you; it comes out alongside Whistle Creek at the Old Monmouth cemetery," Elwood responded confidently.

"That's right . . . then head west for a few miles until you pass the Kerrs Creek Fire Department. In about a third of a mile, turn right onto Sycamore Valley Road . . . it'll eventually become a gravel road after a few miles. Keep your eyes out for a mailbox with Reynolds – she lives in the old Reynolds home place on the left."

"I think I got that," Elwood replied.

Jay laughed, "Or you could go over Big Hill and come in from the other side."

"Don't confuse us with alternate directions," Laura shook her head. "Do we need to call her first; or can we just show up?"

"I'll give her a call so you're not greeted with a shotgun," Jay chuckled. "And let me give you a jar of our award-winning apple butter to take her – freshly made."

A sudden gust of northwest wind brought a quick flurry of snow, as Laura and Elwood scurried toward the car. Jay held Elwood's door open. "One last thing – legend has it that on cold snowy nights like tonight, you can go up to Alphin along Collier's Creek and still hear John Petticrew playing the fiddle. Alphin was where he spent his last few years. I've heard the mournful fiddle there myself many times – I've sat on the bridge and listened to John Petticrew playing to the ballad of Barbara Allen." Then, with a mischievous grin, he added, "Of course, having a bottle of good whiskey next to you helps you hear the song."

† † †

The drive took a good half hour. By the time they arrived at the widow Reynolds' place, the sun already neared the southwestern horizon. A steady wind accentuated the cold temperature – wind chill in the 20s. Elwood maneuvered his Subaru onto a pull-off alongside the gravel road, parking behind a rusting 1990s-era Buick Roadmaster station wagon. The two-story clapboard needed minor repair and paint, but otherwise seemed neatly kept.

A gray-haired, bespectacled, and hunched over woman greeted them on the front porch. She introduced herself as "The Widow Reynolds." Smiling at the gift of apple butter, she quickly invited them inside to get out of the cold and tottered behind with a cane in her hand. Elwood wondered whether she used the cane for walking or as her weapon of choice. She looked every bit to be in her late 80s or early 90s. Her old faded-blue housedress contrasted sharply with her bright red sweatshirt emblazoned on front with "VMI Keydets."

The widow Reynolds led them into a sitting room which had a wood stove that heated not only that room but also the rest of the house. The furniture dated to the widow's grandparents; a small tube television set on a table in one corner, and a card table with a half-finished jigsaw puzzle in another. Uncomfortable was the best that could be said of the chairs. A clay bowl, covered with a towel, set on a chair near the stove.

"Jay tells me you're interested in the Petticrew story," the widow spat out with spunk. "Anyone care for a drink – water, hot tea?" She playfully added, "Maybe some apple cider, though it's on the hard side?"

"Thanks," Laura politely answered, "but we shouldn't stay too long and take up too much of your time." She pointed to the clay bowl next to the stove. "I see you have yeast dough rising, so you're on a time clock."

The widow smiled, "Most city folk wouldn't have known what's in the bowl a'risin'; you must do a fair amount of cooking yourself."

"Cooking is one of my passions," Laura nodded.

"You've cooked up my curiosity as well," the widow relaxed in her chair. "Jay tells me you think you've found a journal that belonged to one of the murdered Petticrew daughters."

"That's right," Elwood replied. "We stumbled upon it in a hidden compartment of an antique dowry box. We're trying to figure out whether it's the real thing – just today we found the Petticrew monument in the Oxford cemetery."

"I'd like to see the journal sometime," the widow countered.

"I wish I'd have brought it with us," Elwood replied. "So, Jay indicated that you're a distant kin of the Petticrews."

"Actually, Rachel Petticrew, the only child who survived the massacre, married a Reynolds. My mother, who was a Reynolds, was a descendent of that family. The story of the massacre has been handed down through several generations now." The widow paused, then smiled. "And, coincidentally, I also married a Reynolds – no relation to my mother."

"I understand the Petticrews settled over on the Collierstown side of House Mountain," Elwood confidently stated, "after living in the Irish Creek area –"

"Where'd you get that information?" the widow interrupted. She confidently declared, "John and Mary Pettigrew came to Rockbridge County after living on a farm between Lynchburg and Rustburg."

Elwood felt embarrassed. "I just assumed it was the Irish Creek area because I knew some Campbells lived in that region. Judith Petticrew in her journal said they came from Campbell country."

"That would be Campbell County," the widow corrected, "that's the name of the county, east of the Blue Ridge, off the southeast corner of Rockbridge County."

Elwood shrugged, red-faced.

The widow pulled a necklace from underneath her sweatshirt, and wrapped her left hand tightly around its large pendant. She looked upward, closed her eyes, and mumbled to herself. After taking a deep breath, she started the story told by her many times previous. "John Petticrew was a quite prosperous farmer over in Campbell County. He had significant land holdings. He took care of his family – his wife Mary, five daughters, and a son. Not only wealthy but also a plain unassuming man respected for his integrity. He was a pious man; he regularly went to church. But, in a sense, he was too trusting. He co-signed loans for friends who went to the same church. When they didn't pay back their notes, John ended up losing everything he'd worked for. He and his family resettled on the Collierstown side of Little House and Big House Mountains, up between the two mountains in the area called the saddle, in about 1843. The small tract of land was owned by John's grandfather. It wasn't being used at that time, because the rest of John's family lived on this side of the House Mountains – in the Kerrs Creek area. The Petticrew family lived in a small secluded log cabin on this land. In order to make ends meet, John took a job with William Alphin who ran a store and distillery along Colliers Creek."

"How far did John have to commute to work?" asked Elwood. His mind drifted – *Maybe we should have stopped by Colliers Creek to see whether the ghost of John Petticrew is playing the fiddle tonight at the bridge next to Alphin's distillery.*

"Miles. He had to walk over rugged terrain. And no horses or mules to help. He'd walk around one side of a mountain, go down the hollow from the saddle to Colliers Creek, then upstream to a place called Alphin – today it's where Collierstown Road becomes Big Hill Road. He stayed overnight at the distillery much of the week, coming home every few days, but most often only on Saturday night."

"That must've been tough on his wife," Laura exclaimed.

The widow tapped her cane on the floor with her right hand; she persisted in grasping her pendant with her left. She smirked, "Someone once told me that John was only a whiskey-maker, but Mary loved his still . . . or is it loved him still?"

She continued to tap her cane in cadence with her self-imposed laughter. Laura and Elwood squirmed in their chairs.

"That's a joke!" the widow finally added.

They joined in courteous amusement. Elwood thought – *Sounds like the type of word game Silas would spout.*

The widow resumed, "Indeed, Mary singlehandedly took care of the farm animals, vegetable garden, and the children. Both John and she were hard workers and never complained. They quickly won the respect of the folks in the Colliers Creek region. Unfortunately, the family had the Andersons as neighbors; James Anderson was a nasty and notorious thief and his wife wasn't much better –"

"Sounds like the Petticrews couldn't catch a break," Elwood interrupted, "with unreliable friends in Campbell County and bad neighbors here."

"That's right," the widow snarled, "James Anderson was a real piece of work. He once got caught in a bear trap stealing corn from a Snider over by Rockbridge Baths. And he was flogged at the county whipping post numerous times for stealing."

"I can imagine that must've worried John Petticrew," added Laura, "he had to go to work, leaving his wife and family to contend with a thief for a neighbor."

"It resulted in bad blood between John Petticrew and James Anderson. John warned him many times to stay off his property. He thought Anderson raided his garden more than once and stole a few of his chickens during nights. Rumor also had it that Mary Petticrew inherited some money about two months before the murders. Anderson may have been ratting around trying to find it."

"Judith alluded to an inheritance in her journal as well," Elwood said. "Do you think John and Mary had some of this cash stashed away?"

"John had supposedly inquired about buying horses and a plot of land next to the cabin," the widow answered, "so I think quite likely. Some claim that it was a quite hefty sum of gold coins."

Both Laura and Elwood were transfixed, by both the story and the spunk of the storyteller. Laura was also mesmerized by the widow Reynolds maintaining her grip on the necklace pendant.

The widow continued, "On Wednesday night, December 16th 1846, a huge snowstorm dumped nearly two feet of snow. It continued into the next day –"

"December 16th – only a few days from today," Elwood thought out loud.

"It was a real blizzard – gale force winds, and temperatures dropping below zero. One of the worst storms ever in this county. The snow drifts were so deep that John couldn't walk home, even on Saturday night. When he returned home on Sunday morning, even before getting to the cabin, he saw a burnt bed sheet and smelled smoke. I can't imagine the dread he felt. John found Mary and five of his children dead, all soot covered, cold and stiff, lying near each other and about five paces from the cabin ashes. Only the chimney stood. It must've been a hellish find and way to die."

Elwood shook his head and mouthed to Laura: "Burning house in a blizzard, the dark fire of hell." The eyes of both moistened. The widow brought her pendant to her lips, kissed it, then resumed her grasp of it.

"Was it determined whether the fire was accidental or whether Anderson might've been involved?" Elwood asked.

"Well, Mary Petticrew was found in a sitting position with her clothes strung about. Her little boy John was lying across her lap in his night clothes. Judith and Margaret lay on the ground facing each other, half clothed. Mary, Judith, and Margaret had blood all over them. The youngest daughters, Letitia and Mary Elizabeth, sat on a log leaning against a stump in their night clothes."

Laura quietly sobbed.

Wiping a tear from his eye, Elwood murmured, "I shudder for John who found his wife and children strewn about, dead and frozen."

"The community summoned the county coroner to a house where the bodies were taken down alongside Colliers Creek. Men were said to have openly wept when they viewed the corpses laid out for burial. The coroner determined that the mother, Mary, met a violet death. She had a deep cut that went from her forehead to behind the ear, as if inflicted by a blow from a metal rod – or maybe a rifle. Cuts and bruises were also on her throat, knees, and legs. Murder was suspected. Feelings in the community ran high for revenge."

"I guess James Anderson was the prime suspect?"

"Indeed, the Colliers Creek community wanted to hang him; but he was nowhere to be found. His wife claimed he left with a friend in the middle of the snowstorm. That seemed incredulous . . . and incriminating to the locals. The sheriff concluded that Anderson traveled during the snowstorm to a place close to where we sit today – where Sycamore Valley Road makes a U-turn back towards Kerrs Creek and becomes Hackens Road – less than a mile from this house. Anderson spent a night there with Billy Bryan, another ne'er do well character. They took off the next day and holed up for more than a week in Augusta County to the north."

The widow slipped her necklace and pendant back under her sweatshirt, as she got up from her chair. She effortlessly added another piece of wood to the stove before Elwood had a chance to offer his help.

Laura noticed that the dough had risen against the cloth, pushing it upward, in the bowl. The widow gladly took her up on her offer to help pinch off roll-sized pieces of the dough to let rise again in glass baking dishes. She admitted it wasn't as easy to pinch now that Mr. Arthur, that is arthritis, lived with her, especially in her fingers. While they worked, Laura and the widow chatted nonstop about baking butterscotch pies, canning green beans, preparing sauerkraut, cooking collard greens, and the best spices for making sausage. Elwood simply watched and listened. In addition, Laura helped the widow ready her dinner of meatloaf and creamed corn for cooking. She then placed the meatloaf in a preheated 375° oven, and set the timer for one hour. The widow gave her a quick hug in appreciation.

The three returned to their chairs in the sitting room – Elwood with a glass of water, Laura with a cup of hot tea, and the widow sipping hard cider. The widow asked Elwood whether he had any more questions.

"I guess they eventually locked up or hanged Anderson for his heinous crime."

The widow paused as she once again gathered her necklace's pendant tightly in her hand. "They should have," she angrily replied, "but it was a continuing tragedy. The sheriff had trouble proving anything; and the Andersons quickly moved a few counties south. The brother of Mary Petticrew claimed to have found some items that belonged to his sister in the Anderson shack. The sheriff finally hauled Anderson and his wife into court five years later. But, by that time John Petticrew was long dead; he died of a broken heart at Alphin's distillery less than two years after his family's massacre. James Anderson was found guilty of murder, but his wife was acquitted. His lawyers appealed and Anderson was re-tried; but by that time most of the witnesses were long gone. The murderous Anderson was acquitted. Justice for Mary and her children was never achieved. Reports surfaced that Anderson finally made a deathbed confession."

"Did the sheriff ever establish a motive for the massacre?" queried Elwood.

"He thought Anderson tried to get Mary to reveal the location of her inherited cash. He knew that John Petticrew wouldn't be home anytime soon because of the snowstorm. Anderson beat her, as well as the two older daughters, trying to get her to talk. After he stole the money, he threw them all out into the blizzard and tried to cover his crime by torching the cabin. John Petticrew was so distraught that he couldn't tell the authorities whether or not any money was missing. Rumor has it that Anderson may have buried the stolen gold near here, when he stopped to meet Billy Bryan. Some claim he was too scared – the possibility of a lynch mob – to come back to retrieve it from its hiding place."

"What a tragedy!" exclaimed Laura.

"And the family even saw more tragedy," the widow added. "The oldest Petticrew daughter, Rachel, survived because she was taking care of her sick grandmother down by Kerrs Creek. Anderson probably went right by that house when he escaped up the hollow here to Billy Bryan's on that fateful night. Rachel eventually married James Reynolds and had two daughters, the oldest of who was stricken with rheumatic fever at an early age.

And, before the youngest daughter was even born, her husband died while working in the woods. She never remarried and raised her daughters with her Reynolds in-laws. Rachel's father-in-law was the uncle of my great-great-grandfather . . . I forget whether it's one or two greats."

"Such a touching and tragic tale," Laura confided. "My heart goes out to the entire Petticrew family."

"Indeed," said the widow Reynolds.

The widow Reynolds finally released her grip on her pendant, hanging from its thick gold chain around her neck. Its metallic sheen and shape captivated Laura. It was more than a simple cross . . . the vertical piece was over two inches long and the horizontal somewhat shorter . . . with a golden number eight about a half-inch high positioned on the vertical piece and centered on the crosspiece.

"Your cross pendant is just enchanting," Laura commented. "Is it a family heirloom? I've never seen anything like it."

"It's been passed down," the widow slowly said, as she clutched it once again in her hand. "It helps me remember Jesus Christ and the Beatitudes, His Blessed Eight."

Elwood and Laura gasped.

"You know, eight has always been my lucky number," the widow continued. "Did you also know that the original building, erected in the 1760s, of the Oxford Presbyterian Church was eight-sided? It was replaced by a limestone structure in the early 1800s."

Laura looked out the window. "It's already dark, and your rolls are probably ready to go into the oven. And your meatloaf will soon be coming out. We need to be going and let you get back to your work. We've already intruded far too long on your time. Besides, my dog will think we deserted him."

As they rose from their chairs, Elwood asked, "One last question – Do you know where the remains, if any, of the Petticrew log cabin are?"

"I've never seen any. I assume it's up Bird Forest Road, since that gravel road goes up to the saddle on the Collierstown side of House Mountain. You can probably find the road on a county map." She thought a bit, then added, "I've heard that

Vernon Entsminger found the remains of a chimney up that way years ago. He lives along Bird Forest Road and has hunted over that area all his life. You might want to talk to him; I have his phone number somewhere."

By the time the widow returned with the phone number written on a piece of paper, Laura and Elwood were waiting by the doorway. She gave the paper to Elwood, then motioned for Laura to bend over a bit. The widow quickly pulled her necklace up over her head and placed it down over Laura's.

"Here, honey, this is for you!"

Chapter Sixteen
FAITH, HOPE, AND LOVE

Two days later, Pastor Elwood Martin slipped into Silas' room at Faithful Care for a visit. Silas sat at his table, slumped over in his wheelchair. Elwood thought Silas' health seemed to be failing more rapidly now. Silas' skin had a yellowish tint, and his eyes a far-away look. Still, he had his ever present puzzles in front of him. And a bouquet of lilies and greenery in his vase.

"Good morning, Elwood," Silas spoke softly. "Doing a letter shuffle – put the letters together to construct the word that answers the clue. Here's the first one: clue is 'the greatest joy.' Letters are 'V,I,G,G,I,N.' What do you think?"

"Actually I got that one before you even gave me the letters – it's G-I-V-I-N-G, giving." Elwood smiled, as he took his usual seat, noticing that Joe the sock monkey sat on Silas' lap.

"Yeah, it should've been an easy one for you. Laura's already provided me with a synopsis of your Sunday sermon – all about giving . . . and doing the right thing," gasped Silas out-of-breath.

"That's right."

"If you don't mind," whispered Silas, "I'm tired and I'm gonna take a nap here in my wheelchair."

"I understand. I'll go down to the nurses' station and see whether I can locate Laura. I need to talk to her anyhow."

Elwood remained sitting at the table as Silas' eyelids shut. Within moments, Elwood heard an erratic but gentle snoring from Silas. He looked down at the puzzle book and saw the next challenges in the letter shuffle:

> H,A,F,T,I – A powerful asset in religion
> P,H,E,O – Never lose it
> V,O,E,L – The greatest force in life

Elwood sat back in his chair and smiled to himself. He looked heavenward. "1 Corinthians 13:13. And now these three remain: faith, hope, and love. But the greatest of these is love."

He prayed for Silas before leaving.

Elwood picked up Laura mid-afternoon after her shift at Faithful Care. They retraced their tracks from two days previous along Buffalo Creek to Effinger. Then, they continued on Collierstown Road and followed Colliers Creek upstream, heading to Collierstown. Elwood had called Vernon Entsminger yesterday as the widow Reynolds had suggested. Vernon initially refused to show them the suspected remains of the Petticrew cabin's chimney. He only relented after Laura convinced Jay, Effinger's retired fire chief, to make the request on their behalf.

Once past the Effinger Fire Department, Elwood told Laura: "I did some research on the Collierstown settlement in the mid-1800s. It was evidently a thriving community with over thirty businesses, mills, and shops . . . as well as a town hall, Masonic Temple, doctors' offices, and school."

"And today, there's not even a convenience store," Laura replied.

"Like Cornwall, it was a booming town in the 1800s, but now busted." He continued, "In 1832, the Lexington-Covington turnpike, the major thoroughfare between Charleston to the west and Richmond to the east, was completed. It was wide enough to allow wheeled wagons and stagecoaches to pass."

"So, was this the road everyone took west over North Mountain?" she asked. "There was no way around the mountain or a pass through it – they had to go over the top."

"Yep. And Collierstown being at the foot of North Mountain was the logical place to stop for almost all the traffic, with a toll station established there. And lots of inns, taverns, restaurants, and blacksmiths."

"No commerce now, just houses and a bunch of churches – Baptist, Methodist, and," Laura sighed, "oddly enough another Presbyterian Church. It's only a couple miles from Oxford. You'd think they'd be in direct competition for members in such a rural area."

"And the two churches are even closer as the crow flies," he snickered, "which I found to be quite interesting. I discovered that the preacher at Oxford in the late 1830s realized the center of population in this area was rapidly moving to Collierstown. So he tried to move his congregation there. He started New Oxford, later to become Collierstown, Presbyterian. His maneuver was so effective that Oxford, except for its cemetery, closed in the early 1840s. I guess that's why the Petticrew monument is at Oxford, instead of the closer Collierstown, Presbyterian. Oxford eventually reopened its doors. I suspect there were plenty of people at that time to populate all churches."

"I guess John Petticrew had no problem getting a job to support his family. The businesses needed labor."

"That's right," he laughed, "I also discovered that whiskey manufacturing was prospering at that time. I'm sure his boss, William Alphin, did quite well at his distillery. In fact, whiskey was one of the largest exports for Rockbridge County in the mid-1800s. The pastor of New Providence Presbyterian Church, at the other end of the county, told me that at one time in the 1800s seven of its eight ruling elders each owned and operated commercial whiskey-making operations. "

"Pre-prohibition," laughed Laura.

Elwood took a sharp right onto Turnpike Road, now a sparsely-traveled road but once the main thoroughfare, then up Bird Forest Road toward the saddle of House Mountain. They

191

drove through rolling pastures, which had been rich farmlands in the 1800s. Bird Forest Road was gravel with a very gentle grade upward, beside a dry, rocky creek bed. Laura got tickled at the sign warning of a one-lane bridge crossing over the creek bed, then a sign indicating a speed limit of 25 mph. The entire road was one-lane; and the Subaru would lose its shock absorbers if one went over 20 mph. They drove past a quaint stone fence separating pasture from road.

After about a mile, the upward slope of the road started to increase more rapidly. They came upon a gravestone marker in the shape of a pinnacle about four feet high in a pasture. It marked a family grave site about fifteen yards off the road. Elwood stopped for a look, but couldn't convince himself to crawl under or over the barbed wire fence to satisfy his curiosity.

Laura stared at the grave marker. Tears welled up inside her. "You know, Silas isn't doing well. His time may be near."

"I know," Elwood replied, "and all I can do is say prayers for him. But he continues with such a good attitude."

"I wish I could be as peaceful," she said with soft tears misting her eyes.

They passed an old deserted church. "To keep people from having to travel all the way to Collierstown Presbyterian," Elwood volunteered, "the church opened a Bird Forest Chapel in this blossoming community in the 1850s."

"Only scattered houses now," she said. "This building looks more recent than a chapel from the mid-1800s."

"I think this is an old Morman church that once served this area," he stated. A red-tailed hawk roosted on the peak of the roof, keenly watching them pass.

The width of the road kept getting narrower and narrower. Rock barriers lined its shoulders. Laura wondered whether this was where the early farmers threw the rocks from their fields. Elwood worried if a car came in the opposite direction someone would have to back up a significant distance. They drove past old log sheds – long abandoned with rusted metals roofs and rot or termites taking them down – several feet from the road on both sides.

They came around a curve and Elwood hit the brakes. The road just ended with a sign that announced "End of State Maintenance." There was barely room to park or turn around. Elwood glanced at his odometer and watch – 3.5 miles from Colliers Creek and 15 minutes. It would have been quite a trip in the old days, probably an hour by horse and two by foot. Straight ahead was a rock gully. A long-abandoned logging trail dog-legged to the left, then headed upward. Another old trail rounded a wooded hill to the left, before heading upward.

Vernon was already waiting for them in his Ford pick-up on this chilly winter day. He spit a chaw of tobacco on the ground before he walked over to greet them. This middle-aged man had a short well-trimmed beard, a ruddy complexion, and balding hair. Laura and Elwood attempted to engage him in small talk. They failed. None of his responses were more than a few words. They quickly surmised he didn't appreciate outsiders in his neck of the woods. Vernon clearly wanted to farm or hunt, not talk, at least not to them.

The sound of a pileated woodpecker hammering on a tree caught Elwood's attention. He glanced upward. Sapsuckers, thrushes, chickadees, finches, sparrows, and other assorted birds flitted about the woods.

They hiked about half an hour uphill through the rocks and forest. Vernon uttered nary a word, as Laura and Elwood struggled to maintain Vernon's pace over the rugged terrain. Elwood couldn't discern a marked trail, although at times it might have been an animal path. They forded a small stream, then popped out into a flat clearing – perhaps a meadow had been there many years ago. Vernon pointed to a heap of rocks.

"As close as I can tell," Vernon said, "I think that's all that remains of the old Petticrew cabin. Nothing else."

Elwood glanced around. "It's certainly located in a beautiful cove. It has a spectacular view of the mountain to the southwest."

"Yep, that's North Mountain."

Elwood walked around the pile of rocks that were once the fireplace. "Have you ever seen any sign of a root cellar anywhere around here?"

"Nope, I've moseyed around a bit, but nothing else," said Vernon, as he spit a wad of dark amber liquid on the ground.

Elwood looked up to the sky, and in particular to the dropping sun in the west-southwest. "I'm trying to figure out where you'll see the last signs of the setting sun on the banks of this little cove."

Vernon stared at Elwood, shook his head, and stuffed another plug of tobacco from his pouch into his cheek.

"It looks like it should be somewhere on the right, or east, side near the rear of the cove," Laura said as she tried to walk a straight line from the setting sun to the back of the cove.

Elwood turned to Vernon: "Supposedly, John Petticrew dug a root cellar in the hillside. I'm just trying to figure out whether it's still there."

"Not where I'd dig a root cellar," growled Vernon. "Too far from the cabin."

"And we have to figure that the setting sun will be just a couple feet further to the south, since we're almost, but not quite, to the winter solstice yet," Laura added.

Vernon and Elwood followed Laura to a spot she deemed to be where Judith described the location of the root cellar's entrance over 150 years ago. They stared at a wall of rocks.

"Don't see anything here, nor nearby," said Vernon.

They poked around for several minutes. Nothing. Finally, they turned to leave, but Elwood caught a reflection of light. Then he saw it. The rock wall was offset from the natural rock formation by about a foot. The entrance to the root cellar was parallel to that wall – it was virtually impossible to see when looking straight at it.

"Well, I'll be," said Vernon.

They slid through sideways about ten feet in single file, then turned toward the hillside. A wooden door had long since decayed. Only metal hinges cluttered the ground. Indeed, a tunnel went several feet into the mountain. But only darkness greeted them.

"I guess we'll have to come back tomorrow with a flashlight," Elwood shrugged. "You can't see an inch in front of you."

Vernon clicked on a small flashlight. "One thing you always carry into the mountains, especially if you're leaving late in the afternoon."

"I hazard to ask what else you're carrying," laughed Elwood.

"Let's just say you also don't have to worry about the likes of a thief like James Anderson up here or a rabid animal," Vernon chuckled as he patted his right hip. "My pistol is always in the holster."

"Somehow, I now feel a lot safer going into this dark cave," sputtered Laura.

All three easily fit into the root cellar, although the men had to bend a bit to avoid bumping their heads on the rock ceiling.

"I don't even want to imagine what the squishy stuff is that I'm stepping on," Laura said. "It's mighty creepy."

"I think I have cobwebs all over my face," added Elwood.

Vernon spotted his flashlight systematically, but quickly, from top to bottom and left to right. Finally, at the far left front corner, he found something.

"Well, all that's in here is this old clay jug," concluded Vernon. He leaned over to pick it up, but as he rose all he had in his hand was the top of the clay jug. "A clay jug in two pieces."

"Anything in the jug?" asked Laura excitedly.

Vernon shone the light to the bottom half of the jug. "Yeah, it looks like a piece of copper metal – with some sort of inscription. It's too dirty to see what it says. How did you know something might've been there?"

"Just a hunch," interjected Elwood. "Let's get out of here."

Once out of the root cellar, Vernon untucked his flannel shirt and wiped slime from the copper. "It says 'Ecclesiastes 4:12.'"

Laura stared at Elwood. But he professed no knowledge of that specific verse.

Vernon kept turning the copper over and over in his hand.

"You know what the verse says, Vernon?" Elwood finally asked.

Vernon wiped his brow with his sleeve. He spat a chaw. "Naw! Only verse I know is the one that says 'of faith, hope, and love; the greatest is love.' I recited it in my wedding vows years ago."

Pastor Martin shook his head in disbelief.

Laura pulled a bag from her jacket pocket and one from her jeans pocket. On the return trip to the dead end of Bird Forest Road, Laura tied red ribbons to tree limbs every fifty feet or so, for their anticipated return trip.

Chapter Seventeen
OPENING DOORS

Near darkness welcomed Elwood, Laura, and Vernon back to the Bird Forest *cul de sac*. A whip-o-will called nearby. Elwood and Laura thanked Vernon profusely for his guidance as well as for his foresight to bring along a flashlight.

Vernon shuffled his feet and added to his chaw. "Y'all should've allowed more time."

They agreed.

Once in his Subaru, Elwood opened his Bible and read from Ecclesiastes 4:12 – "Though one may be overpowered, two can defend themselves. A cord of three strands is not quickly broken."

"So, what's the verse mean?" Laura asked.

Elwood pondered, "There're two of us, instead of one . . . I guess that's good." He cranked the ignition and stared out the windshield. "But a cord of three strands?"

"I guess the more strands that make up a rope, the stronger it is. But so what? I don't need a biblical verse to tell me the obvious," mulled Laura.

"Or maybe the verse wasn't meant to be taken literally, but symbolically," countered Elwood. "Maybe it means we should band together with Vernon to form a team to find the treasure?"

"On the other hand, perhaps a strong three-twined rope is needed to open Judith's door in the root cellar?"

"All this thinking is burning calories," Elwood chuckled, "I'm hungry." He shifted the car into gear. "Let's head back home through Lexington and grab dinner at Niko's Grille."

Laura put her hand on top of Elwood's, still on the gearshift. "Were there any pieces of rope, or cord, in Silas' auction box?"

† † †

Barney danced in circles when Laura and Elwood arrived at the parsonage. His eyes spied the white Styrofoam container in Laura's hand – and his nose immediately smelled left-over hamburger steak with gravy. Going outside could wait in Barney's mind. Barney took his begging stance – sitting upright on his back haunches with his pleading, hungry eyes. He had Laura trained; and a white Styrofoam container meant people food as a treat.

While Laura fed Barney the scraps from dinner at Niko's, Elwood retrieved the Mogan David box from the back porch and dumped its contents on the kitchen table. They plucked out several rope pieces. Only one rope was manufactured from three intertwined strands. Elwood closely inspected the two foot long piece up and down. Nothing.

"Well, that's a dead end," surmised Elwood, then chuckled, "and it's getting late. You and Barney may have to sleep in the spare bed room tonight."

"What're the odds of that happening and no one knowing?" Laura laughed.

"Yeah, the glass house of a preacher," he pouted. "Another few minutes; then I'll take both of you home."

Laura picked up the piece of rope. "Suppose we snip off the ends of the rope? We cut the ends off of the copper pipe and the iron cube."

She searched a kitchen drawer and snatched the scissors. Elwood cut about a half-inch off both ends of the rope – Nothing, other than fraying the newly-formed ends with his cutting motion.

"I'm not sure what I expected," she giggled, "not as though something was going to pop out of the rope's end –"

"Or have a hidden compartment exposed."

Laura slowly unwound the pieces. Nothing. She placed them on the table.

"Well, do you want to put the three strands in the trash or back in the box?" Elwood swung the strands in his hands as he picked them up. The overhead fluorescent light reflected imperfections in the twine.

"Do you see the black streak on each of the strands?" Laura grabbed one and looked at it closer.

Elwood followed Laura's lead and squinted at another one. "It looks like ant tracks running along the strand. If something is written there, its font must be less than one."

"Do you have a magnifying glass?" As soon as the words left her mouth, she realized one was in the pile of stuff from the box on the kitchen table.

Laura collected all three strands and inspected the ant tracks hidden from an external view of the rope. "Well, more verses, Elwood – the first strand says Deuteronomy 8:9, the second Mark 12:42, and the third John 20:19. Grab your Bible."

"Here's the first," Elwood thumbed through his Bible. "A land where bread will not be scarce and you will lack nothing; a land where the rocks are iron and you can dig copper out of the hills."

She put her hand to her mouth. "Prosperity where there's iron and copper?"

"We've already found the iron cube and copper pipe, but no prosperity yet?"

"Maybe we need to look closer at the cube and pipe," Laura responded.

Elwood grabbed the plastic bags with the cube and pipe pieces stored in a kitchen cabinet. They inspected the iron and copper closely; then Laura scrutinized them with the magnifying glass. Nothing.

"Or there might be more iron and copper . . . maybe, rocks in the hills. Did you see any iron or copper in the root cellar?" Laura asked.

"Hmmm, no – but then I wasn't looking for iron and copper there," he said, as he flipped back in the New Testament to the

Gospel of Mark. "But a poor widow came and put in two very small copper coins, worth only a fraction of a penny."

"Just like the iron and copper, we've already encountered a widow. But she gave me a necklace, not coins."

"I sure wish whoever is supplying these clues would make things clearer," he groused.

"Do you have any coins worth less than a penny," ribbed Laura.

"No, but . . . oh, oh," he exclaimed, "I think I remember seeing two coin-like pieces of copper in Silas' box. Perhaps that's what it's referring to."

Laura rooted through the contents strewn about the kitchen table. "Indeed there are two, grimy, nasty-looking round pieces of copper. It looks like something is inscribed on them."

She wiped them off with a paper towel. "One is marked 'iron' and the other 'copper.' The copper-inscribed one is a little bigger and fatter than the iron-inscribed one."

"Could it refer back to the previous verse with the iron and copper rock in the hill . . . or, maybe, the home of the widow Reynolds?"

"Looks like we may need to figure out that at the root cellar, or back at the widow Reynolds' home," Laura replied. "What about the third verse?"

"I know that one without looking it up," he answered. "On the evening of that first day of the week, when the disciples were together, with the doors locked for fear of the Jews, Jesus came and stood with them and said, 'Peace be with you.'"

"Can't imagine that verse referring to something else in the box," she sighed.

"It's the passage where Jesus passes through a wall or through a locked door after his resurrection. Does Jesus come through the wall of the root cellar? . . . or . . . Does one go through a door, without opening the door?"

"Whichever, we may find 'peace.'"

† † †

The next day, Elwood told Laura, when she dropped off Barney for doggie day care, that he wanted to investigate the Petticrew root cellar in somewhat more detail. He planned to make a quick jaunt to the end of Bird Forest Road late morning. Laura reminded him of the biblical verse unleashed from the clay jug – two are safer than one. He hesitated. She wrapped her arms around him and kissed him passionately on his lips. Her argument prevailed.

† † †

The day was relatively warm for December, interestingly enough December 16th. Already by mid-afternoon, the end of Laura's shift, the temperature had soared to over 50°. The forecast called for warm temperatures to continue for the rest of the day, but with some off-and-on rain and perhaps a thunderstorm. A strong cold front was predicted to blow through the area after dark, dropping the temperature precipitously. Fortunately, the wet weather would clear out before the cold front hit.

Elwood came prepared – flashlights, pocket knife, slickers to wear over their light jackets, and the two coin-like pieces of copper.

While waiting for Laura, Elwood decided to visit Silas. Silas' wheelchair sat empty at his table. The daily puzzle page in the newspaper was less than half finished. Joe hugged the flower vase which was filled with a mixture of red, yellow, and white roses. Silas lay on his back in his bed looking near ashen and tired. He coughed. His body rattled.

"Not feeling too good today, Elwood," Silas finally whispered. "It reminds me of three friends who were asked, 'When you're in your casket, and friends and church members are mourning over you, what would you like them to say?' The first guy, Pete, said, 'I'd like them to say that I was a wonderful husband, a fine spiritual leader, and a great family man.'"

"Sounds like a proper response to me."

"And the second, Jim, commented, 'I'd like them to say I was a wonderful teacher and servant of God who made a huge difference in people's lives' –"

"Sounds like something I'd like them to say about me," interrupted Elwood again.

"Then the third, Silas, said, 'I'd like them to say, 'Look, he's moving!'"

"Indeed, that sounds like the Silas I know," Elwood laughed, perhaps too heartily.

"I'm tired and not moving too much," murmured Silas. "I think I'll take a nap. Perhaps a prayer as I drift off would be appreciated."

† † †

Within a half hour after leaving Faithful Care, Elwood and Laura arrived at Bird Forest Road leading them up and up toward the saddle of the House Mountains. It was still warm, but drizzly, when they pulled half off the road at the *cul de sac.* They slipped rain slickers over their light jackets, both wearing jeans and sneakers, to journey to the isolated site of the Petticrew farm.

Even though there wasn't any beaten path, it was relatively easy to follow the red ribbons through the woods. Laura's ribbons definitely didn't define a straight line from the *cul de sac* to the Petticrew homestead. Instead the ribbons took them around rock outcrops, ravines, hollows, and briar patches. At times, they slipped on leafy slick spots created by the persistent drizzle. About fifty yards from the remains of the Petticrew chimney, they jumped over the small stream, the one that a young Judith Petticrew scooped buckets of water for household use over 150 years previously. By the time they arrived at their destination, the clouds had gotten darker and the drizzle had transformed into a steady rain.

They went straight to the root cellar entrance and squirmed inside. It was cool and dry, as expected for a root cellar. They were able to remove their rain slickers and shake off some of the water. With two flashlights, they were able to see a lot more than they did their last visit. Everything was lined in stone, all four sides as well as the top and bottom. Much of the rudimentary mortar had eroded, but the stones had been pieced together like a jigsaw puzzle. Cobwebs galore – Laura swatted them to keep them out of her hair. Animal feces and bones, as well as the remnants of the clay jug, littered much of the floor. The wind, whipping up outside, created an eerie hissing sound through the rocks.

"It's creepy in here, like just out of a B-list horror movie," said Laura uneasily.

"But it's perfect as a root cellar – cool and still dry after more than a century," he replied, "John Petticrew did a heck of a job in building it."

"Maybe," Laura stated, as she focused on an especially large spider web in the corner. "But where's the door into the hillside behind the root cellar wall? Does it lead us to the Petticrew stash of inherited gold, or open the portal to the heavenly gold?"

"Yes, a treasure hunt. Where's the gold?" Elwood dropped to his knees searching for a crack or other sign of a door.

"People would think we're crazy, if they knew we were here looking for a doorway to heaven in an old root cellar." Laura laughed nervously: "I might think we're crazy!"

Elwood didn't hear Laura. He was on a mission with his flashlight, examining every nook and cranny of the stone puzzle. "Well . . . I've been looking all over the walls but see nary a door. If there's one here, Petticrew did a masterful job in camouflaging it, just like he did for the root cellar's entrance."

"Let's try to do this more systematically," Laura suggested. "Why don't you start in the front left corner, and I'll start in the front right corner – scan the flashlight up and down."

Elwood moved to his corner. They followed their flashlights and felt the highlighted rocks and mortar with their fingers, searching for a hidden crevice or crack. Fifteen minutes on their respective sides – Nothing but cold fingers. They started at opposite ends of the back wall.

Suddenly, a muffled crash.

Laura jumped. "Where'd that noise come from?"

"Must be the wind outside, probably knocking a dead limb off a tree," Elwood tried to provide reassurance, albeit with only partial success.

"Sounded like it came from behind the wall," she mumbled.

Moments later, Laura felt something tickling her ankles. She stomped her feet and shone her flashlight on the floor. Nothing.

But five minutes later, Laura excitedly shouted, "I think I have something."

Elwood bounded over to the spot with his flashlight.

"Look here," called Laura. "There's a piece of iron embedded in the rock near the ceiling, and straight down a piece of copper likewise near the floor. And both are slotted, with the copper one being larger. They seem obvious now that I've located them."

"Well, that should also solve the mystery of what to do with the two copper coins – as well as the clue given by the biblical passage from Deuteronomy about iron and copper in the rocks," he snickered.

Elwood excitedly took the two copper coins from his pocket and wiped them off on his shirt. He put the smaller one labeled iron in the iron slot and the larger one in the copper slot. Each coin fit snugly, going about three-quarters of the way into each slot and sticking out a little bit. As soon as the second coin went into its respective slot, they heard a whoosh and a rock door popped open – as if controlled by a spring or a magnet, but with no mechanism visible. The door was narrow and tall, exposing a cubicle about 18 inches wide, a little over 12 inches into the hillside and almost five foot high.

"Well, I don't think both of us are going to fit in here," he quipped. "It'll be close-fitting just for one."

"It makes an old-timey phone booth look like a living room."

Elwood meticulously inspected the sides, bottom, and top of the cubicle with his flashlight. All surfaces were lined with rock just like the main root cellar.

"Obviously, no gold treasure, unless hidden behind yet another wall," he said.

"It creeps me out – looks like a rock casket standing on its end," Laura shuddered. "All we need is to hear chainsaws and see zombies to really freak me out."

"Nothing to be worried about, we may be close to a portal to heaven." Elwood squeezed into the cramped cubicle and waited. Nothing.

"I guess it should close behind you in order for the portal to operate," Laura said.

"We got it open, now we have to figure out how to get it closed."

"I'm not so sure I want to be separated from you," she sputtered.

"Nor I from you, but we both can't fit. How about you try to push the door closed?"

"Okay, I don't like it – but I know you want to see what happens," she replied.

She pushed and pushed – the rock door didn't move.

He shrugged, knocking some dirt from the sides of the cubicle. "Perhaps we should try prayer. I'm reminded of the old saying to thank God for closing doors I'm not strong enough to close and opening doors I'm not strong enough to open."

"Well, I'm definitely not strong enough," Laura echoed.

Elwood was still squeezed into the cubicle. "How about you pull the coins out of the slots?"

She pulled them out one at a time. Once Laura pulled the second coin from its slot, the door snapped shut, quicker even then a slam.

Laura's "Get your fingers and toes out of the way" was lost in the whoosh of the door instantly sealing shut. "Elwood . . . Elwood . . . Elwood . . . Are you okay?"

Silence; she heard her deep breaths echo from the four rock walls. She looked at her watch – 4:32.

She paced, hoping to release her nervous energy. *It'll be getting dark in the next hour . . . I'll give him five minutes in the cubicle, then put the coins back in the slots . . . If he needs more time in there, we can do it again . . . I'm worried, really worried.*

"Elwood . . . Elwood." She must have looked at her watch twenty times in the next five minutes. The ticking of her watch competed with the pounding of her heart.

The watch flipped to 4:37.

She quickly put the two coins back in the two slots. Nothing. She pushed on them. She fiddled with them in the slots. She inserted them in different order. She put them in and out numerous times. Nothing. She beat on the rock door. Nothing. She screamed for Elwood. Nothing. *What should I do? . . . Go get help, but it'll be dark before I get back. . . . What if Elwood gets out while I'm gone? . . . Why did I let him go in there? . . . We should have picked up Vernon to come up here with us.*

Laura sobbed quietly with her hands covering her eyes. Her flashlight was getting dimmer. She turned off both flashlights to save their batteries. She felt alone and scared – as well as scared for Elwood. And it was dark. It was so dark she couldn't see anything, even after giving her eyes time to adjust.

The watch blinked 4:50.

She pulled the coins from their slots and waited, and waited some more. Nothing. She realized the wind no longer hissed through the walls. Silence, just silence. *She needed to listen . . . be silent. Everything was silent. Will God whisper something – anything – to her? She needed to be silent in order to listen to God.* There was plenty of silence, as she sat in the corner of the root cellar with her head hidden in her hands. She felt warmth and comfort touching her, wrapping arms about her, terrifying her. Her imagination ran amok. She said a prayer.

Her watch signaled 5:00.

Laura jumped up and tried the coins in the slots several more times. Nothing. She yelled and screamed for Elwood. Nothing.

She heard a sound – a soft thunder. More rolls of thunder. More minutes passed. A flash of light reflected into the entrance door, followed by a deafening boom.

An immense rumble of thunder shook the root cellar, followed by a hissing whoosh and pop. Laura spun toward the cubicle clicking on her flashlight.

She stared directly at Elwood standing in the open cubicle: "Elwood, you look like you've seen a ghost."

"Ye . . . Yes . . . Yes, the Holy Ghost," he stuttered, "and our Lord and savior Jesus Christ." He had a faraway look in his eyes. "I entered the portal!"

Laura sprung at him with arms open. She thrust a bear hug on him and nuzzled her head into his chest.

A smile came across his pasty face. "And I was only gone, what, less than a minute and you missed me this much – what would I've received if I'd been gone longer?"

"A minute," Laura backed out of the hug and looked at him incredulously: "you were in there for over a half hour, almost forty five minutes. You had me worried sick."

"I'm sorry, so sorry – dear. It felt like less than a minute." Elwood hesitated and sighed, "Actually, I had no sense of time in His presence."

The door slammed shut, startling them both.

"We need to get on our way back to the car," Laura expressed worry. "I need to get out of here – it's beyond scary here."

They exited the root cellar into a wintry mix. Rain, sleet, and snow poured down from the heavens. And dark, heavy black clouds blocked out all semblance of twilight. The temperature had dropped over thirty degrees in the hour they were in the root cellar. The wind had shifted from the northwest, sustained twenty mph winds minimum.

"I guess that cold front blew in sooner than expected," Elwood acknowledged the obvious. "We need to hurry."

They slipped and slid for about twenty yards, passing the remains of the cabin chimney. A flash of light blinded them, though the lightning bolt struck to their rear. Simultaneously, a tremendous explosion and thunder boom shook them to their core. Both Laura and Elwood were tossed like matchsticks to the ground.

Elwood felt blood on his forehead; Laura jammed her wrist into the ground. As they scrambled to their feet and looked back, they saw flames shoot out of the rocks. The root cellar had disappeared. Rocks from the cellar were strewn about. Shrubs and trees smoldered. Elwood and Laura gasped in concert with fear and incredulity.

The wintry mix quickly turned to a full-fledged snowstorm, with the wind lashing it into a blizzard. They could barely see their hands an arms-length away in the near white-out conditions.

Laura took Elwood's hand. "We need to stay together. I hope we'll be able to see the red ribbons to find our way back."

"Keep going downhill," he tried to assuage her fear.

"Flames and a blizzard in this spot," Laura shook her head in fear: "and the same day in December."

At that moment, they stumbled as the terrain dropped. Both tumbled face-first into the small stream. More blood appeared on Elwood's face; and his knee ached. Laura's wrist and ankle throbbed. They crawled out of the stream – wet, cold, and afraid.

Elwood turned to Laura: "We need to pray."

Chapter Eighteen
HERE I AM, LORD

Within the next hour, six inches of wet snow fell. And the snow continued to fall heavily. And the wind howled, feeling like gusts from a hurricane. Laura and Elwood had no idea where they were. They hooked arms to stay together. They thought they had been wandering downhill. But they weren't sure. Going up and down ravines disoriented them. One time they slid head first down a steep slope, much steeper than anyplace encountered on their previous hike to the Petticrew location. It was a struggle to get back up the slope – crawling at times. They worried they were going in circles in the darkness. One flashlight was dead, and the other was fading rapidly.

Their bodies were shivering, having only a light jacket and wet slicker in blustery twenty degree weather. Their feet, as well as their entire bodies, were wet and frozen – their lips dried out and cracked from the wind; their eyes burned; their teeth started to chatter. Both of them were limping and in agonizing pain. They couldn't recognize any landmarks or see any ribbons – only snow-covered trees, rocks, and ground all around in the blowing snow. It was difficult for them to even talk to each other with the wind wailing. They started to worry about survival.

Numerous times Elwood pulled his cell phone from his pocket – No signal. Vernon had told them no cell signal here.

Huddled over, they trudged on.

At last, they saw a faint flashing light and walked toward it – it got brighter as they shuffled closer. They bumped into Elwood's car. Every few steps, Elwood had been hitting the "unlock" button on his car key in his pocket, hoping to be near enough for the car lights to blink. It worked.

Laura checked her watch – 7:56; they had spent over two hours wandering in the wilderness in a blizzard.

† † †

Elwood turned the key in the ignition. The starter ground round-and-round, becoming slower over a ten-second time frame, without firing. Frown lines filled his brow. He turned to Laura to see worry and concern mirrored on her face. After taking a deep breath, he pumped the gas pedal and tried again. The engine begrudgingly fired. They sat quietly until hot air blew out of the Subaru's heater.

They took off their wet socks and shoes to try to warm and dry their feet. It took quite a while for feeling to return to their extremities. Laura inspected their toes and fingers for signs of frostbite, as well as scrutinized their multiple cuts and bruises. The worst of their injuries appeared to be Elwood's laceration on the forehead and a sprained knee, and Laura's badly sprained ankle and wrist.

"Let's see whether we can get this all-wheel-drive Subaru back down off the mountain and to civilization," Elwood confidently stated.

They slowly started down Bird Forest Road. The car kept slipping, but the tires tried to grab the snowy road surface. Under the snow, a layer of ice had formed. It seemed as though the car operated as a sled, while the road with its rock laden sides was the bobsled run. They cruised around a bend in the road. Although the road turned, the car slid straight into a ditch and wedged against a tree. The slide was slow motion – Elwood could see it unfolding, but nothing could be done to prevent it. None of the four tires had anything but ice to grip. The car hit the tree on its driver's side. Impact was sufficiently gentle so the airbags didn't deploy, but hard enough that Elwood's head banged on the side window. Laura examined the resulting cut, which caused the previous cut on his scalp right above the forehead to start bleeding again. He bled like a stuck pig. She curtailed the blood flow with some left-over fast-food napkins found in the console. Elwood tried many maneuvers to free the car – rev forward, rev back, slow forward, slow back, rock back and forth. Every motion seemed to wedge them deeper into the ditch and tighter against the tree.

"I think I have enough gas to last much of the night, hopefully to keep us warm through this blizzard," Elwood sighed.

"I don't think I want to venture outside again until daylight; we don't know whether the next house is ten feet away or a half mile," Laura added, shivering. "We could walk right by a driveway and not see lights from a house, assuming that power is still on."

"I can pull the back seat down and open the interior up to the back, so we can lie down. There's even a woolen blanket in the spare tire compartment that we can use for warmth." He rubbed his hands together.

After Elwood put the back seat down and retrieved the blanket, Laura suggested they get out of their wet clothes – or they'd never stop shaking from the cold. They stripped down to their underwear. Not an easy process due to the close quarters and being on their sore hands and knees. Elwood caught a glance of the jangling cross-with-eight necklace, the gift from the widow Reynolds, which had been hidden under Laura's blouse. They wrapped together in the blanket. With the car heater shooting hot air and their bodies starting to dry, warmth returned. They lay facing toward each other, silent.

Elwood finally broke the stillness: "I'm truly sorry for bringing you into this situation – into what turned out to be a treacherous battle with a snowstorm."

"I came quite willingly," Laura replied. "Who knew that the storm would arrive hours ahead of time? Blame the weather forecaster."

"But I'm truly sorry. I didn't expect us to wander about in a blizzard for more than two hours," he sighed.

"Remember the verse from Ecclesiastes – 'though one may be overpowered, two can defend themselves.' I'm not sure whether either one of us would have survived alone." She chuckled, "Just think of it as a story we can tell friends and family in the future."

"I never imagined that the first night we spend together would be wrapped up in a blanket in the back of my old Subaru," he half-laughed.

"I can't imagine a better way," Laura returned the laugh. She then hesitated before she spoke again: "Well, . . . maybe wrapped up in a beach blanket together – down in Caribbean."

"Just that thought warmed me up." Smiling, he added, "The being together part – I don't care where, when, and how – as long as we're together."

"Gee, Elwood, a woman could almost take that as a proposal," Laura declared.

"I don't have a ring on me," he feigned a frown.

"You could always seal it with a kiss," she smiled.

Their lips came together in a long kiss.

Elwood finally broke the kiss. "Gee. What will my church members think? Here I am lying half-naked with a beautiful lady in the back of my car. Someone could peek through the windows at any moment."

"I'd relish the thought of a good Samaritan stopping by," she laughed. "Besides, you're a pastor. You could preside at our ceremony here in the car and make it official."

"I don't think that would be proper," he grinned. "Plus I'd have to counsel the couple first – whether the bride really approves spending her life in perilous adventures with this normally boring guy."

"Oh, Elwood, you underestimate your traits and charm."

"Yep, the charm of almost getting you lost in a blizzard."

"You know," Laura mused, "I always made snarky comments when the news would report on hikers and travelers getting trapped in snowstorms or the darkness. I'd call them idiots for not knowing the weather conditions or the time of the day."

"I guess you'll have more compassion for the idiots," he smiled. "Now that we be those idiots."

"That's right."

"Yeah – the idiot who was so preoccupied with his own desires – in his desire to see whether the portal to heaven was real, he put the love of his life in danger," he took Laura's hand in his. "And as a result, she had to hike through a blizzard. I still kick myself for being the cause of that pain."

"But that portal is no more – destroyed by a lightning strike. If you would've waited, your opportunity would've evaporated – both figuratively and literally." She paused, then queried, "Do you think the lightning strike was divinely directed at the root cellar?"

"Perhaps instead of whispering, God sometimes yells," he half-laughed.

"I must admit I was scared when the lightning strike lit us up . . . followed by the blizzard . . . followed by our trek down the mountain," she spoke softly. "But I kept remembering your prayer – we had to keep our faith on returning to the car."

"When we went head first down the ravine, I wondered about my faith," he said thoughtfully. "It'd pale in comparison to the faith in God needed by Moses to lead the Israelites across the Red Sea."

They remained silent for several minutes, wrapped in each other's arms. Exhausted, they fell asleep.

† † †

A loud bang – the car backfired. Elwood and Laura went from asleep to fully awake instantaneously. The car's engine rattled, then sputtered and stopped. Out of gas! Silence. Then, a gust of wind whistled, but quickly subsided.

Laura checked her watch – 4:32. Elwood flicked on the dim flashlight. Snow covered all windows except for a few spots on the windshield, evidently protected by an overhanging branch. Snow continued to fall, albeit lightly.

Laura rummaged through the console – a pack of Lance peanut butter crackers and a snack-sized Kit Kat bar. Elwood retrieved a bottle of water from the spare tire compartment. They savored their *impromptu* picnic in quiet darkness.

"Something I've thought about for quite a while," Laura burst out. "How do you think Judith's journal and revelation survived the cabin fire many years ago? And why was her revelation sealed in a copper pipe? Then, even though in the pipe, the copper wouldn't have protected the paper inside from the intense heat of a fire."

"Perhaps Judith kept the journal and revelation stored in the root cellar – and perhaps John Petticrew realized the significance of his daughter's view of heaven in order to warrant its safekeeping in the pipe."

"Perhaps," Laura mused. "But then what about the rest of the stuff from the auction . . . the iron cube, the coded message inside, the rope, the copper coins? It was just like the puzzle you had to go through in order to find the gold in your church cemetery. Could it have been Silas pulling your strings again?"

"I've likewise thought about the hoops we had to jump through to get to this point. But the portal to see Jesus was real. I thought it incredulous at first; but it was real. The puzzle and treasure hunt, though, are certainly Silas' *modus operendi*."

"I guess Judith might've stored her things in the root cellar. And Silas might've stumbled on to them," she added.

"Or perhaps someone else found the things and stored them, creating the various codes to hide their discovery, until they wound up at an estate auction."

"I think Silas knows more than what he's told us," offered Laura. "Do you think he also entered the portal?"

"Good question," he smiled. "If he's seen heaven or been in the presence of Jesus, that fact might explain why he's so good, so pious, so caring. I hope he's feeling better than he did this afternoon. He seemed to be in pain – but he also seemed at peace with letting go."

Once again, quiet reigned.

Elwood solemnly confessed, "Laura, I love you, like I've never loved another in my life . . . even though we've only been together a short time. But before you make a life-long commitment, I need to tell you that God may have plans for me other than at Twin Falls Presbyterian Church."

"I don't understand," Laura replied.

"I need to tell you what happened in the portal behind the Petticrew root cellar."

"I'm all ears; you said you met Jesus," she encouraged.

214

"Perhaps met is the wrong word – I was in the presence of Jesus might be a better way to put it. I felt him there, but I couldn't for the life of me tell you what he looked like. He was just there."

"Interesting," she responded with reverence. "Do you think your mind was playing tricks on you – that you only imagined what you saw?"

"Definitely not," Elwood confided, "it was as real as being here talking to you. . . . Let me go back to the beginning. The ascension to see Jesus was pretty much as Judith described in her revelation. A whoosh after the door closed, a breeze blowing on me, a sweet scent, even a sweet taste in my mouth – it reminded me of the taste after taking the bread and wine at communion. Then the emerging Holy, Holy, Holy announcing the presence of Jesus. I felt Him embrace me with a hug. He said, 'My Father and I have a calling for you.' Almost as a natural reflex, the words 'Here I am, Lord,' came from my heart and out my mouth. My conversation with Jesus turned into a talk with a friend. I asked Him whether He was going to give me a tour of heaven.' But He smiled, 'No. No tour. You'll have to rely on your faith and hope. But after being in My presence, faith in My Father should be easy. We decided you'd be better suited for this calling.' I bowed down in His presence."

Ellwood teared up: "I felt so unworthy in His presence.'

Laura squeezed his hand in hers.

"Jesus told me: 'In your teachings, you preach My Words – if you're the one who's being entrusted with much, much more will be asked – indeed much has now been given to you, for you have been in the presence of the Lord. Much is now expected of you.' I replied once again: 'Here I am, Lord. Tell me my mission.' Jesus said, 'Spread the Word of My Blessed Eight. Go, and provide the Word. Like Paul, be the pinch of yeast that will raise a loaf of bread.'"

Laura quietly grasped her necklace's pendant with her free hand.

Elwood continued, "I then saw the golden road to heaven glistening in the light, slowly fading in the distance as I returned to the portal. I heard Jesus whisper "Peace be with you." The next thing I knew it popped open and I was in your arms instead of in Jesus'."

"Maybe, in doing so, Jesus delivered you to me," Laura smiled, "in addition to the spiritual gold he delivered to you on House Mountain."

Elwood smiled in return, and hugged her.

After a while, he mused, "I can't believe that my Lord compared me to His apostle Paul. I'm so confused about how to proceed on my assigned mission. Paul would know how to proceed, but me –"

"Prayer and Scripture," Laura interjected. "Enter into a dialogue with God. Isn't that what you'd tell your parishioners?"

"I guess I need to practice what I preach," he laughed. "But just so many questions are buzzing about my mind. Do I tell others that I've been in the presence of Jesus? Will they believe me if I told them? They'll think I'm nuts, or even worse that I'm being boastful. Such would draw attention to me and not to Jesus – I need to point to Him, not me. How do I perform the mission? Do I stay at Twin Falls? Do I expand the message of Jesus' Blessed Eight by teaching in a larger church, by becoming a televangelist? What exactly is expected of me? Jesus didn't provide me with a checklist. . . . Excuse me – I realize I'm rambling on and on. It's just so mind-boggling –"

"You may need to slow down," Laura interjected. "I think Jesus has given you a lifetime to complete your mission. I don't think Jesus expects you to finish in the next week."

Elwood took a deep breath. "Maybe I just need to follow the teachings of Paul. I should welcome that God, through Jesus and the Holy Spirit, has given me the freedom to do what I ought to do to spread Jesus' Blessed Eight – not provide me a list of expectations."

"I'd like to be by your side," Laura confessed. "Perhaps it's a divine sign that the widow Reynolds gave me the pendant representing Jesus and His eight Beatitudes."

The temperature in the Subaru was dropping. They were getting chilled. They snuggled closer to each other. Side by side, they fell asleep.

Chapter Nineteen
JOY IS A LIGHT

A Ford pick-up truck rolled to a stop behind Elwood's Subaru. Its engine was left running as the driver jumped out. He shook his head, then spit a stream of tobacco juice leaving a trail of brown, not yellow, snow. He brushed snow from the nearest side window of the Subaru, but snow still fell off its roof when he opened the front passenger door. Sun streamed into the car. Disoriented, Laura and Elwood awoke.

"Hello, anyone in there?"

Elwood turned his bleary eyes toward the door. "Good morning, Vernon. You're a sight for cold, sore eyes!"

"Pastor and Laura, whatcha doing out here? It's freezing in this car," Vernon peered wide-eyed into the back of the car.

"My car not only got stuck but also ran out of gas," Elwood touched his head and winced.

"That's a heck of a cut you have on your forehead, Pastor. Did you spend the night out here in the blizzard?" Vernon caught a glimpse of Elwood's hairy chest and Laura's bare shoulders. He quickly took a step back from the car and, embarrassed, turned his eyes away.

"We're so glad to see you," Laura smiled, "We'll be right out."

"It's not what you think," Elwood appealed to Vernon. Elwood grimaced as he gently rubbed his forehead.

"Not for me to judge," Vernon rolled his eyes. "I'll take you back to my house – It'll be much warmer and comfortable back there."

Once they slipped on their cold, not too wet, clothes, Elwood wiped a patch of fog from the side window. The sun had already risen above the trees to display a bright blue sky. No sign of the departed blizzard beyond lots more than a foot of snow. They also saw Vernon's house. Its driveway entrance was no more than twenty yards from their quiet, cold, stuck, crunched, and out-of-gas Subaru.

Laura crawled out the car. On her first step, her stiff sprained ankle buckled. She found herself once again face down in the snow. Vernon quickly came to her rescue, helping the now-shivering Laura hobble to his truck and wrapping a blanket around her. Elwood didn't even try a solo walk – Vernon threw his arm around Elwood's shoulder to support his slog from car to truck.

Elwood stole a glance back at his car. "I guess better to wedge my Subaru next to the tree instead of whacking into a big rock."

"And good you're far enough off the road to have the snowplow get by. Better to get plowed in than plowed away," Vernon dead-panned.

Dry clothes awaited Laura and Elwood back at Vernon's house. They told his wife they never had a breakfast of scrambled eggs and bacon that tasted better. A generator supplied back-up power to the house; Vernon had already located a tree across the electric line a mile down Bird Forest Road. County schools had announced a snow day for his children, who enjoyed playing the card game Crazy Eights with Laura and Elwood in front of the wood stove for the rest of the morning.

By noontime, Vernon had called a tow truck and confirmed that Collierstown Road had been plowed. He delivered a bedraggled Laura and Elwood to her car, still parked at Faithful Care. They limped into the facility.

† † †

Laura treated Elwood's head gash and cuts, cleaning all with antibiotic rinses and creams before bandaging. From her stash of medications, she retrieved an unlabeled jar of a smelly potion to rub on her and his twisted joints. Another of Sunshine's miracle concoctions. She decided a doctor's visit to treat their sprains wouldn't be needed at this time.

Their relief at being saved from the blizzard quickly abated. The nurse on duty at Faithful Care informed them that Silas died about 5 o'clock the previous afternoon in the midst of a lightning-filled storm of thunder-snow. Laura and Elwood shed tears together. After embracing in a hug, they shared a prayer.

The nurse handed Elwood a small square box, about four inches on each side. Silas had neatly printed "Pastor Elwood Martin" on its top. The box had been found in the back of Silas' sock drawer when the staff cleaned out his room that morning.

Wiping the remnant of tears on his sleeve, Elwood turned to Laura. "Another box. Maybe this will answer some of our questions."

"I suspect not, knowing Silas," she smiled.

He cut the seal to the box with his pocketknife and poured the contents into his hand. He gasped at the sight of a necklace, a heavy gold chain with cross pendant and a sideways eight on the horizontal piece of the cross. Then, a sticky note was stuck on the bottom of the box. In the same print as the box's label was written "PPP BU."

Laura pulled her necklace from underneath her sweatshirt, borrowed from Vernon's wife and displaying the logo "Effinger Fire Department." She placed her pendant next to the one Elwood just received. Virtual twins – identical chains, identical size and make-up of the cross, identical size and make-up of the eight on the cross. With one difference – Laura's eight stood upright on the vertical beam while Elwood's was sideways, like an infinity symbol, on the horizontal beam.

Laura stared, fascinated, at both pendants. "Indeed, more questions."

"Blessed Eight, upright and laid down," Elwood proclaimed, "the Beatitudes, for now and for all times – for infinity or eternity."

"I guess these two are part of a pair." She smiled, "Does that mean we're also together for all times?"

He returned the smile. "Besides our interpretation of eight representing the Beatitudes, the number eight is associated with the beginning of a new life." He took her hand and gave it a gentle squeeze; he looked deeply into her eyes. "Also, as a sign of infinite love. Just look at the eight – neither the upright nor sideways eight has an ending. The pair of necklaces could be a sign of both our new life with God and our new life together."

"I never realized that eight and infinity could be considered two parts of a whole." Laura hugged Elwood with the necklaces between them. Breaking the hug with a quick kiss, she pointed at the note in the box. "P, P, P, space, B, U; yet another puzzle to torment you. A final word from Silas."

† † †

A few days later, a memorial service was held for Silas. The overflow crowd at Twin Falls Presbyterian Church would have made Silas proud – he had touched many lives. Arrangements were made according to Silas' directions in his will, as executed by Dick Dawes, his long-time lawyer.

Elwood presided over the service and eulogy for his dear friend. He started with a reading of the Beatitudes from Matthew 5:1-12, which he offered as a summary of Silas' virtues. All of these assets he summarized in one word, "love," as identified by the apostle Paul in 1 Corinthians 13. Christian love filled Silas. How did Paul define this love? – it is kind, patient, trusts, perseveres, protects, and rejoices in the truth; on the other hand, it is not proud, not envious, not rude, not easily angered, keeps no record of wrongs, and not self-seeking. Elwood also claimed Christian faith and hope, along with a unique sense of humor, filled Silas. Elwood concluded the eulogy with a quote from Adela Rogers St. Johns, an American journalist: "Happiness is a sort of atmosphere you can live in sometimes when you're lucky. Joy is a light that fills you with hope and faith and love." Silas was that light of joy.

According to Silas' wishes, his ashes along with the stuffed body of Joe the sock monkey were returned to New York to be buried next to those of his beloved wife.

Chapter Twenty
OUT OF THE MOUTHS OF CHILDREN

Laura and Elwood spent the next few days limping around on their sprained limbs. Reese Coleman described Elwood's walk as a "hitch in his git-along." Their recovery, though, proceeded relatively rapidly, thanks to Sunshine's salve and Barney's healing licks and nuzzles.

And both missed Silas greatly; Room 79 of Faithful Care would never be the same.

Laura and Elwood also evaded the oft-asked question – What were they doing wandering around the slopes of House Mountain in a blizzard? Hansford Cash even ribbed Elwood by asking him whether he was trying to find Jesus in the wilderness. Elwood responded with a wide grin and "one can find Jesus anywhere and everywhere."

The Sunday morning after Silas' service, Elwood awoke, as every morning since the Bird Forest blizzard, to the re-occurring question swirling in his mind – *How to fulfill his mission of spreading the word of the Blessed Eight?* He lay in bed, lollygagging while the first rays of sun streamed in the windows. *He could preach sermons on the Beatitudes, but such would reach only handfuls of people. Could he make wider impacts with books on the subject? . . . or a Billy Graham- like revival tour? . . . but that wasn't him. Why couldn't he be more*

like Paul, and his charisma, in spreading the gospel? A smile grew – *With Laura at his side, he would find a way.*

The chill in the air quickened Elwood's pace on his walk to the church. As always, the sight of Nettle Mountain on the horizon galvanized his reverence for God's creation. He saw Laura's car in the church's parking lot; warmth flooded his senses. His peripheral vision caught a red-tailed hawk plummeting off a big maple tree behind the church. He watched as it dove near the ground, then glided back up to the large sycamore tree just outside the cemetery. After glowering over the church grounds, it swooped onto the church steeple. *Why did the hawk perch on the church steeple?* Even from the grave, Silas was still playing with his mind.

† † †

Mrs. Leech, the middle school teacher of the Twin Falls Sunday school, was a no-show. She came down with a sudden attack of the stomach flu. At the last moment, the Sunday school superintendent recruited Pastor Martin to be the substitute teacher for the lesson on being a Christian. Elwood emphasized to Joshua, Jaxon, Amber, Meghan, Morgan, Bethany, and Grace to be like you'd like a friend to be to you. In essence, to follow what Jesus identified as the greatest commandment – do onto others as you would have them do unto you . . . or love another, as you would have them love you. In the course of Elwood's discussion with the children, he taught them about the eight Beatitudes that defined the virtues of Christians – those who are humble, desire to do right, kind, righteous, merciful, pure of heart, peacemakers, and stand up for their belief in God.

With only a few minutes left in class, Elwood said to Morgan: "Could you run down to the adult class and have Ms. Armstrong come here? You know who she is?"

"Your girlfriend," Morgan grinned.

Elwood blushed.

Morgan, with Laura in tow, soon returned. Elwood beamed at Laura.

He began, "Ms. Armstrong, we've been talking about the Beatitudes. Could you show the children your necklace?"

Laura promptly pulled her cross-with-eight necklace from underneath her blouse. The children responded with a chorus of oohs and aahs.

Elwood explained, "This necklace symbolizes our lesson on what it means to be a Christian. The cross represents Jesus, our Savior. The number eight signifies His resurrection and our rebirth. It also stands for Jesus' Blessed Eight, the eight Beatitudes, what we need to follow."

"Neat-o." Meghan was enraptured.

"When you go into the sanctuary, look at the baptismal fount," Elwood continued. "Count its number of sides – eight. Baptism represents entering into a covenant with God and Jesus – in essence, your rebirth as a Christian."

Elwood pulled out his cross-with-infinity necklace from under his shirt. "This necklace is exactly like Ms. Armstrong's except the eight on its side means eternity, forever, infinity. Our rebirth under Jesus is everlasting. It's a way to remember the Blessed Eight should be forever followed."

"Gee," Jaxon interjected, "You and Ms. Armstrong have matching necklaces."

"Does this mean you and Ms. Armstrong are gonna get married?" Bethany asked.

Elwood and Laura blushed deep red. Laura looked at Elwood and smiled broadly.

"Ah . . . ah," Elwood stammered. He chuckled, "Well, not really the point I was trying to make. But, in answer to your first question, we do plan to get married this year. About the necklace, I wish I could say I gave Ms. Armstrong's to her; but someone else special gave Ms. Armstrong hers and likewise someone else mine."

"How did they get to be the same then?" Joshua asked.

Laura laughed, "Good question."

"But why do you keep the necklaces hidden?" Grace queried.

Elwood remained speechless. Laura responded, "That's where the person who gave the necklace to me had it."

"But if you're a Christian, aren't you supposed to tell others of your beliefs instead of keeping them hidden?" Grace added.

"Out of the mouth of babes," Elwood muttered as the bell for the end of the class sounded.

Both Elwood and Laura proudly wore their pair of necklaces exposed for all to see during Sunday's worship service, and every day thereafter. They joyfully explained the symbolism to all who asked, as well as those who didn't. And they explained that each necklace was one of a pair, joined forever.

Two Sundays later, Elwood arrived at church to a flurry of activity. Reese Coleman, the church's sexton, was slowly putting the last table in place in the Fellowship Hall, while his wife Mabel arranged tablecloths. Others distributed salt and pepper shakers, tableware, and flowers in preparation for the luncheon after worship service. Elwood found Laura in the kitchen mixing lemonade in a large pitcher and boiling tea bags on the stove. She found time, though, for a warm hug and welcoming kiss.

Minutes before Sunday school was set to begin, Elwood stood greeting Hansford Cash in the hallway outside the sanctuary. Hansford had been ribbing him about a snake skin that Reese had found in the church basement . . . that Hansford had heard Elwood was effective at eliminating snakes. Meanwhile, Peggy Lauderdale proudly beamed and hugged her granddaughter Grace as they exited the sanctuary and passed them in the hallway. The Sunday school start bell sounded.

Elwood drifted into the sanctuary, then up to the pulpit, to do a sound check. He spotted a box next to the pulpit. On top was a handwritten note, seemingly in a young teenager's scrawl:

> *I was entrusted with your $100 several weeks ago.*
> *I purchased the supplies to make these necklaces.*
> *There should be one for each person in church –*
> *maybe for some people to take an extra for someone*
> *they know would like one. It is for them to wear to*
> *remind them of Jesus and His Blessed Eight, the*
> *Beatitudes, forever. They can also spread the Word*

by explaining the meaning of the necklace to others. I hope Jesus will be pleased with what I did with what I was entrusted.

He picked up one – a crudely made wooden cross, about the same dimensions as his, on an inexpensive chain. On one side was glued a plastic charm, an eight . . . and on the other side, another plastic charm, an identical eight, on its side as the infinity symbol. Both Laura's and his necklaces combined into a single reversible necklace.

An inner peace overwhelmed him. He was being shown the way to do much more with the treasure, his spiritual gold, with which he was entrusted. And in that moment of peace, he understood the meaning of Silas' final riddle – *PPP BU* . . . *Peace be with you!*

Elwood wept with joy.

Topics for Discussion
BIRD FOREST

1. As argued by Silas, God's love for us is the basis for one's faith in God. But one could argue that one needs faith in God to realize His love. Is this a chicken-versus-the-egg dilemma as to which comes first? The Apostle's Creed is a statement of one's faith; similarly, provide a statement of God's love.

2. What do you think is meant by "dark fire?"

3. Strange coincidences troubled Pastor Martin throughout this story. How do you explain coincidences?

4. Within months of Judith Petticrew's audience with Jesus, she died a terrible death. Rationalize such with the compassion and grace of God.

5. A quote from Joseph Campbell, an American writer and mythologist, states "We must be willing to get rid of the life we've planned, so as to have the life that is waiting for us." Contrast the life that Pastor Martin had planned versus the one that unfolds for him.

6. Sunshine Clutterbuck was convinced that Pastor Martin had been shown the "sign of Jonah," as described in Matthew 12:39-42, and would be in the presence of Jesus. Pastor Martin initially doubted Sunshine's interpretation of the underlying

theology. Do you believe that Pastor Martin was indeed shown the "sign of Jonah?"

7. The mother of Reid Mackey, a resident of Rockbridge County, claimed there was a 9th Beatitude – "Blessed are those who expect nothing and aren't disappointed." Discuss this 9th Beatitude; and develop your own 9th Beatitude to describe a particular virtue of being a Christian.

8. The initial responses of biblical figures who meet God (Jesus) range from outright fear to doubt to "Here I am, Lord." Summarize the responses of those from Moses to Saul, and compare to that of Pastor Martin. In such meetings, how does God (Jesus, Holy Spirit) reveal but yet conceal? Why do you think God chose Pastor Martin for His mission to spread the message of the Blessed Eight?

9. Why do you think Elwood told Laura of his meeting with Jesus, but told no one else? If you had an audience with Jesus, would you tell others?

10. Pastor Martin is impatient in establishing a pathway for his entrusted mission, to spread the Word of the Blessed Eight. Arnold Glasgow, an American businessman and humorist, has been quoted as saying "The key to everything is patience. You get the chicken by hatching the egg, not by smashing it." Contrast patience versus timeliness in completing God's mission.

11. Who do you believe put together the items and puzzles in the Mogan David box stored in Silas' basement? Provide a rationale for your answer.

12. If you were tasked by Jesus with the mission of spreading the message of the Blessed Eight, how would you do so?

13. Elwood and Laura became historians, in a sense, researching the account of the Petticrew massacre. Friedrick von Schlegel, a German diplomat (1772-1829), defined a historian as "a prophet in reverse." Apply this definition to the findings of Elwood and Laura.

14.   Contrast a life that one lives according to the Ten Commandments (the law) versus according to the Eight Beatitudes (one's faith).

PART 3

SYCAMORE VALLEY

But Jesus went to the Mount of Olives. At dawn he appeared again in the temple courts, where all the people gathered around him, and he sat down to teach them. The teachers of the law and the Pharisees brought in a woman caught in adultery. They made her stand before the group and said to Jesus, "Teacher, this woman was caught in the act of adultery. In the Law, Moses commanded us to stone such women. Now what do you say?" They were using this question as a trap, in order to have a basis for accusing him.

But Jesus bent down and started to write on the ground with his finger. When they kept on questioning him, he straightened up and said to them, "If any one of you is without sin, let him be the first to throw a stone at her." Again he stooped down and wrote on the ground.

At this, those who heard began to go away one at a time, the older ones first, until only Jesus was left, with the woman still standing there. Jesus straightened up and asked her, "Woman, where are they? Has no one condemned you?"

"No one, sir," she said.

"Then neither do I condemn you," Jesus declared. "Go now and leave your life of sin."

— John 8:1-11

Chapter Twenty One
THROWING THE FIRST STONE

Elwood unfastened his seat belt and casually opened the door of his Subaru.

Ba-BANG. A noise echoed from the back of the house.

Barney softly growled from his perch on the car's console; Laura stroked the top of his head and told him to stay. Laura and Elwood looked at each other in surprise.

Ba-BANG . . . Ba-BANG.

After hopping out of the car, Elwood grabbed Laura by her hand and guided her around to the side of the house. They cautiously slipped by overgrown shrubs and sidestepped downed branches, tracking the sounds to the rear. Every few seconds another racket reverberated.

Ba-BANG. A fist-sized rock hit the aluminum garage door of a ramshackle shed.

They saw the back of a scrawny kid bending down to pick up another rock from a pile.

"Hey," Elwood yelled. "What do you think you're doing?"

The boy, about twelve years old, wore grubby jeans, work boots, ratty jacket, and a red baseball hat. He quickly pivoted and flung the rock in his hand at them. Laura and Elwood ducked, covering their heads with their hands. The rock whizzed dangerously close to Elwood's left side before landing harmlessly in a nearby leafless butterfly bush. The kid took off.

"Stop," Elwood shouted, but the youngster never broke stride.

The boy dashed into the scrub brush and, in a flash, disappeared into the woods at the rear of the property.

Laura and Elwood took a deep breath. Both wondered why this kid was throwing rocks in the backyard of the widow Reynolds' home. They warily walked to the shed to investigate, keeping an eye out for more rocks being thrown their way from the woods. The target of all of the boy's rocks, except the last, had clearly been a silhouette of a man on the garage door. The word BUG was painted across his chest. Dents, rips, and holes pock-marked BUG's profile. The head was nearly obliterated. Scattered deposits of rocks at the base of the garage door indicated the boy's target practice had been going on for some time.

Elwood glanced at the back windows of the house. He saw no sign of movement inside. "Let's check whether the widow Reynolds is okay."

Laura walked over and anxiously scrutinized the back door. "I'm surprised she didn't chase him away. No sign of her in the mud room or kitchen. But two window panels are broken. I see a rock on the floor inside."

Elwood and Laura chose a mid-winter day to visit and deliver a meal to the widow Reynolds at her home in Sycamore Valley. They wanted to resolve the issue of the necklaces. *How did she have one necklace, and Silas the other necklace, of a matching set – identical crosses, one with an upright eight superimposed on it, and the other with a sideways eight, or infinity symbol? How had Silas coordinated this ruse, if that was indeed the case, with her? They also wanted to share the writings in Judith Petticrew's journal and revelation.* But, instead of being greeted by the widow Reynolds on her front porch, they were welcomed by a rock-throwing kid in the backyard.

† † †

Elwood and Laura circled back to the front of the house, still no sign of the widow Reynolds. Under overcast skies, the light breeze made them glad they'd worn coats. Their sneakers, though, were caked in mud. The light snow from the previous week had melted, resulting in partially frozen muck masquerading as a yard.

Laura retrieved Barney from the car. She let him jump out to enjoy the plethora of new smells. Elwood had parked his Subaru behind the widow's old Buick Roadmaster station wagon. The Roadmaster was in the same place as it was on their last visit, and probably in the same spot as months ago.

"Hey, Elwood," Laura called out. "I just noticed her car's vanity plate – JPR SSC. I wonder what it means."

Elwood walked to the front of the car and bent over to view the license plate. "That's interesting – I guess the first set of letters must be her initials with R being Reynolds." He tried to scrape some mud off his shoes in the gravel, then laughed, "I fully expected her to identify herself as TWR, The Widow Reynolds, instead of JPR."

Laura laughed in return. "We can see more of the surroundings today than the last time when we visited in the dark. About twenty yards farther down the road I see signs showing that Dug Row Road branches to the right, while Sycamore Valley Road curves to the left and dead ends in 0.77 mile."

She grabbed the Styrofoam container of chicken cordon bleu, broccoli salad, scalloped potatoes, and apple cobbler from the floorboard. Elwood recovered Judith's journal and papers from the back seat. They strolled to the front porch, Barney in tow. Elwood knocked on the door. Nothing. He knocked on the door again. Nothing, not any trace of movement or noise inside. He peaked cautiously through the window. Nothing, no lights.

Elwood pressed his face to the window. "The jigsaw puzzle on the table looks the same as when we last visited over a month ago. Very few, if any, pieces have been added."

"Well, at least you weren't accosted with the barrel of a shotgun," she snickered. "Or whacked by her cane as she came rushing through the front door."

"Maybe she just left for the day – maybe someone picked her up to take her to the store, or doctor appointment, or something."

Laura joined him at the window and gazed inside. "Indeed nothing, doesn't look like any activity inside."

Disappointed, they returned to the car. Looking back at the house, though, they realized its chimney wasn't spewing smoke. Thus, the widow's woodstove wasn't heating her house in the cold weather.

"I'm getting somewhat worried," Elwood grimaced. "Maybe something happened to her in the house, and she couldn't get help."

He returned to the front door and rapped loudly. Nothing. He tried the doorknob. Locked. He walked around the house to recheck the back door.

Momentarily he returned. "It's locked up tight as a drum. No sign of activity. Only things out of place are the two broken window panes on the back door. I guess our rock-thrower wasn't satisfied with just the shed's door."

Laura leaned on the side of the car. "I'm gonna call Jay at the Effinger Fire Department and get the widow's phone number. Then, call her. Maybe she has a cell phone."

"That's good," he responded, "we should've done so before coming to make sure she'd be here."

"Maybe we can come back tomorrow, or this weekend."

"But the more I think of it," Elwood shook his head and sighed, "the more worried I get. I should call the sheriff's office and see whether they can do a wellness check . . . and report the petty vandalism by the kid on the widow's shed. Things just don't feel right."

Once back in their car, Laura pulled a pen and paper from her pocketbook, then dialed Jay's number stored in her list of cell phone contacts. As she asked him about the widow's phone number, her face turned white. Her eyes moistened. The pen and paper remained unused. After less than a minute, she simply said, "Thanks . . . Bye."

Laura sobbed as she turned to Elwood. "The widow died. Jay said the night of the big snowstorm. She died of a heart attack. She'd called 9-1-1, but –"

Barney tried to lick the tears from her eyes. Elwood bent over the car console and squeezed in front of Barney. He gave Laura a gentle hug and a reassuring kiss.

Excusing himself from the car to get some fresh air, he paced a few moments next to the road, then called the sheriff's office. He talked to the dispatcher for several minutes before returning to Laura.

Elwood groaned, "Things get even stranger. I probably got more information than most callers would get – the sheriff's dispatcher on duty was fortunately Joy Bayne, sister of Hansford Cash –"

"Ah, one of your elders at Twin Falls Presbyterian," interjected Laura.

"That's right," he nodded. "She said they'd send a deputy out later today to talk to the boy and the boy's mother. Evidently, they had a previous rock-throwing incident with him before the widow died."

"So, the widow reported him previously."

Elwood shook his head. "The boy's mother complained to the sheriff that the widow shot her son. Allegedly, the widow fired some rat shot into the boy's butt. But there weren't any injuries, not even signs of the boy being shot, just a scared kid. A deputy did an investigation. He found that the boy, Amos Muterspaw from down the road, was trespassing on the widow's property and throwing rocks at her shed and house."

"But why? Did the boy also draw the man's profile on the door? Who's Bug?"

"Amos boasted to the deputy that Bug deserved to be stoned . . . that it was payback. The deputy reported the mother smiled and proudly said, 'That's my boy!'"

Laura sat speechless.

"When the deputy interviewed the widow, she claimed she had a bear problem. She had heard a commotion in her backyard that day and shot at a bear running off into the woods."

"So she couldn't tell a bear from a boy?" Laura seemed puzzled.

"Joy, the dispatcher, laughed when I asked her the same question. The widow took the deputy to her back door; just inside a rifle and a shot gun were propped against the wall of the mud room. One of the back panels had been broken with a rock lying inside. She told him that if she'd known a Muterspaw had been throwing rocks in her backyard, she would've shot him between the eyes with her 0.32 caliber Winchester – it'd been used for such before. And she said she uses the shotgun just to shoo off critters and varmints."

"That doesn't sound like the kindly old lady we met the last time." Laura wondered, "What did she mean the rifle had been used 'for such' before?"

Elwood shrugged his shoulders. "Evidently, the deputy was concerned about the widow's eyesight and access to firepower. He pointed out a small piece of cloth flapping in the wind and stuck on a tree branch about fifty yards away in the back yard. The widow picked up her Winchester and in an instant – bulls eye obliterating the piece of cloth."

Laura gulped.

"The deputy quickly concluded that the widow could take care of herself. He warned the boy's mother to have her kid stay off the widow's property and cut out the mischief – because, next time, the widow might not be as forgiving."

† † †

As Elwood and Laura drove away from the widow Reynolds' house, they passed next to a dry creek bed lined by lots of large and gnarly sycamore trees. Elwood admired the vitality of these sycamores to sprout up between rocks, defying all odds for their survival. This area was indeed appropriately named Sycamore Valley.

Meanwhile, Laura held her gold cross-and-eight pendant, which had been given her by the widow Reynolds, tightly in her hand. A peaceful quiet descended upon them as they contemplated the passing of the widow. She had been a spry and feisty old lady; they hadn't considered she'd been near death during their one previous visit.

They passed a hardscrabble house stuck between the road and the rocks, sycamores, and creek bed on their right. Wafts of burning firewood from its chimney soon permeated the air and their car.

Elwood saw him first. The boy with the red ball cap stared at them from his high vantage point – about twenty feet up a sycamore and sitting on a large limb arching over the road. Elwood noticed a smirk on the kid's face, then saw a rock the size of a softball in his hand.

Elwood slammed on his brakes. He reflexively threw out his right arm to keep Barney from being tossed off the console. Laura's seat belt grabbed against her chest, as her eyes scanned for the problem. The Subaru skidded on the gravel to a sudden stop.

The rock thudded onto the gravel road about two yards in front of the car.

Elwood took several deep breaths. Laura sat quiet and wide-eyed. Barney scrambled to regain his footing. Elwood got his next glimpse of the kid half-way down the tree, scrambling in his get-away. Elwood stared – *What is it about this Muterspaw boy and throwing rocks?*

† † †

Laura found the widow Reynolds' obituary on-line. She threw up her arms. "You'll never guess the widow's full name?"

"No idea. Just JPR from her license plate, or JP Reynolds."

"Hint – what were the initials on Silas' box he gave you."

"Oh, no," Elwood moaned, "J.P. – Judith Petticrew Reynolds."

Her obituary had been published in the same issue of *The Lexington News-Gazette* as Silas'. No viewing, funeral, or memorial services were mentioned, although arrangements were handled by the local Sutherland Funeral Home and Crematory.

She sat back in her chair. "Just a short, inconspicuous obituary. It's no wonder we didn't see it. Because she died the same day as Silas, we were preoccupied with our recovery from our jaunt through the woods up House Mountain's saddle . . . and with the death of Silas."

Elwood looked over Laura's shoulder at the computer screen. "Her age is listed as 89 yrs and 4 mos, just like ages were reported at the old Petticrew monument."

"Curiously, also the same age as Silas," chuckled Laura. "Same day of passing, same copy of newspaper."

Elwood laughed, "Now you're instigating my compulsions; you're pointing out coincidences to torment me."

"And it says she was predeceased by her parents Calvin and Elizabeth, her husband Samuel, . . . and that she was the last of her family. Then its final line states – 'She had a brother Simon and has one special dog-kin cousin.'"

"I'm looking at that last line – weird, definitely weird?" Elwood threw up his hands. "Why 'she had a brother' instead of predeceased by her brother with the rest of her family? Or is the brother still living? And what's dog kin?"

Laura resumed chuckling. "I've never heard of dog kin, much less seen a reference to one in an obituary. Instead of being short and sweet, the obituary is short and ended odd."

"It's also strange not to have any type of memorial service," Elwood shrugged. "Even if no relatives, she must've had friends."

"I'm also puzzled by her license plate. I guess her husband 'Samuel' could be one of the 'S's in the 'SSC' part," Laura smiled. "But then wouldn't he have been a Samuel Reynolds. Where's his 'R'?"

"Come to think of it, oddness abounds," Elwood kissed Laura on the cheek. His thoughts drifted back to the Muterspaw boy – *Now he's beyond odd.*

† † †

Several days later, Elwood visited Wayne McPherson, the owner-operator of the local Sutherland Funeral Home and Crematory. As usual, Wayne complimented him about the fellowship receptions after burials in the Twin Falls Presbyterian Church's cemetery – that Mabel Coleman served the best fried chicken anywhere, and now Laura made a banana pudding "to die for." On the other hand, Elwood nonchalantly queried Wayne about the funeral arrangements for the widow Judith Reynolds.

Wayne told him that the widow had made all the pre-arrangements herself and prepaid everything a decade earlier. He had no interaction with anyone else in terms of handling the body. He confided to Elwood that wasn't really out of the ordinary. In his career, he'd seen lots of bizarre arrangements and funerals; one just last week had ended in a fist fight with the police making several arrests. In the case of the widow Reynolds, he simply followed the instructions that had been given. No visitors. She was cremated. Her ashes dispersed about the Petticrew monument in Oxford Presbyterian Church's cemetery.

Wayne asked Elwood whether he'd ever heard of the massacred Petticrew family from the 1800s. Elwood rolled his eyes and nodded a yes. He fought off the urge to hold the pendant on the necklace given him by Silas. Then, Wayne expressed his bewilderment at the widow's final stipulation – that half her ashes be scattered in a figure eight in front of the monument, and the other half strewn as a sideways figure eight on the opposite side of the monument. As he spread the ashes, he repeated "Jesus' Blessed Eight forever" according to her instructions. Elwood grabbed the pendant.

While still holding onto his pendant, Elwood asked, "The last line of her obituary mentioned a brother Simon and one special dog-kin cousin . . . What does –"

"That part was really strange," Wayne interrupted, "This last line addition came in the mail a few days before her death. First time I'd heard from her in over ten years."

Elwood opened his mouth but no words came out.

Finally, he stuttered, "Her br . . . bro . . . brother."

"Never knew she had or has a brother," countered Wayne, "and didn't really know too much about her either. I saw her at community dinners at the Effinger Fire Department – that's about it."

"What's 'dog kin?'" groaned Elwood.

"I print what I'm given." Wayne shrugged his shoulders.

Chapter Twenty Two
THROWING THE SECOND STONE

Elwood did double duty, dog-sitting while working on Sunday's sermon. After composing his conclusion, he practice preached some lines to Barney. Barney stared at Elwood, his head lying between his feet. Elwood paused in his preaching, then shook his head. He scribbled a few lines on another piece of paper. But he immediately balled up the paper and tossed it toward the waste basket. Barney bounded off the office's easy chair, eager to play fetch.

Ding-dinga-ding . . . Ding-dinga-ding . . . Ding-dinga-ding.

Elwood jumped up from his desk chair in his office at the parsonage. Barney scampered to the front door in full barking mode.

Ding-dinga-ding . . . Ding-dinga-ding . . . Ding-dinga-ding.

Elwood opened the front door. Barney's barking transformed into a low growl. He crouched in a defensive position behind Elwood's right leg and continued to growl.

The woman at the front door was about fifty, but looked older. She wore hiking boots, cargo pants, flannel shirt, and a hat straight out of *Crocodile Dundee*. Her grayish-brown hair was pulled back in a ponytail. She could easily have been mistaken for a hiker who'd taken a wrong turn off the Appalachian Trail at the top of the mountain.

"Good afternoon, Elwood," she scowled. "May I come in?"

"Do we have anything to discuss?" Elwood remained firmly entrenched in the doorway, blocking entry. "I thought you were in North Dakota."

"You know I don't like dogs," she snarled, "especially in the house getting their hair all over the furniture. What's that mutt doing here?"

Barney transformed his growl back to a bark. Elwood crouched down to comfort Barney. The woman danced past Elwood and surged into the hallway. The stench of cheap beer followed along with her.

"Well, Dot," Elwood sizzled, "I don't see that you have any voice in what comes into the parsonage anymore." *What a change in appearance from when she was my wife –* Elwood thought *– from being prim and proper as a minister's wife to this mountain look. But her demeanor hadn't changed from her last year at the parsonage. She still wore her perpetual scowl as a badge of honor. And everyone had to do it her way or the highway.*

Ignoring his comment, Dot put her hands on her hips and glared. "You need to amend the terms of our divorce. We can work out a more equitable amount without going through our lawyers. I want more money than the piddling amount you send me every month."

"I provide you with more than enough alimony," Elwood calmly stated. "And I've covered our daughter's college tuition and expenses as well."

Dot seethed, "She's not our daughter. She's my daughter."

"Yeah – you're always quick to remind me that Arany's my step-daughter. You seem to forget that both of us, not just you, raised her. I still consider her family, even though you've done everything possible to turn her away from me."

"Well, now that she's graduated, you can use that tuition money to supplement my alimony payments."

"Not the terms of our settlement," Elwood snidely countered.

Dot scowled, "You can afford more money, you cheapskate. After all, you're awash with money; you're a millionaire."

Elwood laughed, which made Dot's face turn red and her muscles tense. "Correction, Dot – as I've told you too many times to count on the phone, the church recently acquired an endowment of millions. I haven't. I still draw the same salary."

"You're a liar as well as an idiot."

Barney sharply barked.

Dot sneered, "Shut up that mutt!"

"The dog's name is Barney; he's a wonderful judge of character," snickered Elwood.

"I guess I'm gonna have to see my lawyer after all," Dot raged, tapping her foot. "I thought we could actually discuss this civilly, but you're just being pig-headed."

"Remember you're the one that left."

"It was your fault. You left no room for me in your life." She stomped the floor. "You loved your God more than me."

"I think we've had this discussion many times before," he refuted. "As I tried to explain to you, you turned away from God embittered."

"Oh, shut up! You'll hear from my lawyer."

"I guess, then, we have nothing further to discuss," he shrugged his shoulders, and hastily herded her back onto the porch.

Laura's car pulled into the driveway. Barney flew past Dot and Elwood to greet Laura. He spun round and round and excitedly barked.

Elwood smiled at Dot. "I'll be having dinner with my fiancée tonight."

"So that's why you didn't want to invite me inside. You've already replaced me with some floozy. You didn't waste any time," Dot sneered. "Now that you're a millionaire, you're attracting all sorts of gold-diggers."

Elwood cringed as he introduced Dot and Laura to each other. Dot glowered as she quickly inspected Laura from top to bottom several times. Laura extended a welcoming hand. Dot refused the hand.

"Dot, if you'd like to stay for supper," Laura frowned, "I'll be cooking meatloaf, sweet potato casserole, and green beans to go along with –"

"What're you doing in my house?" Dot demanded.

Laura took a step back from Dot.

Elwood took a step closer to Dot. "First, Dot, it's not your house. And second, Laura isn't leaving, you are."

"Perhaps it might be best if I drive around for a bit," whispered Laura as she scooped Barney up in her arms. Barney licked her face, as she stroked his back.

Elwood gently hugged her. "No, just stay. Dot is leaving."

Dot pointed at Laura. "She's just trailer trash – she needs to get out of here."

"Dot, you need to apologize to Laura." Elwood felt exasperated, his eyes pleading to Laura to stay quiet and remain calm.

Dot turned to Laura and pointed to the engagement ring that Laura sported. "My ring was bigger. The old coot is getting cheaper as he gets older and richer. But then he always was selfish." She re-focused her view to their necklaces. "What a ridiculous pair of pendants? I guess you both think they look just darling, but they make you look like a pair of goofballs."

Laura shook her head in disbelief. She opened her mouth to speak, but immediately realized the folly in that.

Dot turned and stomped off the porch to her car.

"How's Arany doing?" Elwood asked.

Dot didn't break stride: "You just stay out of her life."

Elwood persisted, "I think I have the right to know. I helped raise her. I baptized her, gave her first communion, taught her how to drive a car, paid for her college tuition."

As Dot opened the car door, she leered at Elwood. "You also tried to poison her mind with your God, as well as corrupt my mind. We need no God. We've both joined the Church of the Ethical Society."

Elwood shook his head in disbelief.

"At least I don't have to listen to your crap anymore!" Dot yelled. "Have fun with your hussy and that fleabag of a mutt."

She leaned down in back of her car door, picked up an egg-sized stone from the driveway, and hurled it at the front porch. "You'll pay up one way or the other!"

Elwood quickly stepped in front of Laura, as the stone ricocheted through the rose bush in front of the porch before dribbling to a stop at his feet. The car door slammed. Dot's car kicked up more stones as it sped away.

"Was she always that bitter?" Laura asked, gently breaking her hug with Elwood. "You never told me much about her. I didn't feel it was my place to pry. I just wanted to go forward and not open old wounds."

"She changed in the last year of our marriage," Elwood sighed deeply, picking up the stone on the porch and tossing it back into the driveway. "That last year, she'd get particularly upset when people called with problems. She wanted me to tell them to go take a hike. Since she left, she seems to be mad at everything – and takes it out on me."

"Sorry about that," Laura offered.

"No, I should be sorry," he exhaled, as he opened the door for Laura and Barney to enter the house. "I should have taken Dot to task calling you names, but I knew it would only have escalated her anger. I suspect you smelled the alcohol on her. So telling her to calm down would work about as well as trying to baptize a cat."

Laura suggested they take a walk with Barney to make better use of the remaining daylight before dusk. Dinner could wait. The dead end road that passed by the parsonage morphed into an old logging trail into the forest. Barney scurried ahead of them, trying to find the scent of some critter to chase. Laura and Elwood bantered about their respective days at work, when not admiring the chickadee in the thicket, the initials carved into the large beech tree, the angry caws of a flock of crows harassing a hawk, or the moss-lined banks of a babbling brook. Next to the water, they watched Barney alternately digging furiously at a hole and sticking his nose therein. Hand in hand, they enjoyed the company of each other.

Once back to the house and in the kitchen, Laura chopped portions of a green pepper and an onion to add to the ground beef for meatloaf. Elwood scrubbed a few sweet potatoes, then added them to a pot of boiling water. Their discussion turned back to Dot and the source of her anger.

"In our last year together, she continuously fussed about God and me; I'm not sure which one caught the brunt of her wrath," he confessed. "She also complained about the lifestyle of a preacher's wife – she thought God should reward us financially for being good stewards of His Word at Twin Falls." Elwood hesitated, then added, "But, on the other hand, let's just say she didn't go alone when she left. I suspect that for this last year she was having an affair and she used our standard of living as her excuse. Others told me that she had found someone with lots of money to promise her all the luxuries she thought she deserved; they moved to North Dakota. He also got her into the party scene, lots of alcohol and drugs. Then, I heard he traded her in for a younger model after a year or two there. It only fueled her bitterness."

"Money can't buy happiness," said Laura.

Elwood nodded in agreement.

She added some breadcrumbs, catsup, and an egg to the meatloaf mixture. "By the way, what's the Church of the Ethical Society?"

He groaned, "A branch of the secular humanists –"

"Oh," she interrupted, "they're the ones who claim you can be good without God and that nature is supreme. Humans are capable of being ethical without any God."

"That's right," he nodded. "They believe there's no God-given standard for morality, ethical behavior, and social justice. There's no absolute or universal moral truth. Human reasoning provides a set of rational moral principles. As a result, this church is all about self-fulfillment. These people gather in their need for community and to celebrate their belief in humanity, not God."

"And in doing so, they justify the current human-centric world without the need for a God and our savior."

"I'm distressed that Dot's led Arany astray into this cult," Elwood hung his head.

They continued quietly performing their kitchen tasks – Laura molding the meatloaf into form and placing it on a pan for the oven, Elwood draining the water from the potatoes and peeling their skins. Both Laura and Elwood were comfortable in their moment of silence.

"You never mention any contact with Arany," she gently inquired. "I hope Arany isn't embittered like her mother."

Elwood sighed, "I married Dot when Arany was two years old, but had known her since her birth when Dot was a single mother. Arany always called me 'Daddy.' I was the only father she knew. Dot, to my knowledge, never identified the birth father to anyone, not even Arany. I told Dot she deserved to know. Dot wouldn't let me adopt her – so Arany kept Dot's maiden name, Aldott."

Elwood took a seat at the kitchen table, enjoying the smells of meatloaf baking, while Laura cut up the peeled sweet potatoes. He continued, "Anyway, Arany's a good kid. I haven't heard from her since she left for college, except for one note. Both she and her mother left at about the same time. She wants to please her mother more than anything else. Her lack of contact with me is probably her path of least resistance. She gave no response to my many phone calls, cards, and letters. The note I received after her first year at college apologized for not contacting me. She profusely thanked me for everything, then rambled on and on begging me not to tell her mother about her note. She also begged me not to contact her – that it made things worse with her mother. I felt helpless. I accepted her dilemma."

Laura took a step to Elwood and gave him a quick kiss on the forehead. They hugged and rocked in place. Elwood felt comfort in Laura's arms.

"She has the freedom to choose her destiny," he said, with his eyes moist. "I hope Arany eventually returns."

"I don't think I ever heard anyone else with the name of Arany. It's certainly not a common name."

"Dot said she named her after Arany's grandmother. It was a family name; they had immigrated from Eastern Europe. Arany was appropriately named. She had the same unique color of naturally blonde hair – a flaxen yellow, with an almost metallic glowing sheen – as her grandmother."

"Is Arany still at college?"

"She just graduated from Pacific Coast College, after the winter semester, with a major in environmental protectionism. I think the major was to appease her mother. Not sure how it'll help her get a job. But she was always quite smart and savvy, as well as filled with common sense. She was drawn to math and science. In particular, she got along quite well with Silas in church – they talked of puzzles as well as science stuff. He pulled strings to get her a summer job at VMI in the chemistry department while she was in high school." Elwood beamed at his memories and closed his eyes. "She had a charming smile; she curled her left upper lip to indicate a playful displeasure. To go along with her flaxen hair, she had turquoise-colored eyes, a unique shade of blue-green."

"Smart as well as beautiful, quite a combination," Laura smiled.

Elwood turned white, almost as if he had seen a ghost. He nervously combed through his hair with his hands. He gasped, "I just remembered. When Arany was in middle school, she wrote a history paper on the use of the base eight system, instead of the decimal system, in some ancient civilization. They just counted with their eight fingers, ignoring their thumbs. They considered their numbers sacred – called them their Blessed Eight."

"Oh, wow – another Blessed Eight," Laura repeated. She involuntarily grabbed for the pendant on her necklace, and added, "Coincidentally!"

They smiled at each other.

Elwood stared at Laura with incredulity on his face. He muttered, "But then I also remember a term paper she wrote for English in high school. Its title – the concept of infinity." He reached for his pendant.

Chapter Twenty Three
EIGHT

Several weeks later Pastor Martin publicized the title for his upcoming sermon on the Twin Falls Presbyterian Church sign next to the Jonah-and-the-whale sculpture. "8," the announcement said.

In his initial preparations that week, he sat at his office desk with Barney at his feet. His mind kept mulling over and over his calling from Jesus – *Spread My Word of the Blessed Eight.* For the longest time, he couldn't concentrate on organizing his sermon. He prayed – *Provide me with direction . . . How am I to spread Your Word of the Blessed Eight?* He fretted – *Certainly, it's more than through a sermon, or a series of sermons . . . Jesus has entrusted me with much, so much more will be expected from me . . . But I'm just clueless how to proceed.* He rocked back and forth in his office chair. He sighed – *No answer!* He laughed – *Maybe a busy signal?* Barney jumping onto the office's easy chair broke his chain of thought.

Elwood grabbed his pendant tightly in his hand. The coincidental gifts of matching gold necklaces, the Blessed Eight on a cross given by the widow Reynolds to Laura paired with infinity on an identical cross given to him by Silas, served to confirm his calling. He looked upward – *The message is clear . . . Follow Jesus' Blessed Eight and your rebirth is everlasting, in this life and the next.* Then, he frowned – *But I haven't spread His Word very effectively . . . I have to do more than distributing wooden crosses with upright eight on one side and sideways eight on the flip side . . . That's only a first step.* He jumped from his chair, smiling – *Maybe I need to start a new church, the Church of the Blessed Eight.* He quickly shook off this thought – *Breaking the church into smaller pieces isn't the right approach . . . Instead, I need to unite all churches under the banner of the Blessed Eight . . . But, I'm not a charismatic leader.* He kneeled on the floor and prayed – *Here I am, Lord . . . Guide me!*

Barney barked. He stared pitifully at Elwood. The clock read a few minutes after noon; time for Barney's snack and some outside time. A blank piece of paper still sat on Elwood's desk pad.

† † †

This Sunday Pastor Martin bellowed a question to the congregation: "If you could teach only one thing as a Christian minister, what would you teach?" He paused, giving his flock a moment to think about their answer.

"Perhaps you'd teach the Ten Commandments, the rules that God gave Moses for his people to follow. This list of 'Thou shalt nots' told his people what not to do, the evils to avoid. But the apostle Paul preached to early Christians not to blindly follow the laws, for the people tended to follow the letter, as interpreted by the priests, instead of the spirit of the laws."

He looked upward, then smiled, "Perhaps instead of the Ten Commandments, you would teach 'Do unto others how you would want them to do to you' – what Jesus considered the greatest commandment. Another law, but at least it replaces 'what not to do' with 'what to do.' I'm sure the disciples wondered whether Jesus could be more specific. Are there any limits? Do unto me by giving me money." He gave a half-laugh.

He paused. Less than two minutes into his sermon and Ed Painter had already checked his watch twice.

"Perhaps you'd teach the way to everlasting life is through Jesus Christ," Elwood continued. "But even the disciples wanted more guidance – what is the Way through Jesus Christ?" He roared, "I contend today that the one lesson you need is '8.' The one thing to teach is the Blessed Eight – the eight Beatitudes of Jesus in which he describes the eight virtues of being a Christian."

At that moment, eight tee-shirt clad individuals burst through the sanctuary's side door. Music poured from the speakers as the eight whooped and yelled, gathering in the front of the sanctuary. Each wore a cross necklace with an eight and an infinity symbol on opposite sides. Their matching tee shirts read "8" in the front and the same-sized sideways "8," the infinity symbol, on the back. Below the "8" were the words "HUMBLE, RIGHTEOUS, KIND, LOVING, MERCIFUL, FAITHFUL, PEACEFUL, HOPEFUL" in smaller font; and below the infinity were the words "JOYFUL PATH." The eight people paired into couples in a square, as Elwood called to square dance music. They circled round, they promenaded, they swung their partners, they do-si-doed, they allemanded, and they stomped their feet to the upbeat song of "May the Circle be Unbroken." As quickly as the four couples entered, they danced out the side door.

Pastor Martin returned to the pulpit. "The basic unit of a square dance is eight. Jesus gave eight characteristics of a person who follows his way with his Beatitudes. These eight were given in His Sermon on the Mount, coincidentally delivered during the eight-day Feast of the Tabernacles. This Blessed Eight defined Christian love, defined what we 'ought to do.' It was a simple, but unique, message, summarized by the apostle Paul in his teaching in his first letter to the Corinthians, chapter thirteen, describing Christian love."

Elwood enumerated each of the traits described in each of the Beatitudes. Poor in spirit meant to be humble, to realize that all gifts and blessings come from the grace of God. Those who mourn described those who desired to do right; they mourned our sinful nature which led to a desire to seek truth. The meek were the kind and gentle; they were obedient and submissive to the will of God. The righteous sought to fulfill God's will in their hearts, not simply to observe the law, but as an expression of Christian love. Merciful people had a loving disposition to those in distress – compassion and forgiveness. The pure of heart were free of selfish intentions and self-seeking desires.

The peacemaker displayed not only friendship to others but also preserved peace between God and man. And finally, those persecuted for the sake of righteousness were those who stand up for their belief in God and Jesus Christ leading to a hope for everlasting life. In each case, Elwood provided more explanations, but summarized the eight by holding up the front of the tee shirt – humble, righteous, kind, loving, merciful, faithful, peaceful, and hopeful. These were the eight characteristics of a Christian, the way to emulate Jesus Christ.

"You're never going to achieve perfection, you're not going to achieve a sin-free life," roared Elwood. "You're always going to fall short. But it's about your mind-set; you want to take on these characteristics of an ideal Christian."

At this point, Elwood paused. Ed Painter was still checking his watch every minute. Reese Coleman slept soundly in his designated seat on the back pew. Contagious yawns spread throughout the congregation. In the third row, Faye Tolley and Blanche Linkenhoker had been whispering to each other since the square dance ended.

Trying to regain everyone's attention, Elwood thundered, "Here in the middle of my sermon, let me read today's Scripture from the Gospel of John 8:1-11." He recited the story of the adulterer presented to Jesus by the Jewish teachers. The law told them to stone her. He picked up a walnut-sized stone setting on his pulpit. "They tried to trap Jesus into contradicting the law, to show mercy. Instead he announced, 'whoever is without sin let him throw the first stone.'" Elwood mimicked a baseball pitcher. He pretended he was getting ready to throw the stone out into the congregation. His mind momentarily flipped – *Amos Muterspaw would throw the stone.* But Elwood stopped mid-stride and put down the stone. "A remarkable response from Jesus – though, how does this fit in with this sermon? Neither the woman nor the potential stoners possessed the characteristics described in the Beatitudes."

He picked up the stone again and juggled it from hand to hand. "But Jesus saw a woman who wanted to conquer her sin, who had a good heart and wanted to start a new life in which she followed the eight Beatitudes. Jesus directed her to another chance, a rebirth. 'Go and do not sin anymore.' You'll have a rebirth if you're willing to ask God to forgive sin. Why does eight signify rebirth? The baptismal fount has eight sides; Noah was the 8th person to step off the ark onto the earth to start a new life; the resurrection of Jesus happened on Easter on the first, or in another sense eighth, day of the week. Eight in the bible signifies rebirth, renewal, and resurrection. Like octaves in music, after middle C, the 8th note begins the musical cycle anew. Eight represents a new beginning, a new order, a new creation with Jesus. What is your prize for this rebirth following the eight Beatitudes? It's joy – a joyful path to heaven."

Elwood scanned the congregation – even more yawns. Ed Painter now stared at his watch. Harry Whitmer's head tilted backwards and his lips moved silently; he was counting carved acorns in the sanctuary ceiling's woodwork.

"Not only is this a new birth, but it's also man's true born-again event when he's resurrected from the dead into eternal life," Elwood proclaimed. "Turn eight on its side and you get the infinity symbol; you get life forever, joy forever. Both the eight and the infinity symbol have no beginning and no ending."

On cue, the organist played "I Danced in the Morning," an upbeat hymn that tracked the life of Jesus Christ. Once again the eight square dancers burst through the side door. One set of four danced in a line down the right side of the sanctuary, while the other four danced and skipped a line down the other side to the rear. Elwood bellowed, "Grab onto the chain as they pass by your pew. And dance, dance, dance. Follow the life of Jesus on a joyful path to a forever life." People grabbed the hand of the last person in the chain. It extended from the side aisle, then merged into a double chain coming down the center aisle. Reese Coleman woke and joined in. Even Joe Clemmer grabbed onto the chain and slowly scooted along in his walker.

The singing and dancing ended with the final chorus of the song. Everyone stood in the aisles of the sanctuary. Elwood ripped off his tie and dress shirt, exposing his tee shirt matching the eight and infinity of the square dancers. He raised his arms to the sky, "As the hymn says, Jesus is the life that'll never,

never die, and he'll live in you, if you'll live in Him. Live your life in accord to the Blessed Eight, the eight Beatitudes . . . focus on love . . . it'll lead to your rebirth into the way of Jesus . . . the joyful path to forever life in Heaven. What a joy . . . it's a reason to dance. From the Beatitudes to the cross to everlasting life. Wear your necklaces and now your tee shirts – upright eight and sideways eight. Amen."

† † †

That night, Elwood was sullen. He shared his concerns with Laura as they sat watching the nightly news after dinner. "I think I missed my target today with my sermon."

"Come now, Elwood. Everyone enjoyed the dancing and music – it spread lots of joy."

"My point exactly," Elwood whined. "After the service, everyone complimented me about the sermon, but more specifically about the choreography – the square dancing, music, line dancing, entertainment, and happiness."

"So . . ."

"They missed the underlying and more important message – they had to strive for the eight virtues of a Christian, to be reborn in Jesus to attain this everlasting joy," he sighed. "I failed in explaining the importance of the Blessed Eight. Most people were bored; I even had Harry Whitmer counting acorns well before the end of the sermon."

"Don't be so hard on yourself," she nuzzled into his shoulder.

"Remember God gave a similar call to John Petticrew through the portal. He was called to spread the Word of the Blessed Eight, but evidently never acted on it beyond his own family."

"I think you may be reading too much between the lines," she spoke softly to him. "He might have done more."

"Within a few months, he lost his family in a horrendous disaster and died a broken man. I worry that I may likewise lose everything if I fail – after all, much is expected of those who are given much. Most of the people didn't listen to the message, only to the theatrics."

Laura thought for a few moments before she responded, "Maybe they actually heard more than you thought."

Elwood sighed, "I'm reminded of a story I read this past week about FDR. He was tired of meet-and-greet events at the White House and complained that no one ever listened or paid attention to what he said – he could say anything. So he decided to do an experiment. As the people would file by, he would shake their hand, smile, and mumble, 'Good evening, I murdered my grandmother this morning.' The people would file by, shake his hand, smile, and robotically respond, 'Fine, and how are you;' 'So pleased to meet you;' and 'It's a wonderful day.' That's what I felt like today, everyone was simply nodding in agreement about the eight Beatitudes, the Blessed Eight. I could've said anything. How can I do better?"

Laura gave Elwood a gentle hug. "Be patient. Listen to God. Be silent, as Silas' clever riddle preached. You tell me about your prayers, but they sound like monologues. Perhaps you need some silence in your prayers to give God a chance to respond."

"Who's the preacher here?" Elwood laughed and gave Laura a big bear hug.

Laura whispered in his ear: "Today in Sunday school, Hansford Cash recounted the old adage – If God brings you to it, He'll bring you through it."

Chapter Twenty Four
HOMECOMINGS

During the next several months, Pastor Martin continued to preach about the Blessed Eight and distribute eight-and-infinity cross necklaces. He penned the article "The Power of Eight" for the magazine *Christian Thought Today*, which resulted in a handful of invitations to speak at churches and conferences. He also spent many hours organizing a workshop on the subject at Twin Falls Presbyterian Church. Less than thirty participants registered and even less showed up. His spotlight on the Blessed Eight just wouldn't take off. He agonized over his lack of appeal in delivering the message. Prayer helped, but the concern – *Jesus expecting more from him because he has been given more; and him not living up to His expectations* – continually nagged him.

And nary a week passed by that the Presbyter, Royster Van Guiden, or one of his minions didn't pester Elwood on the phone or stop by for an unscheduled visit. Elwood kept getting assigned to every inconsequential time-consuming Presbytery committee or study. At every opportunity, the Presbytery showed its underlying displeasure with him and Twin Falls Presbyterian Church for not sharing Silas' gift of ten million dollars with them. But, without fanfare, Twin Falls had already started to allocate several gifts locally and regionally to the needy. They also pledged long-term support to a local couple starting a mission in Albania. In addition, Laura's program on supplying meals for the elderly and shut-ins had also blossomed.

Laura and Elwood drew closer together, making plans for their wedding at Twin Falls Presbyterian Church.

† † †

The 8th of August was a typical Shenandoah Valley summer day – hot, hazy, and humid. That morning Elwood, Troy, Harry, Ed, Preston, and Charlie guided an armada of pick-up trucks moving furniture and boxes from Laura's rented house to the parsonage. Meanwhile, the ladies of the church escorted Laura to a beauty salon.

At the appointed time, Laura and Elwood strolled from the parsonage to the church. Barney scampered alongside. For the first time in his life, Elwood wore a tuxedo – white with a yellow vest and bow tie. Barney sported a matching bow tie on his collar. Laura looked absolutely enchanting in her simple, light yellow, knee-length dress. Both bore their cross necklaces. Elwood never saw the splendor of Nettle Mountain or the hawk on the church steeple during that walk; he was totally mesmerized by the beauty of Laura.

Barney sat next to Elwood in the front of the sanctuary. When Barney heard a change in the music and saw Laura enter from the narthex, he dashed to escort her down the center aisle. As Rev. M. L. Stokes, Jr., who officiated the ceremony, later joked: "This wedding was a first; not only was a dog an attendant in a wedding, but also the attendant for both the groom and the bride."

Rev. Stokes opened the ceremony with a prayer, then misspoke in welcoming the guests to a baptism instead of a wedding. The audience giggled, as Rev. Stokes sputtered to correct himself. Elwood and Laura radiated joy, focused on each other and oblivious to the gaffe. Elwood vowed to Laura – If you live to be a hundred, I want to live to be a hundred minus one day, so I never have to live without you – paraphrasing a quote from Winnie the Pooh. He also promised to be the right partner for Laura for the rest of his life. Laura pledged to Elwood that although he wasn't her first love, he'd be her last love.

They saw in each other everything that was good and beautiful. The best times of their lives were yet to come.

The subsequent reception featured a barbeque dinner, with entertainment by Hansford, Preston, and Harry on the guitar, fiddle, and bass respectively. Hansford also arranged for the caterer to present the bride and groom with a burnt and smoking pot of barbeque, in order for them to start their marriage in the same manner as their first date. A blaring smoke alarm accompanied its delivery. He wisely decided, though, against releasing a snake at the festivities.

Laura and Barney moved into the parsonage with Elwood. Laura had only been renting and had no real financial assets – and, on the other hand, no debts. At one time she and her first husband owned their own home, but it had long since been sold to pay for his extensive medical bills. Neither did Elwood have a real nest egg – his savings depleted to nothingness by tuition and alimony. Both knew that God would provide.

Two days after their wedding, Elwood pulled into the parsonage's driveway after a late afternoon counseling visit to the struggling Clifton family. It was a hot day; the Clifton house had no air conditioning. He was tired and sweaty, and glad to see that Laura's car was already in the driveway. He heard Barney's barking announcing his arrival.

Elwood opened the door, only to see a girl running full gallop down the hallway toward him. About four feet from him, the girl started her jump. Elwood only had time to drop his papers, brace himself, and open his arms. A smiling Arany was quickly enveloped into his arms. His eyes moistened. Each whispered how much they had missed and loved each other. Laura stood back and admired the joyous reunion.

"Daddy, can I stay with y'all for a time. Laura already said it's OK. I'm so sorry that I wasn't here for your wedding. But I didn't know. Mother tells me nothing. I like Laura. I'm still looking for a job. I missed you so much," Arany rambled on nonstop.

"Slow down, Arany – of course you can stay," Elwood looked into her eyes with overwhelming happiness. "We have a lot of catching up."

Arany felt like a prodigal daughter. And Elwood felt the joy of the prodigal daughter's father. Laura prepared a feast that night – Arany's favorite – roast beef with gravy, mashed potatoes, creamed peas, and blackberry cobbler with ice cream.

Over dinner Arany told Laura and her father that she'd finally confronted her mother. She wanted to live her own life. The final straw for Arany had been the discovery at graduation that Dot had skimmed from the monthly room and board money Elwood sent, forcing her to make ends meet by taking an extra part-time job. Dot was unapologetic, only furious about losing part of her income. Now, her mother's wrath was being further fueled by her returning home to Elwood. But Arany resolved not to continue living under Dot's thumb.

"I hope mother doesn't show up here," Arany admitted. "I'm hoping her new boyfriend keeps her occupied for a while."

Laura noted the sincerity and humbleness with which Arany spoke. Her long, flaxen, and golden hair was stunning, and her blue-green eyes picturesque; she was as beautiful as Elwood had described. She had a delightful personality.

Laura smiled, "Elwood and I confronted your mother's ire during her short visit a couple months ago."

"She does have a way of acting out her anger," Elwood confided. "I expect even more rage and demands in future phone calls."

"During the times I visited mother, she also kept dragging me off to see tree-huggers," Arany groaned. "She wanted me to scrap Christianity and become a Secular Humanist like her. I finally couldn't keep up with the façade of her secular humanists; I needed to return to my God."

"And I'm also glad you returned home," Elwood smiled, "to both your fathers."

"By the way, y'know what Silas told me?" Arany grinned. "Secular Humanism is a non-prophet organization."

Laura and Elwood chuckled.

Arany couldn't talk fast enough; she wanted to catch up on all four years in one night. "By the way, I did keep in contact with Silas. Mother didn't say I couldn't, but only because I didn't ask for permission. She would've thrown a hissy fit if she knew. Silas kept me somewhat informed about you, daddy. I was so worried about you for the first couple years when you were alone. Silas said you weren't doing that well. Then I hadn't heard from Silas for quite a while; and I found out he died several months ago. I'm just so sorry. Silas was like an anchor for my faith."

"Indeed Silas was special to say the least," Elwood agreed.

"And Silas kept encouraging me to come home. I was just so worried that you wouldn't forgive me for turning my back on you. But Silas told me about the special mathematical equation – about one plus three equals four."

Elwood nodded, "One of his favorites."

"Yep, he told everyone about that equation," Laura laughed. "One cross plus three nails equals four given."

"I still remember the last joke that Silas told me," Arany added. "When the cannibals ate the missionary, they got a taste of religion. He loved his puns."

They all retreated to the living room, leaving the cleaning of dinner dishes for later. Laura and Arany relaxed on the couch with Barney nuzzled between them, getting belly rubs from one side, then rolling over to get them from the other. Elwood sat in his recliner and observed – *Barney likes Arany . . . Problem solved of who'll keep Barney during the upcoming honeymoon.*

Arany continued talking with Laura and Elwood late into the night. She concentrated on her college experiences. Even though her major was environmental protectionism, a major stipulated by her mother, she took enough courses to have been a chemistry major. Her grandmother, who she was named after, was also a chemist. Arany helped a professor on a research project determining the chemical basis for how the skin of an octopus changed color. The chromatophore in its skin detects light and responds to it. No eyes or brain are required. The octopus can become all hues between yellow and brown. It not only camouflages itself but also communicates its emotions – mad, calm, and afraid, among others – by its color.

Elwood thought – *Octopus, an eight-legged creature! Eight – coincidence?*

Arany also shared she'd enrolled, unbeknownst to her mother, in courses in religions and Christianity. Rising from the couch to finally part for her bedroom, she asked her daddy whether she could work with the youth at Twin Falls, just like Silas mentored her when she was a pre-teen.

† † †

The next morning, before Laura and Elwood had risen, Arany had already finished the Sudoku and some of the word games on the puzzle page of *The Roanoke Times*. She was working on the crossword puzzle, when Elwood grabbed a cup of coffee.

"Hey, daddy, this is pretty nifty. The clue for 5-across is 'Noon on a sundial' and is three letters. So the answer is 'X-I-I.' Then, 5-down's clue is 'Picture of health?' The word has to start with an 'X' . . . and it has four letters. The clue ends with a question mark – you know what that means?"

"Silas taught me well. It means the answer is clever or funny. It also means I probably won't understand the clue." Elwood took a seat at the kitchen table and sipped the hot coffee.

"So what's the answer?" Arany chuckled.

"Give me a break. I haven't had my coffee yet."

"Let's go with 'X-R-A-Y.'"

Elwood forced a smile to complement his eye roll.

A few moments later, Arany blurted, "It looks like the puzzle has even more words starting with the letter 'X.' Pretty slick. 45-across is 'X-E-N-O-N' as the answer to 'Noble gas.' You'll like 45-down, daddy. It's four letters and has to start with 'X' . . . with the clue 'Opening day?' The clue ends with a question mark; once again it means –"

"Clever or funny," Elwood interjected. He took a sip of coffee and shrugged, "X-day."

"You can do better," Arany shook her head.

"That's as good as it gets this early in the morning," Elwood replied.

"Well, it looks like 'X-M-A-S' will fit," Arany giggled.

"Oh!" Elwood got up from the table to get a coffee refill. He gave Arany a quick kiss on the cheek as he passed by. "I guess cleverness, like beauty, is in the eye of the beholder."

Arany stuck her pencil behind her ear and picked up a slim paperback called *Pun Phun*. She laughed, "Silas told me to keep your mind alert with puzzles, daddy . . . that you really enjoy them."

Laura's entering the kitchen distracted Elwood. She grabbed a few eggs and butter from the refrigerator and a fry pan from the cabinet. Elwood stole a kiss, then returned to his coffee.

"Hey, daddy, you know – two silk worms named Jim and Bill had a race. Guess who won?"

"A 50-50 chance in getting it right," Elwood shook his head. "Let's say Bill."

"They ended in a tie," laughed Arany. "Here's another one – two hats were hanging on a hat rack in the hallway. Guess what one hat said to the other?"

Elwood looked at Laura who was already fast at work at the stove. "Why do I feel like I'm back in room 79 of Faithful Care?"

"The hat said, 'You stay here, I'll go on a head.'"

† † †

Laura and Elwood enjoyed their five-day honeymoon to New York City. They had time to relish each other's company, and took in some shows and the sites. On their last day there, they decided to pay their respects to Silas at his gravesite in suburban New York City.

It was a huge cemetery. They stopped by its office to get directions to the grave. Once they reached the tombstone, they looked at each other, mouths agape.

The names on the tombstone – Julie Patricia Clark and Simon Silas Clark. The date of death for both – 17 December 1953.

"Well, I didn't expect that," Laura said. She turned to Elwood and shrugged, "Do I have to point out the obvious to you?"

"I see it," Elwood rubbed his chin. "The tombstone lists Silas' date of death as the same as his wife Patty's over sixty years ago. I guess they must've made a mistake. Or maybe Silas, at the time of Patty's death, considered this date his emotional death."

"Maybe," countered Laura, "but it also doesn't look like the ground has been disturbed for the past six decades either. Strange!"

"Could be that they haven't buried him yet," suggested Elwood. "Maybe the body, or rather his ashes, sits in storage."

"They've had a whole spring and summer to get it done," Laura stated. She paced in front of the stone.

"Let's stop at the cemetery office on the way back out and find out," Elwood suggested. "But let's pray before we leave."

Elwood started to kneel, but Laura's knees remained unbent.

She stared at the tombstone. "Did you notice the other oddities?"

Elwood straightened, then glanced back at the grave. "You mean that Patty and Silas both went by their middle names. I never even realized that Silas' first name was actually Simon."

Laura pointed at the engraving on the stone. "Have you heard the name Simon before?" She hesitated and gasped, "And 17 December as a day of death?"

"Oh, so that is —"

"And the initials of Patty and Silas?" Laura interrupted.

"Let's see. JP . . . SSC!"

After prayer, they stopped at the cemetery's office, hoping for some answers. While Laura and Elwood stood at the counter, the caretaker checked the computer at his desk. "It says here that Simon Silas Clark was buried quite a while ago, the same time as his wife, over sixty years ago."

"No way," Laura and Elwood exclaimed together.

The caretaker pointed at the computer screen. "That's what it says."

"He just died months ago, not decades ago," Elwood corrected the caretaker. "He was a member of my congregation for many years, and a patient at my wife's nursing home for the year before he died."

"You must be mistaken." The caretaker pecked at a few computer keys. "We've been scanning obituaries and related news articles into the computer – to help families who do genealogical research. Previously such items were only kept in a manila folder or file. In this case, we have an image of a news clipping – it shows that Simon Clark died at the age of twenty-two with his wife in a tragic car accident."

The caretaker motioned them to his desk. He turned his computer screen toward Laura and Elwood for them to read. They saw the relevant details: a car crash during a snowstorm on the night of 17 December 1953, the car was hit by a truck travelling at high speed, the car burst into flames. Julie (Patty) was trapped in the burning car, while Simon (Silas) was thrown from the car into a snow bank. Both were pronounced dead at the scene.

Laura and Elwood turned white as ghosts.

Elwood finally stammered to no one in particular. "If Silas died over sixty years ago, who's the Silas I've known for these sixty years?"

"Or if we've known the real Silas, who's buried in the grave?" responded Laura.

"And if Silas' grave is a fake, is Patty's as well? Did both die or did both live? Who, if anyone, is buried there? I'm confused," Elwood rambled.

"And what's the connection between the real or fake Silas and the widow Reynolds? After all, they had matching necklaces . . . and her vanity license plate. Then all the other coincidences," Laura grabbed Elwood's arm.

"I have no idea what you're talking about," the caretaker laughed. "But the two of you aren't the first to inquire about Simon Silas Clark this year."

Both Laura and Elwood snapped to attention.

"I have a note on the computer that an attorney by the name of Dawes stopped by in January to scatter some ashes at that gravesite," the caretaker said matter-of-factly.

"You're kidding."

"Yeah, now that I see the note, it's jogged my memory. We usually require ashes to be buried, but this guy had special permission from management to scatter the ashes. And I had to accompany him to the site. He was well-dressed. He scattered the ashes in a figure eight on top of the gravesite. Then turned 90 degrees and made another figure eight sideways across the gravesite. All the time he kept mumbling something. I thought he was loco. I seem to always remember the really weird ones."

Both Laura and Elwood grasped their pendants.

The caretaker scratched his forehead. "Then, the guy showed me the urn and asked whether that looked like half the ashes; he took off with the remaining half. Nice set of wheels – a bright red Lexus, as I remember."

Laura and Elwood looked at each other, speechless.

"One last thing," the caretaker jumped from his chair and opened the bottom drawer of a dilapidated file cabinet. He pulled Joe the sock monkey from the paper chaos in the rear of the drawer. "The crazy guy also wanted to bury this stuffed animal at the gravesite. I told him 'No way,' that instead I'd bury it in a filing cabinet. You wanna take it off my hands."

With tears misting her eyes, Laura reached for Joe. "He needs to come home."

Elwood pulled his cell phone from his pocket and dialed Dick Dawes. Throughout the conversation, Laura observed Elwood shaking his head and thrumming his fingers on the car's dashboard. She held Joe tightly in her arms.

After Elwood got off the phone, he looked at Laura. "First, he said he can't confirm or deny anything as Silas' lawyer, because of client confidentiality. But then he laughed and disclosed that he could tell me Silas' estate paid for two trips, one to New York City and another to near Collierstown. He took both trips in his red Lexus. He continued to chuckle throughout our conversation – it was quite frustrating. He ended by saying Silas can even reach out to us beyond the grave."

Chapter Twenty Five
THROWING THE BLUE STONE

Laura and Elwood settled into the routine of a married working couple upon returning from their honeymoon. Most nights their conversations drifted to the mystery surrounding Silas' burial. But no answers or explanations. They also confided with Arany their story of the Petticrew massacre, the widow Reynolds, the portal, the necklaces, and their survival in a blizzard. Meanwhile, Barney enjoyed his belly scratches, pets, and games of "catch me if you can" during these family discussions.

Joe the sock monkey found a new home guarding the "Stump Your Pastor" question box at Twin Falls Presbyterian Church. Laura deemed, and Elwood agreed, the location appropriate as a reminder of Silas.

† † †

Then, two weeks after the honeymoon, Laura and Elwood had just sat down to a lunch at the parsonage, when Barney started barking.

Ding-dinga-ding . . . Ding-dinga-ding . . . Ding-dinga-ding.

Elwood returned from answering the door with Attorney Dawes, briefcase in hand. Laura extended an invitation to join them for lunch. Although initially declining, he couldn't resist the chicken salad on toast with a side of potato salad – all, of course, freshly made.

Midway through the meal, he opened his briefcase and pulled out a file. "I insinuated in our last conversation that you might expect a surprise from Silas. Here it is – both of you are named in Silas' will or, as Silas called it, a dead giveaway. However, before I open this file, Silas demanded I ask you a question, which you have to answer correctly in order to initiate the procedure."

Laura and Elwood looked incredulously at each other. Elwood turned to Mr. Dawes and smiled, "I don't think I ever heard about taking a quiz in order to inherit something."

Mr. Dawes laughed, "This is Silas you're talking about."

"I guess we shouldn't expect anything less from him," Laura chuckled.

Mr. Dawes glanced down at the front of the file and read, "If you throw a blue stone into the Red Sea, what will it become?"

"Unbelievable," Elwood threw up his arms. "Even from his grave, he's confounding me with his wretched riddles. Do I get a hint?"

"Silas anticipated that you'd ask for a hint; so he wrote down – 'not a color.'"

Elwood sputtered, "Blue stone in Red Sea. Moses parted the Red Sea, but he had a staff not a stone. It doesn't make sense. Why is the color of the stone mentioned, but the answer doesn't have anything to do with color?" He grimaced, mumbled to himself, and reared back in the kitchen chair.

"Wet," Laura said softly and smiled.

Dick Dawes gave her a thumb up. He then delivered the news that they were named in Silas' will as the heir to his house, land, and much of his financial holdings. He handed them the file that transferred the deed to the property at Midvale, keys to the house, and a record of bank accounts – all listed as a wedding present to them. Laura noted that the date on the will was a month before she had asked Elwood out on their first date.

Elwood shook his head: "God works in mysterious ways."

"And Silas also left a trail of mysterious behavior," added Laura.

Attorney Dawes left with a full belly and a smile on his face, leaving Laura and Elwood in shock at their sudden windfall.

By that evening Laura's and Elwood's surprise morphed into concern. Both worried whether it was ethically proper for them to inherit or receive a gift from Silas. It just didn't feel right. Elwood fretted whether a preacher should receive wealth, or an inheritance, from a parishioner. He felt okay about the gift of the small "J.P." box, but all of Silas' property was another story. Faithful Care, Laura's employer, also had a policy for staff not to accept gifts from residents, although a gift from a deceased resident or estate put that in a gray area.

Arany was excited. She suggested they move into Silas' house immediately. It had more space, was in better repair, and was more modern. The current parsonage could then be used as a conference center for the church or a hang-out for the youth. She was already making an impact as an unpaid youth adviser at Twin Falls – in addition to her part-time job as quality control chemist at a local craft brewery.

Elwood called a special meeting of the ruling elders the following Sunday after worship service. He announced his and Laura's inheritance from Silas, as well as expressed his concerns.

Hansford Cash blurted, "If Silas had left his Midvale house to me, I'd already have moved in. I was his friend; you were his friend – what's the difference?"

The rest of the session nodded in agreement.

That evening, having gotten a new Frisbee, Arany played fetch with Barney in the back yard of the parsonage. Her cell phone buzzed. Her mother's number. After her mother's first few words were spoken, she realized her mother was drunk and mad – a bad combination. The conversation started badly and went quickly downhill from there. Dot demanded Arany send her money because Arany now had a job and had no expenses, mooching off Elwood. When Arany refused, Dot called her worthless just like Elwood. Arany abruptly hung up, sat down on the ground, and cried. Barney snuggled into her lap.

Moments later, the phone at the parsonage rang. Dot ranted and bellyached at Elwood about increasing his alimony payments to her. She already knew about his inheritance of Silas' property and money, and accused him of still hiding his previous ten million dollar bonanza in assets. Elwood tried to reason with her.

"You'd better pay up . . . or I warn you, you're toast . . . I can destroy you in more ways than you can imagine," she threatened.

Elwood sighed. He hung up.

† † †

Most every evening for the next week, Laura, Elwood, and Arany could be found cleaning the Midvale house and grounds. But, after much moral wrangling, Laura and Elwood decided to transfer Silas' property and money to Twin Falls Presbyterian Church. The inheritance just didn't feel right to them. They would still move to Silas' Midvale estate, but as the church's new parsonage, not their own house.

† † †

Attorney Dawes agreed to meet them at the parsonage to get the paperwork signed. He timed his visit for another lunch – he didn't think twice about joining them for a tuna salad melt over sourdough bread with a side of macaroni salad. All, of course, freshly home-made by Laura. As a special treat, she served butterscotch pie as dessert. "Just scrumptious," the lawyer moaned, as he rubbed his full stomach.

After lunch, Mr. Dawes opened his briefcase. "Silas said you might decide not to accept his gift. But, in order to do so, he said you had to answer another riddle correctly."

"Is that legal?" Elwood nearly exploded.

"Once again, this is Silas we're talking about," Mr. Dawes laughed.

"Okay, give it to us," Laura smiled.

Attorney Dawes opened an envelope and unfolded a piece of paper. He looked at Elwood. "You should be able to get this one since you're a preacher." He read, "Name the three parts to a good sermon."

"There's lots of ways I could answer that," Elwood threw up his arms. "Does Silas have a hint for me?"

"Indeed," Mr. Dawes responded, "He has one part being a good beginning and a second part being a good ending."

"Well, I guess the third part would be a good middle," Elwood smiled, relieved.

"Oh Elwood, dear," Laura chuckled, "you gotta think like Silas. The last part is that you have to keep the beginning and ending close together."

"Bingo," Dick Dawes gave Laura a pat on the back.

Elwood shook his fist in the air and roared, "I'll be up there some day with you, Silas."

Attorney Dawes agreed to drop off the retitled deeds and official financial transfers by Friday afternoon, so Elwood could present them to the church session at their scheduled meeting on Sunday following worship service. Elwood and Laura would keep the transfer a surprise until then.

Laughing, Mr. Dawes opened another envelope. Therein was a short handwritten note by Silas for Elwood and Laura. He read, "Laura and Elwood Martin must keep the 'J.P.' box and associated cardboard box, the oil painting and water color in the living room of the Midvale house, and – "

"The wedding portrait of Patty and Silas, and the picture of Lazarus being raised from the dead?" interrupted Elwood quizzically. "But why?"

Dick Dawes hesitated, then finished, "And the contents of the wall safe in the Midvale house."

"What wall safe?" exclaimed Laura and Elwood in unison.

Chapter Twenty Six
IRIDIUM

Laura and Elwood stared at the wedding portrait of Patty and Silas hanging over the fireplace mantle. The room was furnished comfortably with a sofa, love seat, and several recliners linked together by a patterned rug on its oak floors. Lamps populated several end tables; books were on shelves on one wall. The painting of the bride and groom was clearly meant to be the focal point of the room. Elwood shuffled up to the picture, stuck his face a couple inches from its bottom right corner, and squinted at the artist's signature. It was just a scrawl, illegible. He shrugged and returned to Laura, who gave him a quick kiss on his cheek.

Barney jumped up onto the love seat, his new favorite hangout in this house.

Laura stood admiring the portrait. "You know, Silas was handsome as a young man. As he told you previously, he might've given you a run for the money in courting me if he'd been younger," she teased.

Elwood smiled, "You're not supposed to be gawking at a young Silas; you're supposed to be determining why Silas wanted us to have the picture."

"And to keep an eye out for the wall safe," added Laura. "Maybe, just like in the movies, it's behind the portrait over the mantle." She pulled the picture out a bit, and looked at the wall behind it. Nothing.

They walked to the other wall to inspect the original water color of Lazarus. It was a captivating representation of Jesus greeting a resurrected Lazarus. Elwood inspected the artist's signature, while Laura stared intently at Lazarus.

"It's the same scrawl as the wedding portrait," he concluded. "The same artist painted both the portrait and this water color."

Laura kept looking at Lazarus speechless, ignoring Elwood's comment.

Elwood added, "What do you think, Laura? Is it significant that the same artist with an unreadable signature painted both pictures?"

Laura paid no heed to Elwood; she kept staring – then she removed the picture from the wall so that she could get a better view of it. Lazarus entranced her.

Elwood squealed, "The safe!" He pointed to the space on the wall where the picture had hung.

"You found it," Laura said, oddly uninterested. She momentarily looked up from the picture before resuming her stare at Lazarus. "But here's something else," she shoved the picture in front of Elwood. "Take a good look at the face of Lazarus."

Elwood's eyes opened wide. He gasped, "It's a young Silas, just like the wedding portrait."

"Why would the artist have used Silas as the model for Lazarus?"

"Sometimes people put information about the artist on the reverse side," he countered.

Laura slowly flipped the picture. A yellowed envelope was taped to the back. She opened the envelope. Two newspaper clippings slid into her hand. The first was identical to the one they read at the cemetery office outside New York City – about the car accident on 17 December 1953 taking the lives of Patty and Silas Clark. The second was a clipping from the same newspaper one day later – headline "Modern Day Lazarus." Laura and Elwood turned to each other, eyes wide open, flabbergasted. Although Silas had been pronounced dead at the scene of the accident, a medic detected a weak pulse on the drive to the morgue in the ambulance. The medic performed CPR and brought Silas back to life, as good as new. The doctors speculated that being kept cold in a snow bank after the accident acted as a preservative for his brain. Silas' first words when he awoke were "Jesus loves me!"

Elwood exhaled deeply. "Wow – what a story."

"That explains why Silas was the model for Lazarus in the water color picture," Laura stated reverently. "Why didn't he ever share this story with us?"

"Yet another of Silas' mysteries," replied Elwood.

After a few minutes of reflection, they turned their attention to the newly discovered wall safe. It was a modern Brinco safe with keypad, obviously opened by punching in a proper sequence of numbers. They then circled around to a closet on the opposite side of the wall. Elwood rapped his knuckles all around the sheetrock, while Laura estimated the wall thickness. The wall safe was embedded within a virtual fortress of steel and concrete. They returned to the keypad and glared at it.

"Guess Silas is gonna torment us some more. What's the number sequence?" Elwood groaned. He stuck his hands in his pockets and jiggled his keys.

"Perhaps you could call Sam to crack this safe as well," Laura kidded.

"Silas never left me his phone number or address. I wonder whether Sam was really his godson." He griped, "It's never easy with Silas' shenanigans. What's the puzzle this time? And yet another safe!"

Laura exclaimed, "12-17-53." She tried that sequence of numbers. Nothing.

Elwood tried 12-17-1953. Nothing.

She thought for a moment, pulled out her cell phone, then tapped in the code of 72889. Nothing. She explained, "The numbers on the phone keypad for PATTY."

"What other numbers might have significance to Silas?" he mulled.

Over the next half hour, they punched numerical sequences for birthdays, names, places, and addresses into the keypad. They finally realized a new approach would be needed; trial and error wasn't getting them anywhere. Because the safe's model and serial number were clearly identified on its front, Elwood called Brinco, the manufacturer, and explained the situation with a now deceased owner of the safe. The customer service representative transferred Elwood's call to a supervisor, who then turned the request over to management. That person conveyed the bad news to Elwood. This particular safe was specially made so there was no way to circumvent the code and to break into the safe without destroying its contents. The only thing he could tell Elwood was that all their safes had eight-digit codes. He laughed – 100 million different number sequences.

Elwood shook his hands in the air. "Geez, Silas and his safes . . . and his challenges."

"He'd be laughing at us if he were here," Laura chuckled, "perhaps even give us a frustrating clue."

"That's the truth," he admitted. "Maybe we can assign Arany the task of figuring out this puzzle. She seems to think a lot like Silas."

After spending the next hour mindlessly cleaning the kitchen while mulling over yet more potential safe combinations, Laura and Elwood decided to leave for the day. Barney jumped off his spot on the love seat, stopped in front of the fireplace, looked about the mantle, and gave a few quick barks.

"What's got Barney stirred up?" Elwood wondered.

Laura shrugged, "Maybe he's feeling ignored," as Barney scooted to her. But he turned and gave a few more barks directed to the fireplace area."

They had just closed the front door, when Laura got Elwood to turn back and unlock it. She hurried back into the living room and wiggled the wedding portrait off its hanger. She turned over the painting. A notecard was taped to its back. Elwood pulled it off, and they both stared at it –

$IrCl_2$
IrO_4^+
$Ir_4(CO)_{12}$
IrF_6

$$Ir(CO)Cl(H)_2(P[C_2H_5]_3)_2$$
$$Ir(mesityl)_3O$$
$$IrTe_2$$
$$IrO_4$$

Elwood sighed, "Chemical gibberish?"

Laura and Elwood showed the notecard to Arany when she returned home from her job that night. Arany pointed out that "Ir" is the chemical symbol for iridium, a precious metal like platinum and gold. Further, she guessed that Silas with his metallurgy background might be fascinated by the metal, but the eight chemical formulas were compounds and complexes.

"Interesting?" Arany pondered. "What's Silas trying to tell us?"

Saturday afternoon, Elwood thought it strange to get a phone call from Hansford Cash informing him that an emergency meeting of the session was in progress and requesting his presence. Hansford would not say anything more – after all, Elwood realized he was supposed to be present as moderator for all meetings of the ruling elders of the church. He wrapped both his paint brush and roller in plastic. Re-painting a bedroom of Silas' Midvale home a gray "moon-glow" color would have to wait as he rushed over to Twin Falls Presbyterian Church. He left Arany painting the trim in another bedroom. Laura was vacuuming and cleaning the pantry. Barney, as usual, perched on the love seat in the living room. On his way out the door, Elwood picked up the new deed to the Midvale property to give to the session – perhaps they wouldn't have to meet on Sunday.

Within a few minutes, Elwood opened the door of the church conference room to find Hansford, Peggy, Preston, Alice Jane, Ed, and Etta congregated around the table along with the Presbyter and Associate Presbyter from Roanoke. When he walked in, the heads of the six ruling elders looked down on the table. The Presbyter, Rev. Royster Van Guilder, scowled and directed Elwood to take a seat. Elwood quickly surmised that trouble brewed.

Rev. Van Guilder abruptly announced to Elwood that the ruling elders of the church had just voted to dismiss him as pastor of Twin Falls. He would receive his salary for one year as severance.

Elwood scanned around the table; all heads remained down – still no eye contact. He shook his head and mumbled, "Why?"

Rev. Van Guilder responded, "It's come to our attention that you used undue influence and pressure on one of your parishioners, Silas Clark, to inherit his estate. There are other issues as well. You stand accused of emotionally abusing your ex-wife Dot, and, in the privacy of your home, of disavowing the divinity of Jesus. Definitely not the behavior this or any church wants for its preacher."

"None of that's true!" Elwood exclaimed, much too loudly.

"We have evidence," Rev. Van Guilder shouted back defiantly.

"Not very good evidence, because it's not true," Elwood sighed. "It all sounds like something a vengeful ex-wife would spew."

"We can't reveal all our sources – but they're credible. Your ex-wife provided a notarized, sworn statement. She said she didn't mind being identified as a complainant," the Presbyter stated.

"Or it's what you want to be credible. Dot is mad and would say anything to bring me down. Just because she swore to it, doesn't mean it's true."

"Be that as it may, you've been replaced as the minister of Twin Falls by our Associate Presbyter, Rev. Rohrbaugh."

"What're my options for appeal? I've been railroaded," yelled Elwood.

"The Presbytery and its Judicial Council will decide your future within the church, and whether you will work in a UAPC church again – but the session has already decided to replace you here. It's their decision. According to UAPC regulations, you and your family can't attend services here. It's a clean break."

"I'm sure it was only the session's decision after you browbeat them to make it," snarled Elwood.

Still none of the six ruling elders would look up from the table. They remained mute.

Elwood shook his head, "I'm sure this also has nothing to do with the ten million dollars that Twin Falls has in its bank account. Put your own person in charge of that endowment."

"You should leave," Rev. Van Guilder scowled.

"By the way," Elwood turned to Hansford, "here's a copy of the deed to Silas' property at Midvale in the name of the church. Also, all his other financial accounts have been transferred to the church. The deed's already been filed at the courthouse. It's a gift from Laura and me to Twin Falls." He growled, "Obviously, I must have exerted undue influence on Silas in order for us to inherit his property, only to turn around and donate it to the church. It's all so logical." He turned to the Presbyter and sarcastically added, "I'm also sure you checked with Dick Dawes, Silas' lawyer, to confirm this alleged coercion."

Hansford glared at Rev. Van Guilden, "Was Attorney Dawes one of your sources?"

"It doesn't matter," he evasively answered. "It's a done deal. The vote's been taken; it will not be undone."

"We'll be out of the parsonage within the week." Elwood angrily stomped out of the meeting, slamming the door behind him.

Hansford handed the deed to Peggy. She gasped, "What've we done?"

† † †

In the middle of a brush stroke, Arany screamed, "I got it!" She'd been listening to music on her head set, as she painted the trim of a bedroom white – all the while pondering *Why iridium?* Recalling a brief moment in her Advanced Inorganic Chemistry class from the prior year precipitated connections in her mind. The professor reported that a recent study had identified new oxidation states, or valences, of iridium. It extended the known oxidation states of iridium from 0 to +9 (as well as a couple of negative ones), the only element to have that property. 0 to 9 were the numbers on the safe's keypad; the oxidation state of iridium in each of the listed eight compounds or complexes must be the code. Tossing her paint brush aside, she pulled the notecard from her back pocket and determined the oxidation numbers for iridium in each compound or complex in Silas' list – deciphering the numerical sequence: 2-9-0-6-3-5-4-8.

Arany ran downstairs, skipping every other step, yelling for Laura to join her at the safe. Barney also came running. While Laura watched, Arany punched in the numbers. The LED light blinked green and the electronic lock sprung the safe's door open. Laura and Arany jumped up and down and hugged in eager anticipation. Laura suggested they wait until Elwood came back – they looked at each other: "Nope, let's do it now! We can't wait."

There were three large, unlabeled, manila envelopes in the safe. Arany reached into the safe, touched the top envelope, then slowly retreated her hand.

She laughed, "No matter how much you push the envelope, it'll still be stationary."

Laura shook her head and rolled her eyes. She grabbed the top envelope and opened it. A house key along with some legal papers spilled out. They unfolded the papers – the will of Judith Petticrew Reynolds, and the deed to her house on Sycamore Valley Road and surrounding 196.97 acres signed over to Laura and Elwood Martin. The will also left her bank account with over $100,000 therein, the contents of her house, and most other worldly possessions to Laura and Elwood Martin.

Both Laura and Arany were momentarily speechless.

Arany finally asked, "Is this the widow Reynolds?"

Laura nodded.

"I thought you only met her one time. Why would she leave you and daddy her farm and a boatload of money? And why would her will be in Silas' safe?"

Laura shrugged her shoulders. She turned to the last page of the deed transfer – dated the same day as Silas' will, the month before she and Elwood had even gone out together. She then spotted the signature scrawl on the will – identical to the ones on the portrait painting and the water color. The widow, Judith Petticrew Reynolds, had been the artist.

Laura was still in a state of shock when Arany opened the second envelope in the stack. A key tumbled out of this one as well. Arany pulled out a car title for a 1992 Buick Roadmaster. She pointed out the transfer section on the title to Laura – the car had been transferred to Arany Aldott.

Arany stammered, "She . . . she didn't even know me. Wh . . . why?"

Laura stared at the paper. "It's parked in front of her house."

"An old car," Arany laughed. "The two of you get land, house, and money; and I just get an old station wagon."

"I'm not sure when it was last moved. It's kinda beat up," Laura laughed. "At least you have a set of wheels now, no more borrowing ours."

"But why . . . why? I never met her. Why would she leave me her car?"

Laura collected the last envelope from the safe. She pulled two single sheets of paper from it. They quickly identified two birth certificates – one for Simon Silas Clark, and another for Judith Petticrew Clark, same date of birth to the same parents, Calvin Ambrose Clark and Elizabeth Petticrew (nee Reynolds) Clark. The widow Reynolds was the twin sister of Simon, or Silas. The coincidence hit Laura – both of them born and died on the same days.

At that moment, Elwood walked like a zombie through the doorway of the Midvale house to see two excited women.

Despair collided with delight.

Chapter Twenty Seven
A STONE NOT THROWN

A disheartened Pastor Elwood Martin pulled his car into the spot behind the old Buick Roadmaster. He closed his eyes and sighed before exiting. His first sight, though, was a spectacular view of Hog Back Mountain rising on the horizon behind the widow Reynolds' house. Perhaps he had simply traded Nettle for Hog Back Mountain to welcome him every day. As Laura circled around the car, he caught her hand.

"Are you up to the challenge of an old farmhouse?" He forced an upbeat smile.

Laura returned the smile and nodded.

Barney spotted a feral tabby cat stalking its next meal in a nearby ditch next to the road. Barney took off as fast as his stubby little legs could take him; he quickly realized the futility of his chase as the cat loped into the brush. Nose to the ground, he moseyed back to Elwood, Laura, and Arany along the gravel Sycamore Valley Road, but made numerous detours with every new scent.

"Hardly any traffic along this road for Barney to contend with," Laura commented.

"And the cars can't go too fast on this gravel," Elwood agreed.

"We're in the middle of the nowhere," Arany laughed, "rocks, sycamores, lots of other trees, and more rocks everywhere." She glared at the Roadmaster, then walked to it and swept her hand over its hood. "And I get one old car. What a windfall?"

Elwood and Laura started to walk to the house, while Arany kicked at her car's back tire. It was near flat. Suddenly, she smiled, "Hey, daddy, you know what happened when the wheel was invented?"

Elwood stopped in mid-stride.

"It caused a revolution." Arany's self-induced laugh initiated laughter from all.

The next week was hectic for Laura, Elwood, and Arany. They worked on multiple fronts – boxing and moving personal objects and furniture from the parsonage into temporary storage, sprucing up the widow Reynolds' house and grounds, and meeting with contractors to formulate plans for modernizing the bathrooms, kitchen, and heating system.

As per the instructions of the Presbyter and their new pastor, Rev. Rohrbaugh, previously the Associate Presbyter, the Twin Falls congregation essentially shunned the three of them. There were two exceptions, Troy Montgomery and Harry Whitmer, the robust young lumberjack and farmer respectively, who volunteered their trucks and strong backs to help with their move. Both were vocal in their support for Pastor Martin and in their scorn for the Presbytery. The rest of the Twin Falls membership had been thrown into total disarray by the espoused revelations about their minister and the takeover of its church by the Valley Presbytery.

Laura worried about Elwood. She knew his anguish at being fired as pastor for no good reason – the lies, deceit, and greed of others. On the other hand, he fretted that being married to an ex-pastor wasn't what Laura had expected. But instead of driving them apart, their situation drove them closer together. It's almost as though Silas and his sister, the widow Reynolds, anticipated all these happenings. As one door closed, another one opened – not just metaphorically, but also in reality. Elwood's concerns soon changed to fulfilling his call to spread the word of the Blessed Eight without a church. Laura suggested supportively he use the next year as a paid sabbatical to plan the way.

Barney enjoyed his new digs, lots of fresh places to investigate. He continued to play hide and seek with the feral cat; the cat would come into view, taunt Barney, then run and hide. Another relatively tame white, fuzzy cat also showed up, but refused to run when Barney darted back and forth at it. Instead it tormented Barney by rubbing against him. When in the house, Barney perched on a chair, next to the shotgun and Winchester of the widow, in the mud room so he could continuously survey the back yard as he mimicked sleeping.

Arany, in her youthful exuberance, was ready for any new adventure devoid of her mother. She cheerfully bounced around the house, spouting her Silas-like, witty sayings to Laura and Elwood. As Laura tried to decide upon which wall to hang the water color of Lazarus, Arany turned to Elwood and spontaneously asked, "Daddy, what did one wall say to the other?"

Elwood rolled his eyes and mumbled, "Not another one."

"I'll meet you at the corner."

Troy helped Arany inflate the tires of her old Buick Roadmaster. Fortunately they weren't dry-rotted. He replaced the battery and filled the gas tank. At its first crank by Arany, it started, bellowing black smoke out its exhaust for the first few minutes. It was a sight to behold, a big boxy station wagon of faded blue color with faux wooden panels on the sides. She and Troy took it for a spin around a big circle of several miles – up Dug Row Road, then down Chestnut Grove Trail, and back Sycamore Valley Road. It rode like a tank, and got about the same gas mileage. But she now had her own wheels.

† † †

The news rocked Sunshine Clutterbuck's world; every cell in her body seemed to quiver uncontrollably. A telephone call from her sister delivered the message on the Saturday morning the week after the firing of Pastor Martin. Her sister had found out from a niece whose cousin was told by a friend of Alice Jane Grant. Sunshine ran outside and wailed, then fell to her knees and prayed. She locked herself in her bedroom, reading and re-reading chapter 23 of the Gospel of Matthew. Jesus spoke of the evil of false teachers.

Clarence went without a cooked meal that night. When he smelled incense oozing from around the bedroom door, he realized the futility of even knocking.

Before the crack of dawn on Sunday morning, Sunshine quietly tiptoed past a sleeping Clarence on the living room couch. She cranked Ole Brownie, and within the hour rolled into the empty parking lot at Twin Falls Presbyterian Church. The church doors were unlocked. Reese Coleman had already performed this task and returned home to Mabel for breakfast.

Silence and gloom greeted Sunshine. Nary a bird announced the sunrise hidden behind overcast skies. The dank smell of rotting hay in a neighboring field rose up in the still air.

Sunshine marched to the front door of the church with a poster in one hand and a hammer and spike in the other. She nailed the poster to the door, as she envisioned Martin Luther doing over 500 years previously. Printed in magic marker –

PEOPLE OF
TWIN FALLS PRESBYTERIAN CHURCH

GOD sent YOU a PROPHET OF TRUTH:
Pastor Martin was shown the sign of Jonah.
He has been and is in the presence of Jesus.
But you flogged him, then chased him from your church.

NOW BEWARE of FALSE PROPHETS:
Van Guilder and Rohrbaugh are full of hypocrisy
and wickedness. Their hearts covet earthly
treasures. They use gifts of gold to exalt themselves.

WOE onto You

Sunshine stood back, then leaned forward to straighten the poster. She kicked at the concrete step in displeasure; the poster needed something to draw attention to it. She went inside, looking for a colored ribbon to put on the spike. Her wandering through the hallways and exploring the rooms yielded nothing. Eventually, she arrived at the adults' classroom and saw Joe watching over a box. Perfect. Now, Joe the sock monkey hung on the spike and pointed to the message. Unbeknownst to Sunshine, she also afforded instant credibility to her posting – the stamp of approval by Silas. Later, each churchgoer read the poster before entering the church, and none took it down.

Sunshine hesitated before she jumped back into Ole Brownie. She glanced back at the church, shook her head in disgust and anger, spat on the ground, and stooped to pick up a stone. Her arm went back to fling the stone at a stained glass window. She stopped, then dropped the stone harmlessly to the ground. She turned to Ole Brownie, "I shan't be the one to throw the first stone."

Chapter Twenty Eight
WHO THREW THE FIRST STONE

The second week after moving into the widow Reynolds' house, Laura and Elwood were visited by a neighbor, Debbie Ford, bringing a chili-mac casserole as a housewarming gift – a country welcome. Debbie was a pleasant, middle-aged woman, who had lived down the road from the widow Reynolds for the past ten years. She admitted, though, she had very little contact with the widow who preferred a hermit-like existence. Others had told Debbie that after losing her husband at a very young age, she lived in this same house for most of her life. In her early days, she worked as a chemist, first at Lees Carpet, then at Kennametal, before retirement. Debbie confided that the few times she'd visited the widow, she'd been either cooking or reading a science magazine.

As Laura and Elwood saw her to the door, Debbie paused and threw a hand up in the air. "Oh, one more thing – some old guy did visit her periodically. Never did recognize the car, though, so he wasn't from this neck of the woods."

Laura and Elwood smiled at each other knowingly. "Probably her twin brother," Elwood replied.

"Oh, I didn't know she even had any relatives," Debbie exclaimed. "But he hadn't visited in the last year or so."

"That makes sense," Laura nodded, "he wasn't driving, confined to Faithful Care."

When Debbie reached the front porch, she laughed and pointed to the Buick Roadmaster. "When you saw this car on the road, you'd better give her a wide berth. You'd just see two eyes peering out over top of the steering wheel, looking straight ahead and with the pedal to the metal."

† † †

Over the course of next few weeks, Troy Montgomery, the young lumberjack from the Twin Falls congregation, became a fixture at the Sycamore Valley house. A couple times each week, he'd arrive with chainsaw and other tools in hand to tackle the trees and overgrowth in its yards – slowly expanding the grounds to its once respectable condition. Other days, he'd repair the sheds surrounding the house, or replace the floorboards and railing of its porch. There was plenty to keep him busy, helping his friends Laura and Elwood with their fixer-upper farm.

The only compensation he'd take was a dinner, homemade by Laura, with the family each week. Interestingly, his garb for these dinners evolved from his distinctive bib overalls, flannel shirt, boots, and NASCAR ball cap – to blue jeans, pullover, sneakers, and generic ball cap – then to khakis, button-down shirt, loafers, and a hint of aftershave. Likewise, his after-dinner activity changed from talking to Elwood to taking walks with Arany.

† † †

Laura and Elwood left early in the morning. They scheduled an appointment with a sales representative at Spencer Home Center in Lexington to choose new tile for the bathrooms, and linoleum, cabinets, sink, faucets, and counter for the kitchen. Their next stop was Keiser Appliances in Buena Vista to look at a possible new refrigerator, stove, and dishwasher. They left Arany sleeping; she had the day off, after working the weekend.

Arany floated in the nether-land between sleep and wake. Rays of morning sunlight burst helter-skelter through her partially closed bedroom curtains. Smells of Laura cooking biscuits and frying sausage for breakfast still permeated the house. She lifted her head slightly and peeked out of her eyelids to glimpse Barney lying next to her feet. He was on his back with all four of his feet straight up, whimpering softly in a dream. It was a perfect day to lollygag in bed.

Ba-BANG . . . Ba-BANG

She staggered out of bed – *What's that banging? Workmen aren't supposed to be here this morning.* Groggily, she stumbled to her second floor window. Her eyes tried to adjust to the bright light outside, while her hands found it impossible to open the old window sealed shut from decades of non-use.

Ba-BANG . . . Ba-BANG

The sound echoed. Rocks were being thrown against the shed door at BUG's profile.

Arany yelled, "Hey!" She rapped on the window at the scraggly tween boy with a red baseball hat. He looked at Arany and scowled. He considered tossing the rock then in his hand at the upstairs window, but thought better.

Arany, still in her pajamas, raced with Barney downstairs to the mud room. When she opened the back door to yell at the kid again, Barney slipped out. He took off after the boy, who was last seen hurtling through the brush at the rear of the backyard. Arany saw the widow's guns still propped up next to the back door. She reached for the shot gun, but thought better. Barney pranced back to Arany, convinced he'd successfully chased off the intruder.

Her hands kept shaking, although petting Barney had a calming effect. Eventually, she shared the sausage biscuits, which Laura had left behind for her breakfast, with him. She then walked out to the backyard, basking in the warmth of the early sun but irritated at being awoken by the stone-throwing Amos Muterspaw. Her father had warned her of the activities of this knucklehead. She picked up a stone from his pile, juggled it, then threw it back on the ground. She looked up at the sky – puffy clouds, no chance of rain, and mild temperatures – a perfect day to head her Roadmaster tank into Lexington for a good cleaning at the self-service car wash. Perhaps that'd soothe her rudely awakened nerves.

She passed the Muterspaw house, not more than a shack, which sat along the dry creek bed to the right side of the road.

The trashy possessions, though, normally decorating its front yard weren't there. The windows now lacked curtains; and the house looked empty. She caught a glimpse of a beater pickup truck pulling a U-haul trailer and leaving its driveway. The boy wearing the red baseball hat sat on the truck's passenger side. *Good riddance!*

Arany shoved many quarters into the pay slots to cleanse her car's exterior. Washing the dirt and grime away highlighted the layer of dull blue paint below. More than two decades of being parked outside guaranteed no glow or sheen to its original coat of paint. Rust splotches decorated its wheel wells. Vacuuming its inside sucked up deposits of dirt, gravel, leaves, and debris. She opened the back of the wagon and lifted the compartment that contained the jack and spare tire. There in the middle of the spare tire was a cheap metal lockbox, the size of a small toaster, with "ARANY" written in magic marker on top.

Her legs went wobbly; her mind befuddled at the sight of "ARANY" on the box. She felt faint and sat on the blacktop.

She tried to open the box. It was locked – no key in sight or in the glove compartment. She shook it; something rattled inside. She raced back home, pushing the old Roadmaster to the speed limit.

Arany plopped the metal lockbox on the kitchen table. *What tools did she need to pick a lock?* She rationalized, though, there was no need to save the lockbox as it had no inherent value. She went outside and used the Muterspaw kid's stockpile of rocks to thwack the box's lock with a stone that fit snugly into her hand. She succeeded in bending the top, causing it to pop open after about ten good thumps with the stone.

The box contained a stack of newspaper clippings and a photograph paper-clipped together, along with a key. The number 758 was stamped on one side of the key's head, while "FNEB" was printed with permanent magic marker on the other side. Arany flipped through the clippings. They dated to the early 1930s and reported on the killing of two Muterspaw brothers by Joseph Reynolds, and his subsequent trial for the murders. Chills went up her spine. The picture was definitely old, faded black and white, showing a girl and a boy, probably about ten or so years old, in their Sunday finest. Her attention was quickly drawn to their necklaces – the girl had a gold necklace with a cross-eight pendant, and the boy one with a cross-infinity pendant – the same ones that Laura and her dad now sported. She flipped over the picture. In a scrawl that was hard to decipher, she read: "Me and Simon. Gifts from cousin Joe Reynolds (Joe's father, Lewis, is brother to my grandpa Charlie). We are the treasure keepers."

"Keepers of what treasure? The necklaces?" Arany mumbled to herself.

She flung herself into the task of putting together the story of Joseph Reynolds from the news clippings. She struggled, though, to concentrate with thoughts gushing through her mind – *What does the widow want me to glean from the story? Why did the widow Reynolds address the lockbox to me, not Laura and my dad? At least, Laura and my dad would now know from whence their matching pendants originated.* But for every question answered another one popped up. *And what does key #758 open?*

Laura and Elwood arrived home late afternoon. Arany excitedly greeted them at the door. She didn't want to hear of tile choices, new appliances, or renovation schedules; she just wanted them to sit down and listen to the story of the lockbox hidden in her Roadmaster. She allowed them a few moments to pour glasses of fresh lemonade over ice; but she used that time to jabber about the Muterspaw boy throwing rocks at BUG again that morning.

After herding Laura and her dad into the living room, she started, "This happened on Tuesday afternoon, on the 22nd of December in 1931. Joseph Reynolds lived about three miles north of the Kerrs Creek post office on the road leading north from Midland Trail. He rented a farm near the base of Hog Back Mountain from Mrs. Susan Bane. As close as I can tell, it must be very close to where this house of the widow Reynolds now stands, and we sit, along the current Sycamore Valley Road."

Laura and Elwood nodded.

Arany continued, "The Muterspaw family lived just beyond the Reynolds farm, further up Sycamore Valley. They were related by marriage. Ida Muterspaw was the wife of Joseph Reynolds. One of her brothers had been Andrew Muterspaw who was married to a woman named Maggie. Andrew Muterspaw, though, had been killed years earlier when a tree which he was cutting down fell on him. Maggie lived on the Muterspaw farm with their grown sons."

"Whoa there," Elwood put up his hand. "Let's see whether I have this straight. Maggie Muterspaw was the sister-in-law of Ida and Joseph Reynolds."

"That's right," Arany smiled, "and Joseph Reynolds was 61 years old with a long black beard, and a farmer. Allegedly, that morning, Maggie Muterspaw along with her daughter-in-law Katy went onto the Reynolds farm to cut a Christmas tree. Joseph Reynolds chased the women off. No one knows for sure whether they were just ordered off and told not to come back, or whether they were removed by force."

"I wonder why he didn't want them to cut a Christmas tree," Laura asked. "It's not like he would've had a Christmas tree farm back then."

"Especially if they're related," Elwood agreed, taking a sip of lemonade.

Arany shuffled the clippings. "There must have been some underlying bad blood between the families predating this Christmas tree incident. Anyway, the three sons of Maggie Muterspaw were Amos age 31 –"

"Amos Muterspaw," Laura interrupted, almost choking on a swallow of lemonade.

"As in the same name as our red-capped, stone-throwing marauder," added Elwood.

"Coincidence?" chuckled Laura.

"Along with Amos were Estill, nicknamed 'James' age 28, and Andy, or Andrew, Jr., age 18," continued Arany, smiling. "Maggie's three sons returned to the Reynolds farm to confront him. Reynolds claims he was cutting wood near his house, sees the boys coming down the road, goes back to his house, and retrieves his rifle. The skirmish occurs with Reynolds in his field and the boys, who are his nephews, downhill on the road about thirty yards away. What happened next had no witnesses, but neighbors arrived on the scene soon afterwards. There's controversy on whether the boys threw the first stones, or Reynolds fired the first shot."

"They threw stones!" exclaimed Elwood, now enraptured with the story.

"The question is," offered Arany, "whether they threw the first stone to start the whole skirmish or stoning."

"This is starting to sound like a replay of John 8:7," Elwood snickered, "or the stone-throwing of our modern-day Amos Muterspaw at the shed here."

"The Muterspaw version, according to Amos' dying statement and Andy, claims that James was shot first without warning by Joseph Reynolds." Arany paused as she checked with a news clipping, "It says he used a 0.32 caliber Winchester rifle. He was –"

"Whoa, again," Elwood threw up his hand. "Could that be the rifle in our mud room?"

Laura gulped, "Remember the widow told the deputy that her Winchester had been used 'for such' previously."

"Probably not a coincidence?" Elwood rose from his chair. He paced momentarily before walking to the mud room, collecting the Winchester, and storing it on the top shelf of a hallway closet.

Arany continued, "James Muterspaw was killed instantly when the bullet hit him in his forehead. Amos and Andy retaliated by throwing rocks at Reynolds for protection, then ran. Amos was shot in the back as he ran. He continued a short distance before he collapsed. A neighbor, William Ruley, took him to the Jackson Hospital in Lexington, where he died that night. Reynolds also shot at and missed Andy while he ran away. But the story was told differently by Joseph Reynolds. He claims the three brothers unloaded a barrage of rocks at him from the road while he stood in the field. He shot James in self-defense, as he was being rocked. In fact, he was struck in the mouth by a rock thrown by Amos and knocked down. He then shot Amos as Amos was picking up another rock. Reynolds maintains he would have shot Andy if his gun hadn't jammed. He alleges only shooting twice."

"All this just three days before Christmas," said Elwood.

"And over a Christmas tree – definitely not the Christmas spirit," Laura added.

"Joseph Reynolds took off and couldn't be found by the Sheriff and others that night. But he voluntarily turned himself in at the jail the next morning. Amos Muterspaw had been shot under his right shoulder with the bullet puncturing his lungs. But the coroner couldn't ascertain the entry versus exit wound – that is, whether he was shot in the back or from the front. Amos and 'James' Muterspaw, both carpenters by trade, were then buried in a common grave in the nearby New Monmouth Presbyterian Church cemetery. 'James' was survived by his wife Katy and a five-year old child. The burial services were attended by an immense number of people. The presiding minister for the burial was Rev. Gardner from an Adventist church in Clifton Forge, with the assisting minister Rev. Weathers from New Monmouth." Arany paused as she picked up her notes.

"What happened to Joseph Reynolds?" asked Elwood.

"I'm getting to that part," replied Arany. She paged through her notes, then continued, "He was charged with the murder of Amos and 'James' and the attempted murder on Andy. He went on trial in February 1932, first for the murder of Amos in Rockbridge Circuit Court in Lexington."

"Talk about a speedy trial – that's less than two months later," Laura remarked.

"And the trial drew a lot of interest with standing room only in the courtroom," Arany continued. "The jurors were taken to the scene of the killing on the second afternoon of the two-day trial. He was found guilty of voluntary manslaughter, but sentenced to only one year in the state penitentiary. The lesser charge and light prison term were due to neighbors testifying on behalf of Joseph Reynolds that the Muterspaw boys had tormented and harassed him while he lived at the farm. In September 1932 he was tried for the murder of 'James' and the attempted murder of Andy. Once again, the jury found him guilty of voluntary manslaughter, not murder; this time he was given a sentence of 2½ years in the state penitentiary in Richmond."

"Quite a story," Elwood said.

"Why would the widow Reynolds have wanted me to know about it, though?" Arany asked, as she took a deep breath.

"Good question," shrugged Laura.

Arany pulled a clipping from her stack. "Here's the obituary for Joseph Reynolds from 1949. Evidently, he lived for over a decade, until the age of 78, after being released from the penitentiary. He was found dead 'in a barn at his home near the Advent Church in the Sycamore community.' The coroner attributed his death to heart trouble for which he had been treated. His burial was also in the New Monmouth cemetery with three ministers presiding – one from Clifton Forge, another from Kerrs Creek Baptist Church, and the third from New Monmouth. He was survived by several sisters and brothers, sons and daughters, twenty-three grandchildren and eight great-grandchildren."

"So both shooter and victims are buried at New Monmouth," Laura noted.

"Odd that it took three preachers to bury him," added Elwood.

Arany showed the key to Laura and her dad.

Elwood took the key and inspected it. "Its shape and the number on it clearly identify it as one for a safe deposit box." Elwood passed it to Laura.

"I agree," declared Laura, "but what does the 'FNEB' represent?"

"Good question." He returned the key to Arany.

"I saved the best for last," Arany announced. She picked up the old black-and-white photo and handed it to her dad.

Laura leaned over so both she and Elwood looked at the picture together. They gasped.

Elwood finally spoke, "That's Silas and his twin sister, the widow Reynolds, as children wearing our matching necklaces."

"Turn it over," Arany suggested.

Once again, Laura and Elwood stared at the writing, mouths open. This time, Laura broke the silence. She mumbled, "Joe Reynolds? So both the widow and Silas were related to Joe. But keepers of the necklaces – are the necklaces the treasures?"

"Or do the necklaces indicate that the twins are taking over from Joseph Reynolds to be the keepers of some other treasure?" Elwood fumbled with his glass of lemonade.

"But if that's the case," Arany calmly replied, "why did the widow address the lockbox to me instead of y'all?"

Chapter Twenty Nine
FROM BOBRALIN TO MUGRILLA

Troy joined Laura, Elwood, and Arany for dinner the next night. While Arany helped Laura prepare a meal of pork chops, scalloped potatoes, creamed lima beans, and baked apples, Elwood and Troy grabbed glasses of lemonade and retreated to the rocking chairs on the front porch. Sweet smells of blooming honeysuckle from the bushes across Sycamore Valley Road complimented the relaxing warmth of the late afternoon. Barney accompanied the menfolk to the porch, his launching post for chasing cats, rabbits, and other critters from the yard.

Whenever Troy visited, Elwood asked about the Twin Falls congregation; he yearned to be back in the pulpit, but the Presbyter, Rev. Van Guilder, wouldn't even return calls. Troy related the chaotic situation at Twin Falls, with the congregation divided over loyalties to Elwood versus to the Presbytery. Friends on opposite sides of the issue no longer talked. And the proclamation nailed to the front door the previous Sunday only served to fuel the flames of discontent. Reese swore the proclamation wasn't on the door when he unlocked it that morning. No one claimed responsibility, but Elwood knew the culprit. Just one person had ever said he was shown the sign of Jonah. Rumors and gossip ran amok through the congregation. Elwood wiped a tear away with his napkin. He felt helpless; he couldn't right his flock. The Presbytery and UAPC seemed to be in no hurry with the appeal of his dismissal. Van Guilder's secretary would only tell him that his case continued under review. Troy snickered that the Presbytery had become very sensitive to criticism. Rev. Rohrbaugh exploded when he saw the proclamation on the front door after worship service. Van Guilder that same afternoon, supposedly in a fit of rage, personally shredded the proclamation into itty-bitty pieces. Only intervention by Hansford Cash saved Joe the sock monkey from Van Guilder's tantrum.

Elwood and Troy then bemoaned the news reported in the morning's *Roanoke Times*. The Valley Presbytery announced plans to construct a new building for their headquarters in Roanoke. Financing for the structure had recently been secured.

Arany interrupted their discussion. Food was on the table – time to come inside, time for Elwood to put thoughts of the unfairness of his treatment by the Presbytery aside.

The four didn't lack for dinner conversation, with Arany steering talk to lockbox revelations. Each obsessed over a different portion of the mystery. Elwood agonized over Silas, Silas' sister, and Joe Reynolds pulling his strings to embark on yet another treasure hunt. The nature of family relationships – from Joseph 'Joe' Reynolds shooting his nephews in 1931; to the widow Reynolds and her connection to the Petticrew massacre at House Mountain in 1846; to Judith Petticrew Reynolds, the widow, and Silas being brother and sister, and being second cousins to Joseph Reynolds; and the reason for Silas and his sister drawing her and Elwood, and now Arany, into their affairs – was of deepest interest to Laura. Arany focused on the safe deposit key; maybe the contents of the safe deposit box would answer some questions. Or, as Troy countered, pose more questions.

Throughout the dinner, Barney patiently waited next to Arany's chair at the table. He wondered whether scraps of pork would be coming his way.

While Laura and Elwood volunteered to wash the dishes, Arany and Troy went on a short walk through the woods to the rear of the house. They talked of the beauty of the natural surroundings and the happenings of the day. They watched Barney scamper ahead of them.

Even though Arany and Troy had spent lots of time together at the Sycamore Valley property, Troy had yet to ask Arany on a date. He continually worried she deserved someone more educated and refined, not a self-employed lumberjack who towered above her. He feared rejection. As if Barney sensed Troy's indecision, Barney kept barking at him, encouraging him to take the plunge. Finally, with hands shaking and voice quivering, Troy asked Arany for a dinner-movie date. They returned to the house hand in hand. Both were even happier than when they left for the walk.

† † †

After Troy departed for the night, Arany checked the phone book for local banks – Bank of Botetourt, Bank of the James, BB&T, Carter Bank, City National Bank, Cornerstone Bank, DuPont Community Credit Union, SunTrust, Union Bank, and Wells Fargo. None matched the FNEB acronym; neither did any banks in neighboring cities. She searched the internet – dead ends. FNEB stood for a type of ammunition; and FNE Bank might be FiNEx Bank, but it was on the other side of the country. She wondered – *Perhaps it's some other acronym, maybe for a person or phrase?*

Elwood slipped into his recliner to resume reading a biography of Martin Luther, while Laura picked up the most recent issue of *Taste of Home* magazine. Arany continued to fret over the key, mindlessly turning it over and over in her hand. "Perhaps I could waltz into every local bank with the key, and see whether it opens box #758 there," she said to no one in particular.

Elwood laughed, "How many banks would look at you as though you're crazy? Maybe you'd get locked up instead." He squirmed from his chair, went to the adjacent dining room still doubling as a storage room for boxes yet unpacked, and rustled through some. Minutes later, he reappeared displaying a safe deposit key with #192 stamped on its head. He announced, "This is mine for Cornerstone Bank."

Arany compared the two keys. "Numbers stamped in different fonts and the keys are different sizes. Not even close to being a match."

"Cross one bank off your list to visit," Laura giggled.

† † †

When Laura was leaving for work the next morning, she suggested to Elwood that he and Arany explore the New Monmouth Presbyterian Church cemetery. Elwood gave her a puzzled look as he shoveled the last bite of cheese and mushroom omelet into his mouth.

Laura offered, "After all, you found the fictional grave of Turnip and Tater Campbell just outside the Twin Falls cemetery, Patty and Silas' graves in a New York cemetery, and the Petticrew monument in the Oxford cemetery. Joe Reynolds and the Muterspaw brothers are all buried at New Monmouth. You never know what you might find there. You've found success in cemeteries before," she laughed.

"And also found confusion," Elwood scrunched his face, nodded, kissed Laura goodbye, and whispered, "I love you," as she went out the door.

An hour later, Elwood drove Arany to New Monmouth Presbyterian Church, only a few minutes away down Sycamore Valley Road, then toward Lexington on State Route 60, also called West Midland Trail, for a little over a mile. The brick church, whose founding dated back over 250 years, proudly overlooked the road from its knoll on the north side of the road. They were greeted by a colorful red and yellow sign with the logo of a rooster sitting on a cross-like weather vane with the sun in the background – definitely a country church. Its cemetery occupied several acres spreading east from the church's Fellowship Hall to a fence separating it from an adjacent forest, then making a dogleg toward the road. Large maples lined the eastern edge of the cemetery, with smaller trees scattered throughout.

Elwood surveyed the large cemetery; it would be a daunting task to walk the entire area. A swag in the middle rose steeply to its eastern edge and more gradually to the back. Older tombstones mixed with newer ones throughout. They decided to start in the middle and work their way to the rear of the cemetery.

Within the first five minutes, Arany arrived at the fence at the end of their second row walked. She gleefully announced, "Here're the gravestones of Foster Reynolds and Willie Reynolds, one died in 1972 and the other in 1952, both 66 years of age."

Elwood's peripheral vision caught another Reynolds tombstone in the background just underneath a large maple tree. "And there's one for Charles and Grace Reynolds, husband and wife, died in 1951 and 1983 respectively, at ages 74 and 99."

Arany turned onto the next row. "Here's where Audrey Reynolds Wilhelm is buried."

"Definitely no scarcity of Reynolds thus far," Elwood chuckled.

They passed by gravestones showing Smiths, Hostetters, and Moores, among others before stumbling upon one identifying Vera Logan Muterspaw, who died in 2011.

After walking a couple more rows, they came upon another concentration of Reynolds; separate stones for Martha, Albert "Scrub," Harry, Isaac, and Lottie, bumped up against the fence line once again to the east.

Arany pointed to the smallish granite in the middle. "Here it is. 'Joseph H. Reynolds, October 4, 1870 – June 6, 1949' and 'Ida M. Reynolds, August 30, 1870 – November 23, 1939.' I guess the 'M' in his wife's name stands for Muterspaw."

After catching his breath going up the steep rise to the graves, Elwood scanned back to the church. "Interesting, these graves are about as far from the church as you can get in this part of the cemetery. I wonder whether it was intentional on the part of the church."

They continued systematically back and forth following the rows, passing Hughes, Ploggers, more Smiths, Banes and Baynes, Hotingers, and Dunlaps. About twenty minutes later, they came upon a Muterspaw plot. One small stone was engraved with Amos M. Muterspaw and Estill F. [James] Muterspaw, with deaths of both as December 22, 1931. Below the names was the phrase "Rest in Peace." The neighboring grave was that of their father. Andrew T. died in 1913, also young at the age of 39. Other graves were for Rachel and

George Muterspaw, and a relatively large Muterspaw marble memorial spire rose to the height of Arany.

"I wonder how many think Amos and Estill are husband and wife, instead of brothers, especially since they're on the same tombstone," Arany said.

"You're right, not too many would be familiar with the name Estill. I don't blame him for going by the name James. Sort of like the old Johnny Cash song, 'A Boy Named Sue.'"

"There's no sign of the boys' mother, Maggie, next to their father."

Elwood looked around. Then he asked Arany to walk back to the site of Joe Reynolds' tombstone. They faced each other, separated by about six rows of gravestones and offset by about eight grave sites.

Elwood called, "How far would you estimate you're from me?"

Arany did some quick mental calculations. "About thirty yards."

"That's what I'd estimate. Forever in death at the distance that separated them in their shoot-out or stone-out on 22 December 1931, with the brothers slightly downhill from Joe Reynolds."

Elwood turned around and pointed at an elongated spruce tree a few feet uphill from the Muterspaw tombstone. "The only evergreen tree in the cemetery is right here. And the Muterspaw brothers forever in the shadow of a Christmas tree."

As they strolled back to the parking lot, they noticed a car traveling to the lot behind the church. The driver gave a "country wave" as she passed. Elwood thought she might be the pastor of New Monmouth, and proposed they drive around and introduce themselves. There they met Helen Irvine, white-haired and vivacious, and helped her carry some groceries into the church kitchen. She wasn't the pastor, only getting ready for her Fellowship Committee catering a dinner for an upcoming Kerrs Creek Ruritan Club meeting. In the course of their conversation, Elwood confided they'd been looking for and had found the gravestones of Joe Reynolds and his wife, as well as of Amos and Estill "James" Muterspaw.

"Ah, the shooter and the victims," Helen volunteered, as she put a jug of milk and two pounds of butter in the refrigerator.

"You know the story?" Elwood expressed surprise.

"Joe Reynolds was actually my great uncle. My grandmother Bessie Reynolds and he were brother and sister," she admitted. "The shooting happened back in the 1930s, but it was a topic of discussion at family get-togethers when I was a kid growing up. About all I remember is my great uncle Joe shot his nephews in some dispute over a Christmas tree. The nephews had attacked him by throwing stones."

"We came upon some news clippings of the incident when we moved into the home of the widow Reynolds, Judith Petticrew Reynolds, up Sycamore Valley," Arany interjected.

"I've got a file with some news clippings as well," Helen countered. "My granny would sometimes take us to the old Reynolds home place up at the end of Sycamore Valley Road and show us where it all happened."

"Were you any relation to Judith Reynolds, and her twin brother?" asked Elwood.

"Oh, not sure how they fit into the family genealogy, probably just some dog kin, and –"

"Dog kin?" Elwood interrupted. "What's dog kin?"

Helen smiled, "My mother always called anyone past third cousin 'dog kin.'"

Elwood laughed. He addressed Arany, "Well, one mystery solved. In the widow Reynolds' obituary, she was survived by a 'special dog-kin cousin.' Now we know it was just a term for a distant cousin."

"Who's the special cousin?" asked Arany.

"No clue."

"If the widow was a Reynolds, I suspect she had lots of dog kin," snickered Helen. She scurried about putting large cans of green beans on one shelf and boxes of pasta on a serving cart to, as she explained, keep them out of the reach of resident mice.

"Maybe, you can help us out with another puzzle," Arany suggested. "The widow left us with a key to a safe deposit box – identified by FNEB. Any idea what FNEB stands for?"

After a few moments of thought, she answered, "First National Exchange Bank, a local bank years ago; after takeovers it became First Union, then Wachovia, and now Wells Fargo. Still in the same location. Maybe even the same safe deposit boxes, I think."

Elwood glanced at the clock on the wall. They needed to be on their way; workers from Welsh Construction would soon be arriving at the house to start the remodel of one of the bathrooms. He thanked Helen for her help and promised to visit the Sunday worship service at New Monmouth in the near future.

"Might you have any more information about your great uncle Joe Reynolds?" blurted Arany, as they exited the church.

"I've a file that has newspaper clippings as well as other things," Helen answered, locking the church's door behind her. She added, "I haven't looked at it for many years, so I can't be more specific."

Arany's eyes lit up.

Helen correctly interpreted Arany's nonverbal request. "I live only a couple miles away on Bethany Road. You can ride home with me and have a look at the file, then I'll drop you back home in a little bit."

Arany's eyes lit up even brighter.

"I'll see you later," Elwood smiled, as Arany followed Helen to her car.

† † †

Helen offered Arany an iced tea and guided her to a leather sofa in the open living area. Helen's house was positioned to allow spectacular views of House Mountain from its picture windows on the south and Hog Back Mountain from the windows on the west. A mixed breed hound dog by the name of Tucker greeted Arany with sniffs and requests for pets, while Helen disappeared into an adjacent office to search for her file folder.

Helen returned with two manila files. The first contained news clippings – some original and some copies – the same as those in the lockbox. The second file held original compositions, written in young girls' penmanship on undersized and lined notebook paper, from her grandmother Bessie Reynolds' early teenage years.

The composition on top was titled "The Pretty Marmee;" then, upon flipping it over, ended with "Feb 2, 1902, written by a friend, Ressie J. Muterspaw, for Miss Bessie S. Reynolds." Arany shook her head and tapped her fingers on the coffee table. "Now I'm confused. A Muterspaw and a Reynolds friends?"

"You have to realize this was almost thirty years before the shooting," smiled Helen. "Bessie, my grandmother, was a much younger sister of Joe Reynolds. He was already a grown man, out on his own, when she was a child. Ressie Muterspaw was a neighbor girl, who was the sister of Joe's wife as well as the sister of Amos and James Muterspaw's father. My granny would have been about fifteen or sixteen in 1902, and Ressie about the same age, maybe a little younger."

While Helen spoke, Arany skimmed over some of the text. "Hmm. Is 'The Pretty Marmee' supposed to be some sort of poem . . . or story?"

Helen quickly perused it as well. "It looks like a song or ballad. You have to remember that there were no tapes, cassettes, or CDs back then. And not much for entertainment – you couldn't just jump in a car and go to a movie. In this rural area, family, friends, and neighbors congregated on someone's porch and played foot-stompin' music with fiddles, banjos, guitars, mandolins, and whatevers. There were few music books. People memorized the tune and the words. I suspect Ressie transcribed the words to this song while singing it, and shared it with my grandmother."

Arany picked up the next piece of paper. "This one's 'Darling Nelly Gray;' it looks like another song." She turned the paper to its back. "And 'written by Bessie for Everett.'"

"That would be one of her brothers; he went by the nickname 'Buzz.'"

Arany selected yet another. She looked over it more closely; it seemed to catch her attention more than the previous two.

May 4, 1900

Bobralin

1

It was early one morning in the month of May,
When the green buds, they were swelling.
Sweet Willie, he lies on his death bed
For the love of Bobralin.

He sent his servant to Charlestown,
Where she had been recently dwelling.
Mother says you must come down
If your name be Bobralin.

. . .

5

Go mother, go make my bed
Go make it soft and narrow
Sweet Willie, he died for me today,
I'll die for him tomorrow.

Sweet Willie lied in the church yard there
And she was laid by the side of him
Out of her breast there growed a red rose
And out of his a green briar

They grew up to her church steeple top
Till they could grow no higher
And there they twined in a true lovers [k]not
The red rose and the green briar

(repeat) And there they twined in a true lovers [k]not
The red rose and the green briar.

by Bessie for Ressie

"Looks like Ressie and Bessie traded songs."

"I suspect there were lots more that didn't survive the last century."

"Odd names – Bobralin, Nelly Gray, and Marmee," giggled Arany. "They all seem to have the same theme. Lovers are separated, then re-united in death."

Another sheet of paper contained a collection of little ditties written by "Ressie J.M. for BSR." Arany smiled, and read two out loud –

Love me little
Love me big
Love me like
A little fig.

The leaves may wilt
These flowers may die
Your friends may forget
You but never will I.

"One can't deny that Bessie and Ressie were friends," Helen returned the smile.

"And friends with rhyming names – how odd?" Arany chuckled.

"And Bessie's twin sister was named Jessie, although everyone called her Aunt Net – so yet another to rhyme," Helen laughed.

The last piece of writing bore the words of the hymn "We All Might Do Good." Arany was totally fascinated by the bits of local history, especially the interconnection of the Reynolds and Muterspaw families. She wasn't sure what it all meant.

† † †

Helen kept driving past Arany's current home for another mile to the *cul de sac* of Sycamore Valley Road. As she backed the car into a driveway to turn around, Helen told Arany that, when she was a child, some of the Reynolds lived even further up the valley, nearer Hog Back Mountain. But the old road was now a private drive, and fields had reverted back to woodland.

Helen identified a long-abandoned, old, dilapidated log shack near the *cul de sac* as the Reynolds home place where Joe Reynolds, afterwards also one of his sons, lived. On the way down the valley, she pointed out the field in which the shooting allegedly occurred. The land was very steep with the field in the process of being overgrown by brush. Arany believed that the old field might be on the property that her dad and Laura had inherited from the widow Reynolds. She shook her head – *How did the farmers years ago even subsist on these plots of land, especially with lots of rock everywhere?*

Helen also promised Arany that she'd arrange a get together – Arany chuckled softly when Helen said, "with some of my dog kin." Madeline Chittum is a descendent of one of the Muterspaw sisters and a wealth of knowledge on the history of Sycamore Valley. Sharon Holland is a great-granddaughter of Joe Reynolds. Both live nearby, the former on Mohler's Loop just off Sycamore Valley Road, while the latter in one of the first houses entering Sycamore Valley.

Helen pulled into the parking area in front of the Roadmaster. Arany thanked her for taking the time to chronicle the Reynolds-Muterspaw dispute. Helen chuckled, "When it snows this winter, walk up yonder to the bridge over the dry creek bed. My granny Bessie always told me that if you listen real hard, you can still hear her brother Joe playing his fiddle to the tune of 'Barbara Allen.'"

† † †

That afternoon Arany cranked up her old Roadmaster and drove to the Wells Fargo Bank in the center of downtown Lexington. Its customer service manager, Mr. Woody, politely escorted her into the vault with safe deposit boxes. Arany turned to him, as he was finding the signature card in a file box, and asked, "Why can't you keep secrets in a bank?"

Mr. Woody, caught off guard, said, "Uh . . . why not?"

"They have tellers."

He rolled his eyes, but supplied polite laughter. The card indicated that Arany Aldott in addition to Judith P. Reynolds and S. Silas Clark were authorized to have access to the box. She gave him her key, as well as showed her driver's license for identification. He opened the box, slid the drawer out, handed it to her, and inquired whether she'd like to spend some time in a private booth. She peeked into the box and saw only one item – a crudely printed booklet titled, "I Remember." She took the booklet, said "No, thank you," turned, and headed out of the bank vault. Mr. Woody replaced the now empty safe deposit box in slot #758.

Arany scanned the front page as she walked out of the bank, so engrossed that she almost walked into an old man coming through the door into the bank. She sat on a bench in the bank's courtyard scrutinizing the title page and introduction. The booklet was authored by Paulmer (Pete) Bronson Smith and written when he was 79 years old. Some quick calculations revealed it had been printed in 1988, give or take a few years. It had 58 pages – it had been definitely published from a copy typed on an old typewriter, not by a word processor on a computer. She started reading the first page, amidst the sounds of nearby traffic and pedestrians at the corner of Main and Nelson Streets.

> I was born, October 23 – 1909, the only son of Emmett Burkley Smith and Ressie Jane Muterspaw Smith, in Rockbridge Co. near Lexington, Va. In the Kerr's Creek area. . . .

She paused a moment – his mother was Ressie Muterspaw, Bessie Reynolds' best friend in their youth. That would make him first cousins to the brothers who were killed by Bessie's oldest brother Joe Reynolds.

> My father and mother lived on a farm at the upper end of Sycamore Valley. This farm was up against the Hog Back Mountain, the last one at the end of the road. Ha. This farm was so steep the horses, and cows had paths around the hill, so they could reach up and pull the grass down, like off a shelf to eat.
>
> Sycamore Valley was heavily populated when I was a young boy. There was, the Muterspaws, (9)

children, the Steven Smiths (5) children, John Vests (3) children, the Mohler family (5). The Reynolds family (6) a total of 28 adults and children. These families all lived east, south & west of my home. . .

The book told of Pete Smith's growing up in Sycamore Valley. For example, he told of having fun with Lonie and Vernon Hartbarger as a child; then, Buzz Reynolds, brother of Joe and another of Helen's great uncles, making a small banjo for them'all to play with. Pete Smith's memories transported her to a time many decades earlier, when farmers transitioned from horses to tractors during Prohibition and the Great Depression. She sat mesmerized.

After about page ten, Arany decided to head home. Her dad might worry. She never made it inside the house. A rocking chair on the porch beckoned her to read more fascinating experiences of Pete Smith. Then, she came to the next to last printed page in the booklet –

> . . . I remember some time in the 1930's I took my Dad up too the home of Mr. Press Reynolds to have his razor honed, as Mr. Press was good at sharpening tools. While we were there we heard some gun shots coming from down below where Mr. Press lived. We didn't know what they were all-about at that time. When Mr. Press had finished with the razor, Dad and I started home. We had gone perhaps one quarter mile down the mountain road, when we met Mr. Buzz Reynolds, Mr. Press's brother, on his way home. I stopped the car so we could speak to Mr. Buzz; that man was shaking all-over. Dad asked what the trouble was, he said, "By G--, Joe Bug (that is what they all called Joe Reynolds) has kilt the whole d--- gang of Muterspaws; shot all of them. Some reading this remember my Dad had something called Palsy, when excited they get nervous or shakey. At this time I don't know which was the worst, Dad or Mr.

Buzz. We went on down the road about three quarters of a mile, too the place where all this happened and there lay Jim Muterspaw in the road ditch with his brains coming out his forehead between his eyes. This was the most horrible sight I ever looked at. I don't remember who went for the sheriff, but some one did. They found Amos Muterspaw along the road, shot through, and rushed him to the Hospital where he died later. Andy Muterspaw, the younger brother, got away. They said Joe Bug would have killed Andy if his gun would have worked. I believe they said Andy threw a rock at Joe Bug that hit the gun on the magazine and fixed it so the shells wouldn't come out, thus saving his life. This trouble all started over Mrs. Muterspaw, these boys mother, cutting a Christmas tree on the land that Joe Bug had rented. I never knew just what the problem was between Joe Bug and Mrs. Muterspaw, that would call for this kind of homicide, among relatives. One thing I do know, <u>IF</u> some person slapped <u>MY</u> mother, I myself would be ready for a fight. At the trial, in court, something I thought was kind of funny; they ask Joe Bug what caused the shooting, he said, "Andy Muterspaw called me a D--- old MUGRILLA, and throwed a rock at me." HA. As I mentioned early in this writing, Andy could not talk real good, he studdered. These kind of happenings in life, sure causes lots of unhappiness among relatives.

Arany looked up and down Sycamore Valley Road from her perch on the porch. She closed her eyes and imagined being present, like Pete Smith's first-hand description, during the shooting's aftermath. She took a deep breath – *Why did the widow Reynolds want me to read this booklet? And what's a Mugrilla?* Arany gave a deep sigh – *The booklet, at least, identified BUG, the target of the Muterspaw boy on the shed door.*

Pete Smith's story ended one page later –

> Sycamore and the Hakins history includes one man
> hanged him self, one man was supposed too have
> been murdered over a love affair, and two young
> men killed over a simple argument of a Christmas
> tree. . . . I forgot – A Mr. Bayne was struck by
> lighting and killed. I was told the bolt was so
> powerful it knocked the soles off his shoes.

Arany was about to close the book, when she caught sight of
some handwriting on the back of the last page and the inside
back cover. At the bottom was a scrawled signature – the same
that graced the Lazarus water color and the wedding portrait of
Silas and his wife – that of Judith Petticrew Reynolds, Silas'
twin sister, and dated two years previously.

Fortunately, the note was printed in small, block, readable
letters, not in the widow Reynolds' scribbled handwriting –

> Dear Arany,
>
> My good friend Pete Smith did not know about
> another story in Sycamore Valley. When my cousin
> Joe Reynolds was clearing his field around 1910, he
> overturned a large rock and found pieces of a
> leather saddle bag underneath. Nothing was left but
> rotted leather shreds, a metal identification tag – J.
> Anderson, and some gold coin. Joe recognized
> Anderson as the thief who massacred the Petticrew
> family in the saddle of House Mountain a couple
> generations previously. Joe was also related to the
> Reynolds who had married the only surviving
> Petticrew, Rachel. She survived because she had
> been taking care of her grandmother at the base of
> Sycamore Valley.
>
> Joe Reynolds told his wife, Ida, that he discovered
> the gold coins and buried them. But his wife didn't
> keep the secret, she told her sister-in-law and
> neighbor, Maggie Muterspaw. Times were tough in

1930 – a big drought decimated the crops. Maggie kept rooting around for the hidden gold; Joe kept chasing her away. On the day her sons were shot, she claimed she was looking for a Christmas tree.

When Joe got out of jail, he made two cross pendants out of the stolen gold coins, melted and recast them – one with eight on it and one with infinity on it. He knew of the story of John Petticrew and the need to keep the message of the Blessed Eight alive. He gave the necklaces to my twin brother and me for safekeeping, and Simon and I planned to give them to your step-father and his wife for another generation of safekeeping.

But you are to be the keeper of the Petticrew treasure, which was passed from John Petticrew to his daughter Rachel, to her cousin Abraham Jr, to his cousin Joe, to his twin cousins. We are now passing this responsibility of being the keeper of the Petticrew treasure to you. You are indeed a very special cousin.

Also Silas said he left something special for you in my Buick Roadmaster.

Chapter Thirty
CHAPEL ROCK

Arany's discoveries totally fascinated Elwood and Laura. All spent the better part of the evening reading and discussing the booklet of Pete Smith, and the addendum written by the widow Reynolds. The widow's story made their necklaces even more special, as their underlying material could be traced back to the gold inherited by Mary Petticrew in the 1840s.

Laura, in another sense, still felt frustrated. She grumbled about trying to piece together the connection between the Petticrew family and Joe Reynolds, then Joe Reynolds and the twins Silas Clark and Judith Petticrew Reynolds. She spent many hours on the internet and in the library. But she couldn't definitively connect the lines from one generation to the next. Elwood laughed and told her to just accept them as "dog kin." And now, she complained of yet another unknown family connection. Why does the widow Reynolds believe Arany is dog kin to her and her brother Silas? Arany's maternal grandparents definitely immigrated to America from Eastern Europe. Arany even had a picture of her grandmother, also named Arany, as a young adult taken in Budapest. The two Arany's were spitting images of each other – both had beautiful, haunting eyes and golden, flowing hair.

Meanwhile, Arany meticulously searched the Roadmaster for the "something special" from Silas. She rummaged every nook and cranny from glove compartment to trunk. Nothing.

She had Troy check the engine compartment and wheel wells. He even crawled under the car. Nothing. She worried she might have accidently sucked up his gift when vacuuming.

The next evening, Arany and Troy went for a long walk, accompanied by Barney. Their hike, as usual, circled the nearly 200 acres of Reynolds property. Some of this land was open, but most was wooded. All was covered by stones, rocks, and boulders of varying sizes. One could envision where the fields and pastures once existed in the time of Joe Reynolds, but their last vestiges were slowly being overtaken by briars, redbuds, dogwoods, and sumacs. The acreage rose steeply from its frontage along Sycamore Valley Road up to a ridgeline, then dropped even more abruptly on the other side.

Their walk initially paralleled the gravel road as well as the dry, rock-filled creek bed next to it. Sycamore trees and wild rhododendron populated these lower parts. Arany's mind often wandered to thinking about the biblical Zacchaeus climbing a sycamore to garner a look at Jesus passing by, or to the rascal Amos Muterspaw scaling such trees to throw stones. Hardwoods such as maples, oak, beech, butternut, and black walnut lined the trail further uphill. Oddly, few pines and evergreens were on the property. No Christmas trees, if ever there were any.

Barney quickly spotted a squirrel munching on an acorn. He raced it to a nearby tree. But Barney never had a chance; he stood barking up the tree for a while, probably warning the squirrel not to come back down. A few steps later Arany and Troy saw the doe and her fawn that had been hanging around the property. Barney enjoyed chasing them as well. Down the trail at bit, Arany and Troy caught up to Barney. They paused, relishing the quiet except for the gentle rustle of the wind blowing through the leaves. Suddenly, the rat-tat-tat of a pileated woodpecker pecking on a rotted oak tree up the hill broke the silence.

Barney found a box turtle. He smelled all around as the turtle hid in its shell. He started to dig around it. Arany and Troy intently watched. He'd push the turtle with his nose, then dig some more. Barney soon tired of the fruitlessness of his efforts, long before Arany and Troy tired watching, and moved on to his next scent.

They stayed on the pathway skirting the lower edge of the property. About a quarter mile from the house, they passed by the old family cemetery surrounded by a low rock wall. Inside were the two small gravestones for Abraham Reynolds and Rebecca Reynolds, evidently husband and wife, with his birth and death chiseled into the stone as 1792 and 1855, respectively. Smaller stones identified other occupants in the cemetery as unnamed infants and another only as Jacob. Their markers were seriously weather worn. Arany and Troy had spent many days several weeks ago cleaning small trees, brambles, and weeds from this cemetery.

They passed by a huge pile of rocks and stones, as if collected off a field, but now overgrown with brush. The rocks were next to the alleged field where Joe Reynolds shot the Muterspaw brothers. Troy was always wary of snakes, especially rattlers, sunning themselves on the rock surfaces. But autumn had rapidly descended upon the valley, and the weather had turned noticeably cooler, making snakes less likely to be seen.

Today, as they momentarily viewed the rock pile, Arany spoke, "Hey, Troy. Did you hear about the rock quarry that went out of business?"

Troy smiled, "Can't say I did." Troy looked at her flaxen hair blowing in the breeze, and the enchanting smile of his maiden remembering a riddle.

"They hit rock bottom."

Near the far end of the property appeared an old rock-built footer – the foundation of the Adventist Church from the Joe Reynolds era. As always, they spent some time inspecting it. Arany had fallen in love with this location, sitting in a grove of sugar maple trees, which had turned brilliant red and yellow in the brisk fall weather. Arany confided to Troy that she could still hear the words being preached, and the songs resonating, from the ruins of this church in the quiet of the forest.

From there they went uphill toward the ridge. They passed by a low hedge of rocks arranged in a perfect figure eight about twenty feet long and ten feet wide. Then another figure eight of rocks was rotated ninety degrees next to it. Someone, maybe Joe Reynolds, had assembled the eight and the infinity symbol at this place. Whenever Elwood and Laura walked by this formation, they grasped their pendants – the Blessed Eight forever.

Halfway to the ridgeline, they stopped at a wet weather spring. No water trickled out; the weather had been too dry. The mud hole, though, had not yet dried up. Barney searched for a frog he'd seen there in wetter times. Nearby he dug for a while at a groundhog hole. Scottish terriers were definitely varmint hunters.

On top of the ridgeline was a rock formation Arany had appropriately named Chapel Rock. The main part of the creation was a large rectangular rock about the size of a Volkswagon beetle with its top sloping on both sides like a roof; a narrow upright rock abutting that rock's one end rose to a height of about twenty feet high in the shape of a spire. Bushes lined the perimeter of the church portion and vines wound around the steeple – almost as if this faux chapel had been landscaped. Arany climbed on top of the rock's "roof" and breathed in spectacular views of nearby Hog Back Mountain to the north and White Rock Mountain to the west. She had found Chapel Rock to be an invigorating place for prayer, traveling there almost every day to talk to God. Something about Chapel Rock made it special, almost sacred. She confessed to Troy that yesterday she felt a calling from God as she was lying in meditation on the rock.

She continued, "Is it coincidental that both Chapel Rock and a church's foundation are on this property? Our walks as well as my personal hikes here feel like Jesus is walking with us or with me."

"Don't forget the eight and infinity that someone arranged in stone," Troy added.

"When I'm not preoccupied with the Petticrew treasure or what Silas hid in the Roadmaster, I feel a calling to the ministry."

Troy smiled, "You'd make your dad proud."

"But definitely not my mother," she shrugged, then hesitated. "I wonder whether Joe Reynolds ever sat on this rock and pondered or prayed."

"He's certainly a man hard to figure out." Troy raised his eyebrows as he leaned against Chapel Rock next to Arany.

"He must've known about John Petticrew and his fixation on the Blessed Eight. He made necklaces with the eight and infinity."

"And I suspect the rock structures with the eight and infinity here on the property."

"So he must have been a believer –"

"But yet also a killer," interrupted Troy.

"But why?" questioned Arany. "Surely not just because of refusing his in-laws a Christmas tree, being called a Mugrilla, whatever that might be, or discovering them trying to find his hidden gold coins?"

"It sure seems a drastic act for a seemingly pious man," answered Troy. "I keep thinking of the old saying – Sticks and stones may break my bones, but words will never break me."

"Why would a seemingly good man be a killer?" Arany stared at the splendor of Hog Back Mountain from her perch. "But then I think of people like Moses and David, both killers who repented their ways and were recruited to do the work of God. Moses had killed, then was called by God to lead the Jews out of Egypt. David had the husband of Bathsheba killed – and God called him to be a king. Did Joe Reynolds likewise have a higher calling?"

† † †

Helen Irvine arranged an all-women gathering for Arany and Laura to meet her friends, Madeline Chittum and Sharon Holland, in Arany's hope to discover more information about Joe Reynolds. Both Madeline and Sharon were widows, the former in her late 70s and a descendent of the Muterspaw family and the latter in her early 70s and the great-

Henry D. Schreiber

granddaughter of Joe Reynolds. They all enjoyed themselves in the informal setting of Helen's living room, sipping on tea and snacking on freshly-made lemon pound cake with cream cheese icing.

Madeline revealed that James Muterspaw, the brother shot dead by Joe Reynolds, had been taken to and laid out on a table in his house, the same house now her home. Both Madeline and Sharon confirmed family tales spinning a history of the Muterspaw boys cussing, rocking, and aggravating Joe Bug Reynolds. Madeline added the Muterspaw boys were a wild bunch; they always had big dances at their house. At that time, churches frowned on dancing as the work of the devil.

Neither Madeline nor Sharon could offer an underlying reason for the family feud other than the Christmas tree incident. Madeline always heard that Maggie Muterspaw told her boys: "If you love your ole Maggie, you'll get me a Christmas tree over there," on the day of the shooting. And even years afterwards, Sharon described an embittered Maggie Muterspaw, one who would never sell anything to a Reynolds.

Both knew Joe Bug Reynolds in their youth, when he was an old man. And both defined his eyes as piercing and his gray beard, which had once been coal black, as flowing. Everyone called him Bug or Joe Bug, but neither knew the origin of the nickname. Madeline pictured him as "a scary sight," while Sharon remembered him as a "kindly old man." Sharon related, "He always had a poke of candy next to his rocker on the porch. He gave out pieces of candy to the kids." Arany shook her head trying to understand the dichotomy of Joe Reynolds – the good and the bad, the scary and the kindness. There was consensus on one of his traits – everyone in both families acknowledged Joe was a crack shot, someone who could shoot the wings off a fly at thirty yards.

Sharon also brought a file folder containing miscellaneous information about her ancestors. A 1900 census listed Joseph Reynolds at age 29 working a farm in Sycamore Valley, already having wife Ida, four kids, and a younger brother living with him. His other younger siblings lived at the home place with his parents E. L., or Lewis, and Sarah. A legal document even showed that Joe guaranteed the mortgage of his father's real estate in 1925 – his warranty consisted of $5 cash, a Ford automobile, one cow, two calves, four hogs, four pigs, 25 barrels of corn, and 60 bundles of fodder. This note of $175 was fully paid and satisfied in 1934, after Joe had served his prison sentences. Interestingly, a copy of another legal document showed that Vernon Hartbarger, another of Joe's nephews and one of Helen Irvine's uncles, was indicted for refusing to appear as a prosecution witness for Joe's trial. The summons was later retracted after the trial.

Laura brought up her problems in tracing the genealogy of the Reynolds family with the other women. Clearly, Joe Reynolds had five siblings – Susan, the twins Jessie and Bessie (Helen's grandmother), Everett ("Buzz" or "Buzzie"), Preston ("Press" or "Pete"), and Baxter. Joe's children were Sadie, Kate (grandmother of Sharon), Gracie, Guy, Lambert ("Lam"), and Albert ("Scrub"). The neighboring Vest and Smith families married into both the Reynolds and the Muterspaw families. But Helen, Madeline, and Sharon all shrugged off Laura's difficulties in connecting Silas and his twin sister to Joe Reynolds, as well as Joe back to the Petticrew family.

Helen smiled, "When I was young, I questioned my mom about her brother's age. I thought he was older, but she said otherwise – that she should know. I argued that granny wasn't living with granddaddy when she claimed, so he had to be older. Mom got very flustered, but you know what she said?"

Laura shook her head.

"She said she got 'em in the woods, just like everything else," laughed Helen, joined by both Madeline and Sharon in her amusement.

"You might need some dashed lines to connect 'dog kin' in family trees instead of those solid lines," added Madeline.

Sharon brushed some pound cake crumbs from her lips and spoke, "My daughter Sherry graduated high school with Joe Tom Reynolds, a real lady's man –"

"That's the guy they call 'Beats,'" interrupted Helen.

"Yep," answered Sharon. "He played the drums in some rock band. But Joe Tom also claimed to be a cousin to Sherry.

327

He said his grandpa was Buzz Reynolds, brother of Joe."
Sharon giggled, followed by laughter from Madeline and Helen.

Arany and Laura looked at each other in confusion. "Am I
missing something?" Arany sheepishly asked.

"Sorry," Sharon replied, "to finish the story, Buzz as well as
his brother Press were both old bachelors, never married."

"But," Helen interjected, "both never lacked for women. So
it's quite believable that he fathered children off the books, not
recorded in the written family genealogy." Sharon and Madeline
nodded in agreement. Helen added, "so Sherry and Joe Tom,
AKA 'Beats,' are dog kin by word of mouth, not by birth
records."

Laura whispered softly to Arany: "From 'Beets' Campbell
to 'Beats' Reynolds – some things you just can't make up.
This'll really bug your dad."

Arany smiled and nodded.

"Speaking of relatives, switching to my dog kin," Madeline
smiled as she faced Arany and Laura. "A couple weeks ago
GinnyLee Muterspaw and her son moved out of the shack down
the road from y'all a bit."

"Yeah, I saw them pull away," Arany nodded. "The boy was
a regular rascal – kept throwing stones at our wood shed where
he'd drawn a profile of Bug Reynolds."

"The boy's Amos Muterspaw – his grandfather was James
Muterspaw, the first one shot by Joe Reynolds. He's as wild and
incorrigible as his grandfather was," Madeline explained.

"Why'd they move away?" Laura asked.

Madeline chuckled, "Evidently, he had discipline problems
at school. He kept throwing stones at other kids. He met his
demise when he hit the principal with one."

✝ ✝ ✝

The following Sunday, Arany, Laura, and Elwood attended
worship service at New Monmouth Presbyterian Church.
Elwood sat uncharacteristically sullen in the pew, memories of
his unjust firing welling up anger. And the Presbytery continued
to delay, delay, and delay in his appeal. He wanted to be in the
pulpit – Now. At that moment, Pastor Casey, the minister of
New Monmouth, bellowed in the midst of his sermon: "God

will give you what you need when you need it, not necessarily what you want when you want it." Elwood smiled and wiped a tear from his eye – *God is whispering to me*. Pastor Casey emphasized that one's joyful path to heaven always contained hardships, before ending with the country saying "Every garden party needs a skunk." *Indeed* – Elwood thought – *a skunk by the name of Van Guider*. Laura gently elbowed him in the ribs; he was laughing too enthusiastically.

Afterwards, Helen introduced Arany to Earl Smith, who as usher had handed a church bulletin to Arany before the service. Earl had been raised in the Hackens area of Sycamore Valley. In the course of their conversation, he told her that his dad, "Dude" Smith, bought boot-strapping molasses from Joe Reynolds in the 1940s, but he really couldn't add anything as to why Joe Reynolds shot the Muterspaw brothers.

But Earl did recall an interesting story: "When I was a youth growing up in the 1930s, quarrels among neighbors were quite common – with firepower being both judge and jury. Once, a friend and I collected hickory nuts on the road not far from my house. A few hours later, old man Ford rode up to my house on his big brown horse. He confronted my dad on our front yard and told him to keep me from gathering the nuts from his hickory tree. Dude told the old man that the road was public property, then walked over to the porch and picked up his shotgun. He pointed the gun at old man Ford and strongly suggested he shut up and get off his property."

With a new sense of purpose Elwood started to write a treatise on the Beatitudes. After penning the first two chapters, he sent them to Luther House, a leading publisher of Christian literature. Not only did their editors provide encouragement in the form of a book contract but also suggested that he write a children's book in conjunction with his project. He threw himself completely into these projects – perhaps he was meant to educate the next generation of preachers and children instead of being a preacher himself. Laura and Arany became his first readers and his enthusiastic cheerleaders.

In feedback to Elwood on a chapter she had read in his children's book, Arany commented, "It's just like reading that new anti-gravity book."

"I don't understand," Elwood scrunched his face in puzzlement.

"Apparently you can't put it down," Arany laughed.

Meanwhile, Arany started a house church, holding Bible study at the Sycamore Valley home, at seven o'clock on Tuesday nights and eleven o'clock on Thursday mornings. She distributed flyers announcing the get-togethers in mailboxes up and down roads in the neighborhood. The gatherings started out small, only one person showing up the first week, but typically increasing by one or two each week thereafter. Attendees then spread the joy of Arany's meetings by word-of-mouth – with youths flocking there on Tuesday nights and retirees in the mornings. Arany blossomed as a humble spiritual leader, with the support of her daddy, Laura, and Troy.

Troy made his mission the clearing of the trees and brush around the Adventist church foundation. The hum of his chainsaw competed with the rat-tat-tat of the woodpeckers. He supported Arany's dream – from her calling to the ministry to its next phase, the construction of an eventual chapel at this location. Although both Troy and Arany had youthful enthusiasm in tackling the project and budding love for each other, they unfortunately lacked the finances required to build the house of praise and worship.

† † †

Arany awoke before Laura and Elwood. She threw a coat over her nightgown and pulled boots on her bare feet. It was a heavy frost for the first day of winter, as she stumbled out the front door to pick up the morning newspaper. Barney, of course, ran aside her, yearning for the opportunity to chase a critter.

Upon returning to the kitchen and pouring a glass of orange juice, she started on the daily crossword puzzle. It was filled with cleverness. The clue for 2-across was "Gets wet with drying?" while that for 13-down was "Area between N and P?" Both had five letters. She scanned down to 22-across, "Book of the unmentioned God?" with five letters. That one she knew.

The only book of the Bible in which God isn't mentioned is the book of "E-S-T-E-R." She chuckled to herself; one could also produce an "E-S-T-E-R" in chemistry upon the reaction of a carboxylic acid with an alcohol. She continued to fill in other words, then smiled as she wrote "T-O-W-E-L" for 2-across and "O-Z-O-N-E" for 13-down.

Elwood popped into the kitchen and groaned, "Good morning," as he fumbled with the coffee maker. Arany blurted, "45-across . . . clue is 'Two-faced God' . . . five letters with the first two being 'J' and 'A.'"

"Believe it or not, I actually know the answer. It's J-A-N-U-S."

"Wow. I'm impressed. I guess we get January from Janus."

"That's right," Elwood responded with a yawn. "Sometimes my course on Greek and Roman mythology back in Seminary is useful. Janus was the Roman god of doors or transitions. He had two faces because one was always looking to the past, while the other to the future."

She finished the puzzle, got up from the table, and went up to her bedroom to get dressed. She splashed a few drops of her new perfume – a subtle, pleasant scent and a gift – around her neck. Troy told her he wished he could take credit for the gift, but Sunshine Clutterbuck unexpectedly stopped by his work site to give him some of her new formulation, "Lavender Magic," for his lady friend.

Troy would soon arrive as they were going on a shopping excursion to the local WalMart. She looked out the window at the profile of BUG on the backyard shed – *I'm looking at Joe Bug Reynolds from the past, but what is he telling me for the future . . . from stones to a supposed treasure.*

† † †

Arany parked her Buick Roadmaster two spaces down from another old Roadmaster at WalMart. As they walked by the car's clone, Troy kidded, "Definitely needs a paint job."

"Just like a Timex, Roadmasters take a lickin' but keep on tickin'."

The other Roadmaster was still there when they finished shopping. Arany cranked the ignition on her Roadmaster and started to back out of the space. Troy had her stop. He jumped out and stared at the other car. He kept looking, going back and forth, at the faux wood panels on the sides of the two Roadmasters.

Arany motioned for him to get back in the car and mouthed, "Let's get going."

Instead, Troy excitedly yelled, "Turn off the car," and waved for her to join him.

He directed Arany to compare the texture of her car's wooden panels to the other car's. Arany rolled her eyes and shrugged, "It's fake wood on both." She poked him in the ribs. "You going crazy or something."

"Only crazy over you," laughed Troy. Arany blushed. He leaned closer to her and took a deep breath. "Maybe the scent of Lavender Magic is driving me crazy."

He pointed again at the wood panels. "But look at the fake wood – they're different, slightly different color and nature of the fake wood grain, they should be the same for the same model of car."

"So what?"

Troy shook his head and mumbled, "Could it be déjà vu all over again?" He pulled out his pocket knife and was about to use it to scrape the wooden panels on Arany's car.

"Whoa, there! You're gonna scratch my car."

"Yeah, as if anyone would notice? Trust me." Troy scraped off a layer of brownish paint to expose a shiny yellow color underneath.

He went to another wooden panel further back on that side. The same metallic yellow beneath the brown.

Arany, now wide-eyed, stuttered, "Does . . . does . . . does this mean what I think?"

"Perhaps instead of calling your car a tank, we should have called it a whale," laughed Troy as he hugged Arany.

Arany grabbed Troy's pocket knife and ran to the other side of the car. She scraped some paint off the panels. "Definitely faux wood," she jumped up and down in glee.

"Just like Silas, to be hiding 'something special' in plain sight," Troy threw up his arms. He did some quick mental calculations. "No wonder you got terrible gas mileage. You've probably been driving around with a million dollars or so of gold in your car's sides."

Arany stopped jumping and stared at the wooden car panels.

Troy pulled his keys from his pocket. He slid one behind a panel and twisted. "It should be easy to pull these panels off the car. And I remember the wholesaler to whom Twin Falls sold Silas' other gold from the whale's belly."

Arany looked upward. "Thank you, Silas."

Chapter Thirty One
FIDDLESTICKS

Weeks later, Arany turned her Buick Roadmaster, free of its faux wooden panels, onto Sycamore Valley Road on her way home. She was almost a millionaire. She could afford a new car, one with better gas mileage. But she couldn't imagine trading in this Roadmaster, which had been so full of unexpected treasures. She'd rather invest the money in her vision, that of a chapel on the foundation of the old Adventist Church in Sycamore Valley. The site had already been cleared by Troy and her. Blueprints and plans were being discussed.

She saw Sharon Holland, bundled up in her coat and scarf, picking up her mail from her box next to the road. Sharon waved her down.

"Do you have a moment?" Sharon asked. Each breath could be seen as a white fog from her mouth in the raw wintry cold. "Come on in the house. I want to show you something that you might find of interest. My daughter reminded me about it the other day."

Once inside, Arany was immediately greeted with a cup of hot tea and a plateful of cookies, and directed to a cozy chair in the living room. The gas fireplace kept the room a toasty temperature. Sharon pointed to a glass case hung on the wall in the room's corner.

"That fiddle was made by my great-grandfather Joe Reynolds," she proudly exclaimed.

"Amazing," Arany set her cup on the end table. She sprung from her chair and dashed to the glass case.

"Grandpa Joe was quite a craftsman," Sharon volunteered. "He also played a mean fiddle; he always played it at family hoe-downs."

Arany stared at the fiddle through the front of the glass case.

"But the really amazing thing is that he made it from scrap wood while he was serving his time in prison," added Sharon.

"What?" Arany pressed her face even closer to the glass case. "I couldn't tell this fiddle from a professionally made one. It . . . It's perfect."

Sharon smiled from ear to ear.

Arany returned to her chair, but continued to look at the fiddle. "So Joe not only played the fiddle, but also built 'em." She nibbled on a cookie.

"Grandpa Joe may have made other fiddles, but this is the only musical instrument that I know he made," Sharon offered. "I guess he had plenty of time to spare in the state pen. I remember that he could build or fix almost anything."

"Helen told me the legend that one can hear your grandpa Joe playing the fiddle from the bridge in our hollow on snowy nights."

"And they're calling for snow later tonight." Sharon chuckled, "I think it helps you to hear the fiddling when you have a jar of moonshine in your hand. They say he plays his favorite song – the ballad of 'Barbara Allen.'"

That night over dinner, Arany shared her chance meeting of Sharon Holland with her dad and Laura. Elwood's eyes lit up. He kept repeating, "Fiddle's made out of scrap wood by Joe Reynolds . . . made out of scrap wood by Joe . . . made out of scrap wood . . . scrap wood." He looked out the window as if in a trance.

Laura made the connection for Arany. "John Petticrew made the beautiful dowry box for his daughter Judith from scrap wood at the distillery where he worked. In it was hidden the journal of Judith. So, it's –"

"Oh, my," Arany exclaimed. "And Joe Reynolds made a beautiful fiddle out of scrap wood in prison. So, could the fiddle likewise have something hidden inside?" With every word spoken, her excitement continued to build. "But where would that something be hidden? It's not like you can build a secret compartment in a fiddle."

Laura caught Elwood's eyes as his eyes returned to the table. She smiled, "Thinking about the Petticrew treasure?"

"We need to call Sharon," Elwood responded. "We need to find out whether we can see the fiddle up close." He bounded up from his dinner chair, leaving half his pork chop uneaten on his plate, and ran to a junk drawer in the kitchen. After ransacking its contents, he scurried to the bathroom where he was heard rumbling through its drawers as well. Barney, from his vantage point on a nearby chair, eyed the half-eaten pork chop.

Within the next hour, all three were in the living room of Sharon Holland. She gladly removed the fiddle from its case and allowed Elwood, and Arany, and Laura, in turn to inspect it. No obvious secret compartments.

"Has anyone ever played this fiddle," Elwood twanged on the fiddle's loose strings and inspected the bow still in the glass case.

"All the time when I was young," Sharon smiled, "but not recently. Not too many fiddle players left in the family."

Elwood then had Laura hold the fiddle in front of him, while he took a penlight and a small cosmetic mirror from his pocket. He stuck the thin mirror into the fiddle's long narrow sound hole while shining the flashlight. He reflected the light first up its neck. Nothing. Then into its body. Nothing. He shrugged in disappointment.

Laura gave him the fiddle and took his penlight and mirror.

"You think I missed something in there," he chuckled.

"No, but I just thought of another possibility." She spent the next several minutes continuously changing the direction and angle of the mirror. Everyone else stared at her in silence. Finally a grin appeared on Laura's face. She gave Arany the fiddle, and the penlight and mirror back to Elwood.

"Orient the mirror so you're looking in the middle of the top board," she told Elwood.

Elwood gasped. "You're right. A series of numbers inscribed on the board."

Arany exhaled and clapped her hands. "No treasure . . . but another puzzle."

"Huh?" Sharon looked confused in all the excitement. Laura explained that the widow Reynolds left a message for Arany that Joe Reynolds had hidden a "treasure" for her. They thought it might have been in the fiddle, but instead the numbers might provide them with some kind of code for the location of the treasure.

Laura rustled through her pocket book and announced to Elwood: "OK, dear. I've found a piece of paper and pen. Read the numbers. Remember you're seeing the mirror image."

Elwood turned to Sharon. "Perhaps it'd be easier if we take a crowbar and pull the fiddle apart to get to the numbers – it's quite a long string. We'll put it back together afterwards."

Sharon sucked in her breath and her eyes bulged.

"Only kidding," Elwood added.

Elwood painstakingly and slowly called out the numbers to Laura –

16532 2362 673 4683 73186 673 653 4332 765

"So what does it mean?" Sharon asked.

"It means we have to solve a code," Elwood answered as he returned the fiddle to Sharon. He turned to Laura: "I guess Joe Reynolds put this one together instead of Silas or his twin sister."

"Maybe Silas learned from the master," Laura chuckled.

Both Laura and Elwood looked at Arany: "It's all yours!"

Arany sat at the kitchen table, a blank piece of paper and the numerical code on a notecard in front of her. She strummed a pencil on the table. She was alone except for Barney lying at her feet. For the past week all attempts at deciphering the message went for naught. Her first observation was that zero and nine weren't used in the code, only one through eight. But was this only serendipity or meaningful? Because the chemical code based on iridium oxidation states had been used to open Silas' safe, she initially focused on sets of eight in chemistry. The numbers might represent the eight elements in a row on the periodic table . . . or octets of electrons in an atom. Nothing – besides which, Joe Reynolds wouldn't have had access to such chemical reasoning in the 1930s. She tried other groups of eight. Nothing.

Suddenly, Arany rationalized – *673 is used twice in the sequence; maybe it's either the common word "the" or "and."* She quickly wrote those letters above the numbers on the paper. Nothing – just the beginnings of gibberish. She scratched her forehead with the pencil's eraser and sighed.

Arany felt Barney stir at her feet. A loud thump on the front door echoed throughout the house. Barney jumped up, barked excitedly, and ran out the kitchen into the living room toward the door. Another set of booming bangs, then a door crashing open, and someone stomped inside. Barney barking evolved to snarling.

Arany stuffed the notecard in her back pocket. Barney kept barking.

"Shut up, ya mutt!" Arany heard as she headed to the foyer through the living room. She immediately recognized the voice, as well as its tone, and wished she could hide. She hesitated before walking on.

"Well. Hello, Arany. Since you wouldn't answer your phone, I had to travel over several states to talk to you."

Arany stood face to face with her angry, drunk mother. Dot wore a stocking hat, an ill-fitting coat, dirty jeans, and carried a heavy walking stick. Her face matched her disheveled clothes. The pupils of her red eyes seemed to bulge out of their sockets.

"Mother, are you okay? You look like you haven't slept in a week. How did you drive here?"

Barney, still growling, retreated behind Arany's legs. His eyes fixated on the bedraggled and threatening Dot.

"I'm fine," Dot shouted, "as if you would care. Shut that dog up. Why do you even leave him in the house?" She pointed her cane threateningly at Barney.

"Mother, you need to leave and sober up. You scare me when you're like this." Arany took a step backwards.

"Not before I get to talk to my daughter," Dot slurred. "I guess you don't want to talk to me because that scumbag Elwood and his floozy wife have poisoned your mind."

"No, they've given me the opportunity to live in peace." Arany's whole body was shaking. Tears trickled down her cheeks.

"I hear you came into some money. I need some. I've come for my share. It's time for you to start supporting me."

"No amount of money will ever bring you happiness," Arany replied defiantly.

Dot moved close enough to Arany that Arany could taste the alcohol on her breath.

"I figure several thousand would be sufficient for all those years I took care of you – but now you just want to toss your mother aside like yesterday's garbage," Dot grimaced.

"Why won't you tell me my birth father?" Arany shot back, with tears flowing.

"Because he's some low life," Dot half-laughed, "just like Elwood."

"Who is he?"

"He ran away with a horrid woman to who knows where," Dot screamed, her face bright red. "One more reason to hate God."

"But who?"

"Some guy by the name of J. T. He actually lived near here, on the other side of Hog Back Mountain," cackled Dot. "They called him 'Beats' Reynolds; he played the drums in some no-name rock band in his spare time."

Arany gasped and connected the dots. "Why don't you come back tomorrow when you feel better?" pleaded Arany without sincerity.

Dot grabbed Arany by the shoulders. "Not until I get some money."

Arany shivered with emotion and sobbed uncontrollably. Tears fell by the bucket. Barney growled louder and nosed Dot's ankle in warning.

"Get away ya mutt." She kicked hard at Barney, hitting him squarely in the nose and sending him sprawling about four feet back.

Arany tried to turn to care for Barney.

Dot shook her: "You listen to me!" She shoved Arany hard.

Arany tumbled awkwardly backwards onto the couch, and shrieked in pain when she knocked her head into the wall. With both hands, Dot raised her cane. Simultaneously, the jaws of a protective Scottish terrier clamped down on Dot's ankle, just when a furious mountain man put a bear hug on her from the rear. He easily picked her off the ground kicking and screaming.

"Maam. I'd advise you to stop kicking," Troy calmly stated. He increased the pressure of the squeeze. The wind escaped from her lungs. Barney relaxed his grip knowing it was no longer needed. "For every future kick, I'll break a rib," Troy added, with a little squeeze.

Dot quieted down.

Troy turned, walked out the front door, and dropped her like a sack of potatoes on the ground in front of the porch. "Maam. I'd advise you never to come back until you're invited."

Dot stared wide-eyed, flat on her back, at the behemoth of a man towering over her with a scowl on his face. He growled, "And if you ever touch Arany again, it'll be your last time."

Dot staggered to her car, coughing and trying to catch her breath. She wasted no time in pushing the gas pedal down and kicking up gravel. Troy made a quick phone call to the Sheriff's Department. He had seen a deputy at the Kerrs Creek Fire Department on his way to Sycamore Valley. Arany sat on the couch, bent over with head in her hands, crying. Barney nosed his head under her hands and started to lick the tears away.

Troy sat down next to her, and gently took her into an all-consuming and comforting hug. He whispered in her ear: "I'm here. That'll never happen again."

She swept away some of the tears, and gave Barney a gentle pet on the side of the face. Then, she leaned into Troy, brushed her hair from her face, and kissed him passionately. Afterwards, she continued to sob softly against Troy's chest. Thoughts swirled from the rage of her mother to the name of her birth father, from her mother's greed to her connection to the Reynolds family, from gold in the Roadmaster's panels to the Petticrew treasure. She tried to come to terms with her emotions.

After about a half-hour of silence, Arany finally spoke, "Troy, will you walk with me to Chapel Rock?"

† † †

Troy lifted Arany onto the top surface of Chapel Rock where she sat while Troy leaned against it holding her hand. Quiet reigned except for the breeze blowing through the leafless trees and the chirping of a nearby chickadee. Arany wanted time to process the encounter with her mother before discussing it with Troy . . . as well as to pray.

Snow clouds started to gather before Arany inhaled deeply and spoke. She told Troy that before her mother arrived, she'd been trying to solve the numerical puzzle from Joe Reynolds' fiddle. Hope churned that its solution would lead her to the Petticrew treasure, for which she'd been assigned to be the keeper. At least her mother finally gave her the reason why she was chosen for this responsibility – her birth father was also a Reynolds, a dog kin cousin of the widow Reynolds, Silas, and also Joe Reynolds. Troy compassionately touched her arm.

"But I hit a dead end with the code," she sighed softly. "It's probably simpler than I'm making it out to be."

Troy's heart fluttered as her flaxen hair twirled gently in the wind and she squeezed his hand. The first snow flake likewise fluttered through the sky. Arany tried to catch it in mid-flight. Troy smiled and calmly confided, "Arany, I agree. I thought about the puzzle on my drive to your house today. I think you may have overlooked the obvious."

"Tell me about it," she beamed against the backdrop of White Rock Mountain.

Troy laughed, "When I was about ten years old, I wanted to play the fiddle like my dad. I nagged him until he gave me a few lessons. But he quickly gave up – said I had no natural rhythm. Then my mother paid for me to take piano lessons; I guess trying to impose some culture on her redneck son. The piano teacher told my mother after about ten lessons, 'Save your money. Your son has no talent, or even ability, to play music.'"

Arany chuckled, "I've noticed your lack of musical ability when you try to sing at church."

Troy exhaled – glad that humor had returned to Arany. "Well, you don't have to pile on . . . to agree so quickly to my lack of musical talent," Troy provided mock outrage.

"Okay," Arany smiled, "you make music with your chainsaw. But what does this have to do with breaking the code?"

"I do remember that music has octaves, eight notes from middle C to high C, so –"

"Hmmm," she pondered, "that makes sense. The numbers were inside a fiddle, so the code breaker should be musical. I was hung up on chemistry. But it means the use of only seven letters . . . but maybe." She pulled out the notecard from her back pocket.

She searched for a pen or pencil. Nothing. Troy found a stubby one, point broken off, in his front pocket.

Arany grinned, "Why can't you write with a broken pencil?"

Thinking initially that Arany was serious, he looked at the pencil. "Well, it's hard –"

"Because it's pointless," Arany interrupted.

With a big smile on his face, he quickly sharpened the pencil with his pocket knife.

Arany wrote:

CDEFGABC
12 34 56 78

She translated the first group of letters. Hopes grew – "caged," an actual word. She continued –

16532   2362   673   4683   73186   673   653   4332   765
CAGED DEAD ABE FACE BECCA ABE AGE FEED BAG

"Well, there're all words," Arany smiled. "Now, what do they mean?"

"Abraham and Rebecca Reynolds are buried in the old family cemetery." Troy returned the smile.

"I guess 'caged dead' must be another way of saying graves," she countered. "After all Joe Reynolds was limited in the letters he could use – he couldn't spell grave in this code."

"Makes sense," he agreed.

"So you go to Abe, or Abraham, Reynolds' grave. Then you face his wife Becca's, or Rebecca's, grave. Then what?"

"Abe's age might be the next phrase," proposed Troy.

"I think I remember that Abraham's age at death was 63 years old. But what then is 'feed bag'?" she asked with anticipation.

"Maybe it means you go the length of 63 feed bags."

"How big is a feed bag?"

They hurried back to the house through the snow flurry, already coating the ground white. They detoured a bit to double check that Abraham Reynolds had indeed died at age 63.

The internet search informed them that most feed bags before 1950 were 100 pound bags, but with sizes varying from a width of 36 to 39 inches and from a length of 43 to 48 inches – although a "standard" feed bag was 39 by 46 inches. 63 feed bags long would be about 241.5 feet, or 80.5 yards. Troy grabbed two shovels, a tape measure, and some small flags from his truck; and they walked through the light snow to the old family cemetery.

Arany stood at the grave stone of Abraham, while Troy lined the tape measure parallel to Rebecca's separate gravestone. He extended the tape measure its full fifty feet and planted a flag. Arany moved ahead to that flag as Troy plodded another fifty feet with the tape measure uphill. They repeated this procedure until they hit the full 241.5 feet, where Troy planted the final flag. He then outlined a circle about twenty feet in diameter – their target range to dig for the Petticrew treasure. Fortunately, no large trees or boulders populated the area.

Light snow continued to fall. Arany playfully threw a snowball at Troy, then fell back first onto the snow at the center of the target area. She outstretched her arms and legs, sweeping them back and forth and shouting, "Let's christen this location properly with snow angels."

Troy followed her lead, falling backwards into the snow and creating a second and much larger snow angel. Both rolled over on their sides, and Troy slid her body to him. Their lips met in a gentle kiss.

They first cleared the target area of underbrush, saplings, and rocks. Then, they dug holes at random locations. Digging was often difficult with roots and rocks galore – some small, many large. No treasure. By the end of the afternoon, the area looked like an exploded mine field. Their bodies were tired, but their enthusiasm wasn't crushed.

Arany suggested, "Let's call it a day. After dinner, let's take some mugs of hot chocolate and sit on the bridge over the dry creek bed. Maybe we'll be able to hear Joe Reynolds playing his fiddle."

† † †

Clear blue skies greeted Arany the next morning. The cold morning quickly warmed; by noon, only splotches of snow remained to dot Sycamore Valley. Troy brought a borrowed metal detector to aid in their renewed search for the treasure. Arany watched Troy methodically tackling the task as she sat on a blanket on top of Chapel Rock about fifty feet from the search area. But by mid-afternoon, the collected treasure consisted only of an old bottle cap and a few nails in the target area, then a piece of barbed wire and a badly rusted horseshoe in an even expanded region.

They went back to the old family graveyard to double check their orientation and direction. Arany noticed that the small gravestone for Rebecca was cattywampus from that of Abraham. Upon closer inspection, Troy discovered that the gravestone for Rebecca had been twisted on its base, probably from a tree falling on it. Originally it seemed to have been parallel to that of Abraham's. So they measured the 63 feed bags in a slightly different direction, only a few degrees change.

They repeated their measuring routine. A few times they had to go around large trees and boulders.

241.5 feet ended smack dab in the middle of Chapel Rock.

Troy scratched the back of his head. "Unless Joe Reynolds had a backhoe or a crane, I don't think he moved this boulder on top of the treasure."

"Perhaps it's buried somewhere around the perimeter of the rock," Arany suggested.

Both Arany and Troy dug round and round the rock. Nothing. The metal detector found twenty-one bottle caps.

Troy chuckled, "Perhaps someone liked to drink beer while at your Chapel Rock."

"Perhaps the treasure isn't something," Arany mused. "Maybe I'm supposed to be the keeper of an idea, like my dad with his Blessed Eight. It's defining me to take an action."

Troy shook his head. "I don't understand?"

"Weeks ago I felt a calling to the ministry . . . I started a house church group . . . I dreamt about rebuilding a chapel on the foundation of the old Adventist church on this property – the place identified in Joe Reynolds' obituary . . . then I was gifted a trove of gold by Silas . . . I commissioned blueprints for this chapel, but have had lingering doubts about getting started on construction." Arany exhaled. With one hand she grabbed Troy's hand, and with the other touched Chapel Rock. "Now the puzzle, the treasure map in a sense, leads us to a rock formation that we've appropriately called 'Chapel Rock.' Are we being led by the Spirit step by step to build the chapel, the treasure for which I am the keeper?"

"When do you want to start?"

Chapter Thirty Two
SYCAMORE VALLEY GOLD

Chapel construction started within the week in a flurry of activity. In several months, by late summer, Arany moved her house church activities to the main room of the chapel, while the chapel's steeple was still being built. The unpretentious sanctuary of the Sycamore Valley Chapel was much like the Adventist Church that once stood at that location. This chapel, though, became known to the locals as the "Chapel of the Golden-Haired Girl."

Arany's happiness periodically turned to sadness upon receipt of rambling and demanding messages from her mother. She ignored them, then became concerned when the messages suddenly stopped. In late summer, a short note arrived in the mail –

> My dearest Arany,
> I'm sorry for all the pain I've caused you these past few years. I've just received my one week AA sobriety chip. I hope you'll find it in your heart to forgive me.
> Love, Mom

Tears of happiness flowed. Arany immediately telephoned. Over the next hour, Dot and Arany reconnected as a mother and a daughter with mutual hope for the future. Arany talked to a transformed mother, one she remembered while growing up at the parsonage. She bubbled with news of the chapel and, of course, her boyfriend Troy who Dot had already encountered. Dot even ended with a heartfelt "Tell Elwood I'm sorry."

Meanwhile, Elwood finished his treatise on the Blessed Eight. Books flew off the shelves; it was a highly acclaimed success. Seldom a week went by that Elwood and Laura weren't invited to another church or conference to disseminate its message. The accompanying children's book likewise became a best-seller. Luther House, his publisher, signed Elwood to write a follow-up book, tentatively titled *Being a Christian*.

† † †

At the conclusion of a Thursday morning Bible study, both Elwood and Arany stood in the back of the sanctuary greeting and talking to participants. An elderly visitor, Marilyn Holzschuh, came up to Arany and expressed admiration for Arany's name and flowing golden locks. In the course of their conversation, they discovered they both had a common heritage; they both traced their grandparents to Eastern Europe. Mrs. Holzschuh had just returned from visiting relatives in Budapest.

Mrs. Holzschuh, with a twinkle in her eye, inquired, "Do you know what Arany means in Hungarian?"

Arany politely shook her head. "I was named after my grandmother Arany." She smiled, "Maybe I can start telling people she's Hungarian instead of Eastern European."

Mrs. Holzschuh pointed to Arany's hair. "It's an appropriate name – it's Hungarian for gold."

"Oh, my," Arany exclaimed. Her mouth opened but couldn't say more.

Another person standing nearby interjected, "Both gold the metal and gold the Arany are definitely precious."

Arany stood red-faced. A group gathered around the exchange.

Mrs. Holzschuh laughed, "And there's even more. Your last name is Aldott." She hesitated, then added, "In Hungarian, it means blessed." She hugged Arany and departed. Elwood looked at his daughter with fatherly pride.

Within moments, all knew their Bible study leader as "Sycamore Valley Gold" or "The Blessed One," much to Arany's embarrassment. They believed that God must have had plans for Arany even at her birth.

The crowd had dwindled to only a few when Sharon Holland approached Arany with a photograph in hand. She handed an old black-and-white picture to Arany. "I thought you might like a picture of my great-grandfather Joe Reynolds."

Arany stared, totally mesmerized. "The eyes . . . the beard."

"I think he must've been in his seventies when this photo was taken," Sharon added.

Arany turned to Elwood. "Daddy, look at this picture of Joe Bug."

At his first glance, Elwood turned white as a ghost. He murmured, "We need to take a trip."

Photograph of Joe Bug Reynolds

Chapter Thirty Three
THE STONE

Elwood and Arany pulled off South River Road in front of Silas' Jonah-and-the-whale sculpture at Twin Falls Presbyterian Church. He grabbed the picture of Joe Bug Reynolds setting on the car's console and ran to the sculpture. Arany lagged behind wondering – *What's this mission of my dad?* Elwood stood opposite Jonah with Joe Bug's picture next to Jonah's face.

"See," he excitedly pointed at Jonah. "Compare to Joe Bug without glasses and hat."

Arany glanced back and forth from the picture to Jonah. She stuttered, "They . . . They're the same."

"Indeed," Elwood nodded, "I knew I'd seen that face every week for many years."

"But what does it mean?" Arany scrunched her face.

"Clearly Silas must've used Joe Bug as the model for his sculpture of Jonah."

"I guess, especially with his long beard, Joe Bug looks like an old Testament prophet," she mulled. "But, daddy, why would Silas have used his cousin as his model?"

Elwood ruffled his hair with his hands as he paced in front of the sculpture. Suddenly, he dropped to his knees under the sculpture of the whale, then stood up in the cavity exposed by the removal of the hidden gold. He rooted around a bit, before focusing on the inside rear of the whale.

"Here it is!" he yelled.

"What?" Arany wondered.

"B.A.? by Bessie," he shouted even louder.

"What're you talking about?" Arany threw her hands up in frustration.

"Notice that Jonah is pointing. I thought I had that figured out a while back – that he had been pointing at the cache of gold in the whale's belly. But maybe that wasn't the real treasure he was pointing to," Elwood rambled in his excitement. "Maybe it had been Joe Bug pointing to the real treasure all along. Come on in here and see."

Elwood popped out of the bottom of the whale and grinned from ear to ear.

Arany maneuvered herself into the belly of the whale and looked to the rear. "You're right. 'B.A.? by Bessie' is inscribed into the brass. Very small, but very clear." She turned and looked back out the whale's mouth. "And Jonah, or Joe Bug, is pointing right at the message."

"Silas must've put it there. In fact, it would've been impossible to see the writing from the whale's mouth. The gold had to have been removed first."

"But what does the message mean?"

Elwood laughed, "This is Silas – a riddle, a puzzle, a code . . . who knows?"

"So the Petticrew treasure might be something other than the chapel?" Arany wiggled back out of the whale's belly.

"And all you have to do is decipher Silas' clue," Elwood continued to laugh. "And it has a question mark, so it must be C-L-E-V-E-R."

Arany sighed, and thought for a moment. "Jonah kept disobeying God, but then begrudgingly followed His instructions. Maybe, likewise, Joe Bug screwed up in his mission, but came through in the end with the Petticrew treasure."

Elwood nodded. They were, though, distracted by a car parking behind Elwood's along South River Road. Peggy Lauderdale quickly jumped out of the car with a look of surprise. Elwood exhaled deeply – *I'm not supposed to be here.* She walked to Elwood. Tears formed in her eyes.

"Oh, Pastor Martin, I'm so glad to see you," she wept softly and stepped into a hug.

"Gee, and I was afraid I'd be kicked off the grounds," smiled Elwood.

"No way. You've been sorely missed," Peggy swept the tears from her eyes with her sleeve. "The ruling elders were going to call you this week."

"Huh?" Elwood stepped back.

"The session finally stood up to the Presbytery and fired Rev. Rohrbaugh before he totally destroyed this church," Peggy snarled. "We're losing members by the droves. His sermons were monotone and the equivalent to taking a sleeping pill. Harry Whitmer had been rating Rev. Rohrbaugh's sermons on his acorn scale from 0 to 73, with 73 being the total number of acorns carved in the sanctuary woodwork. I think Harry counted over 65 every week. But, as you alluded when you left, Rohrbaugh's mission was to raid the coffers of the church for the Presbytery. In that regard, he was very successful."

"I'm sorry," Elwood breathed.

"Will you consider coming back to Twin Falls as our pastor?" pleaded Peggy. "We need you. Can you ever forgive us for turning our backs on you?"

Elwood was taken aback. He, once again, ruffled his hair with his hands as comb. "I never expected such a surprise offer. But I suspect the Presbyter, Rev. Van Guiden, might have something to say about a possible return on my part."

"You don't have to worry about him. For one, Hansford did some research on what he told us about you – it was all a line of bull. Hansford has been a thorn in the side of the Presbytery, Synod, and UAPC ever since, constantly complaining," Peggy seethed. "And secondly, Van Guiden's no longer affiliated with our Presbytery. Can you believe this? – he was actually promoted to a position with the Atlantic Synod of UAPC. I think the Presbytery will allow us to call anyone as pastor, just to get Hansford and the rest of Twin Falls off their backs. Hansford also just got word from Attorney Dawes that the UAPC review of your appeal totally exonerates you from any and all wrongdoing."

"Well, I didn't know," Elwood stammered.

Peggy chuckled, "Hansford actually stomped into the Presbytery offices last week when they balked at us firing Rev. Rohrbaugh. He called them the 'Dark Fire' Presbytery."

Elwood smiled.

"Please, just consider the offer," beseeched Peggy. "We'all miss you something awful. You can continue to write books while you preach."

"Let me talk to Laura tonight," Elwood grinned and hugged Peggy.

"And bring Arany along back too," Peggy added.

Arany smiled and gave Peggy a hug. "I have other plans. You need to come visit Troy and me at Sycamore Valley Chapel."

† † †

That night after dinner, Laura and Elwood retreated to the living room to discuss the offer by Twin Falls Presbyterian Church. Arany figured it'd be a short conversation. Her daddy was already excited by the prospect of returning to the pulpit. Laura would have a shorter commute to her work at Faithful Care. And Twin Falls had this very nice parsonage at Midvale.

Meanwhile, Arany and Troy withdrew to Elwood's office to analyze Silas' latest cryptic message: "B.A.? by Bessie." Arany brought along her file of copies of correspondence between Bessie Reynolds and Ressie Muterspaw, and saved by Helen Irvine. Arany rationalized that this was the Bessie in the clue. On the desk she spread out the poems, limericks, songs, and ballads written back and forth between the two friends around 1900. She scanned everything. Nothing. Troy admired her beauty.

In exasperation, Arany grumbled, "What does 'B.A.?' mean? Is it a question, an uncertainty, a college degree, or a clever clue as in a crossword puzzle?"

"Since this is from Silas, and inspired by Joe Reynolds, I would go with cleverness," Troy snickered.

"But there's nothing, absolutely nothing, with a B.A. on it in anything written or received by Bessie," Arany complained.

"Maybe it's something she wrote that's not in this file," Troy offered. "As I understand, Bessie was Joe Bug's younger sister, as well as Helen's grandmother, as well as Sharon's great aunt. Would anyone else have writings of Bessie?"

"Or maybe it got tossed in the trash years ago," she moaned. "I'll give Helen a call in the morning to see whether she has anything else . . . and maybe Sharon and Madeline also." Arany started to gather her papers. As she did so, the ballad of "Bobralin" written by Bessie for Ressie caught the eye of Troy.

"Just a minute," Troy looked at the words of "Bobralin" more closely. He grimaced as he read. After a few moments, a smile appeared. "You know, the words in this ballad are similar to those I remember in 'Barbara Allen,' the song I wanted my daddy to teach me to play on the fiddle years ago."

"And the song the ghost of Joe Bug supposedly plays on snowy nights up at the bridge," Arany added. "So what?"

Troy took Arany's hands in his. "Say Bessie's 'Bobralin' ten times real fast."

"I don't understand," Arany shrugged.

"Just do it," Troy hugged her and gave her a kiss.

"Bobralin . . . Bobralen . . . Babralen . . . Babra alen . . . Barbra Alen . . . Barbra Allen . . . Barbara Allen . . . oh, my," exclaimed Arany. "Bessie's Barbara Allen or 'B.A.?' She spelled it like she heard it being sung."

"I hate to throw water on this party," Troy chuckled, "but now that we've figured out that 'B.A.? by Bessie' might refer to this 'Bobralin,' so what? How does that direct you to the treasure?"

Arany was already on her smart phone looking up the words to the real "Barbara Allen." "Let's see how the real ballad differs from Bessie's?"

They compared the words.

"The main difference appears to be the final refrain," Troy offered. "The ballad song by Dolly Parton, Bob Dylan, Pete Seeger, and others have the rose and briar intertwining in an old churchyard – the rose from Willie and the briar from Barbara Allen. In Bessie's version, the briar comes from Barbara Allen and the rose from Willie and they intertwine in the true lover's knot up the church steeple."

"That's it!" Arany shouted and jumped into Troy's arms.

"I don't understand," he whispered into her ear.

"Do you have a ladder?"

"I think there's one in the woodshed."

"Let's go and head to Chapel Rock," Arany laughed.

"Are you serious?" Troy looked directly into Arany's smile. "It's pitch dark outside. It's only a sliver of a moon."

"I'll grab the flashlights. You grab the ladder."

Arany and Troy disturbed the quiet of the wilderness. Even with the flashlight leading them, the aluminum ladder would clank, bumping into trees or fall after being caught in grape vines or undergrowth. On the way, Arany explained to Troy that a rose and a briar had indeed intertwined on the steeple portion of Chapel Rock. And that a sacred treasure would more likely be at the top of a steeple, not buried at its base. She couldn't wait until morning.

Troy positioned and stabilized the ladder on the steeple portion of Chapel Rock. He cautiously climbed onto the first rung. Arany caught him by the belt loop.

"I go. You hold," she insisted.

Troy realized that it was no use disagreeing with his strong-willed girlfriend. She ascended, flashlight in one hand.

Moments later Arany scared every creature in the wilderness. She yelled at the top of her lungs: "Laus Deo!" She shone the flashlight down at Troy and explained, "That's what's chiseled into the peak of the rock. Laus Deo – it's Latin for 'Praise be to God.'"

She descended cradling a short piece, but six inch diameter, of threaded steel pipe capped on both ends. It had been in a hole, impossible to see from the ground and hidden by the vines, bored in the rock's peak. Arany bear-hugged the pipe on the walk back to the house. But she soon gave the heavy piece of pipe to Troy to carry. The ladder was left behind for another day.

It was nearly midnight when they arrived at the woodshed.

Troy smiled, "I guess you'd like this opened tonight."

"I'm not going to be able to sleep otherwise," Arany hid her head in Troy's chest.

"It's not gonna be easy," he closely inspected the threads. "Both ends are pretty well rusted shut."

Troy ran to his pick-up truck and gathered a can of WD-40 and a large wrench. He then positioned the pipe in the jaws of an old vise in the woodshed. After spraying the threads on both ends several times, he allowed time for the liquid to diffuse down the threads. He tightened the wrench on the pipe cap and pushed on it. Nothing – no movement. He repeated the steps: spraying, tightening, and pushing. Nothing – the cap wouldn't budge. He tried the cap on the other side of the pipe. Nothing. Troy repositioned the pipe back to the first cap where he deemed the threads less rusted. He wiped his sweaty hands on his pants and tried again with the wrench. Nothing.

Huffing and puffing, Troy looked at Arany. "I could get my oxy-acetylene torch and slice through the pipe, but it'd burn any paper that might be inside."

"No way. I know you can open the cap," Arany implored.

Troy sprayed the threads again. Then he rooted around the piles of wood, scrap, and equipment at the other side of the woodshed. He dug out a three-foot piece of two-inch steel pipe from the pile, smiled, and slid the pipe on the handle of the wrench.

"More leverage," Troy announced to Arany. He leaned on the end of the wrench extension with all his might. He felt the threads give. He rested, then repeated – a little more movement in the cap turning on the pipe. Several more attempts resulted in a full revolution. Troy took off the extension and used just the wrench for a few more revolutions.

He stepped back and looked at Arany. "The honor's all yours."

Arany smiled, stepped up to the wrench, and gave it one last push. Both the cap and the wrench crashed to the floor.

Troy hugged Arany. "I'll wait on the front porch, so you can inspect the treasure on your own."

Arany beamed, and kissed Troy. Tears of joy streamed down her cheeks. She buried her face again into his chest. She said, "Thanks."

Arany looked into the pipe – a piece of paper wrapped around a stone. She pulled the stone from the pipe and turned it over and over in her hands. It was fist-sized, gray, smooth sided, nothing exceptional about it, and fit almost perfectly in the palm of her hand. She could have picked up a similar rock in the back yard . . . or one that Amos Muterspaw had thrown at Bug's profile on this same woodshed. However, it had an odd feel about it – it seemed as though energy flowed from the rock into her body. The sensation combined the magical and the mystical. She pulled out the paper as she slid the rock back into the pipe. The yellowed piece of paper held a handwritten note in old script.

Revelation of John Petticrew

I was in the portal to heaven with Jesus. He told me I could ask Him one question. I said – When the Pharisees asked you about stoning the adulterer because she had broken the law, Scripture says You wrote on the ground. I asked – What did you write? Jesus smiled. He told me – Most people would probably have asked Me to prove that indeed I am Jesus, like doubting Thomas. But you clearly believe in me.

I was then living the scene with Jesus, not just as an observer but a participant. The Pharisees were egging on the crowd. The adulterer looked beautiful, but yet beat up and weary, and scared. Jesus bent down to write with a stick, and made a figure eight, then a sideways eight next to it. He kept retracing all. He whispered to me, "That's what I call a Blessed Eight – no beginning, no ending, forever. I'm just making them wait for my answer." Before Jesus rose, He picked up a stone, showed them the stone, and told the Pharisees, "He who is without sin, throw the first stone." They slowly dispersed, and he told the adulterer to sin no more. Jesus then gave me the stone he had in his hand.

When I reappeared from the portal, I still had the stone in my hand. This divinely held stone is a priceless treasure from above.

Arany spent hours reading and re-reading the revelation, while holding the stone tight to her heart. She was humbled – she was the keeper of this treasure. She knelt in prayer, asking God her next step. *Does she keep the treasure hidden, or does she announce it to a skeptical world?*

An hour before daybreak, Arany slid the paper and stone back inside the pipe, then threaded the cap back onto the pipe. She tightened the cap as best she could with the wrench and carried it to the front porch. Troy, half-asleep, mindlessly rocked on the front porch.

Her kiss woke him. "Troy, can we walk down to the chapel?"

"Of course," he replied, without questioning why.

Arany handed him the pipe to carry, while she manned the flashlight. They slowly walked along Sycamore Valley Road toward the chapel.

Arany reached out and wrapped her free arm around Troy's waist. "Thanks for respecting my role as keeper of the Petticrew treasure."

"The widow Reynolds would've listed me as a co-keeper if she wanted me to see it," he countered. He stopped, then turned toward Arany: "I'm looking at my treasure."

She smiled and gently kissed him.

Troy turned, started walking again, and chuckled, "My only hope is that you appoint our son or daughter to be the next keeper of the Petticrew treasure."

Arany poked Troy in the ribs. "You know, I might consider that a proposal."

"I'd get down on my knees, except I might not be able to get back up carrying this heavy pipe," Troy kidded.

"I'll wait for the ring heavy with diamonds, then," Arany laughed.

"It's in my pocket," confessed Troy.

Once they arrived at the chapel, Troy jumped into the cherry-picker lift, constructed a holder for the pipe at the peak of the steeple, and positioned the pipe there. Arany had him write *Laus Deo* on the wood at the peak. Then he yelled it for the world, or as much of the world awake at near dawn, to hear. Workers were scheduled to arrive early in the morning to finish the steeple roof.

† † †

Elwood walked with Arany along the road to see the completed steeple on the Sycamore Valley Chapel. He stopped at his first sight of the chapel's steeple superimposed on the backdrop of Hog Back Mountain. The view renewed in him a sense of awe in God's creation as well as His praise. The steeple took on a heavenly glow. Elwood walked on. He began whistling the hymn, "The Wonder of It All." Suddenly, a red-tailed hawk swooped down from a sycamore limb and onto the peak of the steeple's new roof.

He turned to Arany. "Why did the hawk sit on the church steeple?"

Topics for Discussion
SYCAMORE VALLEY

1. Life is often unfair. Pastor Elwood Martin was fired as a preacher because of the greed, lies, and revenge of others. But, a quote from Helen Keller says "When one door of happiness closes, another opens; but often we look so long at the closed door that we do not see the one which has opened for us." Explain the closed and open doors that Elwood experiences. Provide examples from your life.

2. Elwood is initially troubled by his lack of success in preaching his message on the Blessed Eight. He packaged his sermon with so much theater that the people only remembered the entertainment. Silas jokes that a sermon should be short. In your opinion, what are the characteristics of a good sermon?

3. Arany had a special place of prayer at Chapel Rock. How do such places aid in one's communication with God?

4. Substance abuse spirals Dot's (the mother of Arany and ex-wife of Elwood) life downward. She goes from emotional cruelty of her daughter to near-physical assault. What step did she need to take in order to reconnect with Arany?

5. Pete Smith had the foresight to write down his remembrances of happenings, people, and growing up in the Sycamore Valley and Hackens community. Who would you like

to have to pen his/her remembrances of your family, church, or community? How do such writings differ from the usual history books?

6. Do you think Joe Reynolds was justified in shooting the Muterspaw brothers?

7. Why do you think Silas used Joe Reynolds as a model for Jonah in his sculpture? Are there similarities in the appearance of bear hunters (a description of this Jonah in the sculpture) and Old Testament prophets? Contrast the imperfections of Joe Reynolds and Jonah.

8. Arany compared Joe Bug Reynolds to Moses and David, in that all had blood on their hands but yet were called to do the work of God. Why does God often call the imperfect to do His work?

9. Pastor Martin sat at church during worship service feeling sorry for himself, for not getting what he wanted. Simultaneously, a line from the sermon stated God supplies what you need and not necessarily what you want. Have you ever listened to God whisper to you with a message that could also be described as coincidental?

10. Rachel Petticrew Reynolds first received "the Petticrew treasure" from her father. Eventually, Joe Bug Reynolds, then Judith Reynolds and Silas Clark, and then Arany Aldott were chosen to be the keepers of the treasure. Were all good choices?

11. Arany, as well as other keepers before her, had several choices with respect to the Petticrew treasure – in essence, publicize it or keep it hidden. In your opinion, did she make the right choice? In a recent novel, *The Shroud Conspiracy* (and sequel, *The Second Coming*) by John Heubusch, the author explores the possibility of extracting Jesus' DNA from the Shroud of Turin. What would be the ramifications of obtaining Jesus' DNA from the Petticrew treasure?

12. If you had an audience with Jesus and could ask Him one question, what would you ask?

13. Other titles proposed for this novel were *The Hawk on the Church Steeple*, *The Riddle of Silas Clark*, *A Whale of a Story*, *Rockbridge Gold*, and *Whispers from God*, among others. What would you have titled this novel?

Acknowledgements

This story incorporates historical facts within a fictional context. *Remarkable Rockbridge: The Story of Rockbridge County, Virginia*, by Charles A. Bodie (Rockbridge Historical Society, 2013), was a helpful source of information on the local history of places such as Cornwall and Collierstown.

PART 1 – NETTLE CREEK: Useful background material on gold mining in the Nettle Creek area was obtained from the pamphlets *Gold*, by Palmer Sweet (Virginia Division of Geology and Mineral Resources, 2007), and *Gold Mineralization, and Tin, Base Metals, and Thorium Anomalies at Yankee Horse Ridge, Irish Creek Tin Area, Rockbridge County, Virginia*, by Richard S. Good (Commonwealth of Virginia - Department of Mines, Minerals, and Energy - Division of Mineral Resources, 1991). The latter publication reported that indeed a Hubbard prospect for gold was worked in the Nettle Creek area in the late 1800s – early 1900s.

I thank Dr. James Squire, the Jamison-Payne professor in Electrical and Computer Engineering at the Virginia Military Institute, for valuable discussions on underground metal detection as well as his review of an early draft of this section for technical accuracy.

PART 2 – BIRD FOREST: The Petticrew memorial, with inscriptions as detailed in this story, is located in the Oxford Presbyterian cemetery. Information on the Petticrew massacre was gleaned from the accounts described in *History Lessons from a Country Church, volume 1*, by Horace Douty (Mariner Media, 2014) and "The House Mountain Tragedy of 1846" by Douglas J. Harwood in the *Proceedings of the Rockbridge Historical Society (XIII)*, and from recollections recorded in //boards.ancestry.com/surnames.pettigrew/120.3.1/mb.ashx.

The *cul de sac* at the end of Bird Forest Road has homes located there. This *cul de sac* isn't as isolated as in this fictional story. As a result, actual access to the saddle of the House Mountains would be on private, not public, land. The location of the homestead of John Petticrew is not known. Dr. Horace Douty has placed it only two miles from John Petticrew's place of work at Alphin (albeit probably along Bird Forest Road), and the Anderson house only 500 yards away.

PART 3 – SYCAMORE VALLEY: The discussion of octopus camouflage was based on the research of Dr. Todd Oakley at the University of California at Santa Barbara (for example: *Science News*, vol 187, #13, 27 June 2015, p. 10).

An extremely valuable source of information on life in Sycamore Valley during this time frame as well as the personal account of the Reynolds-Muterspaw conflict is given in the self-published book *I Remember*, by Paulmer (Pete) Bronson Smith (58 pp, circa 1988). I thank Earl Smith for his stories about growing up in Sycamore Valley; Madeline Chittum for her remembrances on the Reynolds-Muterspaw feud; Sharon Holland for providing access to the Pete Smith Book, the fiddle made by Joe Reynolds in prison, pictures of Joe Reynolds, and an entire file about her great-grandfather Joe Reynolds; and Helen Irvine for furnishing access to her personal collection of the writings by and to her grandmother Bessie Reynolds and relatives, mapping the Reynolds genealogy, and showing locations of the Reynolds and Muterspaw farms in Sycamore Valley.

† † †

I thank the following readers for their invaluable review of early and/or later drafts of the manuscript: Helen Irvine, Florence Connors, Karen Duff, and Dr. Martin Stokes, Jr. Their helpful comments and encouragement were greatly appreciated. I also thank Dr. Martin Stokes, Jr., for his input on Presbyterian policies. In addition, I appreciate the help of Anita Cruze in manuscript preparation, of Alyssa Fisher in cover photography, and of Don Samdahl in publication logistics.

I thank my teacher, coach, and editor Nancy Staub for orchestrating my transition from writing like a scientist to an author of fiction. Her review of several drafts resulted in important improvements in this story.

Finally, I thank my wife Helen Irvine for being my personal literary critic in providing feedback on this story, in cultivating my creative side, and in encouraging me to incorporate my imagination into the real world. In particular, she demanded that

I finish the "whole" story after I thought it was finished at the end of the Nettle Creek installment, then reiterated the same demand after I thought it was once again finished at the end of the Bird Forest installment. She also reached into my mind to paint an artistic depiction of Twin Falls Presbyterian Church.

About the Author

Henry Schreiber is professor emeritus of chemistry at VMI (Virginia Military Institute). He retired in 2014 after 38 years of teaching and research at VMI as the Beverly M. Read '41 Institute Professor in the Arts and Sciences and with the rank of Colonel, Virginia Militia unorganized. His teaching focused on courses about general chemistry, physical chemistry, botanical chemistry, and writing about science. His research spanned the gamut from the nature of the hydrogen bond, to the chemistry of lunar and terrestrial magmas, to chemical constraints on the incorporation of nuclear waste into glass, to coloration and bubble elimination in commercial glasses, and to the development of uniquely colored inflorescences (flowers) in hydrangeas – resulting in the publication of over 130 articles in professional journals.

He received a B.S. in Chemistry from Lebanon Valley College and a Ph.D. in Physical Chemistry from the University of Wisconsin – Madison. Honors during his career include the State Council of Higher Education in Virginia Outstanding Faculty Award.

He lives off Sycamore Valley Road in rural Rockbridge County, Virginia, with his wife Helen Irvine. Coincidentally, in the context of this story, "H" (the first letter in both Henry and Helen) is also the 8th letter of the alphabet.